Armageddon Girl

By C.J. Carella

*To Scott,
For Keeping it Real,*

Published by Fey Dreams Productions, LLC

Copyright @ 2013 Fey Dreams Productions, LLC. All rights reserved. All rights reserved. This material may not be reproduced, displayed, modified or distributed without the express prior written permission of the copyright holder. For permission, contact cjcarella@cjcarella.com

This is a work of fiction. All characters appearing in this work are fictitious. Any resemblance to real persons, living or dead, is purely coincidental.

C.J. Carella

Acknowledgements

Writing may be a solitary occupation, but it's rarely a one-person job. It takes a village to produce a novel. This book wouldn't have made it without the help of many people. The list below is not exhaustive, and my apologies to anybody I left out.

To Carlos and Carmela Martijena, parents extraordinaire, for their constant help and support.

To Joan T. Masters, ex-wife and best friend forever, for making me a better person.

To Igor Buminovich, Jason Bontrager, Erik Fisher, and Scott Palter, for answering assorted questions on history and languages, and double thanks to Scott for all his help and constructive criticism. Any errors and infelicities in this book are mine; there would have been many without those gents' kind help.

To Kevin Siembieda of Palladium Books, who gave me my first full-time writing gig, for the opportunity to make a living doing what I love and for his generous help with this project.

To George Vasilakos of Eden Studios, for all his support.

To MaryAnne Fry and Delia Gable, for being great artists and awesome friends, and to Jesse Belle-Jones for portraying Christine Dark for the cover.

To Scott Coady, gaming buddy, for all his help and support. The Dude Abides.

And last but not least, to the talented folk at www.geekandsundry.com. This book is in many ways my love letter to geek culture, and few things embody that culture like their awesome YouTube channel (http://www.youtube.com/geekandsundry). Thank you for all the inspiration and entertainment.

Carlos J. Martijena-Carella   www.cjcarella.com

Armageddon Girl

Chapter One

Christine Dark

Ann Arbor, Michigan, March 11, 2013

Last stands suck.

Outnumbered a gazillion to one. Bullets and rockets and bolts of energy and angry glares and bad language rained down on her in an epic downpour of malice and destruction. She faced the slings and arrows and magic missiles of outrageous bastards and somehow managed to survive the onslaught. No problem, she told herself, I can handle this. Her counterattacks took the bad guys down in droves, stacked their quivering bodies like cordwood, but for every dozen she struck down, another dozen and a half showed up. The center cannot hold, or in other words we are totally effed up, this is the way the world ends, all banging and whimpering and burning sensations and not so fresh feelings. In the words of the ancients, we're going from suck to blow and it's going to hurt a lot before it is over…

Something bad was behind her, worse than the hordes of murderous men and beasties facing her. She most definitely did not want to turn around. So she turned around.

It was dead, but still deadly. It wore the face of her father.

Armageddon Girl

She had no idea how badly things would have turned out, but luckily her alarm clock saved the day.

"Holy mother of crap!" Christine Dark groaned, and smacked the clock until it stopped beeping like an R2 unit in distress. That had been way intense. Her dreams were usually completely nonsensical dreck or small, anxious things. Showing up for class and realizing you had skipped classes for most of the semester, plus had forgotten to wear pants, that sort of thing. Oh, and the occasional dirty dream involving dark handsome strangers with very skilled hands and mouths. This one had been a Michael Bay does Marvel Comics after smoking a hefty dose of meth kind of thing. She had been in fear of her life, and the weirdest thing was, her dream-self had laughed in the face of death. In real life, Christine didn't laugh even in the face of mild discomfort.

Her heart was racing. She didn't ordinarily wake up feeling like she'd run a marathon. Weirdness. Even after showering and getting dressed, the world did not feel quite right to her, almost as if she was still dreaming. The surreal detached feeling persisted all the way through breakfast with her roommate Sophie. Sophie hadn't spent the night in their dorm room, a not irregular occurrence, and had texted Christine to ask her to meet for breakfast. Christine agreed. She agreed to most of Sophie's requests and suggestions.

"There's a party tonight at the Delta Phi's," Sophie said as soon as Christine sat down with her tray-ful of sensible breakfast food.

"On a Tuesday night?" Christine asked. Most of her attention was on the food in front of her. She was starving and feeling a bit shaky on top of everything else.

"You should come," Sophie continued. She hadn't noticed Christine was feeling off this morning, but Sophie rarely paid attention to matters not pertaining to

Sophie. Normally Christine didn't mind, but her dreamlike state was beginning to be replaced by grumpiness.

Sophie Beaumont was tall, tan and blonde, built to the specs of your typical fourteen year old boy's fantasy female ideal. Christine was short, pale and red-haired, and built to far less impressive specs. The two roommates had blue eyes, but Sophie's were deep and dark blue, while Christine's were pale and tended to go gray when she wasn't in a good mood. Like now, for example. Unreality was giving way to dissatisfaction.

"It should be fun," Sophie added cheerfully.

"You know I don't like that kind of party," Christine replied. "I'll fit in like a Jawa at Rivendell." Doing a little fictional mash-up helped her mood a little, but not enough.

"Like a what where?" Sophie didn't get either reference, of course. Sophie didn't get half of what Christine said, even when she bothered to listen to her. "Never mind. Just come along. Jeff has a friend who's dying to meet you. He's into engineering and stuff, so you can talk math to each other."

"I don't really talk about math during casual conversation," Christine said. She'd rather talk about stuff she was reading, or watching, or playing. Hm. She didn't talk about what she was doing, because she didn't do much other than reading, watching or playing stuff. And thinking. She did do a lot of thinking. Maybe she should be doing stuff more often. Something to think about.

"Earth to Christine," Sophie said. Christine blinked. "You went away inside your own head again. Boys don't like that, you know. You need to pay attention to them, make them feel special."

"I guess. Every one of them is a precious unique snowflake, or something like that, right?" Most conversations with Sophie ended up revolving about boys, and Christine's deficiencies when it came to interactions with said boys. *My freaking life can't pass the Bechdel test*, she thought bitterly.

Sophie smiled indulgently. "Whatever you say, Christine. So, are you coming with me?"

What the heck. She was already having a weird day. Some masochistic impulse drove her to agree to endure an evening of suckitude. "Fine."

* * *

The suckitude, it hurt.

Christine tried to shrink into a corner, but the senior from the Phi Beta Gecko or Whatever House got all up in her grill anyway. His breath smelled of pepperoni-and-cheese pizza, stale beer and a hint of cheap mouthwash. "'Sup?" he said.

"Hi," was her equally suave reply. She probably shouldn't have had so much punch, but she had needed something to take the edge off. The third of a cup she'd downed had taken the edge and a good thirty or forty IQ points right off.

"I said wassup," Phi Beta Gecko repeated in the determined, deliberate tone of the truly drunk.

"Uh, not much? My blood pressure? Gas prices?" None of the answers seemed to satisfy him. He leaned over closer.

"You're kinda hawt," he said. Very flattering. Luckily, his utter disregard for her personal space gave her an opening; she ducked and weaved and got out of the corner and away from him. He was too drunk to give chase. It was clearly time to leave. The night had been a total disaster so far and it could only get worse.

Sophie had tried to get Christine all dressed up in the latest slut wear but Christine had refused. She wasn't wholly opposed to dressing provocatively – the outfit she'd worn at Dragon Con last year had turned many a head – but not when hanging out with the muggles, where she felt like an outsider, exposed, a fish out of water, loser-girl out on a stage where some d-bags would soon empty a bucket of blood over her head. She'd ended up in jeans and a nice silk blouse, and had acquiesced to borrowing Sophie's high-heeled boots. After slathering a copious amount of makeup on Christine's face, Sophie had deemed her fit for public display.

Upon their arrival to the already crowded, loud and rowdy frat house, Sophie introduced her to Jeff's friend Donald or Dominic or Damian: something with a D. Something-with-a-D was kinda cute but there was a mean glint in his eyes that had put Christine off almost immediately. He looked her over and Christine had caught what she thought was either a tiny scowl or a twitch on the corner of his mouth, neither of which felt complimentary. Then she'd stopped being able to notice details like that because Sophie had plucked Christine's glasses right off her face and taken them away. Okay, she probably should have worn contacts to this shindig, but she hated putting the darn things on her eyeballs. In any case, she was half-blind, which didn't help. Some punch-drinking and a few minutes of awkward conversation later, Something-with-a-D had mumbled some excuse and gone away. Sophie and Jeff had disappeared some time before that, so Christine was left alone in a crowd of people she didn't know. If she wasn't so drunk she'd be having an anxiety attack just about now.

Armageddon Girl

She wanted to go home.

Christine looked around for the exit, which wasn't easy in the crowded space. She took another sip of punch and tried to make her way through the inmates of this century's version of *Animal House*. It wasn't easy. People kept bumping into her. One of them bumped her hard enough to knock the remainder of her punch all over her, splashing her blouse and the front of her jeans with artificially flavored grain alcohol. Nothing beat the feeling of syrupy alcoholic fluid running down your clothes.

All in all, she would have been much happier playing *World of Warcraft*, watching that web show about people playing *World of Warcraft*, or quietly reading a novel or *Supernatural* slash fan fic. Or even writing *Supernatural* slash fan fic, which she'd been guilty of. Well, she'd tried, epic-failed, and now she was cold, wet and just plain annoyed. Time to say 'Peace,' head on home and read some *Supernatural* slash fic before going to bed.

The world flickered.

That's the only way she could describe the sensation. For a second or two, everything – the crowd of partygoers, the loud music, the very floor under her high heel boots – went away, came back, went away and came back. It was like a light bulb on its last legs going on and off, but the flickering covered the entire effing spectrum of her senses. *Well, that was weird*, she thought to herself when the sensation stopped. A second later, her bafflement was replaced by the urgent realization that everything she had eaten today, and perhaps the week before, was swirling madly in her stomach and trying to come out the way it had gone in. Her eyes bulging, Christine clapped both hands over her mouth and tried desperately to make it outside.

"Look out, she's gonna hurl," one of the more perceptive Phi Beta Geckos warned the room, and people finally gave her a wide berth, plenty of space to stagger outside just as everything came geysering out her mouth and nose. She hated, hated, *hated* puking. No loved ones around to hold her hair while she did it, either. Christine ended up on her hand and knees on the mostly dead lawn outside the frat house, heaving uncontrollably and hating every second of it. A few partygoers – or more than a few, she really couldn't see very far without her glasses – were looking on with varying degrees of pity, amusement or contempt, dealer's choice; some were probably immortalizing the moment on their smartphones. She must be quite a treat for the eyes, down on all fours and giving the world a great shot of her butt if you didn't mind a little vomit on the side. Hello, YouTube and Vine. Goodbye, dignity. Perfect end point for this particular quest. How could it get any worse?

The universe is always happy to answer that question, and few ever like the answers they get. She really should have known better.

The flickering came back. One second she was on her hands and knees on the lawn, trying not to look at what had been a veggie lasagna some hours and assorted digestive processes ago. The next, things went dark and quiet. Another flicker and she was on her hands and knees on a smooth flat surface with bright spotlights shining right into her eyes, blinding her. And the second after that she was back on the lawn outside the frat house. Absolute OMG WTF moment. Brain aneurysm? LSD-laced Rohypnol in the punch? What?

Christine felt as if something was pulling at her. The nausea came back, now with extra creepy sensations, as if someone's fingers were reaching right through her skull and grabbing her by the medulla oblongata. Some force was dragging her somewhere. She didn't know how she knew that, but she felt it down to her bones. She also felt that wherever that somewhere was, she didn't want to go there. No effing way.

"What the fuck? Where did she go?" somebody yelled. Christine barely heard the words, too busy concentrating on not going wherever she was going in between flickers. Or firing neurons at random while her brain went bye-bye, one or the other. She felt certain she was fighting back somehow, and she had no idea why she felt that. The whole thing was like a bad dream where the craziest crap appeared to make sense. At least the nausea was gone, replaced by a falling sensation, even though she was mere inches from the ground. *If I stumble they're gonna eat me alive*. The Metric lyrics flittered through her head like a bat out of hell.

Something went *pop* inside of her. *This is it*, she thought absently as she felt herself letting go. She was certain she was dying. *Oh, Mom, I'm so sorry...*

She was falling for real now, falling through the ground, through the planet, free fall into utter darkness, where is the light? Isn't there supposed to be a light?

Oblivion.

C.J. Carella

Face-Off

New York City, New York, March 12, 2013

Humans in pain can make the most curious noises.

Case in point: Dan Giamatti, enforcer – soon to be former enforcer – for the D'Agostino crime family. The injuries: three broken ribs; one compound fracture, right forearm; two dislocated fingers, left hand, and several broken teeth. The sound: a panting moan, reaching scream levels only to turn into a strangled heaving gasp when the broken ribs made their presence known. It was a disturbing, pitiful sound. It even bothered me a little, and I was the one who had done the bone breaking.

Giamatti started a new tune, this one something between a wheeze and a sob.

"Can we talk now?" I said reasonably. I had been perfectly willing to have a peaceful conversation with the guy before killing him, but Giamatti had gone for a gun, a knife and finally a hand grenade. The hand grenade had earned him the compound fracture. Luckily for him I had been able to find the pin and put it back before the fucking thing exploded. A grenade explosion would have been a painful inconvenience for me, but rather lethal for him. That was some crazy-ass shit, deploying high explosives indoors, even for our crazy-ass world. Giamatti's reputation as a hard case was well-deserved, but even tough guys could be broken if you applied enough pressure.

"Fuck you, Face-Off," Giamatti blurted, spraying a bloody froth through his broken teeth.

Armageddon Girl

I sighed. It figured; someone crazy enough to go *mano a mano* with a Neo was too crazy to know when to quit. Neos – Neolympians, or parahumans if you really want to get pretentious about it – have been around for close to a hundred years. Sure, most of us aren't godlike unstoppable forces that can take over entire countries single-handedly, but even the weakest among us is stronger and tougher than your average bear. Giamatti should have known better. When I came bursting through the bedroom window, he knew he was dealing with the Faceless Vigilante, or Face-Off, depending on who you ask. He should have tried to talk, or even asked for his lawyer, even if the latter option wouldn't have done him much good. Instead he got into a pissing match with me. He might as well have tried to outwrestle the F train.

I'd been careful not to inflict any permanent damage, which isn't as easy as you think. I'm no heavyweight, but I can still bench press twenty thousand pounds. I could have wrung Giamatti's neck like a chicken's right from the get go, but it would have been harder to have a conversation with him afterward. Instead, I love-tapped him a couple of times, and only started breaking things when he wouldn't stop trying to kill me.

"Just tell me where the girl is, Giamatti," I said. All I got back was more garbled profanities.

Time to apply more pressure. I grabbed Giamatti by an ankle, avoiding his feeble attempts to kick me, and dragged him from the living room of his expensive penthouse to the balcony. I resisted the temptation to smash him through the plate glass sliding door leading outside, and instead opened it before pulling his thrashing body out.

"Okay, Danny, it's truth or flight time."

"Fuck you!"

"Flight it is, then." I swung Giamatti off the balcony. He had time to start a choked howl before he smacked against the side of the building, which didn't help his cracked ribs one bit. I kept my grip on his ankle, so he ended up dangling upside down with nothing but twenty-five stories of New York City air beneath him. I swung him back and forth a few times to make my point. The howls got shriller.

"They've got some good Healer EMTs working for the city, Danny. They can fix everything I've done to you so far. But no Healer is going to put your Humpty Dumpty ass together if I let go of you. Capisce?"

Giamatti nodded frantically. Even hard cases can be afraid of heights.

"So, where were we before you tried to shoot me? Oh, yeah. Where did you take the Jane Doe you kidnapped from the hospital?"

Giamatti spilled the beans most satisfactorily. I leaned over the balcony, still holding him by one leg. There is a trick to doing things like that when you are superhumanly strong but don't weigh much more than a normal human – if I wasn't careful, I'd go over the balcony and we'd both fall to his death; I wouldn't like the experience, but I'd recover after a while. To avoid falling, I had to brace myself carefully against the balcony. No big deal. I'd had a lot of practice and a couple good teachers.

"One more thing, Danny. You really shouldn't have murdered those nurses when you kidnapped the girl." Three nurses and one orderly, to be exact. Giamatti and his goons hadn't left any witnesses behind. "Kidnapping was bad enough, but I'd have given you a pass. Killing four people because they were an inconvenience? You know I can't let that go."

Giamatti didn't say anything to that. He understood what was coming.

I couldn't let the murders go, so I let him go instead.

He howled all the way down.

* * *

Hell's Kitchen isn't what it used to be, but here and there you can still find small bits of Hell.

The warehouse was squatting on a prime piece of real estate, and would likely turn into overpriced condos in the not too distant future. For now, it remained a featureless box of concrete and steel with a two-truck wide loading dock and heavy security doors. From the looks of it, it was a mostly legit warehouse that only occasionally acted as a haven for the kind of stuff the authorities frowned upon, like holding stolen goods or abduction victims.

I walked right to the front door and waved at the security camera mounted above it. I didn't even have to knock before the door opened and a big Italian guy who obviously didn't believe in low-cal meals let me in.

"What are you doin' here, Danny?" he asked me as I walked in. "Thought you were gonna take the night off."

I smiled, and that's when the goombah started to figure out something wasn't right. I was wearing Dan Giamatti's face as well as his clothes, and my build wasn't all that different from his, but the smile didn't look right. I hadn't spent enough time studying Giamatti, mainly because I hadn't even met the guy until a few minutes before I dropped him off a building, and apparently his normal grin didn't look like what I had produced. Or maybe the guy just didn't smile very often. He sure as hell hadn't done any smiling during our time together.

"DG?" the guard said dubiously.

"DG sleeps with the fishes," I said ominously. Well, with the rats at the dumpster he hit at the end of his final descent, but why let reality get in the way of a corny line?

"What the fuck?" The mobster was beginning to catch on that something was very wrong. He soon found out just how wrong things were.

I let Giamatti's face go. His features sank into my head, and the Mafia henchman was now staring into a featureless span of skin. No nose, no eyes, no hair, no ears. That was the face, or lack thereof, I woke up to every morning. It usually made for a great first impression. I could make little kids cry and grown men soil themselves just by being me.

"Motherfuck!" the goombah shouted, looking for all the world like someone who has found a king cobra swimming amongst his morning Cheerios. He went for his gun, which I had to respect, since most people freeze for several seconds when I show them my real face. Unfortunately for him, he didn't notice my fist moving towards his head until the right cross connected and broke his jaw and neck, at which point he stopped noticing anything.

The big guy's body plopped to the ground with the limp finality of those who are never getting up again. I stepped over him, walked into the warehouse and took in the sights. Not much to see: the space was mostly filled with stacks of wooden crates and rows of metal shelves, some empty, some packed with boxes. The place was mostly shrouded in darkness. There was a light by the entrance creating a little island of illumination there, and another on a second level office.

Two men up there had just witnessed their pal's demise. They recognized me, which isn't that surprising; my no-face is fairly well-known.

"Shit, that's Face-Off!" said another big guy in a track suit that could have been the recently departed's brother or cousin and probably was.

"Fuckin' Face-Off!" said his partner, a short skinny rat-faced guy. Nothing wrong with his reflexes; even as he spoke he drew out a huge revolver, a Smith & Wesson .500 Magnum, the kind of wrist breaker some people think will give them a chance against Neos.

I hate the name Face-Off, but since I'm not bonded and licensed, I don't really get a say in what people call me. I don't even own the trademark to (or get any royalties out of) either the Faceless Vigilante or Face-Off, not that there's a big market for stories about freaks with no face. I'm not in this for the money, which is a good thing because I wasn't going to make any. The mass media prefers good-looking guys and girls in tight and skimpy hyper-latex outfits. Last time I was featured in *Buck Comics Presents*, I was the villain of the piece, and one of the New York Guardians beat the crap out of me. None of that happened, but they never pay attention to the angry e-mails I occasionally send to *BCP*'s editors. Oh well, I'm not in this business for the glory, either.

I'm in it because I can't help it. Because the rush you get when you stomp on someone who deserves being stomped becomes addictive after a while.

The little guy with the big gun opened fire. His first shot missed me by a country mile, and the next one was even worse. Idiot. I pulled out my own gun, a sensible Ruger nine millimeter, took aim while the little punk missed me with a third shot, and double-tapped him before he could fire a fourth time. All the while, his friend had been futilely trying to get his own oversized gun out of its shoulder holster. In all the excitement he seemed to have forgotten how to undo the clasp. He saw his little buddy go down and froze, his gun still safely holstered. Sucked to be him: I double-tapped him as well.

Most Neos disdain or positively loathe guns. I myself prefer to punch or kick my targets to death. But since I can't throw fireballs or make people's heads explode with my mind, I need a way to reach out and touch someone beyond arm's length. Guns are fairly effective people-killing tools, especially when you throw in superhuman hand-eye coordination that allows you to hit a target at the maximum theoretical range of a handgun. In other words, the anti-gun caped crusaders can kiss my ass.

Three goons down. I replaced the gun's magazine with a fresh one while I headed for the office. According to Cassandra, there had been five people in the snatch team, including the late Danny Giamatti. One of them was supposed to be a Neo. Where the hell was he? Maybe he had taken the night off like Danny had. My luck was rarely that good, so I wasn't counting on it.

I was halfway up the stairs to the office when I heard a loud crackling noise behind me and realized I'd better be somewhere else very soon. I leaped off the stairs just ahead of a bolt of lightning that would have turned me into a crispy critter if it had hit me. I landed in a rolling tumble and saw my attacker standing by the entrance to the restroom downstairs. Apparently the superhuman member of the snatch team had been in the crapper when I made my grand entrance. I hoped he'd remembered to wash his hands.

Armageddon Girl

The Neo was tall, black and handsome, and looked like a total badass, complete with shaved head, mirror shades, black leather coat and pants, and a combat stance that said 'ex-military' to me. I couldn't identify him off-hand, so he had to be new or really, really discreet. I was hoping he was new.

"Face-Off," he said, a big shit-eating grin on his face. "This is going to be quite the coup." He had a slight French West Indies accent. Haitian, probably, which likely made him a veteran of Papa Doc's bad boy squad. That pack of psychos had been holy terrors before the Freedom Legion went in and cleaned up the whole island a few years ago. That meant he wasn't new, just discreet. Not good.

"Fucking hell," I said while I picked myself off the floor. Giamatti's clothes had gotten more than a bit singed by the near-miss. Too bad; they'd been pretty nice and I really needed a new suit. I'd held on to my gun, but decided to wait a sec before using it. Chances were it'd do me no good to shoot him from this distance anyway; even when they aren't bullet proof (and most of us are at least bullet-resistant), Neos have reflexes like leopards on catnip, so you want to shoot them at point-blank range, preferably in the eye. No wonder so many people hate our guts.

"Allow me to introduce myself," the Neo continued. "You may call me the Lightning King. And tonight I will be your executioner."

"Pleasure," I said, and shot him. I wasn't expecting he'd oblige me and die, but some Neos like to trash talk before a fight. I blame comic books, movies and TV; all that bullshit makes many of them think they're the stars of their own epic tale, never realizing they might just be bit players in someone else's. If they are in the middle of a grandiose spiel, sometimes you can catch them off-guard and put a bullet in their eye.

Not this time. Even as I lined up the shot the Lightning King raised up his hands in a defensive stance. By the time I pulled the trigger, a ball of crackling electricity had appeared in front of him, a big lightning ball, big enough to shield him from head to toe. My bullets went into the lightning ball and did not come out. Fuck.

The Lightning King stopped wasting his breath and got down to business. He threw the giant ball of energy at me. It was moving faster than a baseball pitch but slower than a bullet. If it wasn't for my own leopard-on-catnip reflexes, I would have ended up as a greasy smoking smear on the floor. I leaped out of the ball's way, and it hit one of the metal shelves and exploded, sending up a spray of molten steel, flaming cardboard bits, and shattered jars of pickles.

The smell of electrically fried pickles has to be experienced to be believed.

I cursed Cassandra under my breath while I rolled away. My spiritual guide had mentioned one of the kidnappers had been a Neo, but I'd expected him to be a Type One, a lesser talent who could burn out surveillance cameras and maybe Taser somebody. The Lightning King had to be a Type Two, with enough mojo to take out a SWAT team. That made me the underdog in this little death match. I hate being the underdog. I hate fair fights too, to be honest. A fair fight means you lose half of the time, and in this business losing means they carry you out in a body bag, or in several small evidence bags.

I came to a stop on my hands and knees and realized my suit jacket was no longer singed; it was on fire. I hadn't dodged quite fast enough.

Some people think Neos are impervious to pain. Don't believe that for a second. Pain is too useful a warning system. We may be hard to kill, but we feel everything that happens to us, from a paper cut on up. I've been shot, stabbed, blown up, dipped in acid (don't try that at home, kids) and once had an icepick shoved into my temple and then swirled around inside my brain for good measure, and man did I ever feel that. All of which means I was quite aware that my right arm and back were burning merrily while I dodged a couple more lightning bolts the fucker sent my way. That guy was beginning to piss me off.

I'd dropped my gun sometime during the festivities. I tried to close in on the Lightning King, but he was pretty fast on his feet. He kept his distance and forced me to keep mine by throwing a steady barrage of lightning bolts and flying energy balls. In between dancing around the electrical attacks, I managed to rip off the burning jacket before I got more than a few first and second-degree burns. The burns would be gone in a few seconds – we hurt, but we heal quickly – but I wasn't going to be around in a few seconds if I didn't finish this fight quickly.

A weapon would be nice just about now. I looked around and spotted the little guy's big gun where it must have fallen after he went down. I leaped for the gun as a pretty impressive forked lightning bolt barely missed me and destroyed several boxes of restaurant supplies. I grabbed the gun and rolled on the ground, getting singed by a near-miss. As I leveled the gun at him, the Lightning King created another sphere of energy to protect himself. The shots were swallowed by the crackling energy ball. My guess was the shield was vaporizing the bullets before they could get through, even the big .500 caliber ones I sent his way. Two shots emptied the revolver anyway.

I got an idea even as the revolver made a harmless click on my third trigger pull. I flipped the gun so I had it by the barrel and flung it at the Haitian with all my strength. It hit the sphere, but the energy that will vaporize a seven hundred-grain lead bullet will only partially melt a three-pound chunk of high quality steel.

The oversized revolver was still mostly in one piece when it emerged on the other side of the energy sphere and smacked the Lightning King right in the mouth.

Like I said, Neos feel pain just fine, and nothing will ruin your concentration like having a red-hot three pound piece of metal hitting your face at fastball speeds. A human would have been killed instantly by the impact, but the Lightning King was only stunned for a few seconds. Unfortunately for him, that was more than enough time for me to get into hand to hand range. I was in a piss-poor mood; second degree burns will do that to you. I didn't hold back as I punched and kicked him. You can't when it's a fight for your life and the other guy is as hard to kill as you are. The Haitian tried to fire more electrical blasts my way, but he couldn't aim for shit after I broke both of his arms. By the time I was done, I'd cracked several knuckles in my hands and my feet were sore, but the King was dead, long live the King. He wasn't a pretty sight anymore.

That was the entire crew, unless they'd kept a tactical reserve somewhere. I looked around, but didn't see or hear any signs of life. Several hundred pounds of assorted goods were smoldering, but no major fires had started. I headed back to the office, hoping I'd find the kidnap victim there.

And there she was, lying on a couch, wearing nothing but one of those embarrassing hospital gowns that lace in the back and black panties, plus several dozen feet of duct tape. Somebody had used the better part of a roll of silver duct tape and wrapped her wrists, ankles, arms and legs with it. And also covered her mouth and eyes under even more tape, all wrapped around her head and over her hair. Nice going, fuckers. If she was a vanilla human and started sniffling and clogged up her nose, she would have been dead in short order. Luckily, she seemed to be breathing normally.

That was crazy. Unless these guys were bondage freaks, wrapping someone up in tape like that made no sense, unless they were scared of her. Duct tape in those quantities might subdue one of the less physical Neos, however, especially Type Ones and low-range Twos. Cassandra hadn't mentioned the girl was a Neo, only that she was important. Sometimes Cassandra likes to be cryptic for no good reason.

I ignored the pain in my healing knuckles and pulled off the tape gag and blindfold as gently as I could. The girl stirred and moaned when I pulled the tape off her head, along with a few chunks of hair, but her eyes never opened. Probably drugged as well; these guys really hadn't taken any chances with her.

Under the tape she looked ordinary enough. Most Neos look perfectly human, though – I am one of the freakish exceptions – so that could mean anything. Red hair, pale skin, pretty; she looked awfully young in her current unconscious state. It took a while, but I got her unwrapped and covered her up with a blanket I found in a closet in the office. The chemical burns the tape had left on her skin had begun to heal even in the few seconds since I removed it. Definitely a Neo, then; we can pretty much fully recover from anything that doesn't kill us outright in an indecently short amount of time. That begged the question of what she was doing at a hospital when she was abducted. Most Neos only need medical attention after some serious injury, as in dismemberment serious.

I carefully carried her down to where Giamatti's car awaited. I don't own a car, being a confirmed New Yorker Pedestrian, and Giamatti wouldn't need a ride wherever evil assholes go when they die. It was a nice car, too, a brand-new Tucker Raptor, all tricked up. Too bad I wouldn't be able to hold on to it for long.

I made a little nest with the blanket for the girl. She was sleeping peacefully, and snoring softly. She had a cute snore.

I'd put her somewhere safe and go get some answers from Cassandra.

Armageddon Girl

Chapter Two

Christine Dark

New York City, New York, March 12, 2013

Christine opened her eyes. She was lying in bed in her dorm room. The last thing she remembered was falling into a dark place shortly after experiencing the mother of all acid trips. And puking. There had been a lot of puking involved. Had any of those things really happened?

"Still no signs of consciousness, but all her vitals seem normal, except for an unusually low BP." The voice was young, female and competent-sounding. Christine had watched enough hospital dramas to tell that whoever was talking was a medical professional of some sort. What she couldn't tell was who the heck was saying the words.

The voice seemed to come from somewhere above her head. She looked up, and realized she no longer was in her dorm room but in her old room at home. Well, Mom's home now that Christine had left for college. It was her old room just as she remembered from high school, with the faded Sailor Moon poster over her bed and the bookcases stuffed with paperbacks and hardcovers and the desk with her ancient desktop PC. Except none of that stuff was at Mom's house anymore; she'd boxed up all the books and that PC had gone to the great Circuit City in the sky, replaced with a neat little Dell notebook.

This couldn't be real. She must be dreaming, although she'd never been this aware she was in a dream before.

"It is a dream, my dear, but not an ordinary one." A new voice, but this one was coming from somebody close by. Christine turned and saw a tiny woman – four foot and not too many inches tall – standing by her bedroom door. She'd never seen her before, in dreams or real life, and she hadn't been standing there a moment before, either. The woman had long black hair and a dark complexion that could have been Hispanic or Native American, but her features looked like neither. She didn't look old – late twenties or early thirties, maybe – but something about her said 'old' to Christine. The woman's eyes were sightless solid white orbs. That would have normally creeped the crap out of Christine – and immediately made her feel terribly guilty for feeling that way – but in the dream she wasn't all that bothered by it.

"Uh, hello?" Christine said dubiously.

"I am very sorry to intrude in your mind like this, but I'm afraid this is the only chance we'll have to talk," the woman said. She was smiling, but it was a sad smile. "My name is Cassandra. It is nice to meet you, Christine."

"Nice to meet you. Am I going insane? Are you going to be the imaginary friend I talk to when the meds wear off at the happy place with the padded walls? Or did I die when I was puking my guts out? If I'm dead, are you an angel?" Whenever she felt nervous or uncomfortable – and this was a twofer – Christine either talked too much or shut down completely.

Cassandra started to say something but the voice coming from above came back. "What are you doing here? This is a restricted..." There was a sharp metallic sound, and the voice was cut off.

"Fuck, Danny, why did you go and shoot her?" a man's voice came in.

"I thought you said everybody was going to clear out before we got here." Another male voice, snarling, angry and scary. "Somebody fucked up. Not my problem. No fucking witnesses, *capisce*? Just grab the bitch and let's go."

"I'm sorry," Cassandra said. "This is going to be unpleasant."

Christine was still trying to figure out what the hell the woman was talking about when she felt rough hands grabbing her. She jumped at the touch, but she couldn't see anybody. It was terrifying. A sharp stinging pain on her arm followed, kind of like the last time she donated blood, but much more painful. She looked down and saw blood running from a puncture, right where an IV needle would go. "What's happening to me?"

"Some bad men are taking you from your hospital room. It's my fault. Your physical body is unconscious. Unfortunately, contacting you mentally has raised your awareness enough to experience what is happening around you. Help is on the way, however."

"What..?"

More outside sounds. Another man's voice. "Hey, what are you doing here?" More sharp metallic noises. Gunshots? They didn't sound loud enough, but she thought that's what they were.

Christine was thrown face down on the bed, and realized all of a sudden that she was wearing a hospital gown. Somebody was holding her arms behind her back. There was a tearing sound and she felt clingy tape burning her skin, being wrapped tightly around her arms and legs, over and over, binding them together. More tape covered her mouth, her eyes. She couldn't see, couldn't talk. She felt a sharp flare of pain as someone jabbed a needle on her backside. She screamed, but the sound was muffled by all the tape over her mouth.

"Christine." Cassandra's voice was firm. "Look at me."

She couldn't look at anybody, her eyes were taped shut! But a second later she found herself back in her bed, no longer bound and gagged. Cassandra was sitting on the bed, holding Christine's hand. She could still feel the tape on her skin, but she could move, see…

Talk? "I'm so going to freak the frak out if you don't tell me what's going on!" Christine shouted. Maybe this was a hallucination her brain was making up while in the real world her body was being abused by murderous strangers. Or the whole thing was some delusion and she had finally gone out of her effing gourd. "Freaking out right now!"

Cassandra squeezed her hand. "Please believe me, child. You will be all right. I have seen that much, if nothing else."

It was sheer insanity. Christine was experiencing two sets of feelings at the same time. She was sitting on her old bed in her favorite Hello Kitty pajamas, the ones she had stopped wearing when she was eleven. She was also strewn on the cold and dirty floor of a moving vehicle – probably a van – tied up with duct tape and with her ass hanging out of a freaking hospital gown. She forced herself to concentrate on the Hello Kitty pajamas experience. It was a lot less traumatic that way. "What's happening to me?"

"I had to see you," Cassandra said, which was kind of funny considering her eyes were obviously not in working order. "I wouldn't be able to do this if you were awake. It would be like staring into the sun. You have so much power, child.

I had to see what kind of person you are. I had to see if you can be trusted with all that power."

Power? Several of Christine's teachers had used words like 'gifted' and 'brilliant' when describing her, but even Mr. Gardener, the math teacher who had called her 'a prodigy,' had never referred to her as powerful. So now she was having delusions of grandeur mixed in with an abduction horror fest. It didn't make any sense.

Cassandra started playing a violin she hadn't been holding until just that moment. Trippy. Christine recognized the tune – one of Mozart's sonatas, Number 18, wasn't it? Christine loved music. She'd never quite managed to learn to play any instruments herself, but she'd learned to appreciate music. Mozart in particular fascinated her, with all the mathematical symmetry embedded in his work.

Christine listened to Cassandra's playing and for a while she was able to deal with the other set of sensations without panicking. The music got her through the feeling of being picked up and carried off over someone's shoulder like a sack of potatoes. She was finally dumped on some piece of furniture, like a couch and left alone, still wrapped up in tape. None of that seemed to matter as long as she could be in her old room listening to the strange woman play the violin.

Eventually, however, her brain kept asking questions she couldn't ignore. "Uh, Cassandra?" The music stopped and the blind woman turned towards her. "So, what happens if I cannot be trusted with all that power you were talking about?"

Cassandra's smile vanished altogether, and all that was left was sadness and grim determination. "In that case, I would have to make sure that power was not abused."

I think the nice blind lady just threatened my life, Christine thought. That scared her more than the whole kidnapping bit.

"You seem like a nice young woman, however," Cassandra went on. "You have suffered, mostly small hurts, but they have marked you nonetheless. You have been an outsider, an outcast. That could be dangerous for someone with your potential: the temptation to turn against everyone will be strong. On the other hand, your hurts and disappointments have taught you about suffering and made you sensitive to the pain of others."

The patient's deep feelings of inadequacy and demonstrated inability to fit into normal social patterns led to the creation of elaborate delusional constructs. She fashioned an illusory world where she was powerful and important. The patient's fascination with fantasy fiction and computer games may have contributed to the development of these delusions. Oh, yeah, the psych evaluations just wrote themselves.

Cassandra smiled again, and despite Christine's overwhelming need to believe all of this was just a weird-ass dream, she felt a surge of relief. "You will do, I think. You have a solid core, for which I think we must all thank your mother."

Back in Abduction Land, she heard a bunch of gunshots and other loud noises she could not identify. It sounded like a small war had broken out.

"That's your rescue," Cassandra explained. "A young friend of mine is risking his life to save you."

New pain and discomfort. Someone was taking the duct tape off her. It felt just the way she imagined duct tape would feel coming off her skin, except more painful. Her hair! "Can you tell your friend to watch the hair? 'Cause he's pulling my hair worse than Ellen Weathersby did back in sixth grade." The tape coming off her eyelids was the worst. "Son of a bee! That hurt!"

"I can't contact him while I'm here with you, unfortunately," Cassandra said. "But now you are safe, at least for the time being."

She could feel herself being wrapped up in a blanket, and whoever was carrying her off was being a lot gentler than the previous bunch. Knight in shining armor rescue fantasies annoyed her, but they were better than nightmares about being victimized by maniacs.

"Okay, so I pass the test and I'm the Chosen One and all that good stuff. What now? Do I get to go on a quest to find the Golden Dildo of Gondor or something?" Among all the fear and bewilderment, a brief flash of excitement poked through. A quest? That would actually be, really, really, wicked cool.

The delusions have become so strong the patient may never lead a normal life...

Screw you, imaginary shrink! I'm off to find the Golden Dildo of Gondor and stick it down the nearest Crack of Doom!

Cassandra said nothing, but Christine got the feeling the blind woman could hear her inner dialog just fine. Stupid dream know-it-alls.

"You will see, my dear. It's going to be a difficult time for you. Try to keep in mind you are stronger than you think."

"That should have been 'Stronger than think you are, remember you must try.' And you should be green and about two feet shorter," Christine replied, surprising herself. Smart comebacks weren't her thing; she could think of smart comebacks, but usually minutes or hours after the actual conversations when the comebacks would have been relevant. Her dream self was quicker on her mental feet, apparently. And sassier. She'd always wanted to be sassy and had never made it past awkward and unintentionally funny.

"Sleep now, Christine."

And sleep she did.

C.J. Carella

The Freedom Legion

Atlantic Headquarters, March 13, 2013

It once had been an insignificant island in the Caribbean, somewhere off the coast of Haiti. Now it glittered with half a dozen skyscrapers, a permanent population of over ten thousand people, two universities, and one of the most sophisticated communication and sensor networks on the planet. Overlooking it all was a neoclassic monstrosity on a hill. It loosely resembled the Parthenon but was many times larger; the structure had been called 'the mother of all city halls.' The huge building was the Western Hemisphere's headquarters for the Freedom Legion. Freedom Island was a living symbol of the greatest accomplishments of humanity and parahumanity, working together for the welfare of all. At least that was what all the brochures said. He even believed it on his good days.

Watching from the viewing room on top of the tallest building on the island, the hero of the ages took it all in. After a while he closed his eyes and vividly recalled the ground-breaking ceremony, back in 1953. Europe was still recovering from the war, and the world was still struggling with the war's aftermath. The theme of the ceremony had been 'Never Again.' Never again would the good people of the world allow the horrors of the previous two decades to be unleashed on the helpless and innocent. The Freedom Legion would be beholden to no nation or vested interest. It would be a truly transnational organization dedicated to the benefit of the entire planet. In his mind's eye he saw the gathered leaders and dignitaries of all the great powers. Winston Churchill, who had just regained his seat as Prime Minister, watched the proceedings with a jaundiced eye. Dwight Eisenhower's smile was forced and stiff, and Chiang Kai-shek had not bothered to conceal his scowl while the ceremony concluded and Freedom Island became an independent territory bound by no law but the Legion's. Only the Soviet Union had refused to send a representative to the ceremony, but that failing empire was on its way to irrelevancy even then.

None of the victors of the war approved of the Freedom Legion's internationalist program, but they could not stop it, not when all but a handful members of the Legion had pledged their support to its independence. The will of thirty-three Legionnaires was backed by more raw power than any nation state could command. Without the Legion, Nazi Germany would still dominate Europe. The Legion would ensure no other nation could become a threat of that magnitude ever again. It had been a lofty goal, and on that day he had felt the thrill of possibility, the promise of a great future almost within reach.

"John?"

John Clarke snapped out of his reverie and turned around to greet his old friend. "Kenneth. I thought you were going to skip the press conference."

Kenneth Slaughter, a.k.a. Doc Slaughter, and more recently Brass Man, shook his head. "Artemis asked me to un-skip it. As you know, she can be very persuasive."

"That she is," John said wryly as he shook hands with his friend. The two men were very similar, tall and powerful, broad of shoulder, narrow at the waist, sporting the muscular build of professional athletes. Even the cast of their faces was similar, with firm square jaws and chiseled features generally set in calm and confident expressions. Slaughter's pale blonde hair and sky-blue eyes contrasted with John's dark brown and green, but otherwise they could have been brothers. In all the ways that counted, they were. "Why did she insist on you being here, though? It's going to be the usual dog and pony show." The monthly press conferences at Freedom Island were fairly boring affairs unless some crisis was developing. John suspected he knew the reason, but waited for his friend to confirm those suspicions.

"Artemis – Olivia – is worried about you. As am I," Kenneth said, not wasting any more time on pleasantries. John wasn't surprised. He hadn't spoken with Kenneth for three weeks and had been avoiding him for even longer than that in order to prevent this very conversation. Now he understood why Kenneth had showed up for the press conference: he wanted to make sure John was up for it.

"*Et tu*, Kenneth? I thought a fellow oldster would spare me the touchie-feelie stuff."

"Watch it, youngster. I'm a good decade your senior, and you know it." Kenneth's smile was brief, and his tone became serious again. "We've all noticed it, John. We all feel the temptation to dwell in the past, but of late people have noticed you going into full-fledged fugue states. You were in one just now, weren't you?"

"I was reminiscing, yes," John admitted. He realized with some concern he could not remember how long he had been lost in thought.

"Even when you are paying attention to the here and now, there are other worrisome signs. You seem unusually unfeeling and disengaged. "

"Disengaged? I have been anything but for close to eighty years, Kenneth. You want to worry about disengaged, worry about Janus. He's the one who went on a twenty-year walkabout in outer space." Janus had gone on a twenty-year walkabout in outer space and on his return had chosen not to reveal anything about what he had seen. John didn't know what that meant, except it couldn't possibly be anything good.

"Cassius... yes, he also worries us all. And when we worry about two of the mightiest beings on the planet, we're truly worried. But this is not about Janus. Right now, you are worrying us a great deal."

John shrugged. "I wish you hadn't waited until half an hour before a press conference to bring this up." Underneath the calm façade, he was very worried himself. What Kenneth did not know was that the cold demeanor John was affecting concealed a growing sense of anger and frustration. John was scared of acknowledging this, even to himself. He had managed to repress those feelings, and if the price was to be seen as emotionless, he would gladly pay it.

"Lately it seems like there's never a good time, John. And yes, I know most of that is due to things beyond our control. There's always some crisis to tend to. But the Legion has over two hundred full time members. You can afford to take some time off if you need to."

"Can I? Can I really, Kenneth? Most of those two hundred kids are Type Ones and Twos. Things I can shrug off will *kill* them. Do you want to tell a widow or orphan that their dearly beloved bought the farm because I had to take some time off?"

"All true, but how many will die if your problems get worse?"

John bowed his head, acknowledging defeat. "All right. You win. You are right. Yes, I'm not feeling one hundred percent. And yes, we'll talk about it. Say, dinner at six today?" He had been trying to deal with his troubles on his own, and it clearly wasn't working. Maybe talking to Kenneth would help.

Doc Slaughter visibly relaxed. "I'm glad to hear it, John. Maybe it's simply our version of shell shock. We certainly have experienced enough things to warrant it."

"We called it 'combat fatigue' in my day," John replied.

"Yes, and now it's PTSD, unless they've replaced it with something even more harmless-sounding when I wasn't looking."

"People are softer nowadays, aren't they?"

"In no small part due to our efforts," Kenneth admitted. "I tend to think it's for the best."

"Probably true. See you downstairs?"

Kenneth nodded. "Let's go make our grand entrance. Artemis should be doing the same."

They shook hands, and Kenneth called forth his Brass Man suit of armor. John watched his friend take off, waited a few seconds, and leaped off the balcony.

John let himself fall for some time. He tried to feel the way a normal human would if he was plunging towards the ground a hundred stories below. Fear was a province of mortality. He felt nothing.

A minor act of will, and he soared towards the sky. That had once been a source of elation. He could fly higher and higher and leave the blue planet behind. Once, like Icarus, he had gotten close to the sun, close enough for the heat of its corona to envelop him. He had almost died that time; his internal temperature had risen well beyond the melting point of any earthly material and he had been forced to flee for his life.

Armageddon Girl

Of late, the sun called to him. If he went back, he didn't know if he would turn away from it.

John Clarke, a.k.a. Ultimate, the Invincible Man, flew through the sky, his metallic silver, gold and scarlet costume glittering in the morning sunlight. Once he'd had a cape that fluttered after him, but he had given it up as too childish. The damn thing would get ripped up all the time. No matter. Cape or not, his appearance over the waiting crowd on the ground was greeted with cheers and waves. Amazingly, people never tired of the spectacle of watching a man fly. Brass Man and a woman surrounded by a fiery nimbus joined him in the air. Artemis, the Living Goddess, waved and blew him a kiss as she passed him by. She looked magnificent in her golden breast plate and tiara, her trademark fiery spear held high in her right hand. John smiled. Artemis – Olivia O'Brien to her friends and relatives – always managed to cheer him up. Sometimes he wondered what would have happened if the lady wasn't spoken for, but she was all too married, and to another friend to boot.

It didn't matter anyway. John had not truly wanted another woman since Linda's death.

John dutifully performed some aerial acrobatics with his fellow Legionnaires, to the elation of the spectators below. Other than the press corps there was the usual gathering of tourists – whose financial contributions helped the Legion's ever-growing budget needs – and a number of local residents, who despite working with Neolympians day after day seemed to retain their appetite for the pomp and pageantry of it all. Was he a source of inspiration, or merely titillation? He was no longer sure.

Time to come down to earth and mingle with the mortals.

Ultimate and his companions floated down to the podium and waited for the outburst of applause (mainly from the tourists) to die down. He did the usual dog and pony show, greeting everyone, introducing his fellow spokesmen – spokespeople, he corrected himself – and then ceding the floor to Doc Slaughter for the main fluff pieces: reports of progress assisting the victims of Japan's earthquake, the capture of a cell of anarchist terrorists, and the release of three new pharmaceutical patents (one developed by Kenneth Slaughter himself, the other two by fellow genius inventor Daedalus Smith) into the public domain. One of those three drugs would soon make the HIV virus as irrelevant as smallpox or the common cold (the latter cure being another Daedalus Smith breakthrough).

Artemis took over and delivered statements dealing with some not-so-bright spots. Things in Iraq were getting nasty, with a neo-pagan movement led by several mythology-inspired Neos clashing with the Islamic Brotherhood. A joint Legion-UN mediation team had been beset by assassination attempts from both sides of the dispute. Things remained chaotic in several countries in Africa, thanks to Neolympian warlords stirring old tribal feuds into life. And of course there were the two great bogeymen of international politics.

"Will the Legion support new trading sanctions against the Empire of China?" one of the reporters asked as soon as the floor was open for questions.

Imperial China was one of those nightmares that refused to go away. Four hundred million people lived under the tyranny of the Dragon Emperor. Famine and repression had led to the deaths of millions, and only two brutal wars had prevented the Empire from overrunning the Republic of China.

John found himself flying over a burning city, helplessly watching thousands die under unrelenting artillery fire he was too late to stop. He saw a little girl run into a house seconds before a shell erased it from existence...

"... new sanctions will work?"

John shook his head and returned to the here and now. Those episodes of lost time were becoming more frequent every day. His mind wandered off without warning, especially when he wasn't concentrating on something. John noticed some of the people in the press watching him intently. There already had been rumors circulating that Ultimate was losing it, mostly in the blogosphere, but that was becoming more and more important every day.

Hell, he *was* losing it.

"We are doing our best to build the international consensus needed to deal with rogue nations like the Empire and the Dominion," Kenneth said smoothly. Too smoothly by half. John had been growing steadily more cynical about the two evil empires of the 20th century as they endured and prospered into the 21st. The Dominion of the Ukraine languished under the Iron Tsar, and its influence over Eastern Europe, Russia and the former Soviet states had only grown over the decades. The Chinese Empire had become more cunning after the Second Asian War, and now it could garner several dozen UN votes among smaller countries in Asia, countries that viewed the growing power and influence of the Republic of China with envy and trepidation. When the Dominion and the Empire cooperated (something that was happening with increasing frequency), they often had the votes to render the UN helpless. There was even a movement underway to grant the Empire a seat at the Security Council.

John suddenly realized he had missed another question, this one directed at him. "Can you say that again, Peter?" he said with an apologetic look. *Ultimate: Going Senile?* He could just picture the headline in one of the more lurid periodicals.

Peter Fowler was one of a new generation of independent Hypernet newsies. John admired some of them; their drive reminded him of times past, when he'd been a cub reporter for *The World's Journal* during his all-too-brief attempt at having a normal life. But a few of them had the morals of a vulture and instincts to match. This particular journalist was one of them.

"I asked you how you planned to meet the demands for sensitivity training and closer supervision for senior members of the Legion?"

"Uh, I'm not sure what you mean," John said.

"I'm sure you are aware of accusations of racism, sexism and general cultural insensitivity leveled towards Legion members," Fowler said, apparently forgetting he was supposed to ask questions, not make statements. "There are some, shall we say 'old fashioned' attitudes among your members, and a lack of understanding that we live in a multicultural, more diverse society. The Legion seems to be dominated by white straight males with outdated views on women and minorities."

"I am hearing a lot of comments, many of which I don't agree with, and some which are utter falsehoods, and no questions," John said in a flat tone that people who knew him would take as a sign to ease up, and quickly. He almost blurted out that one of the founding members of the Legion might have been male but also black and gay, and then remembered Janus had never made his sexuality a matter of public record. Wouldn't that be great, outing his friend by accident?

"Here is my question. Don't you think you and other members of the Legion need to do more work to acclimate yourselves to the mores of the 21st century?"

"No, I don't. Next question. Paula?" John gestured to the GNN correspondent, but Fowler kept talking.

"What do you say about claims that your wife left you because she was afraid of you?"

Dead silence.

In a tiny fraction of a second, he could turn Fowler into a thin red mist. So many ways to kill a human. Easier than snuffing a candle. He could kill all of them in the time it took to draw a breath. It would be so easy…

"Ultimate is not going to dignify that kind of question with an answer," Artemis said forcefully, breaking the tense silence. John had no idea how long he had stood there, fantasizing about murdering Fowler and everyone else in the conference room. "Mr. Fowler, this press conference is not a forum for baseless slander," Olivia continued. "Is that understood?"

Everyone was looking at Fowler like something nasty they had accidentally stepped on. "Understood," Fowler said sullenly, blissfully unaware of how close he had come to dying. That was not an exaggeration. John had nearly snapped. He had never been so close to losing control over so small a provocation.

What is happening to me?

Chapter Three

Face-Off

New York City, New York, March 13, 2013

I mostly prefer to be the man without a face. Whenever I'm relaxing by myself or with the handful (okay, three) friends I have, that's how I look. Nobody has figured out how I can breathe, see or talk with a smooth layer of skin, flesh and bone where most people have a pie hole and assorted other orifices. I have no mouth, but people can hear my voice just fine. It's a Neo thing. You wouldn't understand.

On the plus side, I never have to worry about getting my nose broken or someone poking an eye out. On the down side, most people aren't comfortable talking to me when I go blank. It's pretty antisocial. When the damsel in distress woke up, I would definitely put a face on to greet her. Something soothing and friendly, with a full head of hair.

I used to have a regular face, but my stepfather beat it out of me. Sad, isn't it?

At the moment, the girl was sleeping in the basement of the Church of Saint Theodosius, a Ukrainian Orthodox church presided over by one of my few friends. Father Aleksander was a Type One Neo with some minor healing and empathic abilities, abilities he had put to good use ministering to the local Ukrainian community. We had struck a fast friendship during an altercation with some Russian mob stooges that had ended with said stooges in prison after some time in the hospital. Hanging out with the good father always led to interesting conversations and the consumption of some very smooth vodka. Aleksander ran a discreet underground railroad for assorted people in need of a place to hide – refugees from the Dominion and Russia, mostly – and I trusted him to watch over Jane Doe and keep his mouth shut. The man took the concept of sanctuary very seriously.

After leaving her in Father Alex's care, just as the sun was coming out, I went to a diner and enjoyed a tall stack of pancakes, courtesy of the nice wad of cash I'd collected from the mobsters I'd killed that night. I wore one of my regular faces – Tony the wannabe wise guy – in honor of all the Italians I'd recently sent off to their greater reward. After breakfast, I headed to the Bronx to see another friend.

Aleksander had eventually gotten used to talking to me face to no-face, although it had taken quite a bit of vodka to thaw him out. Cassandra, on the other hand, had never had any problems with me. It helped that she was blind as a bat, of course.

I know, a blind seer going by the name of Cassandra. The clichés trip all over themselves. I always poke fun at her about it, and she claims that her name was Cassandra before her parahuman powers manifested themselves. It might even be true.

Of course, she is blind only in a technical sense. Among her many abilities, my spiritual adviser is aware of everything within a three block radius around her. Aware as in she can read a letter inside a sealed envelope, or know how many rats are in the vicinity, and how many fleas are on each of those rats. It's fairly impressive; you learn quickly to never play cards with the woman. And don't ever try to sneak up on her. I tried a couple of times just for shits and giggles, and discovered she is quite fond of practical jokes and homemade traps. One such incident involved several bowling balls and a minor concussion. After that, I just walked up to her front door and knocked politely, at least until I ended up getting my own keys and a room at her place.

Cassandra lives in a boarded-up three-story building in a bad area of the Bronx. From the outside, it looks like the kind of shithole self-respecting junkies would avoid. The inside is a lot cozier, though. Since I don't really have a fixed address, I sleep there more often than not. The front door doesn't look like much but is solid steel and has some unusual characteristics. It was open wide this morning, Cassandra's cute way of letting me know she was expecting me. I walked in and ignored the loud clang as it slammed shut by itself. The first time it had done that had been pretty startling, but I was used to it.

The first floor looks like a condemned building should, complete with dust, peeling paint, cracks along the walls, and an atmosphere of disuse and abandonment that makes most people feel not just that nobody lives there, but that nobody should live there. No junkie has ever tried to set up shop in the building, and teenagers looking for a place to party always give Cassandra's building a wide berth. I'm pretty sure it's a psychic thing my friend does, but she likes her little mysteries, so she's never confirmed or denied it.

Originally there were twelve apartments in the building, but that's down to nine. Cassandra makes her home in the second floor; all the original apartments on that level have had some walls knocked down to turn the whole thing into one big dwelling, a huge apartment covered in rugs and tapestries and flickering in the light of a bunch of candles. Even though the place has electrical power, she uses candles for illumination and doesn't have a TV or computer. My part-time crib is on the third floor, an apartment I've furnished over the years with a combination of Salvation Army furniture, lots of books, mostly second hand (I like to read a lot) and a few choice electronics I've 'liberated' from assorted assholes who had the misfortune to cross my path.

It's a safe house, but it's not my home. I don't really have one of those. When I'm there I'm Cassandra's guest. Same as when I crash at Father Alex's or (far more rarely) at Condor's underground base. When I want to be on my own or am entertaining a lady friend I usually sleep at cheap motels that charge by the hour, or the lady friend's place if we've gotten chummy enough. I only keep stuff I need at Cassandra's, without much in the way of decorations or personal touches.

Cassandra's dwelling, on the other hand, is full of personal touches, a candlelit museum of eclectic tastes. Carpets and tapestries cover the floors and walls, mostly Middle Eastern designs that must have cost a fortune. In between the tapestries there is a lot of artwork, from a few paintings that are either very good replicas of old masterworks or have been liberated from someone or other, to a black velvet Elvis portrait whose eyes seem to follow you everywhere. One large room which I've dubbed the Hall of Knick-Knacks is filled with shelves stacked with little porcelain figurines and display cases with antique jewelry and objects that probably should be in a museum. And like I said, lit candles all over the place, in all shapes and colors. It's a miracle she hasn't burned down the place, but miracles are Cassandra's stock in trade.

That morning, Cassandra was waiting for me in the room with the Elvis portrait in it, relaxing on an ancient-looking armchair and playing something Gypsy-sounding on her violin. My psychic pal is very short and strikingly beautiful, with smooth mahogany skin, high cheekbones and sharp features. She appears to be in her thirties, which doesn't mean anything when you're dealing with Neos, since we either don't age or age very slowly, most likely the former. Most people thought she was black or Hispanic, but I suspected she was something more exotic, some multinational blend I've never been able to identify. I don't ask about that kind of thing, though. It's enough that I know she loves music and laughter, and that she has never turned down anybody who needed her help. Her eyes are covered with a milky pale film, and to avoid making people uncomfortable she usually hides them behind sunglasses. Not when it's just us, though; we are very tolerant of each other's deformities.

I figure she was blind before her powers manifested themselves, since most Neos can recover from crippling injuries. That's another thing I've never asked.

"Hello, Marco," she said as I entered the living room. Cassandra is the only person who knows my legal name is Marco Martinez. Father Aleksander calls me 'my friend,' or 'my young friend' when he's trying to pull rank on me. Condor, a friendly costumed Neo I often work with, just calls me Face. When I'm interacting with most everyone else I'm wearing a fake face and a fake name; when I'm wearing my real no-face people call me Face-Off or profanity-laced versions thereof.

I don't mind that she calls me Marco, although I would like Mark better. It's not my name anymore, but it used to be, and Cassandra lives in the past at least as much as she does in the future, so it's fitting somehow.

I sat down on an overstuffed armchair facing her. "Hey, Cassie." She nodded at me. "I found the girl."

"I know," she said. "I was able to see some of the rescue. The outcome was never in doubt."

"That's nice. It got pretty hairy for a while. The Neo you warned me about turned out to be pretty tough."

"I saw you dealing with him. He was powerful but overconfident. He never had a chance," she concluded.

Working with Cassandra is equal parts helpful and maddening. Much of the time, she lets me know places to be or people to find. Thanks to her, I know where to go to stop trouble or find people who need killing, or at least need a good beating followed by some time behind bars. That works great for me, since it gives me something to do and people I can fuck up and rob with a clean conscience. But she often doesn't tell me the whole story beforehand, and things sometimes end up being more complicated than they first appeared to be. She claims it's the way her visions work and that giving me too much information can actually change the future events she has seen. The paranoid part of me thinks she just likes to make me sweat.

This last escapade made for a good example. "Why didn't you send me to her directly instead of having me beat the location out of Giamatti? Not that I minded doing that. The fucker needed to be put down."

"I wish I could have," she replied. "The problem is simple; it's very difficult for me to sense her location. It's very difficult for me to perceive her at all, as a matter of fact."

The job had been weird from the get go, even by our standards. Early last evening Cassandra had contacted me telepathically, which was unusual in itself. She only does that during emergencies, since she claims it takes a lot out of her.

She told me about a girl being abducted from a hospital, how many perps had been involved and the name of the ringleader. I'd had to find the ringleader and get the girl's location from him. Normally Cassie would have just sent me to the address where the girl was.

"What do you mean? You saw her get kidnapped, right?"

"I wish I could show you how I see things," Cassandra said. She looked distracted, which happened when something in the future caught her fancy. In the flickering candle light, her face looked older than normal. She was clearly exhausted, which was rare enough to worry me a little. "The future is fluid, and the very act of observing it often changes it. I sensed this woman's arrival, and how momentous it would be. Even then, I could not see her directly. I'm seeing the effect she has on the world. She leaves a… I guess you could call it a footprint, or an impression, on the very fabric of reality."

"Great, that clears up everything. I didn't see any scuff marks on the fabric of reality when I saved her. Just an unconscious Neo girl. I would have brought her here, but you told me not to. Didn't tell me why, either."

"I wish it were otherwise, but I cannot have her near me. Her presence would completely overwhelm my senses. From the moment of her arrival, my abilities have been affected."

"Her arrival? What do you mean?"

"Whoever this girl is, she was not in this world twenty-four hours ago."

"Nice. So she's an alien?" That would be a first. Some Neos claimed to be from other planets, but so far every single one of them had turned out to be full of shit, batshit crazy, or both.

"I only know she's not from this world."

"So, like an alien. Or not," I said. "She's a Neo, so she's as human as I am. Unless aliens took her away and just dropped her off. What else could she be? Time traveler? Visitor from a parallel dimension?" You did get some of those every once in a while, and things usually got very messy when they showed up.

Cassandra shook her head. "I'm not sure."

"Now that's something I don't hear every day."

"I know that her presence here is causing the future to warp in ways I can only vaguely glimpse. Things are going to change, perhaps radically, because of her. Things all around the world."

This was getting better and better. "Sounds like a job for Ultimate and his super-pals. In case you've forgotten, Cassie, I'm just a Type Two vigilante. Since when do I handle threats to the world? I can do Brooklyn, Queens, parts of Jersey if I'm pushing it, Manhattan by special request. Acting locally, y'know?"

"We do what is required of us. Or live with the consequences of our inaction."

"I'm getting the warms and fuzzies here. If you're going to share some fortune cookie wisdom with me, do you at least have some leftover Lo Mein I can eat?"

Cassandra smiled. "You shouldn't underestimate yourself, Marco. You are capable of much more than you expect."

I shrugged. I was a freak with some superhuman abilities. I wasn't going to run around saving the planet. If I hadn't joined forces with Cassandra, I'd be jumping over rooftops at night looking for crimes to stop – and believe me, that's one of the most useless things a wannabe hero can do. You could spend a year 'patrolling' and never see anything – the chances of you being at the right place and right time are not quite in the winning-the-lottery range, but they're still pretty small. Supposedly Neos seem to find trouble more often than they should, statistically speaking, but even so it never happens as often as it does in movies or TV. My buddy Condor had a billion bucks worth of police scanners, surveillance cameras illegally installed all over town, and he had tapped into the security system networks of a dozen security companies. He still mostly spent his nights playing *World of Warcraft* while waiting for something to happen. Thanks to Cassandra, I'd been able to do some good, a lot more good than I would have by myself, but I knew my limitations. I wasn't going to save the world. I wasn't even going to save the city.

There'd been a handful of times in my dozen years of vigilantism when something major had menaced New York: natural disasters, or a high-powered Neo on a rampage. That kind of thing happens once every two or three years on average; it sucks, but people have gotten used to it. Dealing with major disasters was the job of the licensed and bonded parahuman team of the city, the Empire State Guardians. The Guardians had full legal enforcement powers, not to mention a sweet license deal that gave them a cut of any income generated by anything with their trademarked likeness, from t-shirts and coffee mugs to movies and video games. They got paid big bucks to save the Big Apple, back up the cops in dicey situations, and preen for the paparazzo in their skin-tight costumes. If the Guardians couldn't handle something, the Freedom Legion would help them out. If the Legion couldn't handle something, it was time to evacuate the city and move to another state. Luckily that hadn't happened.

I mostly watched that kind of thing on TV, or did the superhero version of janitorial work – help people evacuate areas in danger, beat on looters, those kinds of shit jobs. Early in my career, I had tried to join the fray, bright-eyed, bushy-tailed and ready to help. The first time I did, one of the Guardians politely asked me to leave. I wasn't trained to work with a team, she explained, and I would end up getting in the way. The second time I'd tried to lend a hand, another Guardian, an officious prick called Star Eagle, tried to arrest me. I wrapped a light pole around his neck and left, and apparently he was so embarrassed by the incident he didn't press charges. After that I learned to leave well enough alone.

"Capable or not, this doesn't sound like my usual gig, Cassie. If this chick is going to be involved in some major catastrophe, why don't we turn her over to the Guardians or the Legion? They handle that kind of thing all the time. This is way above my pay grade."

"That's not possible. And no, I don't know exactly why." Cassandra frowned. "I don't like seeing only fog and shadows in the future, but that's what I get whenever I try to focus on this woman. Remember, I don't see the future. I see possibilities and probabilities. And she is blocking me somehow, so what I see is fragmented."

"But you have a hunch taking her to the Guardian's HQ is a bad idea." It was a nice HQ, too, a big building with a nice view of Central Park.

"Let me put it this way. When I try to visualize you doing so, all I get is flashes of death. Death everywhere. The whole city and beyond. Death throughout the planet, Marco."

Oh yeah, this was just up my alley. Planetary death? What part of 'above my pay grade' did she not understand? "And if we hold on to her?"

"I see you traveling with her, to many different places. And a great deal of danger wherever you go. The mass deaths are still a probability, but not a certainty. The worst thing is, I think I have seen all of this before, a long time ago, but

I can't remember when." Her normally placid demeanor had been replaced with a bleak expression I'd never seen before. It made me feel queasy. "I hate not being able tell you more, Marco. This is going to be more dangerous than anything you've done before."

When Cassandra saw danger, it meant that in some possible futures I ended up getting killed. Usually that wasn't a big deal, since her visions allowed me to prepare for whatever would have killed me if I wasn't careful. If she couldn't see clearly, I was on my own. I probably should be worried about that, but it felt like too much effort at the moment. I was more concerned about fucking up than dying, to be honest. Fucking up meant people with something to live for ended up dead.

"I managed to mentally communicate with her while she was incapacitated," Cassandra went on. "It was very difficult. The whole experience ended up being rather traumatic for both of us."

"How did you pull that off?"

"With enormous effort and only because she was heavily drugged and even her subconscious abilities were at their lowest ebb. Even so, the task was almost beyond me."

"I better get back to Saint Theodosius before she wakes up, then. If she is such a badass she can make you sweat when she's out cold, I don't know if Father Alex can handle her."

"She does not pose a danger at the moment. I learned as much from my chat with her," Cassandra explained, easing my mind a little. "She's quite a nice young woman, as a matter of fact. Her name is Christine."

"A nice young woman that can end the world. Sounds like my kind of girl." Not really. My kind of girl was not nice at all. I'd been with a nice girl once. That had ended with me cradling her dead body in a cheap motel room. Never again. "So, to sum things up," I continued. "I have to convince this Christine chick to stay away from the authorities, and to go on some sort of quest with me. Sounds perfectly reasonable, not creepy at all." I didn't have much experience dealing with people I wasn't supposed to scare or hurt. How the hell was I supposed to convince her to come along with me?

On top of that, I wasn't crazy about going to far-off places. I'd never been farther away from the city than Jersey and, once, Connecticut. I figured things and people were shit no matter where I went, so I'd never felt any urge to go anywhere. I wasn't sure how I'd handle the world outside the five boroughs. If that was what Cassandra wanted, I'd do it, though. I trusted her.

It never occurred to me that she would lie to me.

Armageddon Girl

Christine Dark

New York City, New York, March 13, 2013

The universe was nothing but darkness and fear. And cold. The universe was nothing but darkness, fear and cold. And pain. Okay, the universe was nothing but darkness, fear, cold and pain...

Christine woke up with a start. Great Oogly Moogly! What time was it? She was going to be late for her test! Going to that stupid party had been the dumbest idea ever. Freaking Sophie and her drinking and promiscuity and Daddy-bought boob job, why did Christine hang out with her at all? Answer: because a bad BFF was better than no BFF at all. What kind of mess had her kinda sorta best-friend-forever gotten Christine into?

She'd had the worst and weirdest nightmare of her life. She didn't want to even think about it, not before she was fully awake and halfway through a hot shower.

The bed felt a lot lumpier than usual; the sheets also felt different. She reached for the glasses on her nightstand, but her hand hit only air, so either she was sleeping upside down or she was in someone else's bed. OMG. Had she and some frat boy..? Had they used protection? Had it been consensual? The idea of some troglodyte from Phi Beta Gecko having his way with her unconscious body almost made her throw up again. She had thrown up earlier last night, hadn't she?

Christine forced herself to take deep breaths and slow down her racing crazy train of thought. When she got anxious her mind sped up and started spinning out of control, and that wouldn't do anybody any good. *Okay, think. It's dark, and don't have my glasses or contacts on, which means I'm blind as a bat. No problem, I still have all my other senses.*

She felt around the bed and found no other occupants, which made sense, since her discombobulated awakening should have woken up anybody with a pulse. After some more feeling around, she found a nightstand on the wrong side of the bed, assuming this was her normal bed, which it clearly wasn't. She felt around that table, but found no eyewear, just a glass of water and a lamp.

"Lamp good, water good." She turned on the lamp and then there was light. The lamp revealed an unusual room, not what she expected a frat boy's lair would look like. It was small, with a fairly low ceiling and very little in the way of furnishings and decorations. On one wall there was an industrial-size golden crucifix, very ornate in a style that reminded her of Greek Byzantine art. The other walls were bare; the room was painted in a light pastel color. Besides the bed and nightstand, the only other furnishing was a plain chair. No mirror, no posters on the walls, no signs of individuality or even fashionable pretend individuality anywhere. So maybe this wasn't a frat boy's place.

Christine continued to take inventory. She was wearing white and pink striped pajamas, a couple sizes too large. For some reason she'd imagined herself wearing her old Hello Kitty pajamas, but that had been part of the weird-ass nightmare. Christine didn't own any pajamas, hadn't since she was a child; she was a t-shirt and sweatpants or undies in bed kind of girl. Which meant...

Someone else had dressed her.

Armageddon Girl

Roofies. Not effing funny. I'm not a victim. This can't be happening, can't be happening...

Okay. Back to deep breaths. Slow down, brain. Please.

Christine tried to think things through logically. Logic and math were great tools, might as well use them. Solve the equation, figure out how things work, win valuable prizes. All right. She didn't think striped pajamas and a big Byzantine cross fit with a date rapist profile. And she didn't feel sore or in pain. In fact, she felt better than she ever had. Her eyesight, for example, was a lot better than it could be without glasses. She could make out every detail on the cross on the wall, for example, and normally without her glasses she would have been hard pressed to identify the object on the wall as a cross. Okay, not that bad but still, her vision hadn't been this good since she was a child.

So somebody had roofied her, dressed her up in pajamas, and improved her eyesight? Let's be logical and discard facts not in evidence. Pajamas, fact. Better eyesight, fact. Roofies, open question. What was the last thing she remembered before waking up here? See? Logic, step by step, cause and effect and we'll be fit as a fiddle in two shakes of a lamb's leg and let's see how many metaphors and similes I can stack in one sentence...

I said slow down, brain!

She lay back on the bed – it was definitely lumpier than the one in her dorm room – and tried to remember the previous night. She'd had that strange dream the night before, which had left her feeling weirded out enough to go with Sophie to the stupid frat party. She had meant to hang out, nurse one drink, see if Jeff's friend was a nice guy, assuming nice guys weren't extinct, then go home and be in bed by one a.m. at the latest. She remembered getting more than a little tipsy. And then…

She had experienced the world flickering in and out of existence. She had thrown up; that memory was burned vividly into her cortex. And she had fallen through the world, or felt like she had. It had to be drugs. She had just said no to those during high school. She'd smoked pot a couple of times in college, but it mostly made her paranoid and her train of thought even more frantic, which sucked, so she'd avoided even contact highs like the plague. But there was no telling what devil's cocktail some fraternity d-bag had slipped into her drink; what had it done to her most prized possession, her mind?

Breathe in, breathe out. What happened next?

The dream. Talking to a strange woman and at the same time being kidnapped from a hospital room, as if reality had gone split-screen on her. It had ended with her being the Chosen One or something like that, all very ponderous and important. Some more weird dreams after, stuff about darkness and pain and stuff she couldn't remember. And then she woke up.

"That wasn't as helpful as I hoped," Christine said to herself. She was her own best audience, so she talked to herself quite a bit, much to the detriment of her social life. "Oh, I know something else. I really, really need to pee."

She got up and saw that someone had left a pair of fuzzy bunny slippers on the floor. That made her feel a bit better. What kind of evil psycho would leave fuzzy bunny slippers for her? *The really, really sick and twisted kind,* her brain helpfully suggested. When she got out of there, Christine was going to punish her brain with a marathon run of *Jersey Shore* episodes.

Hello, door. Locked or not? She tried it, and the door opened. It led to a hallway, a staircase to her right, a room at the other end of the hallway, and – thank you Jesus, Buddha and Great Pumpkin – clearly marked public restrooms on her left. The whole place had a public building vibe, like a library or a community center. She ducked into the ladies' room and did her business.

Christine looked in the restroom's mirror after splashing some water on her face. Not much to look at. Red hair and blue-gray eyes, pale skin that burned under any sort of direct sunlight, a face that Sophie insisted was pretty but that Christine could find a dozen things wrong with in as many seconds of looking. She was skinny – slender, dummy, Sophie kept telling her – but not supermodel skinny. Some guy at the party had told her she looked quote kinda hawt unquote, but that was probably a combination of Sophie's makeup application skills – all of said makeup was gone except for some smudged eye shadow – and Grade-A beer goggles. Neither of her ex-boyfriends had ever praised her looks except in the most cursory way and they'd both dumped her for prettier girls. Sophie was full of it. It didn't matter. Looks didn't last long; brains might not last forever, but they tended to keep on running a good while longer.

Christine had done up her hair for the party, but it was thoroughly messed up. It looked like someone had stuck gum in her hair and then ripped it off. Not having a brush or a comb available, she ran her hands through it, and found something stuck on it. It wasn't gum; she managed to extricate it and found herself looking at a piece of duct tape.

The frakking dream had involved duct tape. She almost had a panic attack right then and there.

Let's focus on the positive, shall we? I may have been duct taped at some point, but I'm not anymore. That's good. So maybe, just maybe, I was in trouble, maybe even in distress, but I've been rescued. Yeah, let's go with that, but be prepared to run and scream if anything seems amiss.

A man was waiting for her in the hallway when she came out of the bathroom.

He was an older gentleman, at least forty-something or older, with a full beard and somewhat scraggly features. And tall, six feet or close to it, which made Christine feel fairly tiny and vulnerable. He was wearing a smaller version of the cross in the bedroom over his gray turtleneck. Under the circumstances, running into him should have made her scream in terror, but she wasn't scared of him even at first glance. Despite his size, his kind if somewhat tired eyes and deep laugh lines, visible even through the thick beard, comforted her somehow. She felt safe around him, which was weird since she rarely felt safe around strangers, especially ones that towered over her.

"Glad to see you are awake," the man said. His voice was gruff and had a hint of an accent. Russian or Eastern European, maybe.

"Are you an Orthodox priest?" Christine asked. Not 'Where am I?' or 'Who are you?' That's how she rolled, and she had learned to accept herself.

"Yes, I am," he replied, unfazed by the question. "I am Father Aleksander. You are in the Church of Saint Theodosius in New York City."

"New York? I was in Ann Arbor last night! That's in Michigan, by the way, and it's like a bazillion hour drive from here. Did they fly me here? I was in a hospital, am I okay? Why am I in church? I was raised Presbyterian, by the way, not Orthodox, but in any case why any church? And…" Christine forced herself to stop talking. "Sorry. I get away from myself sometimes."

Father Aleksander smiled. "That is quite all right. I wish I could be more helpful, but I don't have all the answers to those questions. I will tell you what I can, and a friend of mine will tell you more. Would you like to have something to eat or drink while we talk?"

"Now that you mention it, I'm starving. And can I keep these slippers? They're really comfy."

C.J. Carella

The Freedom Legion

Atlantic Headquarters, March 13, 2013

Olivia O'Brien traded the burnished metal armor of Artemis for business-casual attire. Her office had a changing room with a closet whose space was filled by a combination of colorful costumes and austere business suits. That in a nutshell defined life in the Legion: a combination of circus performing, being a firefighter or soldier, and working as an executive at a large corporation. She came out of the changing room and smiled towards her assistant. "Let's get started, shall we?"

Cecilia Ramirez was supposed to be a normal human, but her attention to detail, skill in maneuvering through bureaucratic mazes, and uncanny ability to gather and remember information from a myriad of sources bordered on the superhuman. She had been Olivia's executive assistant for eight years, and she was invaluable as an aide – and as a friend. The petite Bolivian-American woman glanced at her E-tablet before starting. "The meeting with BC Multimedia to discuss next year's new licensing projects has been confirmed for 2 to 3 p.m. They mostly want to talk about a new lineup for the *Legion Unlimited* MMO."

Once upon a time, Buck Comics had been a small New York company best known for its *Action Tales* comic book series. In 1938 that comic book started to chronicle (and embellish rather radically) Ultimate's adventures, and the rest was history. Now BC Multimedia owned multiple movie studios, publishing houses and software companies, and it lavishly marketed everything related to the Freedom Legion. The relationship had been mutually beneficial for the most part; licensing fees funded a significant percentage of the Legion's budget. Most of the licensing process was left to the many civilian managers working for the organization, but BC's people always wanted some face time with actual Legion members.

Olivia checked the appointment on her tablet's calendar. "An hour sounds good, and don't let me go over it, please." BC's people tended to ramble on if left unchecked. Better to give them a tight deadline. She enjoyed talking to them for the most part – even after becoming a large corporation, BC's management was still dominated by actual fans of the Legion – but she only had a limited amount of time to give them. She reminded herself to change into her costume for that meeting, just to make them happy.

"Of course. Your presence has been requested a 3:30 pm at the Gymnasium. General sparring with the advanced students. ."

"Good, I could use the workout." Even better, she could keep the costume for the sparring session.

The sparring session would be both an outlet to release some pent-up energy and an opportunity to watch some potential Legionnaires. There were several promising new students she wanted to see in action before considering their candidacy to the Legion. In addition to serving as the Legion's headquarters on the Western Hemisphere, the island also hosted the Freedom Institute. The Institute was the premiere Neolympian training school, where young parahumans from all around the world could learn to control and refine their abilities, as well as study the ethics and responsibilities involved in being one of those select few. Most students blessedly took their lessons to heart and became useful and productive members of society. A large percentage of them ended up becoming full-time or reserve members of the Legion.

Thinking about the Institute reminded Olivia of the press conference that morning and the accusations Fowler had leveled towards the legion. 'Sensitivity training' indeed! She didn't know what kind of game that little bastard Fowler was playing. The comment about Linda leaving John had been particularly malicious. Yes, there had been a brief separation, but Linda Lamar had never been afraid of her husband. If anything Ultimate – John – had been the one in fear, always worried about keeping his wife safe. The accusation had been deliberately provocative. It was almost as if Fowler had wanted Ultimate to attack him.

What worried Olivia was that during Fowler's diatribe she had actually thought John was going to react violently. She had known her friend long enough to read his body language and to see the minute tension in his shoulders and face that indicated he was about to do something. If she hadn't intervened and shut Fowler up, she didn't know what might have happened. A man who had spent the better part of a century learning to control his powers and his temper couldn't be so easily provoked, could he? When you added that morning's incident to all the strangeness of the previous month, it was clear that something was very wrong.

Olivia realized Cecilia was waiting for her to stop woolgathering – her assistant was quite adept at sensing what was going through Olivia's mind. "Sorry," Olivia said. "I'm a bit worried about the incident with Ultimate this morning."

"Yes, the whole thing smells like a skunk to me," Cecilia said; she'd clearly been giving the matter some thought as well. "I took the liberty of doing some research on the skunk in question, as a matter of fact. Fowler's blog was just picked by GNN, in a fairly lucrative deal for Fowler."

"That explains what the man was doing on the island. It might even explain the slant of the questions," Olivia said ruefully. The Global News Network and its founder Thaddeus Twist were not fans of Neolympians in general and the Freedom Legion in particular. Twist's media empire never missed an opportunity to point out the real, potential and imaginary problems the world's population of parahumans represented. Twist was an otherwise principled and progressive person, but his obsession with the evil Neos did or could do was a constant annoyance, not least because the man's paranoia was not wholly unfounded. "Fowler has become part of the vast anti-Neo conspiracy, then," Olivia said.

Cecilia's eyes twinkled with amusement. 'Vast Neo Conspiracy' had become a common catchphrase among certain circles. The fact that some Neos did engage in all manner of Byzantine plots did not help, of course. "Aren't conspiracies supposed to be secret?" her assistant replied. "Twist doesn't really try to hide his misgivings about parahumanity."

"No, he doesn't. The sad thing is, I agree with many of his concerns," Olivia admitted. "That's one of the reasons we established the Freedom Institute, to help people with powers become responsible citizens."

"You don't have to convince me, Olivia," Cecilia said with a smile before continuing in a more serious tone. "It was fortunate that Fowler picked on Ultimate instead of one of our more... volatile members. I shudder to think how Berserker would have reacted if provoked in that manner."

"Yes," Olivia said blandly. Cecilia didn't know Ultimate very well. Olivia, on the other hand, knew how angry her friend and mentor had been. It worried her a great deal.

She had known John Clarke for her entire adult life. The first time she saw him she had been plain Olivia O'Brien, high school senior from Baltimore, in the long-gone year 1963. Her parents had taken her to attend the March on Washington that celebrated the passage of the Civil Rights Act earlier that year. As the child of a mixed couple, Olivia knew the racial issues dividing the country all too well. Even on the train to D.C. she had seen the ugly stares her parents attracted everywhere they went. That day she hadn't been particularly upset by the sidelong looks, however. For one, she and her parents were not alone; she had never seen so many people of color together on a train before. More importantly, she felt like part of history in the making.

Reverend King had given his immortal speech that day. Janus also had been there, in his colorful Navy blue and gold costume, his half-mask doing little to conceal his race. His own speech had been cool and dispassionate, and Olivia had forgotten most of what he said, but she and the crowd around her had cheered him wildly nonetheless. Everybody knew Janus had quietly convinced several Southern leaders to change some long-standing policies in their localities. Rumor was some of the more radical white supremacists had disappeared without a trace at around the same time. Olivia didn't think Janus would stoop to that kind of direct action, but she wasn't sure. She cheered him enthusiastically nonetheless. Janus had been the first black superhero, the man who had won the war in the Pacific and who had forced the likes of MacArthur and Halsey to dance to his tune by the sheer force of his personality as much as by his raw power. His speech lacked Reverend King's stirring power, but his presence at the march had meant a great deal.

A hush came over the crowd as Janus finished his speech and people noticed Ultimate flying over the gathering. The silver and red costume was unmistakable. Ultimate's deeds in the European front had been glorified far more than Janus' actions in the Pacific; there were rumors that the two Legionnaires were rivals. Would the Invincible Man try to suppress or intimidate the marcher's gathering? The hero had eschewed politics since the Freedom Legion had become an international organization, but his presence over the gathered crowd seemed ominous.

Ultimate had landed next to Reverend King and shaken his hand, and embraced Janus in a brotherly display of affection. He had remained with King and Janus the rest of the day, saying nothing, respectfully standing behind the speakers of the day, but making clear where his sympathies lay. Plenty of people had bemoaned Ultimate's appearance, her parents' included. They had felt it had been a patronizing gesture, and Olivia could see their point. The teenager she had been only saw the world's greatest hero standing up for what was right, however.

Olivia had never been so proud to be an American.

Things had changed quickly after that day, and not for the better. The Chinese Empire had started a war the next year, only weeks after President Kennedy finalized a major troop withdrawal from the Republic of China with the claim that it was 'time to glean the dividends of peace.' As the US and the UN rushed troops back into Asia, that dumb blonde movie star had gone public with the story of her affair with the President. There were accusations that both the war and the scandal were payback for Kennedy's support for the Civil Rights Act and its equally controversial counterpart, the Parahuman Registration Act. Southerners and Neolympians had allegedly joined forces to destroy the President.

Amidst the controversy, on a cloudy day in May of 1964, Olivia had been seized by convulsions on her way home from school and had collapsed unconscious. When she awoke she realized she had grown three inches in height and become a superhuman being. Her parents' support for the Parahuman Registration Act had wavered when it was time for them to send their darling daughter off to a government facility to have her powers tested and recorded, but in the end Olivia herself had decided to do the right thing.

It was there that she had met Ultimate for the second time, or the first if you discounted that glimpse of him floating down from the sky. He had been one of her teachers, a kind and gentle man who had shown her how to control her powers, and more importantly how to accept who and what she was. Over the decades, as their roles changed from teacher and pupil to friends and equals, they had become close. They had stood side by side through battles and wars, weddings and funerals. He had cried on her shoulder the day his wife died. For a while, Olivia had feared grief would do to him what no weapon or parahuman power had, but John had recovered and moved on. Or so she had thought.

Olivia looked at Cecilia. She knew she could trust her friend implicitly, and she needed to tell somebody. She wished she could tell Larry, but confiding in her husband was no longer a possibility. "I first started noticing something wrong with John about a year ago," she finally said. "It started out with little things. Absent-mindedness. Aloofness and coldness. Memory lapses." She could not bring herself to mention the time a few weeks ago when he had called her by his dead wife's name. It had been heart-breaking, embarrassing and disturbing at the same time. "In the last few weeks they've gotten a lot worse."

"You are saying that Ultimate may be having some sort of breakdown." Cecilia said, looking concerned.

"That's what I'm afraid of," Olivia admitted.

'Neo Psychosis' was a pop psychology term, a catch-all phrase that covered a multitude of problems. The fact remained that Neolympians had a higher incidence of psychological problems than normal humans. Some were the obvious result of being granted superhuman abilities, of course. The mere realization one had become an immortal being with godlike powers could unhinge many minds. Other problems were more subtle and included a variety of personality disorders: an addiction to dangerous thrills, sociopathic and narcissistic tendencies, or even megalomania. For the better part of a century, Ultimate's presence had acted as a counterexample, showing the world a compassionate and steady person who retained those qualities despite being one of the most powerful beings on the planet. If he fell, what hope was there for the rest of parahumanity?

A slight tremor shook the building just as she was about to tell Cecilia more about her worries. In the distance, Olivia heard the unmistakable sound of explosions. What was going on?

"What's that?" Cecilia asked, looking out the window behind Olivia.

Olivia swiveled around on her chair just in time to see fire and smoke erupt from the old Freedom Tower, now turned into a museum. "No!" The sky was full of missiles plunging down on their final trajectories. Pillars of smoke in the distance revealed the source of the explosions she had heard. Instincts honed by decades of combat took over. She was already moving and creating a flaming shield when the first cruise missile hit her office window.

The reinforced glass only served to detonate the high-explosive warhead and provide shrapnel for the fiery explosion. The shockwave washed over her, but she had planted her feet and willed herself not to be moved, and she remained standing. She glanced back. Cecilia had been partially shielded from the explosion and the shrapnel by Olivia's shield, but the petite woman had still been knocked down and was lying semi-conscious on the office floor.

More missiles were coming in. Olivia felt the building shake noticeably as it was struck somewhere below her, and saw more missiles flying directly at her. She created and flung a flame spear at the speed of thought, and detonated one of the missiles a hundred yards away. The other two struck, one exploding directly on her shield, and the heavy warhead was powerful enough to knock her back and stun her for a couple of seconds. Parts of the ceiling collapsed over her

When she recovered, Olivia found herself half buried under fallen masonry. Her head was ringing, but her shield had blunted most of the damage and her superhuman physique had weathered the rest. She could hear other explosions. The building shook alarmingly beneath her.

Olivia lifted a reinforced metal beam off her and staggered to her feet, shrugging off pieces of concrete and rebar that would have crushed a normal human being. The office was a raging inferno. There was no sign of Cecilia or any of the other dozen people that worked in her office.

"Cecilia!" she yelled, but her voice was lost in the conflagration and the new explosions. This couldn't be happening! Freedom Island was one of the most highly protected sites on Earth!

Armageddon Girl

The floor gave way, and Olivia fell as the building collapsed around her.

Chapter Four

Face-Off

New York City, New York, March 13, 2013

I leaned back on the subway car seat and thought deep thoughts.

I was wearing the face of one of my old high school teachers so I wouldn't scare the tourists. Mr. Grover had been a mean-looking son of a bitch, and his face fit my mood and convinced people around me to respect my space. My usual costume is a leather jacket (with discreet Hyper-Kevlar inserts), jeans and combat boots, so people only recognize me when I go faceless. While wearing a borrowed face I was just another disgruntled New Yorker.

Yeah, I know. I may be one of the top vigilantes in the Big Apple, but I usually take the subway to get where I'm going. I had dumped Giamatti's car somewhere in the Bronx, just in case the bad guys had a way to track it other than the GPS device I had disabled before driving off with it. By now Giamatti's Tucker Raptor was probably being stripped for parts at some chop shop, and I was back to using my usual mode of transportation. My other method of travel, jumping from rooftop to rooftop, was fine for short trips but not the best way to get around for anything involving more than a few blocks. When I really needed a car, I would steal it: pimps had the best wheels and they rarely called the cops, so they were my go-to people when I wanted a ride. At the moment, the train suited me fine. It gave me time to think.

This job was getting weirder and weirder. Cassandra had sent me off to check on the girl while she figured out the next step. If Christine was up and about I was supposed to learn as much as possible from her while I waited for Cassandra to get in touch with further instructions. My immediate worry was thinking of ways to keep the ex-hostage from contacting the authorities. While I traveled from the East Village to the Bronx and back, she might well have woken up and demanded to be let go. Father Alex wouldn't keep her against her will, and neither would I, for that matter. My only hope would be to convince her it was in her best interests to stay under wraps while we figured who had ordered the kidnapping and why. Which was something that Cassandra would usually know by now, but with the astral plane or whatever being fucked up, we were flying blind. I was not happy.

I got off the subway and headed for Saint Theodosius. If the girl was awake, I'd offer to buy her lunch and see if I could persuade her to hang around. Talking to somebody I hadn't beaten up or otherwise put the fear of God into wasn't my specialty, except when I had a fake face and identity on. Maybe that was the way to go. Pretend to be an undercover cop or something like that. I lie to people all the time, but the idea of deceiving an abduction victim didn't sit well with me. I'd play it by ear and see what happened.

I went to the back entrance of the Church. The door was open, as usual. I could hear Father Aleksander's voice from the kitchen, so I headed there. He was talking to a woman. The damsel in distress must have woken up, then, and at least it didn't sound like she was going to run right away. I walked into the kitchen, still undecided about what to say. I was leaning toward just laying my cards on the table and telling her everything.

Father Aleksander and the girl were sitting by the kitchen table while an inane morning show played on the flat screen TV hanging on the wall. The girl, wearing silly striped pajamas and a bathrobe a few sizes too large for her, was spooning up the last remains of a bowl of soup – borscht by the smell of it. A wrist-comm lay on the table next to her; hopefully she hadn't used it to call the police.

"Hello," I said; not much of an entrance line, but my normal entrance line is 'Freeze, motherfuckers!' and that really didn't fit the setting.

"Ah, there you are," Father Aleksander said amiably. He always knew it was me, no matter what face I had on. "Christine, this is your rescuer, the Faceless Vigilante." Okay, we were going for all the truth and nothing but.

The girl looked at me, and I remembered I was still wearing Mr. Grover's face, which made me look about fifteen years older than I really was, and not a sight for sore eyes at any age. But when her eyes met mine, I forgot about my face. I felt like she was looking through my fake face – through all the faces I could wear. It was like the first time I met Cassandra. This girl – Christine, her name was Christine – could see *me*.

Before I could start to process that first impression, Christine all but leaped from her seat. Next thing I knew she was hugging me like I was her long-lost brother or something.

I usually don't react well when people make sudden moves. I react even worse when people invade my personal space and touch me uninvited. And I most definitely react very badly when someone hugs me without warning. Typical reactions to any of the above range from shoves to harsh language. If I'm in a pissy mood, gunfire isn't out of the question.

Instead, I let her hug me. Nobody had hugged me like that since my childhood days with my mother, not even Aleksander when he got sentimentally drunk. It felt pretty good. Not that I would admit it to save my life. I'm fucking Face-Off. I don't do affectionate.

"Thank you for saving me," Christine said, still clutching me tightly.

"Yeah, sure, no problem," I said awkwardly and lightly patted her back. I wanted to hug her in return, but I couldn't muster the courage to do it, tough guy that I was. Especially not in front of Father Aleksander, whose face seemed to be struggling between expressions of amazement and delight. A second later he looked concerned, but he couldn't say anything because Christine was talking at a few miles a minute.

"Also, thank you for taking me here, Father Aleksander is the nicest guy even if he's not Presbyterian, which is okay. I still don't understand what's going on, but thank you anyway." She let go of me and stepped back, still talking. "But I'm sure we can figure it out and holy crap where is your face."

I realized I had let go of Mr. Grover's features when Christine hugged me. That happens sometimes when I'm startled or lose concentration, both of which had happened this time. No wonder Father Alex had looked concerned. Christine fell silent for a whole second, and I braced myself for the shrieking that was the usual reaction when people caught me being myself. Instead, she stepped close to me. "That's incredible! Is that why they call you the Faceless Vigilante?"

"Well, they mostly call me Face-Off, but yeah," I said.

"Like that old movie with John Travolta and Nick Cage?"

"Uu, I don't remember that movie. And I know who Nicholas Cage is, but John Travolta? You mean Joseph Travolta?" This was turning into the strangest conversation in my life.

"No biggie. Wow, your voice sounds just like before, but you have no mouth. No anything!" She stepped closer, her hands reaching for my head. "May I?"

Typically, people who reach for my face end up with broken fingers, but I found myself saying "Sure." Mind control, it must be some form of mind control.

Christine gently touched my un-face. Her fingers ran down the smooth surface, pausing near the area where my eyes should be. "Does that bother you?"

"No. It's as if I was wearing goggles. I can see you touching the surface, but it doesn't feel as if you were actually touching my eyeballs," I said.

"That's amazing. It feels like touching the back of a skull, but on the front. Has someone done an X-ray of your head? And you can change face shapes, which means you must change your bone structure. We'd have to run an X-ray of your head before and after a shape change. Or an MRI would be better. Holy mother of crap, this is the awesomest thing I've seen!" She was smiling like a kid at a candy store, but all of a sudden she sobered up. "I'm sorry, I don't mean to sound like you're a lab rat or something."

"Oh, ah, it's okay," I said lamely. I wasn't mad at her. I didn't know what I was feeling, other than shell-shocked. I was supposed to be interrogating her, and she was ready to conduct a full parahuman power study on my no-face. Why wasn't she scared of me?

"How can you do that?" she asked me, and there wasn't a trace of fear or disgust in her voice, just open, almost innocent curiosity. "How is it even possible?"

"How can some people fly or pick up tanks? I'm a Neo, of course."

"Neo? Like Keanu Reeves in *The Matrix* movies? 'Take the red pill' Neo?"

More movies I'd never heard of. And I loved going to the movies, usually on weekdays during the day, when I could sit quietly in a mostly empty theater. Cassandra's words came back to me. Christine was some sort of alien, supposedly. Except I was beginning to realize she wasn't from another planet, not exactly.

"I'm sorry, but I've never heard of that movie, either. Neo is short for Neolympian."

"Okay, now it's my turn to never have heard of something," Christine said.

Definitely not from around here. This was going to be interesting. "Neolympians? Parahumans? Superheroes?"

"Superheroes?"

"And super-villains, but most people just prefer to call us Neos."

"I'm going to sit down now," Christine said and went and did it. She was clearly upset, and seeing her like that was upsetting me, which again wasn't like me at all. Other people's problems don't upset me, except for the urge to smack down the people responsible. Christine was looking at the wrist-comm on the table as if it was going to jump up and bite her. "Do you know what this is?" she asked, pointing at it.

"The wrist-comm? It's a wrist-comm. Well, a wrist-comp officially, since you can surf the web with it and write e-mails, but everybody still calls them wrist-comms." I said. One of the most common personal items since the 1970s, and she was looking at it like it was Smith Industries' newest wonder gadget.

"Not a cell phone?"

I had a mental image of a phone inside a prison cell, and almost laughed, but Christine wasn't laughing. "I don't know what a cell phone is," I said.

"Oh, this is not good at all," Christine muttered.

Father Aleksander turned the TV up, interrupting the conversation before I had the chance to break the news to her. Not that I really knew how I was going to do that. Maybe I could say something like 'Welcome to Wonderland.'

"I'm sorry, but something is happening," Father Alex said before I could try the Wonderland line. Sure enough, Special Report banners were flashing and a news anchor had shown up and replaced the morning show.

Christine and I stopped talking and watched history being made.

The Freedom Legion

Atlantic Headquarters, March 13, 2013

The fastest man in the world was a day late and a dollar short.

The attack caught Larry Graham with his pants down, literally. When the first wave of missiles struck, Larry was busy cheating on his wife with a young Legion recruit in an out-of-the-way hiding spot. It was the worst possible time and place.

Even as he lay on his back while Dawn Zhang – code name Dawn Windstorm – rode him like a bronco, Larry didn't think of himself as a bad guy. Weak and contemptible, yes, but not a bad guy. He had loved Olivia O'Brien passionately for over four decades, and he still loved her, just not the way a husband was supposed to love his wife. Larry had been raised to mean the words 'until death do us part.' "Now and forever," he'd whispered to Olivia just before kissing her on their wedding night.

What he hadn't counted on was how long forever would turn out to be.

Back when he'd been regular Joe College Larry at Boston U, he read a great deal about the Greek gods of mythology. He'd done so partly because Greek mythology had been all the rage after the rise of Neolympians, and partly because he'd picked up Greek as his language elective, and a lot of what the Greeks had written down involved their whimsical and oft malicious deities. The relationship between Zeus and Hera particularly fascinated him. Zeus just couldn't keep his hands – and the rest of his anatomy – to himself. He just ended up with one dame after another – human or Olympian, married or a virgin, it was all grist for the mill to the horny bastard. Zeus was the ultimate dirty old man. Even though the tales amused Larry greatly, he had never figured out why Zeus did what he did. Hera must have been the ultimate ball and chain to drive her hubby to such extremes.

On his sophomore year in college, he went from reading about gods to becoming one. He was walking to his next class when he saw an old jalopy about to run over a woman crossing the street, well over a block away. He ran the intervening distance in the blink of an eye and got her out of the way just in time. A new hero was born that day. Larry tried to use Hermes as his code name, but some idiot newsie stuck him with the moniker Swift, and Swift he became.

Larry kept his identity a secret at first. It was 1940 and the war was in full swing, and even with the US remaining neutral, a few incautious New Olympians had been murdered, either by foreign agents or local super-criminals. He wore a mask and made sure Larry Graham remained well away from the limelight. While wearing the mask and costume, however, Swift became a hit with the ladies. It turned out that gods did get all the girls. Larry cut a swath through Beantown's best and brightest, loving every minute of it. He only slowed down when he joined the Freedom Legion shortly after Pearl Harbor, and that only because Doc Slaughter gave him a pointed talk about the image the Legion had to maintain.

Larry had been more discreet while he went to war, but even as he helped the Allies march through France, the Low Countries and Germany he rarely had to sleep alone. After the Legion became an international organization, he revealed his identity to the world, and Larry Graham became a celebrity. He dated movie stars and fashion models. He finally understood where Zeus was coming from.

Armageddon Girl

He had thought he understood, at least. When Olivia came around, his world view turned upside down. They met in another continent, another war. Olivia was one of the most beautiful women he'd ever seen, with *cafe au lait* skin, deep emerald eyes and a dazzling smile that turned ladies' man Larry into a fool for love. Her exotic looks, her bravery and strength, the hidden vulnerability beneath, they had swept him off his feet. He'd turned his back on twenty-odd years as a happy bachelor, wooed her – yes, at first he had only thought about getting in her pants, but that had changed quickly – and eventually won her heart. In the midst of the death and destruction of the First Asian War, he made her his bride. He had never been happier.

For a while.

Forever was such a long time.

A year had become ten, had become twenty. On their twentieth anniversary, she looked as beautiful as ever. Nothing had changed. Nothing had fucking changed at all. That is, nothing except how he felt.

Little things grew and became big things. Habits and mannerisms that once had been charming became annoying. He knew what she would say or do in almost every situation, and vice versa. Jokes that had made her laugh now only brought about tolerant smiles or annoyed grimaces. They got on each other's nerves. She wanted to talk about their problems. He most definitely didn't.

It wasn't all bad, of course. Rome didn't collapse in one day. Their work in the Legion had often kept them apart for weeks or even months at a time, and their reunions had been sweet. Their love would spark and rekindle, and things would once again be well. For a while. For some time. For a week or a month, or even a whole year.

But not forever.

Forever. The word became hateful. As twenty years together became thirty, Larry had fully understood Zeus' plight. Even if Hera had been the sweetest, most beautiful woman in the world, he would have gotten sick of her, given enough time. Immortals could not be monogamous, he decided. At least Larry couldn't be monogamous, not for longer than a lengthy prison term he couldn't. He never could figure out how John Clarke managed to stay faithful to his woman. That smug, self-righteous stick in the mud never strayed; Larry had watched him carefully over the years, sure his fidelity was an act, and had found nothing. He even arranged a couple of blatant opportunities for John, 'chance' encounters with very interested women, to no avail. Ultimate seemed to be perfectly happy with his rapidly aging vanilla wife. Larry envied John bitterly for that, and despised him as much as he despised himself. Unlike John, he hadn't been able to resist when opportunities presented themselves.

It had started slowly, in fits and starts. A night with a secret agent in Minsk during a covert operation, followed by months of guilt and, perversely enough, a renewed passion for Olivia, which, as always, did not last. Discreet call girls while on station in Beijing. A particularly wild fling with Chastity Baal – and boy, didn't that almost let the cat out of the bag! And many more. Larry always regretted the affairs, always came crawling back to Olivia. She never suspected anything, or if she did, she kept her suspicions to herself. Of late, Larry had come to resent that. Why didn't she know something was wrong?

The one-night stands and short-lived affairs had become a habit after a while. Larry had thought about coming clean and taking things to their logical conclusion. That was when he discovered another aspect of the tragedy of Zeus. The marriage, flawed and hollow as it was, had become part of his identity. He could not conceive of not being married to Olivia. The thought of their parting ways simply terrified him. That realization had led to almost a year of fidelity.

On the eleventh month, Dawn Zhang had joined the Freedom Legion and Larry's downfall had begun.

Dawn was twenty-two, of mixed Chinese and European ancestry, tall and slender and utterly beautiful. Her hair had turned platinum blond the day her ability to control and create winds manifested itself. Her smile melted Larry's heart. Feelings he had not experienced since the beginning of his relationship with Olivia came back with a vengeance.

It was a complete disaster. She was a junior member of the Legion. He was one of her instructors, in a position of power over her, which made fraternization a clear violation of the Legion's by-laws. She was in her early twenties and he had just celebrated his ninety-first birthday. They had nothing in common; the music she listened to was excruciating noise to him, and his cultural background was prehistoric twaddle to her. And yet his old jokes had made her laugh, possibly because they were so old she'd never heard of them. And Dawn's initial hero worship had turned into friendship and mutual attraction. A late night's conversation had ended with a kiss. Things had snowballed quickly after that.

Having an affair in the days of goggle-cams and wrist-comps was hard enough. Having an affair in the Atlantic Headquarters of the Freedom Legion, one of the most heavily guarded and watched facilities on the planet, was a heroic undertaking. Rank hath its privileges, fortunately, and Larry was a Founder, with access to the highest level codes and overrides. They had found secret times and places to be together, and the sneakiness of it all had only added spice to the whole thing.

Larry and Dawn had been in the throes of passion – or, as Dawn put it, screwing like two minks in heat – in a little-used subterranean hangar where several obsolete Legion aircraft gathered dust before being decommissioned. The hangar was deep enough underground and far enough away from the central headquarters that neither of them even noticed the first few explosions. It was only when the hangar lights dimmed and were replaced by red emergency lights that Larry realized something was wrong. Dawn paused her pounding for a second, and Larry grabbed her, got on top and finished what they had started. Whatever was happening topside, some things just couldn't be interrupted.

Larry's post-coital aftermath was normally pleasant and lazy. Now as sex faded away dread filled him. The hangar shook noticeably.

"We're under attack!" Dawn shouted needlessly as she groped around for her uniform. Larry did not waste his breath while he poured himself into his iconic blue and yellow jumpsuit. Comic book mythology to the contrary, he was only the fastest man in the world when he ran; getting dressed took as long for him as for any highly agile Neo. In other words, it was a matter of seconds, but not the blink of an eye.

He didn't wait for Dawn. The calculating part of his mind that was always on, even in times of passion or stress, figured that it would be best if they joined the action separately. They were fifty feet underground but luckily even this mostly mothballed hangar had fast-deployment hydraulic catapults. He stepped into a cylindrical chamber and was launched up like a cannonball. He emerged from the hangar already moving at a good fifty miles an hour.

When his feet hit the ground, he raised that speed tenfold in one second.

Swift's power had two main components. First, he created a frictionless force field around him that made him nearly invulnerable in addition to reducing air drag. To achieve higher speeds, the force field changed and he became intangible, no longer subject to friction and able to move at five or six times the speed of sound without unleashing a devastating sonic boom in his wake. All those powers only worked when he ran or spun in place, for reasons nobody had been able to fathom. The mechanisms behind his abilities remained a mystery. A liberal arts major, Larry had never been much for the hard sciences, and he didn't care much about how his powers worked.

All he cared about was his speed, and all the tricks he could play with it.

Inside the field, the world slowed to a crawl. A cruise missile floated lazily overhead. Larry altered his trajectory and he shot up into the air, intercepting the missile and becoming solid just as he met his target, obliterating it. As he emerged from the explosion, he turned insubstantial again and ran through the air until he caught another missile and destroyed it. Neither explosion made an impression on him; he was back on the ground a fraction of a second later. Unfortunately those had been the only missiles within his reach, and too many of them had already struck their targets.

Where the Freedom Building had once stood there was nothing but a billowing cloud of dust and smoke.

Olivia had been there. He had memorized her schedule, the better to plan his date with Dawn.

Larry screamed his wife's name and charged into the burning ruin.

C.J. Carella

Christine Dark

New York City, New York, March 13, 2013

The TV report convinced Christine she wasn't in Kansas anymore.

Father Aleksander had served her some truly excellent borsch. While she devoured it, he explained that she had been found unconscious in Central Park two nights ago and taken to New York-Presbyterian Hospital. There, he continued as she slurped on, some Mafia guys had abducted her. An associate of Father Aleksander had rescued her from her captors and brought her to the church, where a parishioner who happened to be a nurse had checked her out and dressed her in the funky pajamas. Father Alex called her rescuer the Faceless Vigilante, which sounded rather silly, but he had said the name very seriously.

The account matched her memories of the dream much too closely; that almost freaked her out all over again. Somehow she managed to keep her cool. Father Aleksander's friendly demeanor helped calm her down, or maybe his borsch's secret ingredient was a generous helping of Xanax. She was scared, but the fear wasn't overwhelming her, and that was so unlike her it added an extra scary layer to the whole thing. It was so weird she had to set it aside for the moment. Christine concentrated on eating and listening and tried not to dwell on anything right away.

Things got even weirder when she asked to borrow a phone.

"You can use my wrist-comm," Aleksander said. He unstrapped a weird cell phone from his wrist and handed it to her. Okay, so maybe that's what they called them in the Ukraine or whatever.

The phone wasn't like any mobile device Christine had seen, and she had changed plans on a nearly seasonal basis since age sixteen; between her and Sophie they had tried everything under the sun, including all the I-stuff Apple gleefully pushed out every year. The device she was holding was clearly meant to be worn strapped on your wrist, like an old-school wristwatch. It was bigger than your typical smart phone, and it had a flip cover over a screen that lit up, with the date and time on the top, a row of icons off to one side, and a colorful background picture of an ancient church. It had a keyboard and the screen was touch-sensitive; the whole thing was fairly user-friendly, although not quite like anything else she had ever used before.

Christine decided to try Sophie's number first, to try and find out what the frak had happened the night of the party. It was also one of the only three numbers she had memorized, the other two being her own and her mother's. She really didn't want to call Mom, not until she figured out what was going on.

"I'm sorry," the wrist-phone or comm or whatever said in a pleasant female voice. "Your call cannot be completed as dialed. Please make sure to enumerate the area code and the eight digit number you are trying to reach."

Eight digit number? Christine typed the number again – and got the same message. She tried to punch a 1 before the area code to make it to eleven digits, and she got a slightly different message that pretty much said the same thing. "I don't think the phone is working," she said.

"Are you sure? It seems to be in working order."

"Phone numbers are seven digits long," Christine said. "With the area code, that makes ten."

Father Aleksander looked confused. "That's quite wrong, I'm sorry to say. Phone numbers are eight digits long, eleven with the area code."

Christine gently put the wrist-phone thingy down and had some more some soup while she tried to think things through.

Explanation Number One: The good Father was out of his freaking gourd, kind eyes or not, and he'd probably put that useless talking wrist thingy together with a pieces of discarded I-Phones and baling wire. She wasn't in New York, she was probably in some abandoned church in Michigan, and any second now Aleksander and the Faceless Vigilante, who probably was a leather-clad gimp living in a steamer trunk in the next room, would grab her and do unspeakable things while they sang a jaunty song from *Oklahoma*.

Explanation Number Two: Christine's brain had been scrambled by some roofie combo last night, and she'd apparently forgotten a few facts of life, such as phone numbers having one more digit than she remembered and that the latest mobile devices had wrist straps. The damage was probably permanent and she'd spend the rest of her life painting pleasant watercolors in some innocuously-named institution with beautiful lawns and tall walls where they played soothing Enya tunes in the background.

Explanation Number Three: This was all a dream, and she was in a hospital, or lying unconscious on the frat house lawn, dreaming of Ukrainian Orthodox priests and wrist-comms and cabbage and kings. She would either wake up eventually, or check Explanation Two, except add more Enya, eliminate watercolor painting or any activity and, for an added bonus, orderlies rolling over her comatose body checking for bedsores every other week. With her luck one of the orderlies would be called Buck and he'd be there to... you know.

There was an Explanation Number Four, but she didn't want to go there. Might as well enjoy the borsch and watch the boob tube, which was playing *Live! With Regis and Betsy*, which was weird because Regis had retired a while back and weirder still because there was no sign of Kelly Ripa or even Kathy Lee anywhere and she had no clue who Betsy was. Whatever she did, she would not explore Explanation Number Four, because that way lay madness.

The arrival of the Faceless Vigilante had stopped her brain from shooting up into the stratosphere for a whole three seconds or so. One look at him and she'd known several facts with total conviction: she could trust him with her life, he wasn't nearly as old as he looked, and she was going to hug him like his name was Teddy and it was stuffed bear season. Which led to discovering his real face was impossibly featureless. Which should have freaked the frak out of her, but somehow didn't. *The crazy is strong with this one, this one being me.* Either she had quietly flipped out or her weirdness threshold had been exceeded to the point that her her freak-out engine was out of gas. Explanation One was discarded, which left Explanations Two or Three, but Four was beginning to poke its crazy little head from the corner of her mind she had consigned it to. People like Face-Off didn't exist in her world. Which meant...

The news report came in, and that did the trick. Especially when they switched to a live report from the observation deck of the World Trade Center.

The fact that the live report also showed several people in colorful costumes flying through the air in the best comic book tradition was only icing on the crazy cake.

Explanation Four: She was in a different world, where superheroes were real and Keanu Reeves wasn't, where John Travolta was named Joseph, and people wore their cell phones on their wrists like people used to do with watches. Where Faceless Vigilantes could be literally faceless. Among God only knew how many other different things.

Face-Off and Father Aleksander watched the news intently until they went to a commercial break. For Pan Am Airlines. Which Christine only recognized from a short-lived TV show about an airline that no longer existed. In her world. No longer existed in her world. She had the sickening realization she was going to be using those words a lot. Her world. She wasn't in her world anymore.

"Guys?" They turned to her. "My brain is about to explode. I don't normally do this before noon. Or at all. But could I have something alcoholic in a glass? Or an IV bag, I'm not picky. Pretty please?"

Armageddon Girl

Chapter Five

The Freedom Legion

Atlantic Headquarters, March 13, 2013

Kenneth Slaughter rushed towards the sound of the guns.

Off to his left, both the Freedom Tower and the Freedom Building were collapsing under multiple missile impacts. Up ahead, dozens of aerial platforms moved in a precise death dance, firing missiles from external launchers and maneuvering off to let following waves move into position for their own strikes. The swarm of projectiles reached out towards the still-standing buildings or targeted some of the running or flying individuals trying to defend the island. The attack was all beautifully coordinated, human ingenuity used for efficient death dealing.

The paradox had never been lost on Kenneth. He had become intimately aware of it in 1917, when he had been a terrified young man forcing himself to climb up a trench wall and charge towards massed machine guns and artillery, exquisitely crafted tools designed for the single purpose of ending life.

Even worse, he had learned he himself was quite capable of murder.

One night Kenneth had been in a trench raid that ended disastrously, flares dispelling the darkness, machine guns mowing down the rest of his squad. He had found himself alone and surrounded by enemies. He tried to surrender but an angry and terrified soldier, no older than he was, had stabbed him with a bayonet. The sudden agony and the outraged sense of betrayal had overwhelmed Kenneth. The world had dissolved into a red haze. When he regained his senses, he was the only living thing in the trench, surrounded by the bloody remains of twenty-three men he had slaughtered in his frenzied state. The incident had terrified him. He had resolved to forever bury his inner beast under a rational, emotionless façade. More importantly, he had devoted his life to seeking some form of redemption.

Over the ensuing decades, Kenneth had applied his superhuman talents toward finding a way to bring true peace to humanity. He had finally accepted that killing was an inherent part of the human condition, impossible to remove without destroying humanity itself. Since then, he had done his best to minimize the evil that men would invariably do.

The attack had found him in his underground lab, where he had been performing a routine review of the sixteen projects he was currently overseeing. Like all Genius-Type Neolympians, Kenneth was given to flashes of intuition that allowed him to envision amazing breakthroughs in a variety of scientific fields. His projects ran the gamut from high-energy physics to biotechnology. The development process was the main obstacle for Neolympians, who all tended to suffer from the scientific equivalent of short attention spans. Kenneth had long learned to pass on his ideas to teams of normal but patient scientists and engineers who would proceed to bring his visions to fruition. He still needed to periodically revisit the ongoing projects to make sure his subalterns didn't miss some important detail that could derail a project.

The reason Genius-Types could produce so many breakthroughs in different fields was not a product of intelligence or education, Kenneth had concluded after years of observing his own talents. It was a psychic ability to identify the right answer without having to resort to the game of trial and error that normal scientists had to play. Furthermore, many Neolympian inventions were really not actual technological developments but artifacts created by the same mysterious force that gave parahumans their powers. Those creations could not be duplicated or mass-produced, and telling the two kinds of inventions apart often took a great deal of work.

To Kenneth's eternal regret, all the technological wonders and miraculous creations of the Neolympian era had not stopped murder. If anything, they had made killing easier than ever before.

The evidence was literally exploding all around him.

As he emerged from the underground laboratory, Kenneth activated his own signature artifact, the Brass Man suit that had earned him his second code name. In the Thirties, he had been Doc Slaughter, one of the mystery men who battled evil during the chaotic years of the Great Depression. Under that name he had helped found the Freedom Legion during World War Two. A generation later, he developed his suit of powered armor, and the press dubbed him Brass Man and treated him almost as a completely separate persona. In some ways, the distinction was correct. His personality underwent some changes when he was behind the armor suit, becoming even more dispassionate and machine-like. It probably was a coping mechanism, necessary when he found himself wielding even more power than normal.

From hidden compartments in his belt, shoulders and boots, metal bands emerged and wrapped themselves around his limbs, head and torso, the flexible organic metal hardening into unyielding armor strips once all its pieces were in place. Doc Slaughter became a living bronze figure, a thing of overlapping plates and decorative rivets gleaming in the reflected sunlight and explosive flashes around him. Brass Man leaped and took flight, the propulsion jets built into several points of the armor suit giving him better acceleration and maneuverability than the most advanced fighter aircraft.

Becoming Brass Man was a heady experience. The sensor suite built into the armor flooded him with information only a mind as adept at his could assimilate. While in his armor his strength and durability were the equal or superior of most Type Two parahumans. He would need all the power at his disposal to help deal with the current situation.

The attackers were using waves of unmanned drones. A quick sensor sweep revealed their capabilities: they were low speed but high stealth weapon platforms, each armed with half a dozen cruise missiles. His sensors also detected the source of the attack, a flying vessel the size of a pocket battleship; that vessel had launched the drones. Freedom Island was guarded by one of the most sophisticated air defense systems in the world, but somehow the flying carrier ship had managed to get close enough to attack while remaining undetected. The first strike had destroyed or disabled most defense systems; the second one had struck buildings full of innocent civilians.

First things first. Twin balls of plasma shot out of his gauntlets, hitting a pair of drones dead center and vaporizing them. The plasma explosion also generated a large electro-magnetic pulse that fried the electronic systems of another half-dozen pods around the initial targets. Three more shots took care of seventeen drones. A part of him felt a rush of savage elation and wished the drones had been piloted by the murderers who had seen fit to attack innocent civilians. He pushed the dark emotions deeper down, where they could not bother him.

Other Legion members were on the offensive as well. Daedalus Smith flashed past Kenneth in his Myrmidon battle armor. Kenneth suppressed a surge of irritation at the sight. Daedalus had built his own armor suit not too long after Kenneth had become Brass Man. Kenneth could not deny the Myrmidon armor was highly effective and more powerful than his own, but the constant games of one-upmanship Daedalus insisted on playing got on Kenneth's nerves, not that he ever let his feelings show. The Myrmidon soared through the drones and blew up several of them with a barrage of charged particle beams.

Behind the two armored warriors, other Legionnaires were dealing with the remaining cruise missiles. Dawn Windstorm surrounded herself with a tornado that intercepted several rockets and sent them spinning down into the sea. Hyperia the Invincible Woman chased down another missile and detonated it before it reached its target; she emerged from the fiery explosion unscathed and looking for more targets. From the ground, a couple dozen other Legion members and advanced Freedom Institute students were engaging the last remaining targets with a myriad powers ranging from telekinesis to laser beams.

The battle was not entirely one-sided, however. Some of the missiles were targeting Legion members. Kenneth's sensors coolly listed a growing casualty list,

Legionnaires killed or injured by direct hits or buried under collapsing buildings. The injured would most likely survive; Neolympians could recover from almost anything that did not kill them instantly. There dead could not be brought back, however.

All of the missiles and most of the drones were destroyed after a brief but brutal battle. The few survivors headed back to the carrier vessel, presumably to rearm. The carrier was moving as well, continuing on a direct heading toward Freedom Island. Kenneth flew towards the ship.

He was not alone. Telekinetic adept Mind Hawk had picked up four other Legionnaires – Gun Bunny, Shocking Susan, the Illusionist and Hercules Seven – and headed directly towards the flying carrier. The assault team had pulled ahead while Kenneth dealt with the drones. Kenneth followed them even as his sensors picked up Ultimate flying behind and rapidly overtaking him. Kenneth felt a familiar pang of envy. It shamed him to admit it, but a part of him was jealous of the Invincible Man. Even in his battle suit, Kenneth would never wield the sheer power that the likes of Ultimate and Janus had been blessed with. Perhaps it was better that way. The temptation to use such power for the betterment of mankind, whether or not mankind agreed, might have been too much for him to resist.

Kenneth shrugged off the unworthy emotion and concentrated on the task at hand. One of the dozen screens glowing on the inside of the helmet showed a schematic of the huge tender vessel. Thousands of tons of metal were kept aloft by six anti-gravity devices. The devices had been developed by the Dominion of the Ukraine decades ago, but remained rare and hideously expensive; they were artifacts, each hand-made by the handful of Neolympians with the gift to make such things. Their power requirements were massive, and only a nuclear power plant or some parahuman-created equivalent could meet them. Sure enough, his sensors detected the tell-tale particle emissions of a fission reactor placed near the center of the vessel.

Ultimate flew past him, moving at supersonic speeds and still accelerating. A second later Hyperia also overtook Kenneth. They would quickly catch up with Mind Hawk and his team. Myrmidon was flying in a wide arc in an attempt to get on the other side of the vessel should it or any of its crew try to escape in that direction. That put him out of action for the time being, but Ultimate and the assault team would be able to deal with anything they encountered. They would need to be careful not to damage the ship's nuclear power plant, however.

"Brass Man to attack elements," Kenneth said through his comm system. "Be advised, there is a nuclear reactor inside the vessel. Try to capture it intact if possible."

"Roger that." Ultimate sounded like his own self. John was always calmest during emergencies. It was only during the interludes between times of crisis that his mind seemed to feed on itself.

There was a brief flurry of acknowledgments from the other Legionnaires as they flew closer to their target – and came into range of its defensive systems. The tender ship was more than a carrier: it boasted its own formidable armaments. Two dozen heavy air to air missile launchers and a storm of auto cannon and laser fire reached out towards the approaching Legionnaires. Ultimate just flew through the barrage. Depleted uranium slugs and megawatt-laser beams bounced off him like so many raindrops.

Kenneth's armor was nowhere near as resilient, so he had to maneuver around the worst of it and use his plasma guns to knock down missiles before they could hit him. A few near misses and a direct hit with a high-intensity laser made Kenneth grunt with pain. The armor absorbed most of the damage, but the residual heat that got through would have knocked out or killed a human pilot.

Mind Hawk's attack group was shielded by an energy bubble, courtesy of Shocking Susan. They seemed to be weathering the attacks just fine, and had nearly reached the craft. The Invincible Man got there first: he flew straight into the side of the ship and plowed through its battleship-grade armor plating as if it was cardboard. The rest of the attack group entered through the breach Ultimate had made.

The ship exploded a fraction of a second later. The nuclear reactor inside the vessel had been more than a power source: it was also a weapon.

A small sun was born over the Caribbean.

Searing light and heat washed over Kenneth, blinding him. He could smell his own flesh being roasted. He had time for a brief scream before the blast wave from the nuclear explosion swatted him from the sky and sent him crashing into the sea.

C.J. Carella

Hunters and Hunted

New York City, New York, March 13, 2013

Vincent Bufalino – ever since becoming a made man, he had insisted on being called Vincent, and people called him Vinnie or Vin at their peril – stared sourly at the security camera footage on his computer screen and puffed furiously on his Cuban cigar.

"Fuckin' Face-Off," Dominic D'Onofrio, Vincent's second-hand man, muttered under his breath as he and Vincent watched Face-Off kill the Lightning King on the screen one more time. Vincent had blown close to a million bucks bringing the Lightning King into the States and setting him up as an enforcer, and the colored freak had lasted all of three months before the faceless fucker wasted him. Fucking Neos. Vincent hated Neos, despite the fact that he technically was one of them. Just a Type One, though, barely better than a normal human. Sure, he'd taken his gifts and put them to good use, but he still hated the freaks, not least because he'd gotten the short end of the stick when they were handing out super powers.

"Yeah, that fucker really screwed us." How badly, Vincent wasn't sure, but he feared it would be as bad as it could get. He'd gambled and lost, and he didn't know if he could cover his stake.

"We gotta find 'em," Vincent growled. "Him and the girl. Shit, I don't care if I never lay eyes on his ugly mug, but we gotta find the girl, Dom."

"We'll find her, Vincent," Dom said, but Vincent could tell Dom was just going along. There was no way they would find her in time. Vincent had thought he could get a better deal if he played the angles, and now he'd lost big time. Fucking Neos were supposed to be luckier than regular folk on top of all their abilities, but his luck had been all bad this time.

Doing business with the Russians was always a bad idea. They were bugfuck crazy, for one, and you never knew if they were doing something for the money or if they were working for that crazy metal-headed freak running the show back in the Motherland. But they had a lot of money and special toys, so it was hard to turn them down. Especially because if you turned them down the crazy fucks might take offense and decide that your head would work great as a bowling ball.

So when they had offered a good payday for a simple snatch and grab – okay, not so simple, at a freaking hospital, but easy enough – Vincent had seen no reason to decline. The Russians had been respectful and had come to him instead of trying to do business on his turf without his say so. Russians weren't short of muscle but they didn't do well outside Brooklyn, and Vincent had contacts everywhere. He had half a dozen rackets running out of New York-Presbyterian, so grabbing some skirt out of there sounded easy enough. Everybody wins, nobody gets hurt.

When the details of the job started coming out, however, Vincent had gotten suspicious. And greedy, let's not mince words. The job was more complicated than it had sounded at first, and Vincent had smelled a bigger payoff. For one, the girl had to be kept heavily sedated and trussed up like a Thanksgiving turkey. That could only mean she was a Neo. As soon as he figured that out, Vincent had done two things right away: he'd sent out one his own Neos and his top enforcer, Danny Giamatti, along on the job, and he'd started figuring out the angles.

He was supposed to drop off the girl somewhere in Brighton Beach as soon as they got her, but Vincent had decided to delay the delivery for a bit, and see if he could renegotiate the contract, sweeten the deal a little. He would hold on to the girl and claim there had been some complications, so now the job wasn't worth his while unless the Russians upped the ante. The Russians would be pissed, but they would pay up. They might be crazy, but Vincent ran most of Manhattan and the surrounding areas. They weren't crazy enough to start something just because they'd been shortchanged a little bit. Vincent wasn't even going to ask for much more, just a couple of concessions here and there, get his foot in the door on some of the Russian rackets, like those new ray guns they were getting from the Ukraine. They were going for fifteen grand a piece, and word was they would deep-fry a guy no matter how much body armor he was wearing. Vincent was already collecting taxes on any transaction the Russkies did on his turf, but he wanted a real piece of the action. So instead of delivering the girl, he'd told Giamatti to sit on her and made a few phone calls to get things rolling on the negotiations.

It had been a nice plan, except things had gotten fucked up from the get go.

First, Giamatti had gone off the reservation and killed four civilians at the hospital, the stupid mook. It should have been an easy in-and-out job. Vincent had greased the wheels with the hospital people so they knew to get out of the way and be on a break when Giamatti and his boys showed up. Somehow someone had zigged when they were supposed to zag, and Giamatti had started shooting people like this was a fucking Asian War. Okay, that had been bad, but not the end of the world. In fact, it even gave Vincent a perfect excuse to demand a better deal. But then Giamatti had decided to take the night off instead of staying with the skirt he was supposed to be watching – which normally wouldn't have been a big deal, granted – and fucking Face-Off had been waiting for him at his place. Why Face-Off had decided to go after Giamatti tonight of all nights, Vincent didn't know.

He had some suspicions, though.

Face-Off mostly went after small-time assholes, especially guys who killed or hurt civilians – gang bangers, serial killers, sick fucks that had little or nothing to do with Vincent's rackets. Vincent's people usually didn't bother civilians; they mainly went after others in their business – competitors or traitors, assholes nobody was going to make a fuss about. That kept his dealings off the radar of vigilante types like Face-Off or Condor. Once in a while things went wrong; usually that meant one of Vincent's guys had decided to break the rules, and then vigilantes would step in and mess things up. If things got too serious, Vincent had his own Neo muscle ready at hand, although most of the time his freaks were there to impress the *paisans* and deal with the competition.

Thing was, Face-Off *knew* stuff, stuff he had no business knowing. Not too long ago, the faceless fuck had found out one of Vincent's guys had been running a snuff film racket using girls nobody would miss. That was something *Vincent* hadn't had a clue about until Face-Off shut down the whole operation and put three of his people behind bars and four others in the morgue. While cleaning up the mess afterward, Vincent had gone over the operation, and the security had been tight. The seven guys involved had been careful, and left no witnesses or clues behind. And yet Face-Off had just strolled in like he knew every little detail.

He probably had some Neo juju that let him know things, clairvoyance or something. And that had to be how he'd found Giamatti, and then the girl. Vincent fucking hated Neos. You never knew what kind of shit they could pull on you.

Things had gone from bad to downright horrible. Face-Off had whacked everybody at the warehouse, including the expensive Type Two Neo Vincent had sent along, and made off with the girl. Vincent had known something was wrong when Giamatti didn't check in, but by the time he sent some guys to the warehouse, it was too late. The only good thing about the situation was that Face-Off wasn't the type to go to the cops, not that it mattered much at this point.

Vincent had already set up a sit-down with the Russians to renegotiate the deal, and now he didn't have the girl to deliver. He'd figured on working things out in a few hours, tops. The Russians had sounded like they wanted the girl very soon; the whole job had been set up in less than a day. There was no way Vincent was going to be able to find her before the Russians figured he either didn't have her or was trying to screw them. When they did, the shit would hit the fan.

Like all Neos, Vincent hadn't gotten any older after reaching full adulthood. He'd been born in 1935, and he looked like he was in his thirties; if he dressed up like the asshole kids did nowadays, he might even pass for someone in his twenties. His top lieutenant Dominic was the grandson of the original Dom, who had retired to Florida and died of a stroke during a shuffleboard game. Vincent was not going to die during a shuffleboard game, but that didn't mean he was going to live forever, either. His years of experience had gotten him where he was, at the head of the D'Agostino family, wiping out all the original D'Agostinos along the way. He ran New York and all of Jersey that mattered. But this kind of screw-up was how heads of families got cut off.

He could delay the Russians for a bit, but soon enough they'd know. If the girl was important enough, this could mean war. At the very least, there would be retaliation. They might even decide to go after him personally. That would be crazy, but the Russians had cornered the market on crazy for a long time.

Vincent had a great big house – 'the manor' his wife called it – out by the Catskills, but he spent maybe three days a week there. His home away from home – not counting the three apartments he kept for his mistresses – was hidden under an old restaurant in Little Italy. That was the heart of his turf, the place he had grown up in. He'd single-handedly kept the Chinks from moving into the neighborhood, and kept the place Italian, the way it was meant to be. He'd owned *La Trattoria* for close to five decades, turned the small eatery into one of the best restaurants on Canal Street. The restaurant proper only occupied a small portion of the entire city block that served as Vincent's headquarters. He had offices, a hidden fortified bunker that only a few made guys knew about, and a nice little apartment that would go for a few million if he ever wanted to sell it. The hidden bunker was where he held important meetings, where had had signed many a death warrant, and where, on three occasions, had done the deed himself.

He should be safe there. The best defense was secrecy. People knew he owned the restaurant and that he ate there all the time. Only a handful of people – two of them were in the room with him – knew about the secret bunker belowground. To enter it, he had to go into a basement on Spring Street with a hidden door leading into a tunnel. He'd had to grease a lot of palms with assorted city workers to get it done, and afterwards he'd quietly disposed of everyone involved in the project. On top of that, Vincent always had a pretty impressive Neo bodyguard around. He and Dom were as safe as could be. Of course, he couldn't stay in the bunker forever. Going to the mattresses only worked for a while. But if he could string the Russians along, maybe he could fix things.

"Dom, let's get things going. Start with Jerk-Off. Send the guys out to find any known associates, friends, anybody he fucking hangs out with. See if anybody knows where he could be." That was probably just pissing in the wind, but he had to start somewhere. "Next, find me a Neo tracker. There's one guy in Atlantic City and another in Newark, they can find people with their minds."

"Yeah, I know those guys," Dom said. "They're expensive."

"Get them both. We need to find that little bitch quick, before the Russians figure out we fucked up."

Dom nodded and started talking on his comm. Vincent left him to it and walked to the bar. The bunker office had all the amenities and his bodyguard could mix a killer Bloody Mary in addition to his other skills. "The usual, Tor."

"Yes, Mr. Bufalino," Toreador replied, his Spanish accent still noticeable despite having lived almost twenty years in the US. He was a real Spaniard from Spain, not some jumped-up Mexican or Cuban like the people doing the dishes at *La Trattoria*. Pretty classy guy, knew how to show respect. He also was a trained Neo assassin and a veteran of the Second Asian War. Vincent should have sent him on the job instead of Giamatti and that lightning-throwing punk, but he never felt safe when Toreador wasn't around. He was a guy Vincent could trust.

Toreador had been on the run from the Freedom Legion, something about war crimes during the Asian War. Stupid shit, really; hadn't they gone over there to kill gooks? What did they think would happen? Vincent had recruited him and given him a whole new identity and a place in the organization. Toreador was alive and free because of Vincent, and he never forgot it.

Vincent got his Bloody Mary and drank it while he thought on the best way to go about the situation. He'd let the Russians stew for a bit, let them call him first, and try to stall. If that didn't work, maybe it would be best to hit them first, before they knew what was going on. If the girl was so valuable to them, he should find out why. Maybe it was something he could use. He smiled. Yeah, he was in deep shit, but if he played his cards right he might come out of it smelling like a rose. He was Vincent Bufalino, and he owned Manhattan.

The smile vanished from his face when the bunker's reinforced door started to burn. "What the fuck?"

The door was built like a vault door, reinforced metal with multiple locking rods. The inside was covered with wood paneling. The paneling was smoking and smoldering. Something hot enough to cut through reinforced steel was drawing a blazing line through the entrance's locking mechanism. The stench of burning wood and melting metal filled the room. Someone was using a blowtorch on the door, or a Neo was doing a blowtorch impression on the door. Either way, it meant they had found Vincent's hideout. Only Dominic and Toreador were with him. Chances were he was fucked, with no way out.

Vincent was many things, but not a coward. There was a weapons locker in the office, and he and Dominic hurriedly armed themselves with Thompson M10 submachine guns, big heavy fuckers that fired a fifty-caliber cartridge. The big bastards kicked like mules even with their advanced recoil suppression system, but they would take down anything smaller than an armored truck or a heavy-duty Neo. Toreador didn't take a gun. Instead, he concentrated and a metallic black fluid flowed from his pores and covered him from head to toe, turning him into an ebony statue of living metal. Twenty-inch blades of the same black material grew out around his hands. Whoever came through that door was going to get a warm reception.

The smoke in the room cleared fairly quickly. High-end air scrubbers built into the bunker saw to that. When the door swung open, the invader was clearly visible. "Mr. Bufalino," the man said. "I'd like to speak with you. Will you do me the courtesy of not shooting at me until I say my piece?" The man's voice was deep and had a faint Russian accent.

"Yeah, sure," Vincent said. "We can hear you fine from the door. But take a step in here and we're gonna light you up."

"Fair enough." The stranger stood on the threshold. He was a short and skinny fuck, maybe five six; he would weigh a buck forty soaking wet if he was human, which he sure as shit wasn't. His face was a curious mixture of old and young, with deep wrinkles on his forehead and the sides of his mouth, but bright blue eyes that sparkled with good humor and an otherwise youthful complexion. His hair was silver-white and parted down the middle in a style that had been old-fashioned before Vincent had been born. All his clothes were snow-white, from a well-tailored suit down to his shoes. His skin was naturally pale but the guy had also powdered it to look as white as a mime's. The fucking *finnochio* was the whitest guy Vincent had ever seen.

"You may call me Archangel," the man in white continued. "I've been sent here for the girl. The organization I represent does not like it when their associates renege on their promises."

"The girl ain't here," Vincent said. "If we all calm down and talk about it, I'm sure we can work things out."

"All I need from you is her location. Tell me, and I will go in peace. We are not pleased with your actions but they are forgivable, if you give us the girl."

Lying would do no good. "I don't have her," Vincent admitted. "A vigilante took her. A shithead by the name of Face-Off; I'm sure you've heard of him. I got my people working on it. We'll find him, and her, I swear. I just need a little time. I'll deliver her to your people, as agreed. At no extra charge," he added hopefully.

"That will not be necessary. Unfortunately, your failure to deliver her as promised cannot be overlooked."

"Overlook this, motherfucker!" Vincent fired off a long burst in the middle of his sentence. Dominic fired a second later. The recoil pushed Vincent's gun up and half of the shots hit only the wall and the ceiling, but at least three or four rounds hit the pasty-white freak dead-center in the chest. Dominic also scored several hits.

The man in white did not fall. The fucker was bulletproof.

Vincent had emptied the sub gun. He reached for a fresh clip as the intruder strolled into the room. Toreador rushed to intercept him, his black blades weaving a complex pattern as he swung them so quickly they became a blur. The man in white squared off with the Spanish assassin, the kind of thing comic book assholes loved to put in their covers. Vincent would have appreciated the spectacle a lot more if his life didn't depend on the outcome.

Toreador moved with the grace and speed of the bullfighter he once had been, but there was power behind his movements. Vincent had seen those solid black blades cut through metal plates as if they were made of cheese, and soft cheese at that. Even bulletproof Neos should fear them.

The intruder produced his own sword, a thing of solid energy that shone like the heart of a lightning bolt, its light so intense it left afterimages in Vincent's eyes as the man in white swung his weapon as swiftly as Toreador wielded his. There was a flurry of combat, so quick that even Vincent's enhanced hand-eye coordination could barely follow it, and Toreador jumped back. One of his blades was gone; so was the hand that had been attached to it, severed at the wrist. There was a brief spurt of blood from the stump before the living metal armor covered it and sealed the wound. For the first time in his life, Vincent saw Toreador look hesitant. The Spanish assassin held his remaining blade in a defensive posture and backed away. The man in white stood his ground, smiling mockingly.

Toreador's retreat had unmasked the intruder. Dominic fired another burst from his Thompson. The shots did nothing. The man in white turned to Dominic, gestured at him with his free hand and unleashed a solid beam of light the same intense cyan color as his sword. Dominic didn't have time to scream. He fell limply to the ground, but not before Vince could see the saucer-size hole the beam had charred all the way through his lieutenant's chest.

Dominic's death had bought Toreador some time, and presented him with an apparent opening. The Spaniard pounced like a cat and unleashed a storm of cuts and thrusts. For a moment, the man in white was on the defensive, and Toreador even managed to score a couple of hits, drawing blood and marring the Russian's clothing. Vincent felt hope for a whole three seconds. On the fourth second, Toreador's body fell to the ground; the Spaniard's severed head went spinning off and hit a wall with a sickening wet sound.

The Russian turned towards Vincent. The cuts he had sustained no longer bled. A second later, his suit was impeccably white again, no trace of blood anywhere.

"Wait," Vincent said. "Wait! You can't do this. Don't you know who I am? I own Manhattan! This means war!"

The man in white said nothing. His smile never wavered as he walked towards Vincent, sword poised to strike.

I fucking hate Neos, was Vincent's last thought.

Face-Off

New York City, New York, March 13, 2013

Christine took the generous shot of vodka Father Alex poured for her and downed it in one gulp. She started coughing and sputtering almost immediately. I turned off the TV while she recovered from the coughing fit. The news from Freedom Island could wait. An attack on the Freedom Legion's headquarters was pretty big news, but the Legion always came out on top, the self-righteous pricks.

"Take it easy," I said, and patted her lightly on the back. She got the coughing under control and leaned back on her chair.

"I'm okay," she replied. "I think I needed that. Okay, maybe not needed, but wanted it. Or thought I wanted it. Now I'm not so sure." She took a deep breath, and I braced myself for another verbal avalanche, but instead of babbling she exhaled slowly and closed her eyes. I glanced at Father Aleksander, who seemed to be deep in thought, and back at Christine, who had opened her eyes again.

"Relaxation technique," she explained. "Tense up breathing in, loosen up breathing out. I feel a little better now."

"That's good," I said, mainly to try and keep her from chattering up a storm again. It didn't work.

"Okay. The Many Worlds Interpretation must be true," she said. She looked at our blank faces – well, mine would have been blank regardless – and went on to explain. "You know, quantum mechanics. Do you know about wave function collapses, that sort of thing?"

I read a lot, but mostly historical and pulp fiction. I knew what quantum mechanics were, in the sense that I had heard the term before, but I'd be damned if I could explain what the words meant. "All Greek to me," I said admitted.

"I speak Greek," Father Aleksander said. "But I still don't understand."

"Okay, no problem. Layman's terms. Sorry, I'm kind of a nerd," she said with a nervous smile. She looked like she smiled nervously a lot, and my heart went out to her a little bit. "Okay, say I flip a coin. It can come up heads or tails, right? Right. According to some theories, there is a universe where it will come up heads and another where it will come up tails. One universe for each possible outcome. Okay, that's not the most accurate explanation but it's good enough for now."

"You're talking about parallel universes," I said. "Yeah, we know about those. A few years back, L.A. got hit by an army of weird South African Nazis who'd gated in from an alternate Earth where they had taken over the world. They made a big mess before they got kicked back to where they belonged."

"Yes, that's it. Wow, Nazis from another universe? So this place really is a freaking comic book world come to life. Holy crap!"

"And you are from a parallel universe," I said. "I was trying to figure out a way to tell you, actually."

"That's kinda funny, since people that know me are always saying I must be from a different planet. In my reality, there are no Neos. No people with superpowers, unless you count doping and steroids, damn you, Lance Armstrong."

No Neos? Interesting. Maybe they were better off without us freaks.

Christine wasn't done talking, of course. "Neos, where did they come from? When did they show up? It'd be neat to find the point of divergence, or points of divergence, between your world and mine. Can't be too far back in history. New

York is New York, you're speaking English, the US is the US. So…" She paused and the nervous grin came up again. "I guess you need me to stop talking now."

If I had a mouth, I would have smiled back. "Just a little bit," I said, not unkindly; normally I would have told someone talking that much to shut the fuck up already, but I really didn't want to hurt her feelings. Very strange. "Okay, let's see," I went on. I'd been a Neo fanboy long before I became a freak with no face, so answering her question wasn't much of a chore for me. "The earliest Mystery Men appeared during the Roaring Twenties. There was one confirmed Neo during World War I, a German flyboy, Von Richthofen. The guy got shot in the face a few thousand feet in the air, crashed his plane, and walked away from it. There were stories about some American guy with the French Foreign Legion, but those weren't confirmed. More Neos showed up during the Nineteen Twenties; the real flashy and powerful ones appeared during the Thirties. The Berlin Olympics of 1936 was the big turning point; that's when the term 'Neolympian' was used for the first time. Adolf Hitler unveiled the Teutonic Knights during the Olympics, made a big splash. The Knights could do things most people back then thought were impossible; bend steel with their bare hands, fly, that kind of stuff."

I waited to see if Christine was about to launch into another stream of consciousness tirade, but she was listening raptly, so I kept talking. "Hitler was the first to recruit Neos and put them to work out in the open. He also dressed them up in costumes and gave them code names. The US had a bunch of Neos – we still have the largest concentration of freaks on the planet, for no reason anybody can think of – and some of them had been featured in pulp magazines and radio shows, but it took a while to figure out they weren't just very talented normals.

Then came Ultimate, the Invincible Man, in 1938. He got his own comic book, *Action Tales*, not too long before the Germans were rolling through Poland."

"Okay. World War Two, both here and in my world, check. Since you're not speaking German, I'm guessing the good guys won?"

"Yep. Germany and Japan surrendered in 1945. By then most of the Teutonic Knights were captured or dead. Same with the Kami Warriors of Japan – well, they were all dead."

"Wow. Wowie-wow. Okay, I can see we could spend hours talking about this. Later. I mean, we most definitely will, later. Let's get to current events for a sec. Who's President?"

"John Colletta," I replied, and saw Father Aleksander frown. I hoped we wouldn't get into a political argument.

"That crazy wrestler," Father Alex said disapprovingly.

"That crazy war hero," I replied, and turned to Christine. "Never mind him. Colletta's a good man. He beat JFK Jr. and that bozo from Florida who ran for the GOP; Colletta ran on the Reform Party ticket, and both Democrats and Republicans are a bit sore about the election. He's also our second Neo President."

"JFK Jr. – you mean John-John is alive? He died when I was a kid in my world. My mom cried."

"Serves the Democrats right, sending the kid of a one-termer to run for the Presidency," I said.

"One-termer? That's kinda harsh, isn't it? Or… wait, JFK Senior wasn't assassinated?"

"Unless you mean character assassination, nope. He just lost in '64 to the first Neo President: Ray Stephens, a.k.a. The Patriot."

"Okay, so we could spend hours talking about current affairs, too, 'cause we're going to have to go back to historical events to make sense of the current affairs. My head's so going to explode. Why don't we talk about me for a second? We can start with, what the eff am I doing here?"

"We don't know. Somebody or something brought you here, some trans-dimensional portal or para-temporal machine is my guess. Like those Afrikaner Nazis in L.A., or the Magister in his fucking teleporting Porta Potty."

"You're serious. A teleporting Porta Potty."

"I didn't invent it. Thanks to him, people get paranoid at construction sites, concerts and anywhere else you need to use those fucking things. You never know when you go take a crap whether or not you'll find yourself in a whole different universe. Don't ask me why he didn't go for something more sensible, like a car or a telephone booth." Now I was talking up a storm. She wasn't just a chatterbox, she was contagious.

Christine started to say something, stopped herself and shook her head. "Later. Okay, let's say some super-nutjob brought me here. Why? Sorry. You don't know, of course, you'd have to find out which super-nut brought me here. But some goons took me from the hospital, right? And you rescued me, thank God. So you do know who's behind all of this."

"Well, not really," I said apologetically. "They were local Mafia muscle, and I don't see how they could have grabbed you from another universe. Somebody must have hired them when you landed in New York."

"They didn't know who hired them? You didn't ask them?"

"I, ah, sort of killed them before I had the chance."

Christine looked shocked. "You killed them?"

"They had already murdered four people. I didn't want one of them getting to you. And one of them was a Neo himself, a pretty heavy-duty one." And – this I didn't say – I was in a bad mood, and some people just need killing. And here I was, justifying my actions to someone I'd just met, and feeling – guilty?

"I'm not going to get all judgmental and stuff, because I don't know all the facts, and also because you saved me from guys who clearly weren't very nice. But killing is something pretty final, and you sounded kinda casual about it, but I'm going to stop now."

"I concur," Father Aleksander said. "And I've had similar arguments with my young friend here. But perhaps there is a better time for that, no?"

Christine nodded bleakly. "Okay. Setting aside morality, it's going to be hard to find out who hired them, now that they can't tell us anything, on account of their being dead."

First she made me feel like shit, and now she made me feel like a dumbass. I normally didn't give a damn what people thought about me, so this was worrisome. You start doubting yourself out in the streets, and someone's going to strangle you with your own guts while you ponder the whys and wherefores of your actions. I had to admit to myself that I had been a little too kill-happy at the warehouse. Then again, I normally got all my info from my psychic pal; I didn't need to interrogate criminals very often. Giamatti had been a special case, though I'm sure he hadn't felt very special on his way down from the penthouse.

"I normally get all my info from an associate of mine. Her name's Cassandra."

Christine's face lit up at the mention of my psychic pal and I felt another grin forming up behind my blank face, not a common occurrence. "Cassandra! Yes, she came to me in a dream vision thingy when you rescued me. She seemed pretty cool," she added.

I nodded. "She is. She would normally know who did this and why, or at least give me some good clues, but she said that you are somehow interfering with her visions."

"Yes, she said something like that in the dream. Holy crap, I'm in other people's visions and they are visiting me in my dreams. I'm probably crazy, but I might as well go with the flow." She paused for a second and her eyes went wide. "Wait, my glasses, I don't need them anymore. I'm the Amazing Tobey Maguire! And I got roughed up during the kidnapping, but I feel fine now." Her eyes got wirder. "I'm one of you, aren't I? A Neo? But how? I'm not from a super-world like you…" She paused again, and her eyes got wide enough I worried her eyeballs would pop out. "Holy crap, it's my freaking father. He's a freaking freak from another reality! I can't freaking believe it!"

"Ah, Christine?" I tried to break in, but she was having none of it. Her stream of consciousness was more of a waterfall of consciousness now.

"Oh, God, please don't let it be the Porta Potty guy! My dad is a freak from another world who travels around in a Porta Potty? It can't be." She turned to me. "Quick, who else can travel between worlds? There's more than one, right?"

"Well, the Magister is the best-known Neo with trans-dimensional abilities, but he's not the only one. There is Marcus Magus, and of course the Traveler, he claims he's been around since Victorian times, but everybody's pretty sure he's full of shit and he just stole the name from H.G. Wells. But wait, are you sure that..?"

"That my crazy father is a Neo from this world? Absolutely. I always knew something was seriously wrong with him. And not just because he knocked up my mom and disappeared, and nobody can ever find him, except when he shows up once every blue moon to check on me. Oh, God, that rat bastard!"

"You're sort of jumping to conclusions, aren't you? Although it does seem to fit."

"He'd better not be Porta Potty Man! I'll kill him!"

"Probably not," I said reassuringly. "The Magister isn't much for one-night stands, according to the stories. He mostly drags some girl or another through assorted adventures through space-time, then dumps her and gets someone else, and nobody's claimed he knocked them up as far as I know. He's fucking creepy, but I don't think he's the guy."

"Okay. Or I'm going to need another shot of vodka."

"Besides, maybe it's not your father. Neos who have kids — and not many do — have mostly human children. I think the chance of having a Neo child is something like twenty-five percent when both parents are Neos, and something much lower when only one parent is parahuman. It could have been a naturally-occurring mutation. Nobody knows where Neos came from in the first place. Maybe you're the first one on your planet."

"Maybe. Another thing, when do you get powers if you're a Neo? I mean, there's been plenty of times when I've wished I could set somebody on fire. Like every day when I was in high school, but I've never gone Carrie or Firestarter on anybody."

"Neo powers manifest at different times for different people," I explained. "Usually after puberty, although there are exceptions, and usually before middle age, but again, there's exceptions there too. As far as I know, there's no hard and fast rules, either, sometimes a potential Neo just wakes up with super powers, sometimes a traumatic event triggers them. I figure your abilities triggered when you crossed over. That's why you've fully recovered from the kidnapping. All Neos heal fast."

'Which leads to my next question: what are my super-powers? Other than 20-20 vision and healing fast. Should I try to concentrate and set something on fire, or something like that?"

"Let's take it one step at a time," I said quickly before she actually tried to set something on fire. There had been some tragic incidents along those lines. "Usually when powers manifest it's pretty obvious, but you were unconscious at the time. Just don't try anything right now, okay? You might accidentally set me or the good father on fire."

"Oh, God, okay, I see your point."

I could tell that Father Aleksander wasn't crazy about all the taking of the Lord's name in vain Christine favored, but he was restraining himself from saying something. I'd also caught him smiling while watching Christine and me talking. I wasn't sure why.

"At the very least, you can interfere with precognitive and clairvoyant abilities," I went on. Jesus H. Christ, I'd never spoken for so long with somebody I'd just met except when doing undercover work. "That's why Cassandra wanted you as far from her as possible while she tried to figure things out. And you might be able to travel between worlds, in which case nobody brought you here, you did it yourself."

"But if I did it myself, why did someone try to kidnap me?"

"Point. And we still don't know why you appeared in Central Park. If someone was bringing you here, why wouldn't they drag you directly to their home base?"

I shrugged. "Not enough information. We can make guesses until the cows come home, but we need information. Cassandra is working on it; meanwhile we can learn more about you. Your powers, for one."

"So where can I learn about my powers?"

"Well, I do know a guy."

Chapter Six

The Freedom Legion

Caribbean Sea, March 13, 2013

After a while, he dreamed.

"Clarke! John Clarke!"

He turned around and saw her for the first time, standing in the bullpen of *The World's Journal*. She was beautiful, and angry, and beautiful when she was angry. Her fiery red hair and blazing blue-grey eyes expressed her anger beautifully. She walked determinedly toward him, a rolled-up newspaper in her hand.

"Yes, I'm talking to you, buster! You stole my story. Nobody steals Linda Lamar's stories, let alone some upstate small-town bumpkin fresh off the farm! Who do you think you are?"

"Ma'am?" he said, confused and bewildered. He had no idea what she was talking about. For one, his father wasn't a farmer, but a doctor, albeit a small town doctor.

She poked his chest with the rolled-up newspaper. "Don't ma'am me, you gaping chimpanzee! I spent three weeks working on the O'Doule brothers and their extortion racket! I was about to write a whole feature on it, and what happens? Some mystery man busts them up, and you write about it!" She poked him again. "You get a Page One byline and a job at the *Journal*! What do I get? Not a heck of a lot! Thanks for nothing, buster! You pull that stunt on me again, you're going to be walking funny for a week!" She stalked off before he could formulate a reply.

That had been the first time.

"John, please go away."

That had been the last time.

The pallid scarecrow on the hospital bed was ninety-three years old. Linda Lamar had endured three cancer operations, a heart transplant and every measure modern medicine had developed against old age and death. She had been shot nine times, stabbed six times, and had lived through more narrow escapes than possibly any other normal human being. She had celebrated her ninetieth birthday singing and dancing, looking like a vigorous woman in her early sixties. The collapse had happened two years later and it had been sudden and total, as if a dam had broken and let all the ravages of time flow at last.

"I can't bear to have you look at me like this. Before, it was all right, but now…"

He gently shushed her and held her hand, weeping silently as he watched her go. He whispered the only three words that mattered, and she whispered them back. At the end he had seen her fear, and had been overwhelmed by despair. For all his power, he had not been able to help her. She died in fear and pain, and he couldn't make it better.

Slow mocking applause started behind him.

"Pathetic."

The hospital room was gone. John now stood in one of the many lairs of his greatest foe.

Hiram Hades clapped his hands a few more times. "You are so very weak, for a man who can move mountains," he said with a contemptuous smile. "She didn't die of cancer, or even old age. What did finally kill her? It was your ethics, boy. Your moral cowardice did her in."

"I did everything I could," John said. The words sounded hollow and false even as he spoke them.

"Buffalo chips. Daedalus Smith offered you an alternative. All you had to do was take him up on it."

"Cloning a full adult body is illegal!" John snapped back. "And a brain transplant would have resulted in the clone's death! Linda wouldn't have wanted to live by murdering an innocent."

"Ah, but you never asked her, did you?" Hiram said triumphantly. "You didn't dare tempt her with the chance of youth and vitality. You were afraid she might have asked for it, begged you for it."

John didn't say anything.

"They call you the Defender of Liberty, but you never gave her the freedom to choose. You knew better than her, of course. She was only human, and you are a living god. The only difference between you and me, boy, is that I never hid my certainty than I was better than the mortal rabble beneath us."

"You may have been better than them, but you weren't better than me," John growled, and the scenery shifted again. Another lair, this one high in the Peruvian mountains. Hiram was there as well, lying broken and bleeding at John's feet. Hiram's adamantine black armor and all his gadgets and artifacts lay shattered and scattered around him. He was dying, but his mocking smile still showed through his bleeding mouth and splintered teeth.

"That was the day you finally grew some balls, boy. How many lives would have been spared if you had done what was necessary the first time you beat me?"

"I wised up. You would have gotten the death penalty in any case, but I couldn't risk you escaping while you went to trial. You had done it too many times before."

"So you stepped on my neck until it snapped, and all my cybernetics and healing systems could not put Humpty Dumpty back together again. It was your finest moment, Ultimate. But you squandered it and went back to your old phony persona, merciful and compassionate when all you really want is to kick apart the miserable anthills humanity has erected. You let people who are your inferiors in every way tell you what to do, mock you and insult you. You think your restraint makes you better than they are, when all you are doing is bringing yourself down to their level. Pathetic."

"So what should I do, then? Become like you? Kill and destroy, only to end up dead and unlamented?"

"I tried to rule humankind and lost," Hiram admitted. "But think about it, boy. You could try and win."

John started to reply, but cold water filled his throat, his lungs.

He woke up at the bottom of the sea, surrounded by the darkness, cold and pressure of the deep. His body had been brutally battered, burned and irradiated by the explosion, but he was recovering quickly. His costume had been mostly torn off, but he was fine, physically, at least.

John was not much given to introspection, not until the last few months. He had grieved Linda and moved on, acknowledging his regrets and losses but not obsessively dwelling on them. Recently, however, it seemed like the past was all he could think about.

He needed to do something about this.

Armageddon Girl

Christine Dark

New York City, New York, March 13, 2013

"It's freaking surreal," Christine whispered to herself as she strolled through the brave new world she'd found herself in.

She'd never been a fashionista, something that Sophie was never reluctant to remind her of, but there were things that just jumped at you. Men's hats, for example: about one third of the people over thirty she saw on her way to the subway wore them. Old-style hats, the kind of thing she'd last seen on *Mad Men*. Her uncle Pete had once joked that JFK had killed the hat industry by refusing to wear one, and that maybe people should have looked for a disgruntled hatter at the grassy knoll. Maybe JFK turning into a disgraced one-term president instead of the Martyr of Camelot had changed fashion history along with capital-H history. Neat theory, and probably wrong, of course. Other than hats, she noticed more men of all ages wearing button-down shirts. T-shirts were there aplenty, though, and a lot of them seemed to have stylized insignias for assorted superheroes. She saw dozens of red-on-silver 'U' symbols, which must stand for Ultimate, who certainly seemed to be a popular guy. Comic-book t-shirts weren't just for children or geeks on this planet. That cheered her up quite a bit.

She didn't see any Face-Off merch anywhere. Her rescuer didn't seem to be much for self-promotion. Or maybe he had a lousy publicist.

Women wore skirts and dresses of all lengths, from micro-minis to down-to-the-ankle numbers, wIth a mInority in jeans or slacks, and a larger minority wearing tight and shiny leggings in various colors, including several people who really, really shouldn't be wearing anything tight or shiny. A lot of them also favored 80s style big hair, with lots of product to keep it just so. It made her shoulder length, just-hanging-there hair seem drab, and she'd been lucky to get a hair brush from Father Aleksander to undo some of the damage her abductors had inflicted on it.

Since Christine couldn't really go out on the street wearing striped pajamas and fuzzy slippers, Father Aleksander had let her rummage through the church's donation box clothes selection. She'd ended up in faded blue jeans, sneakers, a plain t-shirt and a pink sweater. One of the priest's parishioners had also dropped off some new underwear for her, so at least that wasn't second hand. She didn't stand out much, and nobody was going to mistake her for a fashion model, so that was okay. As long as they didn't figure out she was an alien from another dimension, she'd be happy.

Cars looked different, too. Christine was into cars even less than she was into fashion, but she did notice a ton of electric cars on the streets, noticeable because they made a funny buzzing sound which Face-Off explained was built in so they wouldn't sneak up on people. Some brands she recognized – Ford and General Motors – and others she didn't, like Tucker. Whatever company Tucker was, it made a lot of cars in this world. The foreign cars she could see were European (mostly German Mercedes), a few Japanese models and lots of others she'd never heard of, like Donfeng and Fujian Motors, which Face-Off explained were Chinese. "Made by the good Chinese of the Republic of China," he added. "As opposed to the evil Chinese of the Chinese Empire." Which definitely would merit a whole other conversation sometime soon.

People were on the phone as they walked, same as in her world, but most of them were using the wrist-thingies instead, and most of them were Skype-ing or whatever they called it here, using screens on said wrist-thingies. She had no idea how people could walk and do video conferencing at the same time but they seemed to manage just fine. A lot of people were also wearing goggles or mirror shades with antennas on the side, which were the most common alternative to the wrist-thingies.

They were in Times Square, which was as crowded as the one in her universe, and had just as many neon signs and giant screens. At first glance most of the buildings and stores she could see were pretty similar to the ones in her world. This Times Square also had flying guys in leotards, though.

"Flying dude. That's a flying dude over there," she blurted out.

"Stop staring, you look like a tourist," Face-Off said in an amused tone.

"I *am* a tourist. Do you know him?" she asked. Flying Dude cut an impressive figure in his skin-tight red and yellow costume and shiny full face helmet in the same colors. Color-coordination was a must in superhero world, apparently.

"Little bit. Name's Star Eagle. He's a prick."

"Bummer."

Face-Off had a face on right now, as well as hair, which he could grow and remove at will. He looked a bit like Christian Bale. Christine wanted to ask him if Christian Bale existed in this world, but she had way too many questions ahead of that one. Maybe when she had a chance she'd check Imdb.com and find out, assuming they had Imdb.com in this world, which was yet another question on the list. She'd managed to ask only about a dozen questions on the subway trip to Times Square, which left her with about three or four hundred to go.

The subway cars in this world were a bit cleaner and more comfortable than back home: the cars were more like the ones in the London Underground, which she had seen firsthand on a trip with her mother and one of her few rich boyfriends. The trip had been a last-ditch attempt by the boyfriend to impress her mom, an attempt that had failed rather messily. The sights had been awesome, but the drama had spoiled much of the fun. London had been cool and different, but she'd never been as culture-shocked as she was now. The combination of familiar sights and stuff straight out of Bizarro Sunnydale was making her head spin.

Christine tried not to stare at the flying dude, which wasn't easy to do, as he kept circling Times Square and performing aerial maneuvers, to the delight of hundreds of picture-snapping tourists. The local New Yorkers hardly spared him a glance, which went to show that New Yorkers were the same throughout the multiverse. After a while, they walked out of Times Square and left Star Eagle the flying prick behind.

"I don't want to sound like a nine-year old, but are we there yet?" she asked Face-Off. "I need to sit down and process all this stuff."

"We're close. Just another couple of blocks."

"Okey-dokey," Christine said, somewhat uncertainly. A part of her still wasn't a hundred percent sure she wasn't imagining the whole thing. On the other hand, if her imagination was that good, she might have to start writing movie scripts as soon as she woke up. She turned her attention on the tourists. They were an international bunch, lots of Chinese and East Indian ones, plus the usual assortment from every continent. A few were using their wrist-thingies to take the pictures, but most of them were using dedicated cameras or some sort of goggle-built devices.

"So what's the deal with the wrist-thingies?" she asked, trying to at least cross a few more questions off as they walked. "Back home we have cell phones, and we keep them in our pocket, or purse, belt-holder or even fanny packs."

"Not much to tell. We've had wrist-comms here for over fifty years, and wrist-comps for about twenty. I think the first one who started using them was a Chicago police detective back in the 1940s, Richard something or other. It wasn't a phone, just a two-way radio, but a few years later he started using a wrist communicator with a TV screen. Someone started calling them wrist-comms, and after a couple decades everybody started using them. I keep mine in a pocket, though. Having an electronic gizmo strapped to your wrist while you're punching people out isn't a good idea."

"Interesting." Christine's brain had been getting bored of watching stuff like a slack-jawed yokel, and it jumped at the chance to work on a new problem. Wrist TV-phones for fifty years, that was way older than cell phones in her world. Older than personal computers; had PCs developed earlier in this world, too? Add another question to the list, darn it.

Speaking of worlds, she needed to have some shorthand when thinking about them. Christine decided to name her world Earth Prime. Her current location in the multiverse would thereafter be known as Earth Alpha. There you go, neither world would have to feel bad or marginalized.

"I wish we had more time so I could show you the town properly," Face-Off said. "Maybe after this is over, we can take some time off and you can play tourist and I can play local guide, unless you're in a rush to get back home."

"That'd be cool," she said. Except for the whole kidnapping thing, and luckily she'd mostly slept through that, this whole situation was pretty freaking awesome. She definitely wanted to get all her questions answered and Earth Alpha was an uber-geek wonderland. She wasn't into comic books all that much; she'd gone through a short-lived *X-Men* movie madness phase, but had outgrown it early in life. She was still burning to know how superheroes would work in real life, even if this wouldn't have been her choice of alternate universe to visit. If given her druthers, which nobody was handing out so far, she'd have stumbled into one of her guilty-pleasure fantasy romance worlds, complete with bare-chested silent and strong men with hidden sensitive sides (although, to be honest with herself, those worlds would also be sorely lacking in basic sanitation and other modern conveniences, and people would be somewhat more rapey than she'd like).

Come to think of it, she had a silent and strong male companion right by her side, if not all that bare-chested, and he kinda-sorta had just asked her out on a kinda-sorta date. Face-Off wasn't a muscle-bound type, and he had no flowing hair or soulful eyes – or any kind of hair or eyes when he was himself, but on the other hand he could look like anybody he wanted to, which meant she could get flowing hair and soulful eyes a la carte. Not that she really wanted to hook up at the moment, especially with a very strange stranger.

Christine knew few actual facts about her rescuer, but she was certain about a couple things about him. Face-Off was in a lot of pain, and there was a lot of pent-up rage inside him. Something bad had happened to him, or lots of bad somethings. She didn't know why she felt so sure about that; they hadn't had an

Oprah-style interview or anything, and he hadn't really volunteered much information about himself. She suspected that one of her Neolympian powers was some sort of super-empathy.

Her Christine-sense also told her that Face-Off was a pretty lonely guy, something she could sympathize with. She'd never been good at making friends. In high-school she'd been a total nerd; her love of books, computer games and obscure TV shows and movies had been her first social strike. A brutal acne outbreak and braces that didn't come out until her seventeenth birthday had pretty much been strikes two and three. Throw in her absent-mindedness and endless chattering whenever she got nervous, except when she got so nervous she just shut down and couldn't speak at all, and it all added up to a perfect pariah paella recipe. In college she'd gotten a bit better, but even there half of her friends were people she'd never seen except as avatars on online games. Agreeing to go to the fateful frat party had been an impulsive last-ditch attempt to come out of her shell, and instead she'd ended up in another world, shell and all.

Speaking of absent-mindedness, she barely noticed Face-Off had led her to an elevator to the subway. They got on the elevator, and Face-Off started pushing its buttons in a complex pattern. Now that she was paying attention to her surroundings, Christine followed the pattern and memorized it. It was a thirteen number combo punched in a rapid fashion. The elevator went down, and down, at least two levels lower than it should have. Pretty neat. Christine wondered how somebody had managed to build entire elevator levels on the down-low, and sighed. The last thing she needed was more questions.

The elevator doors opened up into total darkness. Face-Off produced a flashlight out of a coat pocket and turned it on, casting a small island of light ahead of them. From what little she could see, they were in a disused section of the subway system. The concrete floor was covered with dirt and assorted detritus, and she was pretty sure she saw a couple of rats the size of Boston terriers scurrying about. Yuck.

"Looks cozy," she said, trying to sound nonchalant. Her voice broke halfway through 'cozy,' so she failed miserably.

"All part of the ambiance," Face-Off said without a trace of chalant in his voice. "This is an entrance to my buddy's secret lair, and he doesn't exactly roll out the red carpet for visitors."

"But you guys are friends, so it's okay, right?"

"Yeah. Haven't seen him in a while, but he's good people. We've worked together a lot, and he's the go-to guy for Neos who need to learn about their abilities but don't want to go into the system. He was my teacher."

"System, as in prison?" Christine asked as they walked into the darkness, down an old tunnel with old and rusting railroad tracks running along its length. This wasn't her idea of a good time; talking about something, anything, helped her anxiety a little.

"Not quite that bad. Every Neo is supposed to register into the Parahuman National Database, get tested for powers and mental defects, get a background check and all his shots like a good doggie, and if he or she is deemed fit to be out in the wild, he's free to go."

"Oh, okay. That doesn't sound too bad."

"You have to provide them with your fingerprints, blood type, DNA samples and a Kirlian Aura impression. If the government ever wants to find you, the database makes it easier than a Google search."

"Okay, I can see why people might object," Christine said. She felt unreasonably happy to hear Earth Alpha had Google.

"Yeah, a lot of us object. They still haven't made it a crime to avoid registration, but somebody is always introducing a bill in Congress to make it illegal. For now, it just means unregistered people using their powers can be prosecuted even if they don't harm anybody."

"Yikes." Christine wasn't thrilled to find out her rescuer was in effect a criminal.

Face-Off stopped walking, and she bumped into him. "Hey, I know this isn't fair to you, tagging along with an illegal like me," he said. "If you want to turn yourself over to the authorities, they'll hook you up with a parahuman counselor and social worker, and you'll probably end up having the Empire State Guardians or even the Freedom Legion looking over your case. I would have put you in touch with them after I rescued you, but Cassandra told me it would be a bad idea. I trust her judgment, but it's up to you."

"That's cool. I mean, thank you, but I'll stick around for now. I know I can trust you not to intentionally hurt me; I also know you will stop anybody who tries to hurt me; you might hurt them more than you need to, but I guess I can handle that. The killing stuff still bothers me, though. To quote a wise guy: 'Do not be too eager to deal out death in the name of justice.'"

"'Even the wise cannot see all ends,'" Face-Off finished the quote, surprising her. "So they have *Lord of the Rings* in your universe, too," he added, and she could somehow sense a nice smile behind his no-face.

"Yes! Speaking of *Lord of the Rings*, are we going to be wandering around this pretty good simulation of the Mines of Moria for too much longer? I'm starting to get dark- and creepy-phobic. My last name may be Dark, but I'm not a fan of it, not really."

"Almost there. But sometimes my pal likes to play tricks on his guests, so be on the lookout for anything," Face-Off said. "As a matter of fact..." He whirled around and shone his flashlight back the way they'd come. Christine turned around and caught something moving away from the light, bigger than any rat could be.

"Getting sloppy, Face," a voice said from the darkness. A female voice. "I could have tagged you and your girlfriend half a dozen times."

"Fucking hell. Is that you, Kestrel?"

"Aw, you still remember me after all this time. I'm Condor's new official sidekick. Congratulate me."

"Congrats," Face-Off replied. He didn't sound very enthused at all.

"Friend of yours?" Christine whispered.

"Sort of," he said. He spoke towards Kestrel's voice, searching for her with the flashlight. "So are you the welcoming committee?"

"I just wanted to say hi personally."

A figure came hurtling out of the darkness and attacked Face-Off with a flurry of punches and kicks, knocking the flashlight out of his hand. In the brief flashes of illumination the spinning flashlight provided, Christine caught a glimpse of a woman in a black latex catsuit, thigh-high boots and a stylized bird mask, also black. She was getting positively medieval on Face-Off, who was on the defensive, blocking and dodging blows like a stunt-man in a *Crouching Tiger, Hidden Dragon* sequel, minus the flying leaps. A few seconds into the fight, the flashlight hit something and broke, plunging everybody into darkness.

Christine could still hear the sounds of a fight, but now she couldn't see anything. Not only was she a non-fan of being in the dark, but now she was in total darkness while bad things were happening pretty close by. She didn't like it one bit. She wanted, no, *needed* to see what was going on.

And just like that, she did.

It wasn't like normal sight at all. The Kung-Fu Fighting duo in front of her looked like two figures made of multicolored swirling lights, mostly reds and yellows in a multitude of hues. The tunnel outlines were rendered in a flat and dead grayscale tone, with little splashes of color here and there which she instantly knew were rats and some of the larger roaches and spiders in the area. She also knew that the woman attacking Face-Off was enjoying the violence with an almost – or maybe not so almost – sexual passion. Face-Off, on the other hand, was mildly amused and resigned to go along with the fight. This was Kestrel's idea of a friendly greeting, but underlying that was also a test of strength, the kind of macho posturing that Christine thought was mostly a guy thing.

Now that she could see (or sense, or whatever) the fight, it wasn't that scary at all. The dynamic dumbos were trading punches that could break bones on a normal person, but they weren't getting hurt; she knew that just the same way she knew what they were feeling. That is, she didn't have a clue how she knew those things, just that she knew them. Christine set the mystery aside, figuring she would go insane if she thought about it too much. Instead, she watched the fight and waited for it to stop.

"Hey, lovebirds!" said somebody behind Christine. "Cut it out or I'm going to turn a hose on you!" Light – the real deal, not the weird stuff she was seeing with something other than her eyes – shone out, also behind her. Her normal vision returned as soon as there was enough light to see by, and the multicolor sensory input went away. Interesting.

A door had opened off one of the tunnel sides, and a man stood by it. He was tall and athletic, and was wearing a black, gray and silver outfit that seemed to be equal parts rubber, chain mail and metal plates. A silver helmet with a different bird design covered most of his face. He had a big flashlight he was using to illuminate them.

Kestrel stopped her attack on Face-Off as suddenly as she had started it. "Good workout, killer," she said in a sultry voice. Christine had never been able to pull a sultry voice in her life: the few times she'd tried people thought she was having a stroke. Unfairly or not, she started hating Kestrel just a little bit.

"Yeah, was it good for you, baby?" Face-Off said sarcastically. Those two had history together, Christine realized, the kind of history that involves bumping uglies followed by throwing plates and other stuff at each other. She felt a slight pang of jealousy, followed by a not-so-slight burst of annoyance. Yeah, let's be the cliché damsel in distress getting all clingy Klingon on her knight in shining no-face. Not cool at all, Dark.

"Face. Good to see you, bud," Condor said, walking up. The two shook hands and Condor clapped Face-Off lightly on the shoulder. Christine figured Face-Off didn't hug it out with most people, even friends like Condor.

"I see you've met my new partner," Condor said. Kestrel moved to Condor's side and draped herself around him in a way that indicated their relationship involved a lot more than kicking criminal ass together. *Kestrel the Super-Slut*, Christine thought. *Just great.*

"Condor, this is my friend Christine," Face-Off said. Condor offered his hand, and Christine shook it politely. She sensed that Condor wasn't a bad man, not exactly, but he had a healthy – or perhaps slightly unhealthy – ego, and even with Kestrel all over him, he still managed to check Christine out; she got the feeling the guy had gleaned her dress and cup size with one quick glance. Even without her new over-sensitiveness power, she could tell the guy gave off God's Gift to Women vibes. Under that there was a darker undercurrent, but Christine didn't try to study it too closely; she felt like she was snooping way too much already.

"And you've already met Kestrel," Face-Off continued. Kestrel looked Christine over but didn't offer to shake her hand. It took her one look to pass judgment on Christine, who didn't need super-empathy to know what the judgment had been: plain awkward girl, not a threat, someone to be mocked or otherwise ignored. Some things didn't change across universes. There was a lot more about Kestrel than that, of course. Even a cursory peek with her new Christine-sense picked up a toxic emotional stew that left her reeling and without any desire to look any further.

"Any friend of Face is a friend of mine," Condor said.

"Too bad all of Face's friends can fit in the back of a rickshaw," Kestrel added.

"Yeah, I love you too, K," Face-Off replied. He turned back to Condor. "Now that we're done with all the pleasantries, can we get to work? Christine could use some help."

"I told you I would help, Face," Condor replied. "If we all step into my lair, I'll set up my equipment and we can do a full scan and all the basic power tests."

Hopefully they would be grading the tests on a curve.

Chapter Seven

The Freedom Legion

Atlantic Headquarters, March 13, 2013

Buried alive.

Olivia O'Brien regained consciousness in total darkness. Concrete and metal pressed down on her, hundreds of tons of it. She tried to draw a breath and inhaled a mouthful of dirt instead. For a second, panic overwhelmed her, and she trashed against her prison. Something shifted above, and the pressure above her increased. Olivia stopped moving, and forced herself to think.

She wasn't in any immediate danger. Neolympians could not be suffocated, a fact that had baffled and infuriated biologists for decades. Lack of oxygen could cause temporary unconsciousness in parahumans, but sooner or later the same mysterious force behind their powers took over and restarted their metabolism, releasing oxygen by breaking down carbon dioxide in their system.

Olivia had been in similar situations before. Wars and battles against parahumans often led to collapsing structures. Usually she was strong enough to dig herself out. She wouldn't be doing so this time, not with much of a skyscraper piled up on top of her. She could lift a tank over her head, but she couldn't move hundreds of tons of metal and stone, and even if she could, she would risk accidentally crushing any human survivors. She would have to wait for rescue teams to reach her.

That gave her time to think, and to grieve. Cecilia was gone, and so were hundreds of people she had known, worked with, befriended. It had been twenty years since the Second Asian War, the last time she had lost so many people in so brief a time. Without wishing to do so, she found herself remembering the bad old times.

1991. China. The Middle Kingdom had been a battleground for five decades, the site of two major wars and countless lesser skirmishes. This was no lesser skirmish. The Emperor and fifty armored divisions had burst out from the Dragon Wall and lunged toward Beijing. The Freedom Legion had assembled to defend the sovereign capital from the invaders.

Olivia flew over the battlefield, her flaming bolts shattering T-95 tanks; Brass Man, Myrmidon and the dozen other flying heroes that made up Second Squad followed her lead. They had already scoured the skies clean of all Imperial Air Force aircraft. Down below, her husband Swift darted through the enemy forces, sending armored vehicles flying like discarded toys. The Patriot, hastily recalled into service, followed in Larry's wake, leading Third through Fifth Squads, dozens of ground combat specialists, each of them able to fight a tank platoon single-handedly. Above her First Squad – the most powerful Legionnaires, including Ultimate, Janus and Hyperia – battled the Emperor himself and his Celestial Warriors; their struggle generated energy discharges capable of leveling entire city blocks. Behind her, the Seventh and Eight Squads of the Freedom Legion waited in reserve, ready to counter any breakthrough into the hastily assembled Chinese and UN defensive forces that stood between the Imperial horde and a city of eighteen million people.

An intense flash of light above her was swiftly followed by a wave of overpressure that almost knocked her off the sky. Later she found out the massive explosion had scattered First Squad miles in every direction, temporarily removing its members from the fight. The explosion had also obliterated the Emperor's remaining Celestial Warriors. Olivia looked up and saw the Dragon Emperor, a tall man in a green-and-gold robe, surrounded by a coruscating flux of elemental energies. Held high in his hands was a miniature star, too bright to look at directly.

"No," Olivia whispered, a prayer more than anything else. Like so many prayers, it had gone unanswered.

The Dragon Emperor flung the energy sphere down towards the rear of the defensive lines. It struck Seventh Squad's positions.

"No!" Her scream was lost in an apocalyptic explosion.

The blast was later determined to have an explosive force equivalent to ten kilotons of TNT. Only one member of Seventh Squad survived. The other fourteen men and women, all friends and comrades, were lost, along with six thousand ROC and UN troops killed and three times as many wounded.

Olivia screamed in wordless rage as she flew towards the Emperor. His elemental aura had faded somewhat, his power drained by the massive release of energy. Her flaming spears struck him again and again, sending him spinning in the air. Her rage fueled her powers to levels she had never reached before or since.

Maybe she managed to hurt him in his weakened state. Maybe he sensed First Squad rallying and coming back. For whatever reason, the Emperor fled, leaving behind over half a million Imperial soldiers to be killed or captured in the ensuing days. After the mopping up operations, the Legion held funerals for its fallen members: Olivia endured a heartbreaking parade of family members, friends and other loved ones paying their final respects to the dead.

It would happen again. More neatly lined coffins, some draped in the national flags of the deceased's countries of origin, others in the blazon of the Legion. More grieving men, women and children in black or the funereal colors of a dozen other cultures, some sobbing quietly, others in mute agony. Some looking at her with hatred for daring to survive what had killed so many others.

"Artemis. This is Daedalus. Can you read me?"

Her cochlear implant had survived the explosions and the ensuing building collapse. She subvocalized a response. "I read you, Daedalus. I'm safe for the time being. Please concentrate on other survivors first."

"Way ahead of you, Olivia," Daedalus said. "You're the last one. Larry is clearing a path towards your position. Stand by."

Now that she had been dragged back to the here and now, Olivia could hear and feel the sounds of Larry using his abilities to liquefy stone and metal, opening a tunnel into the debris. Sweet Larry, who still loved her even if he couldn't help straying with other women. None of that mattered, of course. She had dead friends to bury – and to avenge.

Olivia waited for her husband while nursing thoughts of retribution.

Face-Off

New York City, New York, March 13, 2013

"Just lie down on the table and relax," Condor said in his best public servant voice. "The scans will only take a couple of minutes."

"Okey-dokey," Christine said dubiously. She tried to smile but couldn't quite pull it off. "I'm not big on doctor visits and stuff like that. I'm glad I get to keep my clothes on, at least."

"Nothing to worry about," Condor replied. "The scans are non-intrusive. You'll be safe as houses."

"I'll be right here," I added, trying to sound reassuring. I suck at being reassuring; I'm much better at being intimidating and threatening. She managed to smile at me, so I guess I did well enough.

Christine lay on the examination table. An assortment of scanners and cameras loomed over it. Condor gently lowered a brain-scan helmet over her head and adjusted it. I stayed close by for moral support, and Christine grabbed my hand and squeezed it. I gave her a gentle squeeze back and she relaxed a bit.

"So what sort of scanners do you use?" Christine asked. "MRI's? Thermal Imaging? Sound waves?"

"All of those, sure, and a couple others," Condor said. "Okay, we're all set. We're going to go into the other room and run the tests, okay?"

She let go of my hand. "Do I get a lollypop afterward?" she asked. "Just kidding. Actually, a lollypop would be nice."

Condor chuckled.

We stepped into the monitoring room. We could watch Christine through a glass partition on the wall. She lay back and started doing her breathing exercises.

"Interesting girl," Condor commented as he started the scanning runs. Half a dozen monitors came to life. One of them displayed a thermal image of Christine, another her heart rate, body temperature and assorted other vitals, and so on. Condor had the best equipment money could buy, and some stuff he had invented himself and couldn't be found anywhere else at any price.

"You don't know the half of it," I said. "According to Cassandra, she is very important. She is also not from this world."

"She isn't? She looks pretty ordinary at first glance. Pretty enough, just a bit on the plain side for my taste."

"She's not plain," I blurted out. Condor grinned at me much like Father Alex had. What the hell was wrong with everyone today?

"Well, we'll know more about her in a minute," Condor said, watching the monitors. "Her metabolic rate is Neolympian all right. Resting heartbeat is at 35 bpm, which is typical for a Neo; its picking up a little, but that's probably just anxiety. I'll have her brain activity in a few."

"Good. So when did you and Kestrel team up?" I asked Condor while he worked the scanners, trying to sound casual. That pairing could not end well, but I wasn't close enough to Condor to just come out and say it. Luckily, Kestrel had excused herself quickly and left us alone. Having her hanging around while trying to test Christine would have been a pain in the ass; Kestrel didn't get along with other women, not one bit.

"Oh, about three, four months," Condor replied, equally casual. "Not too long after the last time I saw you. She's... well, you know. We get along. Nobody's getting a ring on their finger, and we don't ask many questions about what we do on our own time. And – hey, check out Christine's brain activity. She's definitely a Genius type."

"Sounds about right," I said.

"Aura scan is coming online... Damn, it's maxed out." On another screen, we could see Christine's psychic aura. It glowed blindingly bright, all yellow and white. "That's a high Type Two, or maybe Type Three. My scanners are only up to measuring a 2.7 or so. We've got to be very careful doing the stress tests. My facilities are not really up to handling a Type Three."

I nodded. Type Twos – 2.0 to 2.9 in the Parahuman Ability Scale – were full-fledged superhumans. Type Threes were powerhouses, the kind that can take over a country – or destroy it. There were about five thousand Neos in the planet, but only a couple dozen or so known Type Threes. The planet probably couldn't handle many more than that; there was some question as to whether it could handle the ones already there.

"My first choice would have been to turn her over to the Guardians or even the Legion," I said. "But Cassandra insisted we do this on the QT for now."

"No problem. Cassandra's always right. Besides, those sanctimonious assholes would probably lock her up first and ask questions later."

"Yeah, especially if she's a Type Three."

"Spectrographs are back – she's flesh and blood, no abnormal organs or cell formations. Decent healing factor, fast metabolism, none of them at unusually high levels. Bone density is pretty good; she could bounce a .45 caliber bullet off her skull, but she wouldn't enjoy the experience."

"Yeah, I usually don't," I said dryly.

"Me either, that's why I wear a titanium-Kevlar helmet. Other than her aura, nothing in her readings screams Type Three. Why don't you go get her and meet me at the gym? I'll set up and take some precautions so she doesn't bring the whole complex down if she loses control."

"Sounds like a plan."

I went back to the room and helped Christine off the table. "So how freakish did I turn out to be?" she asked.

"So far, your bones are tough enough to resist bullets, you can heal damage very fast, and you are somewhat stronger than a normal human – we'll find out how much stronger when we do the stress tests. Plus you have a very strong aura, so that means you may have some very powerful abilities. We'll try to discover them during the stress tests, too."

"Wow. Er, how stressful are the stress tests? Is it like a Danger Room kinda dealio? I don't handle confrontations all that well. As in, I tend to panic and go all deer-in-headlights and spazz out."

"No problem. We'll take it easy," I said as I walked her through the high-tech complex. The walls had sensor and weapon pods on every corner. Like I said, Condor had spared no expense.

"So your friend Condor is like super-rich," Christine commented, glancing around.

"You could say that. His father was a major industrialist, and he inherited a controlling interest in a dozen mega-corporations. "

"So why did he decide to become a superhero? Did someone shoot his parents when he was a child or something?"

"Not quite. When he was sixteen or seventeen, a terrorist gang kidnapped him and tortured him for several days. Condor's powers manifested themselves while one of those assholes was trying to carve an anarchy sign on his chest. Things got pretty bad for the kidnappers after that. Since then he's been doing the vigilante thing, just like me."

"Uh-huh. How about his 'sidekick' Kestrel?"

We got on an elevator and started going deeper underground. "Kestrel is... I guess you could call her a bit eccentric. She used to call herself the Kinky Kestrel; besides fighting crime she also runs her own, uh, dungeon."

"Dungeon? Like a lair with monsters and hidden treasure?"

"Well... monsters yeah, I guess. And if you consider whips and chains treasure, then that too."

"Oh. That kind of dungeon. You're saying she is a super-dominatrix, aren't you?"

"Technically, she's a switch. She'll be happy to beat you until you squeal, but she'll also let you beat her up, whip her with a real cat o'nine tails if she feels like it – she will heal the damage almost right away – and if you can afford her hourly rate. Of course, if she says her safe word and you don't stop right away, she'll mess you up. Bad."

"Holy crap. Yuck. I mean, I guess it's okay as long as it's consensual, whatever floats people's boats and all that." Christine gave me a look. "You, ah..."

I chuckled and shook my head. "Not my kind of thing. When I first met her, I thought she was just another vigilante. I learned about her extracurricular interests later. Here is the thing..." I trailed off and considered what else to say.

It had happened early in my career, shortly before meeting Cassandra. I had been just another vigilante looking for trouble, and I had found it in spades. Some mad scientist type – a former high school chemistry teacher of all things – had developed a designer drug (street name Ultimate Drops, U-Drops for short) that temporarily boosted normal humans and gave them Neo-level strength and agility, along with PCP-like immunity to pain and meth-like short temperedness. U-Drops became very popular with the local gangs.

Of course, there were drawbacks. The super-strong users could easily break every bone in their bodies by pushing themselves past human limits, and that was if you didn't keel over from a heart attack or stroke. Other possible side effects included liver and kidney failure, catatonia, permanent insanity and anal leaking.

The Empire State Guardians eventually busted the asshole who'd invented the drug, and luckily the drug was an Artifact, not a Gadget, which meant only the original creator could make it, and it couldn't be mass-produced like an ordinary drug. Every once in a while someone came out with worthless knock-offs that claimed to be the real thing, but so far all of them had turned out to provide few or none of the benefits while keeping all the side effects.

That night, it was just my luck that I tried to bust a dozen bangers hopped to their eyeballs on U-Drops. One of them hit me over the head with a fire hydrant he had ripped right off the sidewalk. He ended up in a wheelchair for his troubles, but I went down for a couple of seconds and his buddies proceeded to stomp me into the pavement with assorted blunt and sharp objects. I might or might not have bounced back and fought them off – all modesty aside, I'm pretty damn tough – but I didn't have to. Kestrel had been passing by and joined in the fun. She kept the bangers off me long enough to recover, and between the two of us we put nine of them in the hospital and three in the graveyard.

Here's one of the not so secret facts about Neolympians: we are adrenaline junkies. Being in dangerous situations gives us a huge rush. Winning a tough fight is like an aphrodisiac. Winning a tough fight with a hot chick fighting alongside you is… well, let's just say I was ready to go by the time we were done. Kestrel and I mopped up the last gang bangers, and then we scrambled up to a rooftop and did some private banging of our own. As a first date, it was great.

We hung out on and off a few times after that and eventually gave the couple thing a try. The sex was damn good, but we didn't have a lot in common besides the obvious stuff, and her kinky side turned me off pretty quickly. I like hurting people, but I don't like hurting people I like. Our personality flaws didn't mesh well, either: she was pushy and abrasive, and I was stubborn and sullen. Cassandra didn't like her one bit, which didn't help one bit; my relationship with Kestrel was one of our main bones of contention when my psychic pal took me under her wing.

After a while we avoided each other's company unless we were kicking the shit out of somebody or fucking like bunnies. Over the course of a couple of years, the avoidance times got longer and longer, and eventually became a permanent thing. I hadn't seen her in years.

I wasn't sure how much of that I wanted to share with someone I'd barely known for a couple hours. A part of me weirdly wanted to share the whole thing with her.

Christine waited quietly a whole six seconds for me to say something, which had to be some kind of record. "Okay, I know it's none of my business," she finally said. "Sorry. It just sounded like you two had a history."

"We did, a few years back. It didn't end well. Irreconcilable differences I think is the legal term." There. Three sentences to encapsulate twenty-six months of heaven, hell and lots of purgatory.

"And now she's with Condor," she said. She didn't say anything else, but I could read between the lines. Yeah, she didn't think that was going to end well, either.

"Condor sounds like he knows the score. He should be okay," I said. I wasn't going to say anything against my friend, especially not to someone I'd just met, no matter how comfortable I felt around her.

"You don't sound all that sure."

I wasn't, but it was none of my business. "Consenting adults. They'll work it out one way or another. Worst case, Condor is just as tough as me, so she probably won't do any lasting physical damage. Mental damage... Neos are all a bit crazy anyways. Who knows, maybe they are made for each other. I'm not a couple's counselor, or an expert in relationships."

I left it at that and didn't share the fact that my last girlfriend had been a stripper with a heart of plutonium and a temper like well-aged dynamite; she'd never even known my real identity, and thought she had hooked up with some local tough guy. That hadn't ended well, either.

Armageddon Girl

The elevator doors opened into a very large chamber. Heavy battleship-grade metal plates covered the walls and ceiling. Dozens of devices stood off in clusters along the walls: a few of them looked like implements of torture, and under the right – or wrong – conditions could be exactly that. I knew them all well; Condor had helped me learn my limits and train my abilities years ago. He did it informally for many 'illegals,' Neos who for one reason or another didn't want to go through normal channels and get their doggie licenses. In my case, it was because the first thing I'd done with my powers was knock my stepfather through a brick wall. Step Dad hadn't survived the experience and if I'd stayed and taken my medicine, the best I could have hoped for was several years in Neo Juvie.

Thanks to Condor, at least a dozen Neos who might have ended up as hardened criminals had gotten their shit together instead and now were out there doing good deeds, or living normal lives if that was their choice. Three of them had gone fully legit, and one of those three was a member in good standing of the Freedom Legion, which is about as legit as you can get.

I looked at Christine as she took it all in.

"I got the butterflies in the stomach thing all of a sudden," she said. "And the dry mouth and the palpitation thingies, too."

"It's going to be okay," I said with a lot more confidence than I felt. None of the people Condor had helped had been a Type Three, although there had been a couple of high Twos.

It was going to get interesting.

C.J. Carella

The Freedom Legion

Near the Dragon Wall, East Kazakhstan, March 13, 2013

Chastity Baal crawled to the top of the rocky hill slowly and carefully. The human eye could notice motion at surprising distances and although this remote part of the Empire of China was sparsely guarded, all it took was a bit of bad luck – an enterprising junior officer deciding to patrol vigorously along the Wall, for example – to unravel the best-laid plans. Upon reaching the bare promontory, she uncased her binoculars and looked down on the scene below.

The Imperial border with East Kazakhstan was protected mainly by mountains that channeled would-be travelers into a few easily-defended passes. One such pass lay below her: the Dragon Wall blocked it quite thoroughly. Even without her binoculars, the hundred-foot tall construct a mile and a half from her position was clearly visible, a glowing featureless expanse that appeared to be made of red glass but wasn't. Even from a mile away, Chastity felt the wall's crimson energy pulsating with a rhythm not dissimilar to a heartbeat. Some said the Dragon Wall was a living thing, or an extension of the Dragon Emperor's mind or soul. Chastity remained agnostic on the subject. It certainly was an awe-inspiring sight, a mute testament of the godlike power of its creator.

Nobody on this side of the Wall knew much about it. It had sprung all along the frontier of the Empire back in 1948, when the Freedom Legion and the Republic of China's Ten Thousand Immortals – a lofty name for the two dozen Neolympians comprising said Immortals – had chased the Emperor and his minions into the Chinese hinterland. It was an energy construct, impenetrable to all but the most powerful conventional weapons, and self-repairing in a matter of minutes even when breached. Travel and commerce were nearly impossible except where and when the Emperor wished. Winston Churchill had called it 'a fiery curtain that shall mar Asia for generations.'

"That is a pretty sight," Celsius said from below. He was watching her binoculars' input through his wrist-comp. "They say you can see the Dragon Wall from space. But didn't they say the same about the old wall, too?"

Chastity ignored her partner's prattle and continued her examination of the area. This remote area of Kazakhstan was thinly populated and had no paved roads. Her team had been inserted via a stealth helicopter flying from a ship disguised as a cargo vessel sailing in the Caspian Sea, hundreds of miles away. It was a complex and costly operation, but it had gotten them to the back door of the Empire, where the local garrison was small and fairly inattentive. Said garrison would consist mainly of people being punished for some infraction or another; the border with Kazakhstan was nobody's idea of a vacation spot. Such guards would likely be lax in pursuing their duties.

Kazakhstan had wrestled its independence from the Soviet Union in 1951, following one of the many brutal revolts instigated by the Dominion of the Ukraine during World War Two. Thousands of ethnic Russians had been massacred and many more thrown out of the country, along with other minorities. The new country had quickly descended into chaos and civil war and ended up as something of a chess board where the Dominion of the Ukraine and the Dragon Empire played their little games against each other, helping this warlord or that and ensuring nobody held onto power for long.

Most of Kazakhstan's border with Imperial China had become a sort of no man's land, lightly populated and without even the corrupt oppression that passed for law and order in the rest of the country. Imperial patrols often operated on the Kazakh side of the Wall, but did so sporadically and mostly along the more populated areas of the border. Thus, this locale was ideal for extracting an important defector, if said defector could make it past the Wall. And if the extraction team did a proper job.

The two-member team was a study in contrasts. Chastity Baal was five feet nine inches tall, athletic and slender, her dirty-blonde hair tied back in a severe ponytail under a desert-pattern camo hat, her hazel eyes currently peering intently through her binoculars. Celsius – nee Howard Kowalski – was two inches shorter, a squat, heavily muscled man with coarse brown hair and neatly trimmed beard. Chastity was cool and distant in her dealings with him, as she always was to people she found lacking in any interesting qualities.

Celsius had started out their partnership with a barely polite come-on attempt, and followed that with thinly-veiled resentment at having to follow her orders. He was a Type Two Neo, after all – a 2.4, he had proudly told her within minutes of making their acquaintance – and Chastity was a mere 1.1, only slightly more formidable than a normal human, and female to boot. His lack of respect for her was but one of Celsius' many failings.

Patience was a paramount virtue when conducting covert operations, a virtue Celsius simply did not have. The man was a reasonably competent Legionnaire for missions involving dash and panache while gallivanting around in colorful costumes, but a complete failure as a covert operative. He had been assigned to this mission to provide backup should something go wrong. Chastity had reluctantly and against her better judgment allowed him to join the operation. She had quickly regretted her acquiescence.

Celsius had been angry about trading his resplendent red and white costume for a set of camo fatigues much like the ones Chastity was wearing. He had adamantly refused to carry a gun, despite Chastity's attempts to explain to him than an unarmed man in the wilds of Kazakhstan would be viewed as a target, which might lead to trouble if some enterprising bandit gang took a swipe at them. Working with someone for the first time wasn't easy in the best of circumstances. Working with a rank amateur who refused to learn was a recipe for disaster.

She preferred to work alone. Tommy Leary, the one person she'd trusted without reservations, had died of old age in 1992, tending bar at the little Boston pub he had purchased shortly before his retirement from a colorful life of crime. Chastity missed Tommy with all her heart, but she had been alone before him and had soldiered on after his passing.

Chastity had thought she herself would have retired peacefully decades ago after a long and eventful life, starting with her experiences as a Caucasian orphan surviving in the rough and tumble streets of Macau. Said orphan grew up into a rather successful international criminal and eventually a reformed do-gooder and occasional freelance consultant for Interpol. The discovery that she was one of the vaunted Neolympians had come as a shock to her, although both her friends and enemies had nodded knowingly upon hearing the news.

Even before realizing she was not aging physically, Chastity had come to the conclusion retirement was not for the likes of her. Immortal or not, living an ordinary life just didn't have any appeal to her, and even if it had, trouble always had a way of finding her even when she did not actively seek it out.

In the ensuing decades, Chastity became involved with the international paragons of the Freedom Legion. She would not don some garish costume and perform heroic deeds in the public eye, but she was quite capable of performing discreet if perhaps dastardly deeds in the service of the greater good. Her membership in the Legion was a secret, which allowed her to continue to use her reputation as semi-retired criminal and her connections with the international underworld for assorted ends. The current assignment, to assist in the defection of a disgruntled Imperial Mandarin, was the kind of operation she excelled at, even if she had been saddled with a partner with little understanding of the way things were done.

"They should've scrapped this mission," Celsius complained after a few blessed minutes of silence. "Someone's nuked the Legion, for fuck's sake! We should be doing something about that, instead of sitting here at the arse end of nowhere."

The report of the attack had come in just as they were getting ready to leave the helicopter. Chastity had filed the information away and moved on. Celsius hadn't. "It may not have occurred to you that the Empire is a very likely suspect in the attack on the Legion, and that an important defector could have vital information on that regard," Chastity said. "It almost certainly has occurred to our superiors."

"Right," Celsius said in a slightly chastened tone. "I'm not used to this, all this waiting doing nothing," he added, the closest thing to an apology Chastity was going to get.

"Nine parts boredom to one part abject terror. That's how this type of operation goes," she explained to him. "If we're lucky, we'll be spared that last part."

"Too bad," he replied. "I wouldn't have minded having a go at one of the Celestials. That would be something, wouldn't it?"

Celsius was a young man, not yet thirty, blessed with more raw power than common sense. He would make a perfect front-line soldier, or better still the rampaging warrior type you sent out first to soak up bullets that might otherwise hit someone useful. Here and now he was a disaster waiting to happen. "If it comes to that, Celsius, we'll probably not face just one Celestial. And our objective is to rescue a defector, not finding out just how great and powerful you are."

Sullen silence was his only response. *"Jhew lun dou,"* Chastity muttered to herself. The Cantonese curse didn't do much to alleviate her mood. The little pig-genitals idiot behind her didn't speak the language, so the insult went unnoticed. After the operation was over she might just have to translate it for him.

The late afternoon started slipping into dusk when she spotted movement at the wall. An opening appeared on the glowing surface and a black sedan – a Fujian Motors model imported from the Empire's hated rival and main trade partner, the Republic of China – emerged from the opening and started down the poorly-maintained dirt road that led into Kazakhstan. "He's coming," she told Celsius, who had settled down for some sleep.

"About bloody time," the Neo grumbled but headed towards their vehicle and started the engine. The defector's car would not last long on those roads; the trip to the waiting helicopter would be made in their modified Jeep Seven. Chastity slowly backed down the slope and joined Celsius. The two vehicles met a quarter of a mile from the Dragon Wall, masked by the rising mountains in between. The sedan veered off and came to a stop as the Jeep approached. Its driver got out and greeted them.

Bao Xia Ming was an unprepossessing man of middle stature. His expensive Hong Kong suit was exquisitely tailored, and he displayed his wealth openly through gaudy rings around almost every finger and a bejeweled gold-cased wrist-comm. One of the rings had the dragon sigil of the Emperor: its wearer could open doors into the Dragon Wall at will, although they unfortunately were attuned only to the person for whom they had been designed. The man's demeanor showed he was someone used to wielding great power and who found the experience of having to drive himself anywhere profoundly demeaning.

Bao stepped forward and shook hands with Celsius, ignoring Chastity completely. Imperial attitudes towards women were rather unenlightened. "Thank you for here being," he said in accented English. "Got to get out, by goddamn. We go now?"

"We go now," Celsius replied sardonically. While they spoke, Chastity had been using one of the many devices in her rather unique wrist-comp to scan the defector for tracking devices. She found three of them; his ornate wrist-comm and two rings.

"You have to leave these items behind," Chastity said in perfect Mandarin, pointing at the jewelry. Bao couldn't have looked more astonished if she had sprouted wings and taken flight. "They all have electronic tracers," she continued. "You must dispose of the Dragon Ring as well; it might also be used to find your location. By now they will know you have crossed the Wall. We must hurry."

"What's going on?" Celsius asked. He spoke only Polish, English and a smattering of Russian, mostly swear words.

Chastity explained while Bao, muttering angrily under his breath, got rid of the expensive jewelry. Bao next demanded his luggage be transferred to the Jeep.

Celsius grabbed the three heavy suitcases and carried them effortlessly to the waiting vehicle. "Come on, let's go!" he yelled at the dignitary. The Jeep finally got underway.

They drove deeper into Kazakhstan. Ideally they would drive all the way to where their helicopter lay in wait. Flying even a stealth vehicle too close to the Dragon Wall was a risky proposition. With any luck, they would reach the landing site and be on their way in under an hour.

Luck was not with them, unfortunately.

Hunters and Hunted

New York City, New York, March 13, 2013

Peter Fowler felt a bit wobbly and light-headed as he walked to his crappy studio apartment from the liquor store, where he had spent more than he could really afford. He needed a drink or ten after his harrowing experience at Freedom Island, though. He'd almost gotten killed twice in one day, and if that didn't warrant getting sloshed, nothing did.

Life as a Hypernet blogger was never easy. Making a decent living at it was nearly impossible unless you were in the top one hundred or so, and the field was crowded with thousands of wannabes. Fowler had started out early, clawed his way up and attracted a small but loyal following. He'd managed to scrape by, although only because his mother would send him a check every other month or so to help cover the bills. Every check came with a handwritten warning in impeccable Palmer script that this was the last time she would help him, and sooner or later that last time would come. Fowler was looking at a future that involved waiting tables to supplement his income. That's when the GNN people had come calling.

GNN had offered to buy his domain name (xw.fowlertalks.net) for the equivalent of five times the advertisement revenue he had made on his best year; it wasn't exactly big money, but it was real money, enough that he wouldn't need to bother his mother for a good long while. More importantly, the network would add his blog to its opinion section and put him on salary as part of its editorial staff. His articles would be viewed by millions of people and he would make at least three times what he had before. Fowler had thought about it for about four seconds before saying yes, never bothering to look for any attached strings.

He'd been in GNN's thrall for a couple of weeks. When the first check came, he'd celebrated by buying a brand-new computer and using it to send a nasty e-mail to his girlfriend. He'd rubbed his success in her face and broken up with her – he could do better now. He'd followed that bit of conspicuous douchebaggery with some wild partying. He had gone a little crazy and managed to blow most of the money before the strings attached to his newfound fortune made their presence known.

Fowler had a lot of pet peeves: he hated the government (any government; he wasn't picky), he hated the mainstream press (who were all lackeys of the government, natch), and he hated Neos. Neos were above the law. They could do whatever the hell they wanted, unless other Neos designed to step in and stop them. And, although this was something he only admitted to himself when he was well and truly drunk, he hated them because he wasn't one of them. Like so many children of the modern world, Fowler had grown up idolizing the costumed freaks and wishing he could join their ranks. In his case the disappointing realization it wasn't going to happen had turned into resentment.

Word from above had come quickly enough. Tone down the anti-government and anti-press stuff, and concentrate on the anti-Neo stuff. Fowler had been indignant for a whole fifteen minutes, until a look at all the crap he had bought with the domain name sale money provided him with a moment of clarity. He'd sold out, plain and simple, and now it was time to sing for his supper. All in all, he didn't particularly mind concentrating on Neos. Those freaks deserved whatever they got.

The strings got pulled again right after he'd gotten invited to Freedom freaking Island to be part of the monthly Legion press conference. The importance of the invitation wasn't lost on him. Few bloggers ever got to join the respectable members of the mainstream media for events of that magnitude. Peter might have sold out, but he hadn't sold out cheaply.

The day before he was supposed to fly to the island with the rest of the press corps, a creepy little man from GNN – he'd said his name was Mr. Night – had dropped by and told Fowler what to ask Ultimate during the press conference. Fowler hadn't been thrilled about being told what to do, but he'd gone along and done his best to make Ultimate lose his shit live on international TV and Hypernet newsfeeds.

The story about Ultimate's wife leaving him was not completely groundless: the power couple had gone through a two year separation back in the 1970s. By then Mrs. Ultimate was getting on in years, being a normal human being. Fowler figured being afraid of Ultimate had nothing to do with it: she was probably not revving up his Ultimate-motor anymore and he'd sent her packing before the bad publicity made him take her back. You couldn't have the Defender of Liberty dumping wifey because she was getting a bit thick in the middle, could you? In any case, the facts didn't matter. If his new bosses wanted him to run with a 'have you stopped beating your wife' angle, that was fine by him.

At least in theory, that was. For a second there he'd thought Ultimate had been mad enough to actually go after him. If the Invincible Man decided to pop

Fowler's head like a pimple, who the hell could stop him? That could have been pretty bad. He'd never been in fear for his life before. Peter had survived, but his performance got him punted off the island via the next available flight that very morning; he left with the impression he was lucky he hadn't had to swim all the way back to New York instead. No buffet lunch or island tours for him, and he guessed he would never get invited back, GNN connections or not.

On the other hand, being thrown out meant he'd dodged yet another bullet. A few hours after the press conference, somebody had bombed the crap out of Freedom Island. Fowler had followed the news, and it looked like several journalists had gotten blown up along with the freaks and their pet humans. He had been spared, but the scathing op-ed he'd spent the flight home writing was useless now. You couldn't blast Ultimate and the Freedom Legion on the same day they had gotten bombed and then nuked. He'd have to come up with a softball piece, get in a few subtle digs while praising the selfless heroes and their human friends. Maybe focus on the human victims of the attack? After all, only a few freaks had died while hundreds of innocent people had been slaughtered right in the raid. Yeah, that could work. He'd think about it after a few drinks.

He was a few steps away from his building's front door when somebody grabbed him and shoved him into a blind alley. Fowler slammed into a trash dumpster; the paper bag he'd been carrying was knocked out of his hands and the sound of breaking glass was quickly followed by the smell of booze.

"Hey! What the fuck..." Peter's words froze in his throat. Three men were blocking the alleyway. They wore leather jackets over silver t-shirts with the letter 'U' in red.

They all had Ultimate rubber masks over their faces.

"You don't fuck with heroes," one of them said, his voice muffled under the rubber mask.

"Hey, man, hey," Fowler replied feebly. He wanted to say something that would make things better. He considered himself a wordsmith. All his words deserted him when he needed them most.

"You don't fuck with heroes," the man repeated. The three moved in on him, brass knuckles in their hands. Fowler had time for one brief scream before one of them punched him in the pit of the stomach, paralyzing and silencing him. Fowler fell and the trio stomped and punched him until he stopped twitching. The attackers spray-painted a slogan on the alley's wall, rushed out and drove off in a van.

A slight man wearing a black suit and sunglasses emerged from behind a dumpster in the alley. There had been nobody there a moment before. He was old and deeply unattractive, with a lopsided smile on his face, an awful thing that most people couldn't look at for long. He sauntered over to Fowler, who was wheezing in agony. The slogan painted on the alley wall over the dying man was simple and to the point: 'Don't Fuck with Ultimate.' The man in black leaned over Fowler. The blogger only had one functioning eye at the moment, but even through the shock and pain he recognized the man looming over him. It was the weird GNN guy who'd given him his marching orders for the interview. Mr. Night, the little man with the creepy smile.

"Help," Fowler tried to say. It came out as a choked, meaningless sound.

"Sorry, little boy," the man said in the reedy voice that had set Fowler's teeth on edge the first time he'd heard it. "Martyrs have to be dead." Mr. Night examined Fowler's injuries with a clinical eye. "You really don't look too bad. You might even recover if given proper medical attention. Can't have that."

Mr. Night's brow furrowed in concentration and Fowler stopped breathing. The blogger tried desperately to force air in his lungs, but nothing happened. "Off you go," Mr. Night said pleasantly.

The last thing Fowler saw was Mr. Night's smiling face. Something dark and inhuman seemed to be floating behind his sunglasses.

He'd escaped death twice that day, but the third time, as everyone knows, is the charm.

* * *

Fowler's body was discovered seconds later. By then Mr. Night was well away from the scene. His work was never done, and even with his little gifts he had to hustle to keep up with his many duties. The little man in the black suit vanished as soon as good Mr. Fowler had breathed his last. He reappeared somewhere not quite in the physical world, wrapped in comforting darkness and pondering about the work of the day.

Great things often came from humble beginnings. The death of an unlamented blogger was of little consequence in and of itself, but it added color to the little tableau Mr. Night was carefully sketching. The paranoids on the web would spread their own pet theories. Fowler had dared to question Ultimate and had paid the ultimate price, pun definitely intended. While few would actually blame Ultimate directly, the death would plant seeds of doubt in the minds of many. It was all part of a delightful scheme to turn the beloved hero of millions into a despised villain. Mr. Night appreciated the beauty of the plan, even if he wasn't Its mastermind.

He wore many figurative hats. To the well-intentioned members of the Foundation for Humanity, he was plain vanilla human Mr. Night, doing his bit to save the world from the growing Neo threat. To the vast Neo conspiracy that sought to rule the world by seizing control of the source of parahumanity's powers, he was a trusted operative, using his strange abilities to carry out the orders of his putative masters. And to his true masters, Mr. Night was a man who had sought knowledge and found it, terrible knowledge that had flensed off his humanity and left him only with a somewhat twisted sense of humor and an overriding purpose. He very much looked forward to the time when he would reveal who and what he really was to his purported employers.

Mr. Night returned to the world he despised, the world of harsh lights and sharp edges where the teeming plague of humanity crawled and sweated and spawned. He longed for the day when the whole planet would be cleansed of the plague of life. There was still much work to do before that blessed event, but the day was creeping closer, very close indeed.

He emerged from a shadowy corner in an office, startling a man working at a computer. The flunky jumped in his seat, spilling coffee all over himself. "Holy shit!" he shouted. "Mr. Night, sir," he went on more respectfully. Everybody at the secret facility had been exposed to Mr. Night's eerie comings and goings for some time now, but nobody had gotten used to them.

"Has the girl been found?" Mr. Night asked. So many things revolved around the little girl from another world. He had caught a brief glimpse of her during the extraction operation, when she had been dragged into this plane of existence.

She was a thing of bright light and colors, hope and power made flesh. He could hardly bear to look at her. Only the knowledge she wouldn't survive the uses the plan had in store for her made her presence tolerable. But he hadn't had to endure said presence for long; the cursed girl had managed to fight off the summoning process and ended up relocating elsewhere.

The flunky visibly hesitated before delivering the bad news. "She was taken from the hospital, but something went wrong. Archangel is still trying to sort things out."

Mr. Night's smile didn't waver. It rarely did, mainly because it was no more a reflection of his actual moods than the flesh and bone he hid behind were representative of what he really was.

"Place a call to Archangel, would you?" he said. The Russian troubleshooter might need help in finding the girl, and Mr. Night would make sure he got it.

The girl was proving to be rather troublesome. If time permitted, he would have to put some effort in making her demise a memorable experience for everyone concerned.

Chapter Eight

Christine Dark

New York City, New York, March 13, 2013

"No way! That's not just impossible, that's ridiculous!"

It turned out that the first weird machine Face-Off had made her get into was, among other things, a scale. A scale which had promptly declared Christine weighed... a lot more than she had. "I've gained forty pounds? WTF!"

Christine had never been a Weight Watcher, and she had been blessed with a darn good metabolism, which had earned the sincere hatred of most women around her. She could eat pizza and other forbidden foods and not gain a pound. Sophie cordially detested her for it, and Christine could understand why, since she'd seen Sophie literally agonize over taking a second bite out of anything with a higher caloric content than a celery stick.

While she didn't indulge in threesomes with Ben and Jerry except when terminally depressed, Christine didn't really watch what she ate. She also didn't care about her weight and appearance as much as most of her friends did. But she still wasn't thrilled to hear she'd somehow put on over forty pounds in the last twenty-four hours. She didn't feel bloated or fatter. Stupid scale.

Bad enough this whole testing thing was giving her flashbacks of P.E. class back in high school. Her P.E. experiences had consisted of equal parts embarrassment, pain and discomfort, with excessive sweating added for good measure. The fact that before the test they'd had her change into a padded gray bodysuit that felt a bit too tight for her taste didn't help, either.

"Ah, I sort of expected that," Face-Off said.

"So what happened? Did I grow two feet? Are my boobs the size of basketballs and I somehow missed it? Is my butt the size of a car?"

"Remember what I said about your bones getting denser and stronger? That also makes them heavier. Neos are usually twenty to fifty percent heavier than a human of the same size. Some are even heavier."

"Well, doh. I should have figured that one out. That's cool, I guess. Nice to be all tough and resilient, but swimming is going to suck – if we are that much denser we should sink like stones."

Face-Off nodded. "Yep. Can't float, can't do the backstroke."

"Bummer. Do many Neos, uh, hulk out?"

"Hulk out?"

"Sorry, cultural reference from the completely fictional superheroes in my world. I mean, get bigger and bulkier than normal."

"Gotcha. A few, yes, but not many. Most Neos look perfectly normal. A few are a bit freakish, like *moi*." He patted his featureless face, but he was grinning underneath, so Christine smiled back at him. "You look perfectly normal," he told her.

That sounded perilously close to 'perfectly plain' to her, but she set that aside. "Okay, got me weighted up and I'm all dense and stuff. What next?"

"If you can grab those handles above your head, we'll see how much weight you can lift and press." She did. "Okay, the machine will start pushing down; just push back against it," Face-Off explained. "If it gets too heavy, just stop and the machine will automatically stop as well."

"Not getting squished sounds good," Christine said as the machine pushed down on her like a vertical version of the Death Star's trash compactor of doom. She pushed back, and a digital readout on the machine started spitting out numbers. A hundred pounds. Pretty impressive, that's like two dozen kittens. Two hundred pounds. *Even nicer, I can bench press a football player.* That sounded kinda dirty. Four hundred pounds, and she could still push back without even working up a sweat. At eight hundred pounds she was beginning to feel a bit of a burn, but she made it to over a thousand pounds before giving up. Half a ton. She could lift half a ton over her head! "So I can pick up a car and throw it at someone?"

"Not quite a car. The average car is about four, five thousand pounds. You could tip over a car, though."

That didn't sound as impressive as picking up a car and tossing it like a kitten, not that she would toss a kitten anywhere. "Bummer. I bet you can throw cars around," she told Face-Off. Guys always loved to show off how big and strong they were. And since when had she started trying to flatter guys? Apparently since right after meeting this particular guy.

"Well, yes," said the guy, not sounding particularly proud or flattered. "It's trickier than it sounds, though. If you don't pick up a car the right way, you usually end up tearing chunks off it instead. At least if you are super-strong but don't have the ability to somehow pick up huge and bulky objects without destroying them. The heavy hitters like Ultimate can grasp things as big as a battleship and use some form of telekinesis to keep it in one piece while they pick them up. Middle-weights like myself, we have to be careful with the stuff we lift."

"So how much can you lift over your head? If you don't mind my asking, that is. Just want to get a feel of how much of a super-womyn I am."

"Uh, about ten tons, maybe a bit more if I push it."

Great. She was a total wimp. "I'm a total wimp."

"Not really," Face-Off replied. "You're stronger than most Type One Neos, and much stronger than a normal human. You can break a normal guy's neck without half trying, so you are going to need lessons on how to fight and manage your strength. If you get excited, you can easily smash furniture, pull doors off their hinges, and so on. No roughhousing for you until you get some training. You could knock somebody out during a pillow fight."

That didn't sound wimpy at all. It sounded a bit scary, as a matter of fact. On the other hand, she had always been easily intimidated by even implied violence, let alone actual violence. Knowing she could pick somebody up by the throat in the inimitable style of Darth Vader was pretty good for her self-esteem, even if she would never do that for real.

"I'm kind of a klutz normally, so it's going to suck if I'm a super-strong klutz."

"We can test you reflexes and hand-eye coordination next. They should be a lot better than they were before your abilities manifested themselves." He led her to another section of the Danger Gym.

Ooh, she was going to be graceful, too? She would love that. Her short stint taking ballet lessons had made her feel like a total Ugly Duckling. Anything that involved pirouetting, jumping and dancing had usually ended in unintentionally hilarious ways. "So how come I don't feel super-agile, not to mention super-strong?"

"It's a Neo thing. Unless you consciously push your body, it somehow restrains itself to the speed and power of a normal human being. If you get startled or angry or scared, though, all bets are off. That's when doors and necks get broken by accident. With some training, you can also learn to turn off your strength consciously, but even then it's still not a good idea to startle a Neo."

"So people really shouldn't throw me any surprise parties," Christine said. "I'll have to mention that next time I update my Facebook page."

The agility testing equipment looked suspiciously like a gymnastics set. Pretty soon Face-Off had her jumping around like it was the Olympics.

One of the first things she learned was that she could jump really far. So far, in fact, that the first time she tried a long jump she overshot her target and smacked into a wall, hard. Which was embarrassing, but didn't hurt as much as it should have. Those extra-heavy bones were paying for themselves already. Once she got used to it, though, she discovered she was graceful like a cat. She could even do jazz hands while prancing on a tight rope, which she'd never been able to do before, much to her shame and sorrow. Her klutz days were over.

"Not bad," Face-Off commented. "Okay, let's take a short break." Christine followed him to a snack and drinks area, and gratefully slurped on some ice tea. Condor appeared from a sliding door on the wall and joined them.

"I've been monitoring your biometrics," Condor said. "Trying to figure out what kind of powers you have."

"Any luck? Am I a healer, tank or DPS? I like playing rogues, so if I can turn invisible and stuff, that'd be awesome."

"DPS?" Face-Off said dubiously, but Condor smiled.

"Damage per second," Condor explained. "Which makes you a gamer chick," he said, eyeing her appreciatively. "They are about as rare as unicorns around here. Kestrel thinks that stuff is for losers. What do you play?"

"Well, mostly *World of Warcraft* – do you guys have that in this world?"

"That's my game too!" Condor said, surprising her. "That's what I usually play when I'm waiting for something to happen – or I did before Kestrel started hanging around. It's not the most popular game around, but I like it. Most people are into *City of Heroes*, which as you can guess is all about costumed freaks like ourselves."

"I guess with people flying around and throwing lightning bolts for real, playing elves and mages isn't all that special. That sucks."

"It's got some appeal. Some people like being in a world without Neos, even if it's only a game."

Christine thought about being a normal person in a world where a select few could throw cars around or fly. It probably wasn't all that great.

"Anyways," Condor said. "As your adrenaline levels went up, I got some interesting energy fluctuations. And when you hit that wall, there was an energy spike. Electro-magnetic and kinetic I think it could be a protective aura of some kind. I'd like to explore that a bit further."

"Okay. Explore it how?"

"Here, let me show you."

Condor led her to a blank section of wall. A bunch of what looked like guns, hoses and those tennis and baseball things that shoot balls at you were lined up facing the wall, some twenty yards away. "Er, this kinda looks like an automated firing squad," she commented, feeling a little nervous.

"That's exactly what it is," Condor said. "Don't worry, we're not firing anything lethal at you, not until we are sure you can handle it. If you can stand over there – yeah, right there is fine. We'll stand over here." Condor and Face-Off walked out of the line of fire and stood by the assortment of missile launchers.

"I'm getting a bit anxious here," Christine said, only half-joking.

"It's okay, Christine," Face-Off said. "Condor did the same thing for me, a while back. He's going to start with things like beach balls and water balloons."

"Yeah, I just love getting smacked with water balloons," Christine muttered. She stood her ground, though. Time to grrl up, grrl.

"Feel free to dodge the attacks if you want to, but try to concentrate on defending against them with your mind."

"How the eff am I supposed to –" A foam ball with something heavy in the middle bounced off her head. It didn't hurt, but it startled her into silence. Another one hit her left boob. "Hey!" She sidestepped the next ball. Now that she was paying attention, she saw they weren't all that fast, at least not at first, and she could duck away from them. But the rate of fire of the ball-launchers started going up. She got smacked on her shoulder; she dodged a couple of shots but walked right into a few more. And they were flying faster now; they were starting to sting a little when they connected. "Hey!"

"Try to concentrate," Condor said, sounding a lot like Mr. Phelps, the d-bag of a P.E. teacher she'd had the misfortune to endure during her last two years of high school. This whole thing was bringing her back to the nasty dodge ball games he liked to organize for his sadistic pleasure.

Okay, concentrate. Smack. Dodging wasn't working so well now that a dozen balls or more were being sent her way in each volley. Smack, smack. She slapped a few balls away, but one got through and got her in the eye. That hurt a bit, and now she was getting mad. Curling into a ball was an option, but if Condor was anything like Mr. Phelps, he'd just kept bouncing balls off her until she snapped out of it. Maybe – smack! She couldn't think, she –

Three or four balls were flying straight at her face. She raised her hands, knowing she wasn't going to get them all, and something appeared between her and the balls. Something like a circular wall: a semi-transparent barrier that sparkled with energy. The balls hit the wall and bounced off, and the smell of ozone and burning plastic filled her nostrils.

"Holy crap!" she said. Unfortunately, the energy wall disappeared a second later and a follow-up ball hit her right in the mouth, pretty hard. "Ow! Dammit!" Her concentration was shot, and she got smacked a few more times. It took her a few seconds, and several more hits, to figure out what she had done. She flexed something within her, and a bigger wall – no, not a wall, a *shield* – appeared in front of her, and this time she stopped all of them.

After holding the shield up for a bit, Christine started learning a few things about it. First of all, she could feel the impacts on its surface, not as if the shield was her skin, but more like feeling rain drops through a jacket – distant and muted, but still there. The balls were not just bouncing off, but were getting burned a little bit – that's where the smell was coming from. It was pretty awesome. *Shields at ninety percent, O Captain! My Captain!*

"Very good, Christine," Condor said, and now he sounded nothing like Mr. Phelps. "I'm going to switch to something a bit harder. Let me know if it gets to be too much."

"Okay," she replied, and another machine started spitting baseballs at her, and these were pretty hard fastballs. She concentrated on her shield, and the baseballs hit it and bounced off. The impacts felt different, harder and focused on a narrower area. She could feel the shield bend slightly as the hits increased in speed and power. As the impacts got harder, the shield drew more power from her.

After a while, the balls started hitting the shield pretty darn hard; if her control slipped those things were going to leave a bruise, or even break something. She looked at the machine shooting at her. Half of the shots seemed to be aimed right at her face, and that wasn't very nice. She glared at it.

There was a loud crack like a gunshot as the machine flew apart in an explosion of metal bits and plastic shards.

"No way!" she shouted. Her concentration fell apart along with her shield and the last baseball from the doomed machine hit her right between the eyes. Things got blurry for a second or three.

"You're okay," Face-Off said when she could focus again. He was leaning over her. She hadn't quite gotten knocked out, but she had ended up on her ass and spaced out for a bit. That fastball had hit hard. Yay for super-bones, or her brains would be leaking out of her nose and ears just about now.

"You're supposed to ask me if I'm okay, not tell me," Christine grumbled as he helped her to her feet. "My skull may be super-strong, but I think I got a concussion."

"No worries, we recover from concussions in a matter of seconds, mostly. Although this guy I know got shot in the eye, bullet lodged in his brain. After a few hours the bullet came right out of the bullet hole, but he had trouble remembering stuff for a few days."

"I can't tell if that was a joke or not," Christine complained.

"Must be my poker face," Face-Off replied, startling a laugh out of her.

"Well, that was special," Condor said as he walked up to them. "I won't charge you for my pitching machine, mostly because I'm grateful you didn't accidentally do that to me or Face-Off here."

"Oh, God, that would have been horrible," Christine said, her good humor vanishing. She normally didn't glare at people, but the idea of her getting angry at somebody and blasting a hole through them made her a little nauseous. Or nauseated. One of those two, or maybe both.

"It's okay," Condor assured her." I was able to measure the energy level of the impact, and it would have been survivable by your average Type Two Neo. It wouldn't have been pleasant, though."

"So how did I do it? I didn't see energy beams coming out of my eyes or what not."

"Most energy beams are invisible to the naked eye. Plasma discharges are visible, but what you unleashed on my poor pitching machine was pure kinetic energy. To be exact you caught one of the baseballs and accelerated it to three thousand feet per second, right into the mechanical pitcher."

Christine did some quick math in her head. Let's assume a five ounce baseball at 3K fps. Don't forget to carry the zero... "That's like sixty thousand joules of energy!"

"Give or take," Condor said, sounding impressed. "Four times the punch of a .50 caliber bullet. I forget you're a Genius, too."

"I'm a Physics major," Christine said. "I can do math; that and being a gaming geek meant I had no prom date, or much of a social life. But I could do math before I became Wonder Womyn. Danica McKellar is my personal idol."

"They didn't have girls like you when I was going to school," Condor said bemusedly.

"Of course, that was back in the Sixties," Face-Off commented.

"As in the Nineteen-Sixties?" Christine blurted out.

"You didn't tell her about Neo longevity," Condor said to Face-Off.

"I was going to get to it, but I've been answering a bazillion other questions all day," Face-Off said. "Sorry, Gramps."

"You're saying Neos – we – don't get old?" Christine broke in.

"Not that you'll notice. I told you about Ultimate coming out in 1938, right? He's still around, and he looks about the same as he did seventy-odd years ago."

"Except the eyes," Condor said. "You can see his age in his eyes."

"Well, I haven't had the honor of looking into his eyes," Face-Off muttered.

"So how old are you?" Christine said. "Sorry, rude." Was he like eighty or something insane like that? Creeposome.

"Twenty-seven this July," Face-Off said. "I'm a newbie."

"And you should respect your elders," Condor said.

"You got it, old-timer."

Christine ignored the byplay. Never getting old. Not the kind of thing you really think about at age twenty-one, except when reading bad vampire romances, something she was guilty of doing on occasion. Go Team Edward, but without having to suck blood or glow in daylight. Kinda neat. Watching every normal friend you have die of old age, not so neat. Maybe not having a lot of friends had an upside.

"You okay?" Face-Off asked her.

"Yeah, just thinking things through. I keep getting hit with information overload, but I figure some meditation time and a hefty dose of anti-psychotics will take care of it."

"Well, no time for either," Condor said. "Now that we know what you can do, we need to get a feel for your limitations and capabilities."

That meant more balls to the face, Christine guessed. "Fun."

C.J. Carella

The Freedom Legion

East Kazakhstan, Kazakhstan, March 13, 2013

Chastity Baal coughed and spat blood onto the sandy oil. A broken rib made its presence known with a sharp jab of pain when she tried to move. Behind her, the flames consuming the burning jeep alternatively crackled and roared. For a few seconds, she didn't know where she was or what had happened.

Ah, yes. The Celestial Warrior.

She had seen the figure rushing towards them faster than the Jeep had been traveling. She started to swerve but the running man had smashed into the vehicle. Metal crumpled and the world spun out of control as the multi-ton vehicle was flung into the air. That was the last thing she remembered.

Celsius had gotten his wish.

Chastity looked around. Bao was crawling away from the ruins of the vehicle, still alive but badly injured. Some fifty feet away from the Jeep, Celsius was confronting the Celestial. The Chinese Neolympian was short but heavily muscled, with a shaved head and eyes that blazed with unnatural light. He was bare-chested and the Imperial Sigil branded into his skin glowed with the same hues as the Dragon Wall. Celsius was unleashing a torrent of fire onto the Celestial, but the flames sputtered away inches away from the target, leaving the Imperial unscathed. The Celestial advanced through the stream of fire, leaning forward like someone pushing into a strong wind.

Armageddon Girl

She reached for the pistol in her belt holster, ignoring the stabs of pain from the broken rib. The Celestial was nearly upon Celsius. The Legionnaire switched tactics and encased the Chinese Neo in a sheath of ice. That stopped the Celestial, but the ice began to crack seconds later under his relentless strength. Celsius' face was contorted with exertion and fear. He knew he wouldn't be able to hold the Celestial for long.

The pistol's 9mm rounds would be useless, but the weapon also had an integral mini-grenade launcher under the barrel. Chastity calmly loaded the launcher as the Celestial broke through the ice and hurled himself at Celsius, who tried to dodge away but wasn't fast enough. The Imperial grabbed the Legionnaire in a grip meant to rend him limb from limb. Chastity took her shot.

The 15mm grenade hit the Celestial on the right temple. Its shaped-charge explosive warhead created a jet of plasma no thicker than a knitting needle, concentrating all its power in the smallest possible surface. It was designed to punch through the protective fields that made some Neos largely invulnerable to conventional weapons. The explosion's flash hid the Celestial's head for a second, and the man staggered but did not fall. When the smoke dissipated, Chastity couldn't see any signs of injury on him. The Celestial's hold on Celsius had not slackened, either. He twisted the Legionnaire's body. Celsius screamed in overwhelming agony and even from fifty feet away Chastity heard the loud crack when his spine broke.

The Celestial Warrior let the limp body drop to the ground as he turned towards Chastity. The Imperial hesitated for a second when he saw he was facing a woman. His angry expression was replaced by a lascivious smile.

Panic flickered inside of her, stirring the animal desire to flee. Fear was an old acquaintance of hers; she had lived with it from an early age, and from an early age had learned to set it aside. Running wasn't an option; it would only provide the Imperial with the thrill of the chase to add a little spice to the main course of rape and murder.

Chastity struggled to her feet, letting go off the useless gun. Only one thing left. She reached for the scabbard built into her right boot and pulled out a dagger. It was a fighting blade, seven inches of high-quality steel, curved and single-edged with an unusual symbol carved along its length, a sinuous interlaced design that Chastity had not been able to identify even after consulting with several experts. The weapon had been a parting gift from a lover. "Keep it with you, kiddo, but don't use it unless you're at death's door," he had told her. "It's a prototype, and it's got flaws. Flaws that might kill you. But if you ever need someone dead, no matter what the cost, this is the tool for the job."

For five years Chastity had kept the dagger around whenever practicable, but had never used it. It was time to see what it could do.

The Celestial reached for her, going for a grapple. She sidestepped the overconfident attack and slashed at him with the dagger, striking his forearm. The protective field that had ignored Celsius' flames and the armor-piercing grenade parted under the impact like an elastic membrane pierced by a scalpel. The blade cut through his flesh and scored the bone beneath. With a cry of surprised pain, he spun away from her. The shocked expression in his face matched her own.

The dagger was glowing. Chastity saw the blood on its edge disappear, absorbed into the weapon; the symbol carved into the blade flared brightly. It appeared to be moving as well, but she had no time to look at it closely. The Celestial charged her again. This time he was all business, intent in destroying the woman who had hurt him. For several seconds, Chastity was too busy dodging a whirlwind of punches and kicks to strike back. She used the knife defensively, presenting a threat to his bare-handed attacks and forcing him to be cautious. The man had been trained well, a rarity for someone who was largely invulnerable to conventional attacks. She did not score another hit on him, but she managed to keep him from striking her.

They broke contact and circled each other warily. The Celestial's shock at being wounded had been replaced with anger, but he was still proceeding coldly and deliberately. She had a slight speed advantage on him, but it would not make a difference if he pressed on with his attacks. Chastity might cut him again, but if one of his blows landed it would kill or at best cripple her, and the fight would be over. She watched her opponent intently, looking for an opening.

That's when she noticed the dark tendrils extending from the Celestial's wound, thin veins of blackness that drank the blood spurting from the slash and spread like a network of roots beneath the man's skin. The tendrils pulsed bright with purple-black hues, and a tingling feeling in the hand holding the dagger matched the rhythm of those pulses. Chastity's eyes widened in surprise.

Sensing her distraction, the Celestial struck. She ducked away from a kick, but wasn't fast enough to completely avoid it. The impact of his foot against her midsection should have sent her broken body flying into the air. Instead, Chastity had her breath knocked out of her and was pushed back a couple of steps. The Imperial warrior tried to follow up his attack, but the graceful maneuver turned into a clumsy stumble. The dark tendrils around the wound had spread further; she saw them creep under the skin of his chest, surrounding the Imperial Sigil, and quickly slither towards his face. The Celestial screamed and his body started convulsing.

Chastity moved closer. In an ordinary fight, she would have cut the man's throat and been done with it. There was nothing ordinary about this. Dark light flowed from the fallen Imperial and reached towards her. Chastity felt its approach as a wave of heat and pressure rushing in her direction like a slow-motion explosion. The dark light coalesced around the dagger and flowed into its blade. Its handle shook and grew hot in her hand. She tried to let go of the weapon, but her fingers wouldn't obey her. The symbol along the dagger's edge was clearly moving now, twisting and turning in a hypnotic pattern, and the metal was humming with a matching rhythm. The Celestial at her feet gave a last galvanic spasm and was still.

Pure agony rushed into the hand holding the dagger and beyond, suffusing her entire body. Chastity had been beaten and tortured dozens of times during her checkered career, with items and techniques ancient and modern. None of those experiences had prepared her for this. Every nerve, every cell in her body burned in a fire that seared without consuming. Worse still, the pain did not overwhelm her consciousness; she remained fully aware. She knew several mental disciplines that allowed her to distance herself from pain and discomfort, but she was overwhelmed too quickly to use them. Her writhing body collapsed next to the man she had killed.

Along with pain, her mind was flooded with alien thoughts and memories. She became a young boy growing up in a family farm until government soldiers with the scarlet markers of the Imperial Guard came to take him away. A kaleidoscope of sensations followed: brutal training sessions, being forced to kill while still a child, steps in a relentless process that leached away all traces of humanity and compassion, a final ceremony in which the young man's body was transformed, granted superhuman powers through the Imperial Sigil carved into his chest.

The fire within her flared up one final time, erasing all thought.

Chastity woke up some indeterminate time later. The pain was gone; the dagger was still in her hand, an inanimate object once more. Her first impulse was to fling it away, but she forced herself to put it back in its scabbard. The weapon had saved her life, after all. As she finally let go of the handle, she felt fresh pain on the palm of her hand. A mark had been burned there. It looked like a combination of the symbol on the blade and the Imperial Sigil. She examined the Celestial's body. The man's face was contorted in a final rictus of agony, and the Imperial Sigil was gone from his chest.

There was no time to think about what had transpired. Imperial troops would be on their way, and perhaps more Celestials. She activated an emergency beacon and went to check on Celsius. The Legionnaire was breathing shallowly, still alive despite having his spine broken. She injected him with a heavy dose of restorative serum. The Doc Slaughter invention would seal internal injuries and speed up the healing process, even the miraculous healing process of Neolympians. Celsius would probably recover.

Bao was next. The Mandarin had two broken legs and painful but non-life threatening burns and scrapes. She set the broken limbs and injected him with a dose of serum. Just as she was done with her ministrations, a low rumbling noise alerted her to the arrival of the stealth helicopter.

Chastity waved at the descending vehicle. Once they were out of danger she might have the leisure time to dwell upon the gift that had saved her life.

She was afraid it had exacted a price she would regret paying.

Face-Off

New York City, New York, March 13, 2013

"So what's the verdict, professor?" I asked Condor. We had taken a dinner break. Christine was washing up and we were having a drink while we waited for dinner. Kestrel had briefly returned during the tests but Condor had sent her off on a Chinese food run. We were sitting in his informal dining room, the one that only seats eight or ten people. He was having wine, something expensive and French. I was drinking beer straight from the bottle. Imported beer, just to be fancy.

"I think we haven't even begun to see what she's capable of," he said. "For starters, she has strong empathic abilities and some sort of multi-spectrum vision. Her physical powers are pretty impressive. Her force field and kinetic attack are at least in 2.6 or 2.7 range, possibly higher. She's scared of her abilities and isn't really pushing them. That isn't unusual, especially when we're dealing with someone who didn't even know Neos existed. Going from her aura readings, I think she's got the potential to be a Type Three, and sooner rather than later."

Some Neos started out at low power levels, but developed them over time. The more they used their abilities, the more powerful they got. Others never improved from their starting point. Everybody had an opinion about why that was the case, and nobody knew anything for sure.

It had been a long but interesting afternoon. Christine's control over her force fields and kinetic blasts had improved surprisingly quickly. By the end of the session she was knocking baseballs out of the air with bolts of pure energy. Her defenses had gotten stronger as well. In addition to the force shields she had a secondary protective field around her that had appeared when Condor switched to heavy attacks. Protective fields were the most common powers among heavy hitters; that's how they could survive massive explosions or military grade heavy weapons. Below a certain threshold, damage was shed without making any impression, not even budging the target. Past that threshold, a fraction of the damage got through the shield, enough to hurt or kill, depending on how tough the Neo was. Nobody knew how either form of protection worked, except that they appeared to violate several physical laws.

"I hope your psychic guide figures out your next step quickly, before whoever is looking for her gets their act together," Condor added. "Anybody trying to use a potential Type Three has to have some serious muscle backing them up."

"That's something I've been thinking about," I said. "The snatch team consisted of a pack of Mob buffoons. Okay, they had a Neo along for the ride, but the whole thing felt like an improvised play to me. Like they didn't expect her to pop up in Central Park and end up in a hospital."

"Sure. If someone or something dragged her from her world to ours, I'd imagine they wanted her to arrive somewhere under their control. A properly staffed and outfitted secret base, for example. She must have gotten away somehow."

"Yep. Something went wrong. They figure out where she is, and they try to grab her quickly, using the local Mafia as subcontractors; that move goes tits up, too."

"Thanks to you and Cassandra," Condor pointed out.

"True. If Cassandra hadn't sent me to get her, Christine might have ended up right where her abductors wanted her. Their move may have been improvised, but it almost worked. My worry is that their next move is not going to be improvised, not if they have any brains. They'll come after her with all the muscle they can put together."

"Hopefully by then we'll be out of town," Condor said. "I'm perfectly willing to go along, mind you. I just happen to love this city, and it's already taken too much damage lately."

I nodded. Neos didn't go on rampages very often, but when they did the results were spectacular. New York had a very high parahuman population, so it ended up getting wrecked more often than most places.

"Epic battles are a lot more epic when they don't generate massive collateral damage," Condor went on. "Ideally somewhere with wide open spaces and nobody around."

"Do you guys get a lot of epic battles?" Christine asked as she came into the dining room. She was wearing the generic black and silver costume Condor provided for his students. She clearly wasn't comfortable wearing tight spandex and knee-high boots – she had sensibly picked a pair without high heels – but I thought she looked great.

Down, boy. You're her bodyguard, not her boyfriend.

"Not as many as they do in the movies or the comics, thankfully," Condor said. "The ones we do get are bad enough."

"I can imagine. Having fights between people who can throw cars around has to be bad for the environment," she said as she sat down next to me.

"Can I get you something to drink?" Condor offered. "I have a nice wine selection, and even a good assortment of beers for my more proletarian friends," he said, looking at me.

"I'll just have a diet soda, please. I'm done with alcohol for a while. Oh, can Neos get drunk? I figure the regeneration thingy would flush alcohol out of our systems pretty quickly, wouldn't it?"

"That's correct," Condor said, giving her an 'I really like you' look. "It's almost impossible for most Neos to get drunk on wine or beer," he continued, handing her a glass filled with Diet Coke and ice. "Hard liquor will do it, but we don't stay drunk very long, and we never get hangovers."

"Wow. That's pretty neat, except for the huge bar tabs," Christine noted before taking a sip of her soda. She looked at her glass. "This doesn't taste like diet at all."

"Why should it taste differently?" Condor asked. "Some people pretend they can tell the difference between diet and regular, but they are full of it."

"In my world diet and regular sodas don't taste anything alike. More Neo super-science at work, I guess."

"The original formulae were developed by a Neo scientist, yes. Diet foods are mostly made of 'mirror molecules' that fool your taste buds but have no nutritional value."

"Which can cause problems sometimes," I added. "Between the diet sodas and diet foods, there've been cases of people literally starving to death even while eating like pigs. That's why there's huge warning labels on all the diet shit, to make sure morons don't kill themselves."

"Now that's pretty amazing. If I brought the formula or recipe or whatever back to my world, I'd become mega-rich, like buy and sell Oprah and J.K. Rowling rich. Funny thing is, I like the way diet soda tastes, even though I know the stuff is terrible for you. This stuff actually tastes too sweet for me. Weird. I don't really gain weight easily anyway – hmm, can we get fat? I figure the super-metabolism and healing must burn calories like crazy."

"Well, it's a complicated situation," Condor said, and I sat back, slurped my beer, and resigned myself to a lecture on Neo biology. "First of all, no amount of food intake would allow for the energy usage even a Type One Neolympian displays. The weakest Neos can recover from near-fatal injuries in a matter of days or even hours, for example. Our bodies get energy from an extra-biological source. Nobody's sure exactly what it is."

"Einstein went crazy trying to figure it out," I said, just to be part of the conversation. I wasn't crazy about the way Christine was looking at Condor. He normally has that effect on women, but in her case it was clearly his brains she found attractive. "He called the source of Neo powers 'spooky energy' and spent the last few years of his life trying to find out where it came from."

"In any case, our energy consumption is supplied by that 'spooky' source of energy. Our digestive system is like a car battery hooked up to a nuclear power plant. It's basically redundant."

"Wait – that means we don't really need to eat," Christine said. "We don't really need to breathe, either, I guess."

"In theory, yes," Condor said, and he looked just like a professor who'd just found his new favorite pupil. "In practice, you will feel hunger pangs if you don't eat, and lack of oxygen will cause temporary unconsciousness, but not death."

"Holy mother of crap. So we can't get fat, then."

"It's not impossible – excess calories above our metabolic base rate will still create fat cells. But it takes something on the order of nine, ten thousand calories a day for an average-size Neo to start putting on weight. If I ate that much and led a sedentary life, I'd probably gain a couple of pounds a month. So if you ever see an obese Neo, and there are a few out there, they must be eating ten or twenty times as much as a normal person over a period of years or decades."

"That's cool. The not needing to breathe thingy is cooler, though."

"It makes breath control games so much safer," Kestrel said, entering the dining room. She was wearing civvies: tight red leggings, an even tighter black tank-top and high heels that accentuated her long legs. Her dark black hair was done differently than the last time I had seen her without a mask, cut short in a pixie-like fashion. The sharp facial features were the same, with a nose that was a bit large for her face but which in combination with her high cheekbones created a striking if not quite beautiful whole. She kissed Condor and sat on his lap. "I can let Condor choke me until the lights go out. It's pretty intense." Kestrel smiled at Christine. "You should try it sometime."

Christine didn't say anything.

"Ease up, Kestrel," I said. "Not everyone is a preevert."

"There aren't any perverts. There are people who dare to try new stuff, and people who don't," Kestrel replied playfully. Condor looked embarrassed but didn't say anything, and I realized his new sidekick had gotten her hooks into him real good. The couple of times Kestrel had gotten me to go along with her S&M games it'd quickly become obvious I wasn't into them. From the look in Condor's eyes, I was pretty sure he'd discovered things about himself he hadn't expected. What a mess.

"Let's play nice," Condor finally said. He was actually blushing a bit. "Dinner is in the kitchen, right?" he asked Kestrel.

She nodded. "I brought dinner and heard some rumors," she said. "Looks like every Russian, Belorussian and Ukrainian gang in the city has gotten new marching orders; they are looking for a pale girl with red hair. There's even a picture of her making the rounds." Kestrel tossed a flier on the table. There was no text on the flier, just a picture of Christine, taken while she was lying on a hospital bed.

"First the Eye-talians, now the Russkies," Condor wondered.

"Or maybe it was the Russians all along," I said. "They don't do that well outside their little enclaves. They might have subcontracted the grab at the hospital."

"Yay. Find me, win valuable prizes," Christine said in a low voice. She didn't look very happy at all.

"Don't worry," I told her. "Condor's lair is very well protected. Nobody's going to find you here." Of course, sooner or later we'd have to leave, and things would get interesting.

My comm started vibrating. It was Cassandra, finally.

Her call wasn't as helpful as I hoped.

Chapter Nine

Christine Dark

New York City, New York, March 13, 2013

The food was good – even in Bizarro universe, you could find good Chinese takeout in New York City – but Christine only picked desultorily at her General Tso's chicken. She was on the verge of an anxiety attack, and she desperately did not want to lose it. Not in front of Face-Off. And certainly not in front of Kestrel and Condor. She might be immune to asphyxiation, but not to embarrassment.

So how do I worry thee, she told herself. *Let me count the ways.*

For starters, the whole super-power bit was beginning to scare the ever living pee out of her.

Christine had never been all that much into superhero comics, except for a brief love affair with *The X-Men* when she was a child. She had been crazy for all the movies (well, until the third movie, when they butchered most everyone), and for a while it had been all about graphic novels and Anna Paquin posters. For the most part, though, she'd been more into fantasy, both sword and sorcery and contemporary dark modes. Dragons and vampires were her thing, not men in tights fighting crime.

The idea of running around in a painted-on costume – the little spandex model Condor had made her wear didn't show too much skin, but it was pretty snug and made her feel like the star of a fetish porn production – didn't exactly thrill her. The idea of fighting crime, or even things like pollution, global warming or offshore drilling sent the butterflies in her stomach into a fluttering frenzy. Christine was perfectly comfortable fighting giant monsters in an online game, but real life confrontations turned her into a wet noodle. No effing way she was going to go around beating on people in a world where cosplay wasn't play at all.

She really wanted to go home. Yes, her life on Earth Prime kinda sucked, but it was a suckitude she could handle. Going to school and dealing with Sophie and worrying she'd graduate with a six-figure student loan and a job at Starbucks, she could handle. Sitting in some underground secret base while a guy with no face who apparently killed people whenever they annoyed him discussed strategy with a genuine All-American Superhero, she couldn't handle all that well. Especially when the All-American Superhero's girlfriend was a crazy S&M skank who every few minutes looked at Christine much the way a cat would look at a particularly tasty tiny critter. Whatever Kestrel was thinking about Christine, she was sure it involved lots of adult toys and not-so-erotic asphyxiation. Even worse, Kestrel and Condor had exchanged a couple of glances that seemed to include Christine. She was afraid that if Face-Off wasn't around the words *ménage a trois* might rear their ugly French heads. Or, since Kestrel wasn't exactly shy, by the time dessert came around the words *ménage a quatre* might pop up.

The worst part was, no matter how scared and desperate to go home she was, she was stuck here. There was the whole question of who had brought her here, and why. Since whoever it was had sent a bunch of mobsters to pick her up at the hospital, she was pretty sure their plans for her did not include a pony, tiara and all-expense paid vacation to Disney World (did they have Disney World in Earth Alpha? *Not now, brain!*). She wanted to go home, but they, whoever they were, had found her there. Nowhere to run, nowhere to hide.

Christine forced herself to bite into a piece of chicken while fighting off her incipient panic attack. Blubbering and demanding to go home wasn't going to help. Let's try some damned Vulcan logic. Something had plucked her from her home, and might well do it again. At least here she had some allies, and she might even be able to protect herself. From the tests Condor had put her through she had more firepower and defenses than your average 25-man raid. She wasn't going to run around in a cape and mask, but she might be able to deal with this situation, hopefully without too much violence, and then go home.

While Christine confronted her anxieties, her new pals continued to discuss the call Face-Off got from Cassandra. Christine had wanted to say hi to her – it would have been nice to talk to her outside dreamland – but the call had been short and abrupt, and her marching orders had left Face-Off angry and bewildered.

Do not contact the authorities. Find the Lurker. Do not contact me again. That had been it. If she had been Face-Off, she would have been peeved off, too. Who the eff was the Lurker?

"All I can tell you is that he hasn't been in New York in decades," Condor told Face-Off. "The Lurker's been working out of Chicago since the Seventies. We teamed up a few times, but the last time was back in '08 or '09. We hunted down a Neo serial killer, a really nasty bastard who liked to travel around. I have no idea where the Lurker is now. He's been off the radar for a while. That's been his M.O.

for a while. Disappears for a year or two, makes a quick kill or two, then disappears again."

"And you have no idea where he goes when he disappears?" Face-Off asked.

"Well, he is the Lurker. He doesn't exactly show off for the press. He might have been in Chicago all along, or walking the earth. Who knows?"

Kestrel spoke in a deep, gravelly voice. "Who sees the darkness in all men's souls? The Lurker does!" She was clearly quoting something.

"The Lurker was one of the first mystery men in the late 1920s and early '30s," Condor explained to Christine. "He even got a radio show very loosely based on his adventures. That was the show's signature catch phrase."

"A radio show and dozens of novels, not to mention a few movie serials, and a really lousy motion picture in the '90s" Face-Off said. "He was my favorite mystery man when I was growing up."

"Yeah, he suits you. You both like to work in the shadows and shoot people," Kestrel commented. "I wonder what else he likes to do in the shadows."

"He's not your type, Kestrel," Condor said. If he was bothered about his girlfriend-sidekick showing interest in other men of mystery, he didn't show it. "The Lurker is all work and no play. The guy's straight like a Mormon and pretty creepy to boot. He's a strange little man. He never took off that gas mask he always wears, even when we were kicking up our heels after the job was done. Doesn't drink, doesn't joke around. And you don't want to ever, ever quote that 'darkness in all men's souls' line to him. He really doesn't like it."

"Yeah, you've only told the story a million times," Face-Off said.

"Uh, I haven't heard it yet," Christine said tentatively.

"Condor tried to be a smartass, and the Lurker punched him through a wall. The end," Face-Off said in a deadpan tone. "There, I saved you a good ten minutes of your life."

"You have no storytelling skills, Face," Condor said.

"I'm just fucking frustrated. Cassandra can be cryptic sometimes, but this one takes the cake. There's probably better instructions in the fortune cookies that came with dinner." As he spoke, Face-Off cracked open a cookie and read the little paper strip inside. "Here we go: 'Hard work you enjoy is not hard work at all.' That's only slightly less helpful than 'Find a superannuated mystery man.' And why him? He's one of the oldest Neos around, sure, but why can he help instead of the Freedom Legion or someone with more juice?"

"We just don't know," Condor said. "Besides, the Legion has problems of its own. I know you've both been too busy to follow the news, but someone nuked them earlier today."

"Nuked?" Christine gasped.

"Yeah. It's pretty bad. I've been checking updates in between the tests. They haven't released a casualty report yet, but it's got to be bad. They are going to be pretty busy dealing with that. Anyway, maybe that's why the Legion can't help. Or maybe it's because they don't know anything about Christine, and somehow the Lurker does."

"The Lurker does!" Kestrel said in her fake Lurker voice. Christine got the feeling that when Kestrel found something funny, she kept picking at it long past its expiration date.

"It doesn't make any sense," Face-Off said. "I was a fan of the guy but he's never been a major player. About my league, maybe, and that ain't the majors, that's for sure," he concluded bitterly.

"He's a strange guy," Condor mused. "And I only saw what he wanted me to see, but he's learned quite a few tricks over the years. Invisibility. Some sort of darkness powers. I think even teleportation, although how much is sleight of hand and how much actual Neo powers I don't know. He might be a lot more capable than we think."

"Cassandra has never steered me wrong before, so I'm not going to start second-guessing her," Face-Off said resignedly. "Just wish she'd just told us why we have to go see Mr. Creepy."

Christine had a sudden nasty thought. "I have one more theory," she said. "Maybe he's my father."

Condor looked at her. "I really hope that's not the case." The expression in his face made Christine shudder. Her dad had been a bit weird and creepy, though. It kinda fit, even if the idea scared her.

"Could be. If he's learned so many new tricks, maybe he can hop to other universes, too. Wish Cassie would just tell us," Face-Off said. "I guess we'll find out when we meet him. We're going to have to go look for the Lurker in Chicago. Got any ideas, Gramps?"

"I have a couple of contacts in Chi-Town that might help," Condor said. "And don't call me Gramps, it's disrespectful."

"Sorry, Gramps. Any ideas on how to get there?"

"I guess I'm going to have to dust off the old Condor Jet."

"No way," Christine said. She hated flying with a passion. She'd actually made her mother and grandfather drive her and her stuff from New Jersey to Michigan rather than get on a freaking plane when she went off to college, and the two round-trip flights she'd taken home since then had been among the worst experiences in her life, up until the last couple of days, of course.

"It's fast, it's stealthy, it's VTOL, and it seats twelve," Condor said. "It's a perfectly serviceable aircraft."

"No freaking way," Christine said, for all the good she knew it would do. They were going to make her fly, her father was probably a creep who walked around wearing a gas mask, and she was going to cosplay whether she wanted to or not. She didn't think things could suck any worse, but she had a feeling she'd be proven wrong about that, too.

C.J. Carella

The Freedom Legion

Atlantic Headquarters, March 13, 2013

"We might as well get started," Daedalus Smith said wearily.

They had done all that could be done for the living. The dead were being slowly extricated from the wreckage. Hyperia and Kenneth had survived the explosion as well, although both had been badly injured. Daedalus had been just far enough away to avoid the worst of it, and his Myrmidon armor had weathered the distant flash and shockwave without taking damage. The others had been too close to the blast.

The Legion's meeting room was in the Freedom Hall, which had survived the attack nearly unscathed. The assault had focused on the office buildings on the island; the attackers had targeted civilians and support staff. John felt ashamed about that. The island's vaunted defenses had been overwhelmed by the opening missile barrage, and the civilian buildings had never been meant to withstand military weapons. Should they have done more to protect the thousands of humans working for the Legion? The aftermath's answer was clearly yes.

Four of the eight Council Members (Kenneth, Olivia, Daedalus Smith and himself) were sitting at the table. The other four (Chasca, Darkling, General Xu and Meteor) were based on the Pacific Headquarters in the Marshall Islands and had holographic avatars in place, linked by the most secure communication systems the Legion could devise. John missed the old days when the entire Legion could meet in a conference room. That was no longer possible; the organization had over two hundred full-time members. A governing Council had been formed in 1962, with eight Councilors elected by the Legion's membership for two-year terms. John had served in the Council every term since then. People trusted him. If they only knew what was going on in his head lately...

"... eight hundred and eighty-three confirmed dead," Kenneth Slaughter was saying. John blinked. He'd somehow blacked out for several seconds. Kenneth was wrapped in bandages, but he had insisted on attending the meeting. "Four hundred and thirty six people suffered severe injuries, and we have about six hundred others with light injuries. The main hospital was one of the facilities hit, so ninety-two critical cases were medevac'd to hospital facilities in Port Au-Prince. Ten Legion members were killed in action. In addition to Mind Hawk's strike team, we lost Hailstorm, Medicine Man, Mesmer..."

John hung his head as Kenneth read the casualty list. Most of the deceased had been acquaintances, good people but relatively new recruits. Mesmer – Jason Merrill – had been with the Legion for fifty years. John had been at Jason's wedding and his son's baptism. Jason had been a friend.

He felt numb.

"All losses, human and parahuman, are painful and regrettable," General Xu's hologram said, his clean-shaven face showing no trace of emotion. Xu was a recent entrant to the Legion, although he had been an active Neolympian since World War Two, best known in the Republic of China as Mao Zhe-Dong's executioner. John had only a vague idea who Zhe-Dong was, but if you heard Xu tell the story, Mao had been as big a threat to the world as the Dragon Emperor. John had serious doubts about that. "I think we should concentrate on the paramount question, however," Xu continued. "Who launched this unprovoked attack on the Legion?"

"Unfortunately, the carrier vessel was thoroughly destroyed, and its remains scattered into the ocean." Kenneth replied. "We have just started redeploying assets from search and rescue operations and tasking them to salvage what we can from the debris. The explosion that obliterated the vessel was in the twenty kiloton range, which means there is going to be very little to recover. The same teams are recovering as much radioactive material as possible. I will have a preliminary environmental impact statement ready for you later tonight."

"Before Doc here buries us in reports and graphs, let's get down to the nitty-gritty," Daedalus Smith broke in. Kenneth and Daedalus were equals in sheer genius and brilliance and near opposites in almost every other way. Where Kenneth was cool and reserved, Daedalus was flamboyant and irreverent. Kenneth led an ascetic life, dedicated to his scientific advancements and helping humanity. Daedalus managed to spend a good deal of his free time in the public eye, a notorious playboy seen with an endless variety of movie stars, singers and other notorious personalities, human and parahuman. They were not friends, and the best one could hope from their interactions was cold civility.

"Long story short, the missiles are Chimp designs," Daedalus continued, his eyes bright with anger. General Xu frowned – the slang term for 'Chinese Imperial' wasn't exactly liked by the Republic of China – but said nothing. Daedalus absent-mindedly pulled at his mustache as he continued. "We salvaged enough pieces from some of the cruise missiles that detonated over the island to identify them. They are designated C-755 types, three hundred mile range, pack a nice 100-pound enhanced explosive warhead, roughly equivalent to ten thousand pounds of TNT. From the video records from my suit, we can identify the flying carrier as a modified ACV-12. I'm sure that sometime between the environmental impact statement and our 'fishing for radioactives' operation we'll gather enough big chunks of the ship to definitely identify it. But let's get real, it's Chimp technology. By tomorrow Doc will have enough evidence to convince a jury, but he already knows I'm right."

Kenneth Slaughter nodded, although he wasn't happy about it. "The preliminary findings do point in that direction. But do let me emphasize the word 'preliminary.'"

"Of course, Doc," Artemis said. She was cool and collected, but John could see the pain in her eyes. As the Public Affairs liaison for the Legion, Olivia had worked closely with most of the civilian staff at Freedom Tower, which had suffered the most casualties in the attack. Many of the dead had been close friends and colleagues of hers. "Still, it does seem clear the attackers were using Imperial technology."

Xu muttered something in Cantonese before speaking out loud. "Insanity! Why would the rebellious provinces attack the Legion in this manner? There has been peace between us for twenty years."

"Yeah, it's probably not an official Chimp operation," Daedalus agreed. "For one, they'd have sent at least a few Celestial Warriors along for the ride. The attack was launched by drones and vanillas."

"'Vanillas' is an insensitive term, Mr. Smith," Chasca said, her voice cold. "So is 'Chimp,' for that matter." The Peruvian beauty was the youngest member of the Council at a mere forty-three years of age, but her forceful personality had made an impact since joining the Council four years ago. She was right, too; 'vanilla' was Neo slang for normal humans, and while not directly derogatory unlike other terms like 'squishy' or 'normy,' it wasn't a compliment, either.

"Sorry, my mistake. Drones and humans, with Imperial technology," Daedalus said without a trace of remorse. "An ACV-12 has a crew of a fifty, but if its systems were automated, it could have been cut down to a handful people, or even remote-controlled from somewhere else. Even if there was a crew, I don't think we'll be able to identify any of them, since they were at ground zero of the explosion. Doubt we're gonna find any pieces big enough to fit in a sandwich bag, and even those are going to be pretty crispy around the edges."

"So there is no evidence of parahuman involvement?" Xu asked.

"Nothing conclusive," Kenneth said. "The vessel had a very sophisticated stealth suite, which might be parahuman in nature. That explains how it was able to approach the island without being detected. Such stealth systems are not standard for any Aerial Carrier Vessel in the Empire's arsenal."

"Yes," Xu agreed. "If the Empire could deploy undetectable flying carriers, we would have known about it." *The Empire would have tried to start another short victorious war*, John mentally translated. The Dragon Emperor's territorial claims included all of China, and pretty much everything east of India up to and including Japan. He had never been content with the territory he controlled, which spanned all of Mongolia and several interior provinces of China. He had sealed those lands behind an energy wall five times as long as the original Great Wall of China. Twice in the last forty years, he had tried to seize more territory, leading to the deaths of millions.

John had faced the Emperor a handful of times. Each time, even fighting side by side with such powerhouses as Janus and Hyperia, he had never been able to earn more than a draw. The man's power was godlike and was matched only by his ambition.

"... should launch Operation Saint George," Meteor was saying. "It's about bloody time, I say. We've been planning it for decades, and all we've done is let the bugger consolidate his power." Meteor had always been a balls-to-the-wall type. John had known him since the war. The British superhero had destroyed the city of Dresden in a firestorm that had killed thousands, and John had beaten him to an inch of his life afterward. He and Meteor did not care for each other, but in the ensuing three quarters of a century had learned to work together. John still tended to disagree with Meteor most of the time, and this was no exception.

"That's not going to work," Daedalus said before John could voice an objection. "I wish it would. You all know I've got plenty of reasons to hate the Chi... the Imperials." Back during the First Asian War, Daedalus had been captured by the Dragon Emperor. It had not been a good experience, and he managed to escape only because his captors had tried to force him to design weapons for them. It was never a good idea to let a Genius-type parahuman near a weapon workshop. "I'd love to see the Chief Imp's head in a trophy case at the Freedom Museum. But even if Operation Saint George does go off without a hitch and we take out ol' Draggy and his WMD arsenal, what do you think is going to happen to the Legion afterward? After we launch a surprise attack on a sovereign nation? 'Cause the only way Saint George has any chance of working is if we attack by surprise."

"Which is why we should strike now," Meteor broke in. His eyes gleamed like molten iron. "We could bloody well do it tonight, they'd never expect us to react so quickly! The Legion is assembled and mobilized; we can launch Saint George in six, eight hours at the most. We can bring Janus in, and he can lead the way. He'll do it too, there's no love lost between him and the Emperor."

"Yeah, we could probably pull it off," Daedalus said. "I'd say a seventy-five percent chance. Do you agree, Doc?"

"If Janus could be convinced to join in, I'd say closer to eighty percent. However...."

Daedalus cut him off. "Yes, however. The UN would blow a gasket. At the very least, we'd lose our seat in the Security Council. Come on, matey," he told Meteor. "You know that plenty of people have been bitching about a non-governmental organization having so much influence, pretty much since we got our seat back in '46. We are always getting accused of being a US puppet, or part of a secret conspiracy to set up a Neolympian world government, sometimes both. We take out the Chief Imp without asking for permission first, and we become the villains of the piece."

"Which we *would* be, if we acted unilaterally," Chasca said. "Our charter allows us to operate only in countries that expressly grant us permission to do so, or when enforcing an official UN resolution. But that is not a problem. If we have evidence the Empire is behind this, the UN will act on it."

"Sure," Daedalus replied, his sneer clearly visible. "It would only take a couple of months of debating the matter. The French would threaten to veto any resolution until we dotted every 'i' and crossed every 't.' You were here when I said Saint George only works as a *surprise* attack, weren't you?"

"That's enough, Daedalus," Olivia said.

"Hey, I'm just pointing out the facts here. And I already said we couldn't go with Saint George. Talk some sense into our limey pyromaniac friend over there."

"Somebody needs to teach you some manners, Mr. Smith," Meteor said.

"ENOUGH!"

The shout was loud enough to make the room shake and the holograms flicker. Everybody froze and looked at John, who was as surprised as everyone else. He had been listening quietly; an eye blink later he was on his feet, the echoes of his voice reverberating in his ears.

He couldn't just stand there looking like an idiot, so he kept talking. "There is no point in debating an attack on the Empire right now. If we find enough evidence linking the Empire to the attack, we can discuss our options. Fair enough?"

"I strongly second tabling any discussion involving an attack on the Empire," General Xu said. "For one, my nation would view such an attack with the utmost concern."

"As would mine," said Darkling, the Korean Mistress of Shadows, who had been quiet throughout the discussion so far. "Another war with the Empire would bring death and destruction throughout Asia, and perhaps the whole world. So let's try to keep the macho posturing down to a dull roar, okay?" Meteor definitely resented the remark, but he kept quiet. Even Daedalus didn't come back with a smartass remark. John's loss of control had shaken everyone up, with good reason.

Normal people could afford to lose their temper once in a while. Even heads of state had that privilege, at least in private. A man who could shatter buildings with his fists had to always keep his emotions in check, however.

The Council agreed to keep the entire Legion on full alert and postpone any discussion on retaliation until more evidence was available. The meeting ended quietly. John had been ready to leave himself, but caught the look in Kenneth's face. *We need to talk* was written all over it. Their planned dinner for that evening had not happened, of course. John remained in the conference room with Kenneth. Olivia stayed behind as well.

"I know," John began as soon as the three of them were alone. "Something is seriously wrong with me."

The relief in his friends' faces was almost insulting, but he could understand it. "The press conference," Olivia said. "I saw how close you were to reacting violently. Whatever is happening, it's been building up for some time, hasn't it?"

John nodded. "And it's more than my temper." He described the blackouts and nightmares. "What do you think, Doc?" he asked Kenneth. "Have I got Neo Psychosis?"

"You know that term is nothing more than popular slang," Kenneth said. "You may simply be experiencing shell shock, like we discussed earlier."

"Even if that's all it is, that's no joke," John said. "My temper's fraying like never before. And I don't understand why it's happening now."

"The timing is suspicious," Kenneth agreed. "But it's happening, and we have to deal with it."

"So what do you think I should do? Resign from the Council? See a shrink? Now, when the Legion has been attacked directly for the first time in over a decade? They *gutted* us, Kenneth. A dozen dead Legionnaires in one day. We haven't suffered losses like that since the Second Asian War. I can't be sidelined now."

"Why not wait until we know what we are facing?" Olivia said. "It was good advice for dealing with the attack, and it's a good idea here, too. Let's get somebody trustworthy to evaluate you, find out what is wrong, and then we – you – can decide what to do."

"Sounds like a plan. Any suggestions as to who to see?" John asked. The idea of meeting with one of the Legion's counselors did not appeal to him.

"Doctor Martin Cohen from Chicago," Kenneth said without hesitation. "He's a very skilled empath and an authority in parahuman psychology. He is the man who convinced me that using surgery to remove violent tendencies in criminals was a terrible mistake, even before the side effects became apparent." Kenneth's regret managed to seep through his seemingly unemotional tone.

"Ah." Doc Slaughter had used his skills as a neurosurgeon to make alterations in the brains of forty-six convicted criminals in an effort to 'cure' them from their criminal tendencies. In all fairness, they all volunteered to undergo the procedure in return for reduced sentences. The operations had been successful, inasmuch as forty-four of the patients had never committed a crime again. The two exceptions had turned into brilliant criminal masterminds of near Neolympian ability. The others... the kindest thing one could say was that they had done very well for several years. Within a decade, however, all had been struck with a wild assortment of mental problems and ended up institutionalized for life. Doc had discontinued the program long before that happened, thankfully, or the toll would have been much worse. The press hadn't really caught on at the time, although back in the 1980s *Rolling Stone* magazine had published a scathing exposé, which in turn had sparked a flurry of lawsuits and a Congressional investigation. It had taken decades for Kenneth to live down his mistake.

"He is the man to see," Kenneth continued. "Very discreet, and not directly affiliated with the Legion, although he has received some grants from us in the past."

"Okay," John agreed. "Is he going to be able to get a read off me?" All parahumans were fairly resistant to psychic powers, and the resistance seemed to be a function of the parahuman's overall power level. Most telepaths and mind-controllers couldn't touch him.

"Probably not, or at least not a detailed one," Kenneth said. "But he does not rely on his powers to diagnose problems. He is a skilled therapist."

"Guess he has a new patient now," John said resignedly. Anything, even confiding in a stranger, was better than this slow dance with madness.

Chapter Ten

Christine Dark

New York City, New York, March 13, 2013

After they had made their plans to fly to Chicago – to be more specific, to fly to Chicago in a home-made, non-FAA certified aircraft that was over thirty years old – Condor and Kestrel had left for some private alone time, which Christine expected would involve whips, chains and edible underwear. Face-Off had led Christine to Condor's rec room. It was big and high-tech like the rest of Condor's Lair, with lots of screens, something that looked like a cross between an X-Box and a military-issue flight simulator seat, six large reclining armchairs and half a dozen lesser game consoles. The room was dominated by a flat screen TV big enough to be used as a dinner table.

"Guess Condor likes to watch his stories in full life-size goodness," Christine commented.

"Yeah, the guy's a big movie buff," Face-Off said. "He's got a big library of laser disks, and just about every pay channel there is. So if there is anything you'd like to watch, I'm sure I can get it for you. Well, stuff from this planet, at least. No John Travolta movies, sorry." He had a mental grin on as he said that. Christine could pick the invisible smiles automatically now. "Or if you want to get some rest, I'll show you to your room and you can catch some Z's."

"Maybe later, it's still early and I spent the last day or so unconscious, so I'm slept out right now."

"No problem. Can I get you anything to drink? I'm going to grab another over-priced foreign beer."

"Another Diet Coke would be great, thank you. Or a regular Coke, I guess."

Christine sat on one of the armchairs. She noticed there was a keyboard and game controller attached to one of the arms. This was a gamer's dream setup. She wanted to open a *World of Warcraft* account and see how this universe's version stacked against hers. If they turned out to be the same, she'd freak out. It was freaky enough that the same game existed in both worlds. Sure, Monopoly and chess would be around, since they predated the appearance of the zany guys in latex, but computer games from the last decade? Maybe there was some sort of telepathic communication between the two worlds, and some ideas got passed on through the collective unconscious or some weird Jungian crap like that. Come to think of it, that might explain why people all of a sudden started creating comic books with costumed heroes in a world where they didn't exist. Maybe the comic book guys and computer nerds from her universe got some sort of visions or psychic seepage from Earth Alpha. If anybody was going to receive messages from another universe it would be geeks.

"Hey," Face-Off said, and Christine jumped a little. "Sorry, I didn't mean to startle you." He handed her a Diet Coke.

"I was lost in thought for a second, that's all. I space out sometimes, as in a lot. All part of the Dark charm."

"No problem." Face-Off sat on another chair and took a sip of his beer. He had to produce another face to do it; Christine recognized the old tough guy he'd looked like when she first met him.

"By the way, what is your name? 'Face' is a little impersonal. You saved my butt; I would kinda like to know your name."

"I have lots of names," Face-Off said, getting up and standing in front of the TV. His face changed, and now she was looking a black-haired man who looked a bit like a younger version of the guy from that Showtime show *Episodes,* what was his name? Matt something. "In Little Italy, I'm Tony." His voice had changed and gotten much more Jersey Shore-like. Even his body language was different, with more hand gestures and nods at nothing in particular. "Tony's a funny guy, a real wiseass. But people like him, 'cause he's always got money to spend, and he sucks at playing cards but he don't mind when he loses."

He whirled on his feet, and when he spun back around he was a thin-faced kid with messy brown hair. "On 137th Street I'm Dean." Dean apparently couldn't stand still; he started doing little hops in place, and he hugged himself and rubbed his upper arms a lot. The way he slouched his shoulders made him look a lot shorter than his usual five ten. His voice was whiny and annoying. "Donny's a junkie, a little dope fiend. He usually has enough cash to pay for his medicine, though, so people don't care if he hangs around."

Another whirl, and now he was a blonde in a crew cut. He looked mean until he smiled. He had a sweet, friendly smile. "Johnny hangs out with the hookers on West 28th. He buys them coffee and donuts, and never tries to pull any shit on them, so they trust him a bit, enough that they will share with him any street gossip they hear. They also know that if they tell Johnny about a pimp who gets too slap-happy with his girls, the pimp will end up having a nasty accident."

"That's pretty awesome," Christine admitted. "You should be in the movies. But those are masks. What about, you know, the real you? I know that's kind of Oprah of me – do you have Oprah here? Never mind – but who are you, really?"

The blank face was back. "This is my face, the only face I've got," he said as he sat back down. The Tony-face appeared for a second while he chugged some beer, then disappeared again. "When I make a face, it is a constant effort, like keeping a muscle clenched. Not a big effort, but you have to concentrate on it all the time. When I relax, this is what you get."

"Uh, were you always like that?" Christine asked.

"Did I scare the shit out of the entire maternity ward when I was born, you mean?" Face-Off said and chuckled. "Nah, nothing so dramatic. There was an incident when I was sixteen. That's when my old face went away. For some reason, I can't bring it back. I've tried to do it off old pictures, and I can't get a grip on it."

When he said 'incident,' her Christine-senses picked up a nasty emotional spike. Whatever the incident had been, it hadn't involved sponge cake and cuddly kittens, unless the kittens had ended up baked into the cake. "Okay," she said, pointedly not asking any questions about the incident. "That's your face. Cool. What's your name?"

He hesitated for a second. "Mark. Marco, if you want to be technical. And if you say 'Polo' I'll... I'll get miffed. Marco Ernesto Martinez. My father was Puerto Rican, my mother Italian. Call me Mark."

"Mark it is," she replied. She raised her Diet Coke to him. "Thanks for saving my butt, Mark."

He raised his beer bottle in return. "Cheers. Pleasure saving you. Now that you're a Type 2.5 or higher, you'll probably end up saving my butt if we get in trouble before we get you home."

Condor had explained to her the whole power classification thingy. It was a nerdy thing to do, assigning numbers to powers and trying to rank them. She could see a couple of geeks at a comic book store or worse, an online forum, having furious arguments about the actual PAS numbers of some superhero or another. Who was stronger, Ultimate or Mighty Mouse? That made her smile, and she explained why to Face-Off – to Mark.

Mark was mentally grinning when she was done. "Oh, yes, we get a lot of that shit. Is so-and-so a 2.7 or a 2.8? Neos are as bad or worse than vanilla humans about it. 'What's your number?' That's the question we ask each other to see where we fit in the Cosmic Pecking Order. The whole thing is ridiculous."

"So what's your number?" Christine said. "Hey, I am a nerd. And a geek, pointdexter, dork – with my last name, I get that one so effing much – you name it. I like linking numbers to things."

"I'm a 2.3 or 2.4. So I usually say 2.4 to puff myself up. Which means you are anywhere between thirty and a hundred percent more powerful than me, supposedly."

"I guess. But I don't know what I'm doing yet, so I'm sure an experienced 2.1 can gank me pretty good."

Mark nodded. "That's part of why I think the rankings are bullshit. There's plenty of cases where Neos beat opponents several times more powerful than them. The whole testing system isn't an exact science, either, and the tests fail big time at predicting how far you can push your powers when you get angry or desperate. Plus some people develop their powers over time, so this year's 1.2 can be next decade's 2.2 or whatever. And the actual powers you have also count for a lot. The electric fucker that tried to kill me when I was rescuing you could hit me from range, so unless I closed the distance he had the advantage, no matter what our numbers were."

"Ranged versus melee, gotcha," Christine said. Her games had the same issues. And unlike games, the world didn't have designers to bitch at about game balance and ask to please nerf the ranged Neo powers so they didn't win every duel. The number one rule of the Reality Game was 'life's unfair.' "So why even bother with the ranking system?"

"It makes people feel a little better, I guess. If you can measure things they aren't quite so scary," Mark said. He made another face – the Christian Bale look-alike this time – and finished off his beer. "So how about you, Christine? What's your story before you got dragged into Olympus 2.0?"

"Me? God, nothing much to tell. Born and raised in New Jersey, mostly around Princeton Junction. Junior in college, Physics major at UM, which meant I was headed for grad school, except I was getting kinda sick of physics, I love the math but the theoretical stuff is more annoying than useful sometimes. That was back when my problems were little things, like wondering if I really wanted to do what I'd been studying for two years, and if I had gone too far to change my mind. Plus there weren't a lot of women in the Physics department, which can really suck. Yeah, you end up being the center of attention sometimes, but it's the wrong kind of attention, you know? And a lot of a-holes thought I didn't belong there because as far as they were concerned only people with dicks can understand the mysteries of the universe.

"Lately I've been playing too many computer games and letting my grades slip; it's almost like I want to fail. But if I do, the a-holes are going to smirk and say the girl couldn't hack it. So should I finish my degree to show them what a-holes they are, even if I'm not sure that's what I want? I was thinking of maybe taking a year off and think things through. Guess I am taking a year off now," she realized out loud.

Mark just sat there, listening and actually paying attention, unlike your typical guy. Usually by that point her dates' eyes glazed over or they interrupted her, either to talk about themselves or to ask some stupid question meant mostly to shut her up. *Except this is not a date, just an ex-victim and her rescuer yakking it up,* her brain dutifully informed her. "And my social life sucked. My roommate Sophie thought that party was one of my last chances of having a normal college experience. I'm not saying I had no social life. I had two serious boyfriends and stuff, but they didn't work out. As in both relationships ended in total disaster. One cheating a-hole and one domineering d-bag." *Smart, let's talk about my exes. Guys love to hear about other guys, said nobody ever.*

Who gives a frak? Her brain retorted. *Are you actually interested in a murderous guy with no face?*

What if I am?

Then I think you have serious problems. Plus it's pretty pathetic, swooning over your rescuer like some loser bimbo. So last century, or even the century before that.

We're just talking, she replied, and realized that outside in the real world, it had gotten pretty quiet. "Sorry," she said. That made it how many times she'd said 'sorry'? A large integer, that was for sure. "Mind wandered off again."

"That's all right," he replied; his mental smile was warm and relaxed. "I was pretty wound up about tomorrow. I don't like doing things without a clear plan, a definite goal, and it's driving me apeshit. This little chat has helped me relax for a bit. And trust me, Cassandra is the queen of the wandering minds. Sometimes she'll stop in mid-sentence and won't say a word, or listen to a word I say, for a good hour or two. I usually grab a book and catch up on my reading until she comes back to earth."

That led to a nice conversation about books; they exchanged favorite titles for a while. Both worlds shared a lot of the same classic authors, like Tolkien and Edgar Rice Burroughs. Things changed radically after World War Two, which made sense. No J.K. Rowling, for example. Stephen King, yes, although his books were very different, except for the Dark Tower series, amusingly enough. George R.R. Martin was around, but he wrote long convoluted novels about the doings of a bunch of fictional Neos instead of fantasy. Supers sold better than dragons in this world, she supposed.

Movies came next. Some actors existed in both worlds – Nicholas Cage, for one, the Olsen twins for another, except in this world they were triplets and one of them was a Neo superhero. Katherine Heigl made rom-coms in both worlds. Bruce Willis, yes, but no Demi More or Ashton Kutcher.

How did that work? If chaos theory was right, very few people born after, say, 1945 should exist in both worlds. Butterfly effect and all that jazz, little changes building up until almost nothing was the same. Oh, well. She wasn't that big a fan of chaos theory. Maybe the butterflies canceled each other out some of the time. When she had the time, she'd have to sit down and try to figure it out. If she ever got back, a careful study of the two timelines would make for a great paper. She might get an A or end up in an insane asylum. Maybe both.

Christine normally didn't talk to near-strangers for hours on end, but next thing she knew, it was well past midnight. Time flies when you're having trans-dimensional comparative pop culture discussions.

C.J. Carella

The Freedom Legion

Atlantic Headquarters, March 14, 2013

Chastity Baal looked at her debriefer with thinly-concealed contempt.

"Can you tell me again how you managed to take down a Celestial?" Swift asked. To have him of all people in charge of her after-mission report made for the perfect topper for this caper. She, the Mandarin and Celsius – whose prognosis remained rather poor – had been flown to the Atlantic Headquarters with undue haste. Going to the Pacific Headquarters would have made far more sense, but politics had overruled common sense, as was the case all too often.

Swift met her stare with his own glare and waited for an answer. Chastity was generally rather discriminating about who she allowed into her life and her bed. Her brief affair with Larry Graham had been a monumental mistake that had haunted her for years. Larry had found her at one of the lowest points in her life – still mourning Tommy, feeling truly alone in the world – and had, if not taken advantage, certainly seized the opportunity she had foolishly offered. He then had had the gall to blame her for his philandering, and had remained a chilly, hostile presence in her life. Fortunately, their work in the Legion very rarely put together. Tonight was a vexing exception.

She waited a few more heartbeats before answering. "I used the special munitions Doctor Slaughter provided," she said, lying by omission. She wasn't ready to discuss the dagger, not until she had a chance to speak with its creator. "Celsius had also engaged the Celestial and possibly weakened him before I finished him off."

"Okay, fine," Swift conceded, speaking loudly to make himself heard over the noise in the background. Heavy machinery was hard at work not very far away from Freedom Hall, where the debriefing was being conducted. The Hall itself had been largely undamaged, but even its normally pristine marble walls and columns were pock-marked with shrapnel. Chastity had gotten a good look at the devastation on the flight in. Freedom Island had been attacked before, but it never had suffered so much damage.

Swift waited for the noise to abate somewhat before continuing. "I'll give Celsius an assist for putting down the Celestial. That might cheer him up if he ever wakes up. Artemis is debriefing Bao right now," Swift added, declining to use his wife's real name in Chastity's presence. Then again, Chastity was depersonalizing Larry by thinking of him in his costumed guise, so perhaps she shouldn't cast stones. "We'll find out what he knows. We're hoping he can tell us if there is any connection between the Empire and the attack."

"The timing of the defection is suspicious," Chastity commented. "We were contacted by Bao six days ago. The attack's preparations would have been on their final stages then. If someone is trying to frame the Empire, the defector would make a perfect tool."

"We're not just going to take Bao's word for it," Swift said dismissively. "We have enough mind-snoops in the Legion to make sure he's telling the whole truth and nothing but. This ain't our first rodeo, you know."

"If the attack came from the Empire, wouldn't it have been more sensible to take Bao to the Pacific Headquarters? That's going to be our forward base of operations if the worst happens." Chastity thought she knew the answer but wanted to see if Swift would admit to it.

He shrugged. "Two of the Pacific Councilors – I think you can figure out who – have a vested interest in not pissing off the Empire. Some of us on this side of the world thought we'd be better off presenting them with solid data. That way they don't have to resist the temptation to massage the info before presenting it to us. The younger crew is a little too willing to do whatever it takes to find a peaceful resolution even when there's none to be found."

Chastity didn't say anything. She hadn't been working with the Legion for very long as Neos measured such things, but even so had become keenly aware of the rift between the 'original' Legionnaires – the founding heroes of World War Two and a select few from the First Asian War – and the younger generations, especially the younger generations from countries other than the US or Great Britain. That rift could turn into something dangerous down the line. She shrugged mentally, unwilling to let Swift see anything she was feeling. She was a covert operator, not a mover and shaker.

"Are we done here?" she asked.

"Yeah. That about covers it." He glanced at the computer. "You're off the clock until 1300 hours tomorrow. Doc will be handing out assignments at Freedom Hall then. Don't let the door hit your ass on your way out."

Chastity rose from her chair and left without saying a word. Dealing with Swift's juvenile behavior could wait. She had someone important to see.

***

"Chastity! What a delightful surprise."

Daedalus Smith looked anything but delighted, but he stepped aside and let Chastity enter his personal quarters at Freedom Hall. The Hall's neoclassic exterior hid a high-tech warren of gleaming corridors, cylindrical elevators and computer terminals every few dozen feet, with sensors and cameras monitoring everything and everyone. The living quarters for the senior members of the Legion were several levels underground and resembled a luxury hotel, featuring hallways covered with thick lavender carpets and decorated with expensive replicas of renowned paintings. Daedalus' room was at the end of one such corridor.

Chastity's former lover was wearing a bathrobe, but he did not look as if he had been sleeping when she came calling. His handsome features were marred by his customary smirk, but his eyes showed no amusement, just cold calculation. She glanced past the richly furnished living room and caught a glimpse of a naked young woman just before she shut the bedroom door.

Daedalus shrugged. "She's a bit shy. Her name's Lydia; she's an emergency medicine specialist. Vanilla, but very athletic. You'd like her." His eyes gleamed with amusement for a second. "Maybe the three of us could have a little party."

"I didn't come here for that," Chastity said as she walked past Daedalus.

"Yeah, I figured as much. So what brings you here unannounced? In case you haven't noticed, we're in the midst of a crisis here. You are dropping by during my allotted four hours of R&R, probably the last I'll get for the rest of the week. So what gives, Chaz?"

"The dagger. I used it in Kazakhstan."

"Oh, yeah? How did it work out for you?"

Chastity lunged at Daedalus and slammed him against a wall, one hand tight around his throat. "What the hell is that thing, Daedalus?"

He pushed against her, to no avail. "My, you seem to have gotten a tad stronger," he said. "Why don't you tell me what happened, Chastity? Then I'll explain as much as I can. And would you mind letting me go? I'm not in the mood to play bottom tonight."

Chastity released him and stepped back. Daedalus absently rubbed his throat and waited for her to speak. "A Celestial attacked us. He took down Celsius. I used the dagger."

"Saved your life, didn't it? Any Celestial would have torn you apart otherwise. They run at 2.5 or higher, mostly higher. Why so mad, then?"

"The dagger did something to the Celestial. It did something to me." Chastity said and showed him her scarred palm. The burn had healed but the symbols seared into her skin remained. "What is that thing?"

"It's a prototype," he said. "It took me ten years, working on and off, to build the damn thing. My own little vorpal blade, snicker-snack. But it didn't work very well for me, so I thought it'd make a great gift for the girl who had everything."

"Stop talking nonsense. You made a magical dagger? I thought your devices were all technological."

"My best toys have nothing to do with any technology humanity can understand," Daedalus said. "Might as well call it magic. My Myrmidon armor cannot be reproduced: the best combat suits Smith Industries builds for the US military have six percent of its firepower and maybe two percent of its defensive capabilities. It's all magic, Chaz."

His infuriating use of a diminutive for her name had been one reason she had left him. His tendency to pontificate for any reason or none was another. "So what does your vorpal blade do? What did it do me?"

"Tell me what happened, and I'll try to explain it to you."

Chastity described the events in Kazakhstan. Daedalus nodded. The calculation in his eyes had been replaced with measured excitement. "Okay. First of all, I picked the right person for the blade. Few people have the strength of will to use the device. I'd probably have ended up dead if I had used it on a Neolympian. The couple of times I tested it proved that rather definitely." Seeing Chastity's glare grow in intensity, he rushed on. "Short form: the dagger absorbed the Chimp's energy matrix. Found the link between him and the Source, severed it and drained all the energy in his body. It tried to do the same to you, but you resisted it, and instead it forged a connection with you. And dumped at least some of the Celestial's power right into your sexy bod, by the way. I'd be careful on my next sparring session if I were you. My guess is you'll find you've gone up several points in the Parahuman Ability Scale. Maybe a full integer."

"What is the Source?"

"It's my pet term for whatever fuels our powers. Einstein's Spooky Energy, or Oppenheimer's Gifts of Shiva, if you will. The dagger was an attempt to manipulate our access to the Source. It was partially successful."

"You knew that if I used the dagger it could kill me."

"I told you to use it only if the alternative was death," Daedalus said without a trace of remorse. "Like I said, it was a prototype. If I perfect the design, there won't be any side effects. I'm still working out the kinks, in between saving the world and building better mousetraps for the edification of the masses."

"So what happens now?"

"That's up to you, my dear. I'm guessing you didn't mention the dagger or what it did to the Celestial in your report, did you?"

"I wanted to talk to you first, and Swift didn't give me a chance to do it before the debriefing. So, no, I didn't say anything."

"Good ol' Swifty. Why the hell did you sleep with him? Larry's a complete fuck-up when it comes to women. One of these days Olivia is going to wake up and snap his neck. At least I'm an honest philanderer who's never going to get married."

Chastity shrugged. "What's done is done."

"So do you forgive me?"

"I don't think you are telling me everything."

"I'm probably telling you too much. If you blab to Doc Slaughter about this, I'll never hear the end of it. His own attempts to find the Source went spectacularly wrong, and now he thinks it's too dangerous to even try to do it. He can be such an old woman about this stuff."

"He's probably right," Chastity said, opening and closing the fingers of her marked hand. She seemed to have full mobility there, but she could feel every contour of the mark on her palm, along with an echo of the pain that had preceded its creation. "What happened with the Celestial… It was wrong, Daedalus. I have killed many times, but what that dagger did to him was much worse than death. I think a part of him is trapped inside the dagger." *Or inside me*, she thought but did not say out loud.

"You're still alive, aren't you? Would you rather have let him kill you, probably after a little rape as an appetizer? Why are you giving your gift horse a full dental checkup, Chaz? Let it go. If you don't want the dagger, I'll be happy to take it off your hands."

"I'd rather hold on to it," she replied, surprising herself. She had gone to Daedalus' apartment resolved to throw the dagger at his feet. Now that she knew he wanted it back, she felt reluctant to part with it.

"No problem. You survived using it once, it'll probably be easier to use it again. We'll be calling you Chastity the God-Slayer in no time."

"Sounds rather pretentious to me."

Daedalus chuckled. "You are one of a kind, Chaz. Why did we ever break up?"

"You wanted more than I wanted to give and far more than you were prepared to give in return. You were a patronizing bastard. And you wouldn't stop calling me Chaz."

"And you were a bit of a bitch, now that I think about it."

She smiled at him. "Always."

"If we are done, I'll get back to schtupping Linda, if you don't mind. The invitation to join us still stands."

"The rejection of the invitation still stands, too. And you said her name was Lydia."

"Close enough."

* * *

Daedalus Smith closed the door after Chastity left and considered things for a few seconds. He probably should have insisted on getting the dagger back from her, but the damage was done. She was Marked and irrevocably linked to the weapon. He shrugged. Giving her that little present had been stupid, but he was somewhat fond of her. He'd given her the dagger in the off-chance she might be one of the few people able to survive its use, and also as an experiment of sorts. The fact that the weapon had worked and hadn't killed her outright was valuable information. As long as she didn't figure things out, everything would be well.

It didn't really matter. Things were already in motion and they would be over one way or another long before Chastity and the dagger became an issue.

Things would have been already over if the fucking girl hadn't escaped.

If Mr. Night and the damn Ukrainians didn't find her soon, he would have to go with Plan B, and that scheme had a much lower chance of success. He was hopeful they would succeed. The target was little more than a child, and wholly ignorant of her abilities and the way this universe worked. She should be easy prey. If she wasn't, he'd go with Plan B and roll the dice. The stakes were well worth the gamble.

Taking over the world wasn't for the faint of heart.

Daedalus forced his customary smirk back into place and strode into the bedroom.

Hunters and Hunted

Chicago, Illinois, March 14, 2013

God is in the details. Take care of enough details, and you could kill God.

Mr. Night tittered at his own witticism. On the next street over, a wino sleeping off his last binge heard the laughter, went into convulsions and choked to death on his own tongue. Mr. Night noted the man's passing with a smile. Another little detail ironed out. Seven billion to go.

He walked the dark streets of Chicago and the few people he passed by got the hell out of his way. The walk was inconvenient, but the same protections he had set around his place of business to prevent pesky interlopers – like one Mr. Damon Trent, a.k.a. the Lurker – from interfering with his business also made teleportation there impossible. He had instead arrived to Chicago in a blind alley a few blocks away. The exertions of this evening's travels had left him feeling a bit peaked, but he managed the walk nonetheless.

The third-floor office in the low-rent building beckoned him. The building was empty at this time of night and most of it was vacant anyway. Although he never misbehaved there – don't shit were you eat was good advice as well as a delightful expression – most people didn't find him an agreeable neighbor. Only one fellow tenant had remained in the building for more than six months after Mr. Night moved into the neighborhood, and he was a sour old accountant, a secret serial killer with a soul as black as coal, just the kind of fellow who would feel warm and cozy in the vicinity of Mr. Night and all his works. One of these days Mr. Night must pay him a friendly visit to get acquainted and exchange stories. The murderous accountant would not survive the experience, but in the end he was yet another detail to iron out.

The receptionist was at her desk when he entered the office. Wanda never left her desk, and would never leave it until he finally released her into that good night. He had recruited her from a local morgue, a nice young woman who had run into a mugger with a sharp knife and a taste for death. Wanda's corpse had been fresh when Mr. Night appropriated it, and she still looked rather nice, if perhaps a teensy bit gray around the edges.

Wanda looked up when he walked in: her eyes were devoid of emotion or personality. The dead woman's soul and consciousness were trapped inside a very special place of Mr. Night's creation, screaming her notional lungs off in utter agony and despair, along with a select few others. The poor girl must be quite insane by now. The thought warmed the cockles of his heart, darn him if it didn't.

"Any messages, my dear?" he asked her politely.

Wanda's dead eyes glanced at the computer on her desk, then back at him. "Mr. Twist left instructions to call him tonight," she said in a pleasant voice.

"Thank you, Wanda. Carry on."

Mr. Night entered his inner sanctum, a small office with no decorations except for hundreds of complex geometric figures only he could see. His energies were at a dangerously low ebb, but here he would replenish them. He sat on an old rolling chair, put his feet up on the desk and enjoyed a moment of peace. Mr. Night nominally worked as the troubleshooter for two different conspiracies. Even for a man of his skills it was akin to juggling a dozen knives while blindfolded.

The current situation wouldn't last much longer, however. The girl's arrival had seen to that.

Her escape from the grasp of one of the conspiracies was troublesome, but he hadn't been surprised. She was a creature of Mr. Night's worst enemy. The girl was a tool designed to destroy everything he had worked so hard to achieve. Unfortunately she was also an indispensable element for the plans of Mr. Night's true superiors. If you juggled knives blindfolded, you'd inevitably get cut. His great adversary had the advantage of having access to both the Source and the Outside. Mr. Night only served the Outside, and his grasp over It was weaker than he wanted to admit, even to himself. Direct action was luckily not his purview. He was much better at pulling strings and letting useful idiots do most of the heavy lifting.

Speaking of useful idiots, he had a call to make. Thaddeus Twist owned the Global News Network, several movie studios and controlling interests in dozens of other corporations around the world. All the wealth and power the man wielded were secretly dedicated to one end: the eradication of Neolympians from the world. Mr. Night had been working for Twist for several years. The billionaire trusted him, and thought he was a loyal human agent. He was wrong on all accounts.

The media magnate wasn't used to be kept waiting, and it was getting late. Mr. Night dialed a very exclusive number, one that led directly to Twist's personal wrist-comm. A few seconds' later, the billionaire's face appeared on the screen.

"Night. Took you long enough. I've been trying to reach you for hours!"

"My apologies, Mr. Twist," he said meekly. It was best to let certain people think they were in charge. "What can I do for you?"

"You could start by telling me you have located Smith's facility."

"I'm afraid I don't have the exact location just yet," Mr. Night lied with great conviction, since he had just returned from said facility. "I am certain it is somewhere in the vicinity of New York City, however."

"New York... Are you sure? If we have to strike there..."

"Some collateral damage is going to be unavoidable, sir," Mr. Night said. "We are talking about saving seven billion humans from the tyranny of five thousand freaks." Twist didn't say anything for several seconds. Mr. Night kept his peace, letting the billionaire convince himself without any further prompting. The man thought he was saving humanity from the Neolympian plague. His intentions were good through and through, and nothing was deadlier than a human convinced he was doing the right thing.

Twist shrugged. "Keep at it, Night. We are going to need that location as soon as possible so we can make arrangements to take it out. Meanwhile we have a war to arrange."

"I will keep in touch, sir."

Twist hung up.

Twist and his followers wanted to save humanity. The second conspiracy he pretended to serve sought absolute power. Both groups were unwittingly doing his bidding and moving closer towards his own goal: a lifeless planet stripped of life and sentience once and for all.

Mr. Night sat back and let the darkness feed him. The dance was on, and he was calling the tune.

Chapter Eleven

Christine Dark

New York City, New York, March 14, 2013

It was late, but Christine was too wired to sleep.

Mark had shown her to a guest bedroom, which was bigger than the dorm room she shared with Sophie back on Earth Prime. The room had a thirty-inch TV-slash-computer computer screen on a big desk with a comfy rolling chair, a king-sized bed, a personal bathroom, and all the amenities of a five-star hotel. Lying on the bed were fresh towels and a very plush bathrobe. He'd wished her a good night and left.

Christine was tired, but there was no way she was going to sleep without checking out Earth Alpha's interwebbies.

The differences and similarities had her head spinning fairly quickly. First of all, this wasn't a home computer but a terminal tied to a bigger system. She wasn't sure if that was the case for all home systems or just Condor's; something else to go on the Giant List o' Questions. Mouse, check, screen, check, keyboard, check, no surprises there. A retina scanner, interesting. When she fired off the computer, the Microsoft logo greeted her and she burst into laughter. The power of the Gated One was truly great!

The graphic user interface wasn't exactly like any she had ever used before, but it was close enough for her to figure it out. She fired off Hypernet Explorer and went surfing. More differences to add to the pile. Not Internet but Hypernet. Not World Wide Web but XanaWeb, which was apparently short for Xanadu Web. On Earth Prime, *Xanadu* had been a crappy '70s movie, as far as she could remember. In this universe web pages were labeled xw.whatever.something instead of www.whatever.something. She tried to open Wikipedia, but instead found Hyperpedia, which was like Wikipedia and the Encyclopedia Britannica combined; Britannica had been absorbed into Hyperpedia back in the 1990s; they had stopped releasing it in printed format in 1996 (she found that out by doing a Hyperperdia search on the origins of Hyperpedia, of course).

Christine grinned like a Cheshire cat on loco weed. This was her chance to pare down the Giant List o' Questions! Wiki, er, Hyper away, oh cyber-explorer!

A few seconds later, she backed away in frustration. To get to the full articles in Hyperpedia, she needed to log on with her XID, whatever that was. She Googled it (yay Google!), and found it was short for Xanadu Identification. Again with freaking Xanadu. *Okay, how do I get one of those, and is it a good idea?* she asked herself.

Well, you could ask the big talking computer Condor uses, her brain answered. *Easier than Google.*

Well done, brain. I will recommend you to all my friends. Out loud: "Computer?"

"Good evening, Christine," the computer said. "You have guest privileges in the Lair. How may I help you?"

Beam me the frak up, Scotty! The computer made Siri sound like a half-wit. "Er, I wanted to know how to get an XID, Also, if I get an XID, will I be risking detection by the bad guys looking for me?"

"Getting an XID requires you to register a username and a biometric signature. It is done at no cost, and is nearly impossible to track, as long as you restrict yourself to passive observation."

"Okay, so I won't start a blog or open a Facebook page," Christine told herself. "Thank you, Computer. You can go away now."

"You are welcome. Good night."

She registered as Nonl33td00d92, which surprisingly wasn't taken. The retina scanner took a picture of her eyeball, and now she had an ID which apparently was good for just about everything in the XanaWeb. And no need to remember a password, since your password was your retinal pattern, which you pretty much carried inside your eye sockets everywhere you went. Neat and neater.

Back to Hyperpedia. Full access granted, I am your Queen and mistress, bow to me and kiss my l33t feet. Okay, she admitted to herself, getting an ID wasn't exactly a hax0r achievement, but still. She wondered how well hackers did in this world. Probably not very, if people with super powers could track them down to their parental-basement hideouts. Having an ID permanently tied to you would also not be helpful to maintaining anonymity. Lots less a-holes with Internet balls throwing virtual feces around, too. Spammers would be on the same boat. A world without spammers and trolls? Talk about paradise!

So many questions, so little time. Maybe a bit of history first? Christine wasn't a big history buff; she'd taken some basic courses, and aced them because acing courses was what she did, and with an eidetic memory remembering dates and places wasn't a big deal to her. Her problem with history was that it wasn't neat, not like mathematics. The dates and events were set in stone, but the causes and effects were debatable at best, and historians disagreed about them as badly as fanboys at a Comic Con. Still, she knew the basics, so she might as well start with World War II and at least catch the Cliff Notes. One of her boyfriends (the domineering d-bag who enjoyed making her feel like shit) had been a history major who specialized in that conflict, so she'd done a bit of extra reading on it in a pathetic attempt to get his approval.

So let's see. 1939. Invasion of Poland, check. In addition to tanks and artillery, the Nazis led their attack with the Teutonic Knights, which included a flying guy who could throw lightning bolts, another that could punch out a tank, and assorted other odds and ends, emphasis on the odd. Apparently some of the Knights had been normal guys in costumes who were used for propaganda purposes. You just couldn't trust Nazis in any universe.

Moving on. Phony War, check, then the Nazis attack France. Battles, Nazis kicking butt and taking names, mostly names like Pierre and Henri. Dunkirk evacuation after the French and Brits get zerged and pwned. British Neo called Meteor fights the Teutonic Knights over Dunkirk and helps protect the evacuation of the retreating Brits. Yadda yadda, the US stays neutral, yadda. Invasion of the Soviet Union in 1941, same as in Earth Prime. Later that year, Pearl Harbor, ditto, except that the Kami Warriors, Japanese superheroes, hit Pearl alongside the fighters and bombers and inflict even more damage.

1942. Freedom Legion is founded and recruits a bunch of US superheroes and mystery men (and women, you sexist pigs). More battles. Slaughter Raid on Japan; that one replaced the Doolittle Raid from Earth Prime. It wasn't a slaughter, it was led by a guy by the name Doc Slaughter. Battle of Midway, check. Neos fought on both sides. One of them, a guy called Janus, sank the battleship *Yamato* and the carrier *Amagi* single-handedly and killed Admiral Yamamoto. That had to hurt. Guadalcanal, check, but the Japanese never come back. Back to Europe. Stalingrad, check. Stalin and most of the Soviet high command get killed. *WTF?* Okay, let's get some details.

The Russians had their own group of super-peeps, called the Heroes of the Revolution (predictable much?). Two of them, Medved (the Bear) and the Hunter, were BFFs. Their bromance ended tragically when the Hunter was executed for defeatism during Stalingrad. Big oops. Bear guy runs all the way to Moscow from Stalingrad, storms the Kremlin, crushes Stalin like a grape and does the same to just about every Soviet leader in Moscow until an armored division and the other Heroes of the Revolution chase him away. Moscow gets pretty battered in the process. The Germans still get reamed at Stalingrad, though.

1943. Very few checks, things are pretty damn different. The Germans and Soviets keep hammering on each other but then both sides start having major problems in the Ukraine. Some guy called the Iron Tsar is arming partisans with effing *ray guns* and building robots and death machines and other fun stuff, and using them on both sides in the name of an independent Ukraine. He also encourages most of the Heroes of the Revolution to defect and raises his own army of Neos, including a scary lady going by the name Baba Yaga who allegedly massacres entire Nazi and Soviet armored divisions by her lonesome. The Soviets just weren't very good at keeping their superheroes happy, apparently.

In the Pacific, the Japanese are getting beaten much faster than in Earth Prime's history. Their Kami Warriors get killed pretty quickly, and Janus, who also happens to be the first black superhero, sinks entire fleets and destroys island garrisons without any help. Elsewhere in Asia, another super-guy, the Dragon Emperor, takes over Mongolia and invades China, killing Japanese, Communist and Nationalist Chinese and anybody else who gets in his way.

1944. D-Day at Normandy, check, but spearheaded by the Freedom Legion. Ultimate the Invincible Man takes out most of the Teutonic Knights. The article insists D-Day could not have gone off without the Legion, which is kinda funny, except on Earth Alpha the Soviets are not doing too well and the Nazis have a lot more troops to defend in the Western Front, so maybe it's not that funny after all. The Iron Tsar and his super-weapon-wielding army take over the Ukraine and chunks of Belarus, Poland, Russia and everywhere unlucky enough to have a border with it. The Ukrainians use some flying saucer-like ships to bomb the crap out of Moscow and assorted other places. The Soviets never get into Eastern Europe except parts of Poland; they are too busy fighting the Iron Tsar.

Late the same year, Hitler gets assassinated by a group of disgruntled officers and the Mind, one of the last Teutonic Knights. It's a tough world for dictators without superhuman powers. The Germans try to negotiate peace, but the Allies are in no mood and the Germans finally surrender unconditionally when Patton and the Legion are about to reach Berlin by April of 1945. The US and Great Britain finish off the Nazis by themselves, mainly thanks to the Freedom Legion. VE Day is a little earlier than on Earth Prime.

A few weeks later in Asia, Janus kills the last of the Kami warriors and has a sit down with Emperor Hirohito, who orders a general surrender. A bunch of military leaders refuse the order, so Janus kills them too, until the rest figure that surrender is the way to go. The US never drops nukes on Japan, although regular bombing had pretty much leveled almost all its cities already.

The post-war settlement was completely different. The Soviet Union gets very little out of the peace settlement, partly because there isn't much of a Soviet Union left after the super-Ukrainians are done pasting them and helping several Soviet Republics to revolt and secede, and partly because a Neo by the name Daedalus Smith unmasks a bunch of Soviet spies embedded in the US late in the war, which makes US president Truman none too eager to let the Soviets get anything good.

The Allies do some skirmishing with the Iron Tsar but are too war-weary to do much about him, and a peace settlement allows the Dominion of the Ukraine to keep most of its territory. The Soviets get kicked out of Poland and are forced to declare Belarus an independent republic, too. There's no Cold War in this world, since the Soviets remain a mess, never develop nuclear weapons, and end up becoming puppets of Ukraine.

There are two Chinas, a Republic and an Empire; the Empire holds Mongolia and the more thinly-populated interior of China, and most of the people and the money stay in the Republic. Mao gets killed by a Chinese Neo and with little Soviet support the Chinese Communists never get anywhere and are hunted down by both the Imperials and Nationalists. The Republic of China becomes a major US ally.

Whew. Christine checked the time; she was beginning to hit the wee hours, and she was getting sleepy. Even Neos needed sleep, or did they? A quick Google search revealed that if they didn't get enough sleep Neos eventually went insane, so yeah, they needed their beauty rest.

But there was so much she needed to know! Just a couple more searches...

Mark found her passed out at her desk the next morning, drooling all over the keyboard. Very embarrassing.

Face-Off

New York City, New York, March 14, 2013

Condor's vessel emerged from the East River like a monstrous sea creature, scaring the shit out of a ferry full of commuters.

"We're going to be on YouTube before breakfast," I grumbled.

"I'd better be. I could use the publicity," Condor replied. "I haven't flown this baby in over a year, so it's good to know it can still make an impression."

"You have maintained it regularly, right?" Christine asked nervously. She clearly didn't like flying very much.

"Of course," Condor said as the ship rose over the river, shedding water like a duck. The Condor Jet was a big, odd-looking thing with a bird design including a beak on its tip, but it could travel under water and in the air, where it could outperform an F-42 fighter. Condor went on in a tour guide voice. "On your left, you can see the Brooklyn Bridge. It looks like we have stopped traffic, but that shouldn't last long. New Yorkers don't impress easily."

"Is the Condor-plane supposed to be vibrating right now?" Christine said. "Because I can feel it vibrating right now."

"The VTOL system does generate a bit of turbulence, unfortunately," Condor said. "As soon as we get some altitude I'll fire off the turbines and it'll be a smooth ride, I promise."

"Okay."

"I've always liked the vibrations myself," Kestrel commented from the copilot seat, and Christine scowled at her. Well, scowled at Kestrel's back. It was a pretty cute scowl, I thought.

I watched the New York skyline as it receded away, and wondered if I would ever see it again. I hoped my friends would be all right without me. Father Alex had agreed to leave town for a few days. My friendship with him was largely a secret, but I didn't want him to take any chances, not if the Russians and Ukrainians were looking for me. I'd spoken briefly with Cassandra that morning, despite her instructions not to contact her. She'd been expecting my call, of course, and assured me she would be fine and proceeded to admonish me not to call again. I still worried.

"Fasten your seat belts, ladies and gents," Condor announced. A few moments later the aircraft started accelerating. The stealth system kicked in, wrapping the aircraft in an energy field that rendered it invisible to radar, cameras and even the old Mark I eyeball. The vibrations stopped and the flight settled into smooth, imperceptible movement. Christine relaxed visibly. "We will arrive in Chicago in one hour and twenty-five minutes. Thank you for flying Condor Airlines."

"That's pretty fast," Christine commented. "We're not going to have time to watch an in-flight movie or anything. Too bad, I kinda wanted to catch Oliver Stone's *True Patriot*."

"Don't bother," I said. "It's full of mistakes, even a few outright lies."

"Oh, okay. I got the basics on the Patriot and how he became President after Kennedy before I fell asleep by the computer. So what's so wrong about the movie?"

"Not much, except it implies a Neo conspiracy destroyed Kennedy's presidency during the First Asian War, which led to his losing the election to Ray Stephens. Kennedy was something of an anti-Neo guy – he pushed the Parahuman Registration Act – but it's kind of a big leap to claim Stephens' victory was a 'bloodless coup.' There are no 'vast Neo conspiracies.'"

"Well, not that we know of," Condor commented. "Of course, if you listen to the wilder conspiracy theories, all Neos are working together to form a planetary government. Blame Daedalus Smith and his stupid 'New World Order' speech back in '81. He might as well have started spouting off about the Illuminati."

"Yikes. I just wanted to watch a movie," Christine said.

"Sorry. It's just that a lot of people hate us, and it pisses me off," I admitted. "The media has a love-hate relationship with Neos. You get the tabloids treating us like superstars on the one hand, and regular newspapers ready to pounce whenever a Neo screws up or commits a crime on the other."

"I can kinda understand people being afraid of Neos," she replied. "I was on Hyperpedia all night, and there's some scary stuff out there. You have the Ukraine and like half of China under Neo dictators, you have that guy in Mexico..."

"*El Presidente*, yeah," I agreed. "But he gets elected democratically every time." Of course, *El Presidente* had been winning elections for over fifty years.

"Sure, but he still pretty much gets to do whatever he wants. I found like twenty parahuman dictators all over the world. Africa, South America, that Papa Doc guy and his army of Neos and zombies in Haiti..."

"The Legion put a stop to that. Now Haiti is a pretty nice place to visit," I said, and belatedly realized I was defending the Legion. Normally I would piss all over those sanctimonious pricks unless they were on fire.

"That's the thing: Neos had to rescue Haiti from other Neos. Muggles – regular people, I mean – don't stand a chance."

"Most Neos do their best not to infringe on the rights of normal humans," Condor said. "And we do our best to hunt down the ones who think they are above human justice. In fact, when we have more time, young lady, you are going to take my course on Parahuman Ethics. It's not quite as long and boring as what properly bonded and licensed Neos get, but it covers the basics. Short version: you are not better than anybody else just because you have powers. If anything, you have an obligation to use those powers for the betterment of all."

"'With great power comes great responsibility,'" Christine said, clearly quoting something.

"Exactly," Condor agreed.

"A very wise man said that in my world. On the other hand, another wise man said 'Power corrupts, and absolute power corrupts absolutely.'"

"We can only hope he was wrong. Because there are a lot of people with great power – over five thousand confirmed Neos – running around. And sure, a lot of people would love to see us gone, but we're here, they'd better get used to it." Christine snorted when Condor said that, for no reason I could fathom.

"She's got a point, though," I felt forced to admit. "Most of what we do is clean up messes other Neos made."

"But we are cleaning up those messes. That's my point."

"I'm sorry I'm being so negative," Christine said. "You guys have been great, and from what I read Neos have done incredible things for the world. I guess whenever someone shows me a silver lining, I start looking for a cloud."

"Can't blame you for that," I said. "This ain't no utopia. It's a miracle some dickhead with more power than sense hasn't blown up the planet. We've had Neo-created plagues, tsunamis, earthquakes and giant monsters, and every couple of years it seems some asshole decides to try and take over the world."

"Could be worse, I guess," Christine said. "It could happen every week."

"We do what we can, and usually the guys who pull that crap don't get a chance to do it twice."

"Oh. In my world's comic books, villains usually keep coming back."

"Here they get the death penalty, and they typically don't come back from that."

'Yikes. Harsh."

"Once you catch somebody after he's killed a couple hundred innocent people, you really don't want to risk him getting out and doing it again."

"Okay, still harsh, but I guess that makes sense."

"I'm pretty sure whoever kidnapped you also has some world-changing plan in the works," I said. "And when I find them, they won't be making any more plans, ever." I was full of shit, and I knew it even before the last words were out of my mouth. I was a holy terror when it came to beating up local gang bangers or Neos in my own weight class, but I wasn't going to stop a planetary conspiracy. At best, I'd die trying, and dying while trying is a loser's way out.

Christine didn't say anything for a while. Just as well.

C.J. Carella

Hunters and Hunted

New York City, New York, March 14, 2013

In retrospect, killing the Mafioso had not been a good idea.

Archangel sat back on his armchair and listened to the local lackeys' excuses. His temporary headquarters was an office that belonged to a pimp from Belarus. The Brooklyn location was more convenient than the secret facility in Manhattan, and closer to his underground contacts, contacts like the very pimp whose office he'd appropriated and the other drug-dealers, racketeers and general scum he was forced to work with until they found the girl. Archangel briefly considered killing one of them *pour encourager les autres*, but resisted the urge. For one, it would make a mess on the carpet. For another, they probably couldn't be any more afraid of him than they already were. Drive too much terror into a man's heart and he became unpredictable.

"We have spread the word, and we have photos of the girl out on the streets," the current lackey said, unaware of his close brush with death. Well, perhaps not wholly unaware, considering how much he was sweating, even for a fat pig from Minsk. Archangel's reputation was well known in certain circles.

Kill one man, and you are a monster. Kill a few thousand, and you become a legend.

"What else?" he asked.

"We are searching for the vigilante, Face-Off. It is not easy. He operates throughout the city, and he can alter his appearance."

Anonymity was a powerful defense. Once a target's location was known, it could be attacked, no matter how well-defended it was. The Mafioso he had killed might have had some idea where this Face-Off was. There was also the matter of retaliation once the Mob found out the fate of their boss. Both points indicated that killing Bufalino had been an error.

He was reluctantly relieved that Mr. Night was not directly overseeing this part of the operation. The disgusting toad would have made some pointed remarks about Archangel's mistakes, and it would have been hard to resist the temptation to cut him down to size. Archangel had tried doing just that once before, shortly after making his acquaintance, and the results had been... suboptimal. Best to avoid the temptation to try again.

He needed more assets. Fortunately, they were due to arrive soon.

Archangel patiently listened to his lackeys' reports, which revealed nothing of much value. The interrogation of a handful of Mafiosi had revealed nothing more than what he already knew or suspected – Bufalino had held on to the girl as a bargaining chip, and the faceless vigilante had taken her. If that imbecile had kept to his part of the bargain, the mission would have been accomplished already. Killing him had been the right thing to do, he decided.

"We have visitors, sir."

"Show them in." The promised reinforcements were here. Archangel watched the newcomers with interest.

The man and woman walked in side by side, looking in different directions so that between them they could scan the whole room. They made an odd couple, a towering bearded Cossack and a petite Japanese female. Archangel knew from the files he had read that they were a couple as well as a team, lovers and killers.

He examined the man most intently at first, for he was a living legend who had changed the history of Archangel's Motherland. The newcomer was a hulking brute, well over seven feet tall, his massive physique hardly concealed under the bulky black overcoat he wore, his brown hair and beard long and casually groomed, framing a harsh Slavic face. Archangel recognized him from old black and white pictures of the man standing over the shattered remains of a Panzer IV, holding the tank's turret over his head like a trophy.

Medved, the Bear, the man who killed Stalin and with him the Soviet Union, met Archangel's eyes unflinchingly.

Strange. Not too long ago, as Neolympians measured such things, Archangel would have charged Medved and slashed him into quivering gobbets of flesh, or tried to. But the young boy who had grown in the dying remnants of the USSR and the chaotic Ukrainian puppet that followed its downfall was long gone now. The boy had become the man known as Archangel, and Archangel now served the Ukrainian overlord who had done as much as this hirsute giant to destroy the *Rodina*. Things changed. One learned to adapt or one was crushed by the changes.

"Medved," Archangel said, nodding his head at the giant. He turned to his companion. "And Lady Shi," he added, acknowledging the woman. "Welcome."

If Lady Shi was offended by being greeted last, she gave no sign of it. She was beautiful like a porcelain doll, her delicate features cold and impassive. Archangel saw the way Medved looked at her, and belatedly realized she was the more dangerous of the two. He had misjudged her, a justifiable blunder given the history surrounding her gigantic companion, but a blunder nonetheless.

"Archangel," Lady Shi said in perfect English. "The Iron Tsar's little hatchet man. You do know my Bear has no love for Russians, do you not?" She smiled, and for a second Archangel caught a glimpse of the madness and fury behind the cool façade. Behind her, Medved tensed slightly, and violence and death became imminent.

One of the men in the room didn't react well to the insult to Archangel. Arseny Bogdanovich was a young hothead, and he instinctively began to reach for his gun. Most likely he wouldn't have pulled out the weapon – only the truly insane drew a gun on Neolympians of this reputation – but nobody had a chance to find out. Lady Shi reacted to the sudden move without ever taking her eyes off Archangel. Her left hand moved with blurring speed and a glowing star-shaped object flew from her outstretched fingers and sliced through Arseny's neck. His severed head landed with a thud on the carpet, followed a second later by the rest of his body.

"Nobody move!" Archangel shouted before things turned into a bloodbath. "Arseny shouldn't have drawn on a guest, even a rude guest."

"My apologies for the rudeness, Archangel-san," Lady Shi said, giving him the bow an equal bestows on another she has offended slightly. "I repay it with the removal of a man who clearly lacked the common sense not to provoke me into action." Her grin widened.

Archangel smiled back. Here was a woman after his own heart, a stone cold killer who loved what she did. He preferred pliable and submissive bed partners, but someone like her would make for a very entertaining diversion. The damn Bear was a lucky man. "You know who I work for, and I know who you work for," he said politely. "Circumstances have forced us to work together. I suggest we make the best of it."

"Yes," Lady Shi said pleasantly, and Medved relaxed minutely. "We all will be the best of henchmen. Our lord and master commands it, and my Bear and I owe him everything."

It was odd that Medved had not ended up in the service of the Iron Tsar like so many former Heroes of the Revolution – and a few Teutonic Knights, for that matter. He would have made a good addition to the Iron Guard. The reports Archangel had read indicated the big Cossack had disappeared after the war and emerged decades later as the agent of a clandestine American organization. That organization was now working with the Tsar, so in effect the Bear was finally serving him. Lady Shi was the Bear's true mistress, however. Archangel would be sure to remember that.

A couple of men removed the mortal remains of the unfortunate Arseny and dropped some newspapers over the pool of blood he'd left behind. The carpet was ruined, of course. Oh, well; it was bound to happen eventually.

"Please, make yourselves comfortable. If you want any refreshments, they will be provided."

"So, you are looking for the woman from another world," Lady Shi said after they sat down and had their drinks served to them. "But she is protected from normal means of scrying, correct?"

"Unfortunately, that is true. Among my men I have a psychic sensitive and a clairvoyant, and neither of them has been able to find her."

"I have some small skill in these matters," Lady Shi said modestly. "But I will not try to find the girl. I will concentrate on her rescuer, the man with no face."

"If he is with her, he is likely protected as well," Archangel objected. In fact, he had tried the exact same thing and his psychic hounds hadn't been able to locate him at all, either.

"My talent also allows me to see where he has been, not just where he is now," Lady Shi explained. "I will lead us to wherever he makes his lair. Perhaps the girl will be there. Or perhaps someone there will be able to tell us what we need to know."

Archangel nodded. "That is good. We are off to a good start."

Chapter Twelve

The Freedom Legion

Atlantic Headquarters, March 14, 2013

He looks so guilty.

Olivia O'Brien tried to look her husband in the eye, but Larry pretended to concentrate on the report on his e-tablet. She sighed and looked out the window of the passenger jet as it prepared for takeoff. They were bound for the Legion's Pacific Headquarters in the Marshall Islands. The hypersonic orbital plane would get them there in a few hours, faster than she could fly on her own, or than Larry could run. Larry would have probably preferred to make the run on his own nonetheless. Anything other than face her. To make matters worse, one of Larry's floozies was sharing the flight with them. Chastity Baal was sitting near the cockpit, busy reviewing the intelligence briefings they had gotten from the Imperial defector. Olivia couldn't even muster the energy to be angry at her. Larry was the man who had betrayed her. And Olivia herself had, by her silence, tacitly condoned his betrayal.

They had barely talked since her rescue, partly because as soon as she was free from the debris Olivia had rushed to take charge of the situation. It was only to be expected, since she was a member of the Council and Larry wasn't, hadn't been since 1988, when he lost his seat to General Xu. Busy as they were, however, they should have been able to find some time to spend together. All of Larry's breaks had happened to take place during times Olivia had duties she could not be spared from. He was clearly avoiding her.

Men – no, let's be fair, she scolded herself, people – clung to their illusions with near Neolympian tenacity. Larry, for example, clearly believed his philandering had gone on unnoticed. Olivia had known for years. She even knew that Larry's latest fling with that Dawn girl was turning into something more serious than his previous affairs.

She had known for years about his infidelity, but pretended not to. In the end, she had preferred to live a lie than to publicly acknowledge the truth.

There were many reasons for her inaction, so many good reasons. The scandal would affect the Legion and provide fodder for tabloids and blogs everywhere. Artemis was a living symbol, a role model for women and especially women of color around the world. Pride was at work as well: she could not tolerate being perceived as weak, pathetic, a victim. Part of it was simple denial. If she pretended it was not so, maybe it would not be so.

And part of it, much as it disgusted her, was the fact that she still loved Larry. Even now, she felt sorry for him. His guilt for being away cheating on her while missiles were flying towards her office made her sad and furious at the same time. Worse yet, it also made her afraid that Larry was considering confessing to his infidelities. She had no idea what she would do if he did come out with the truth. Pretend to be surprised, and repay his lying with her own dishonesty? Admit she knew, and reveal her own complicity in their sham of a marriage? Maybe it would be best if Larry kept his secrets to himself and they marched on for another decade or three. Better to do as he was pretending to and concentrate on real world problems, the kind that could be met openly with force.

Olivia checked her own e-tablet. Daedalus Smith had uploaded the latest data on the carrier vessel. It was an Imperial Chinese model, just as he had said. A recently decommissioned one, with all three ships of its class supposedly dismantled and broken up for parts half a decade ago. Their contragravity drives alone were worth billions of dollars and should have been sold off or installed on new vessels. How had their attackers gotten hold of an entire ship? Even the notoriously corrupt Imperials wouldn't have allowed an entire warship to disappear, no matter how many palms were greased along the way. The penalty for such a crime would be unspeakable: the Dragon Emperor prided himself in the skill of his torturers. To steal the ship and smuggle it out of the country should have been impossible.

And yet, according to the defector they had interrogated, and who was now sitting sullenly a few seats behind Olivia, that was exactly what had happened. The theft – the word didn't do justice to the seizure of something worth close to a quarter of a trillion dollars – had supposedly happened slowly and in carefully planned stages. Key components had been taken from the disassembled vessels and smuggled to a yet unknown location where some third party had used them to build their own ship. Someone had managed to accomplish the impossible, which was not surprising in the Parahuman Era. Neolympians did impossible things on a regular basis.

If a parahuman was involved, however, why had the attack been conducted by mere humans? If any Neolympians had been on the vessel, they had left no remains, not that there was much left to uncover. A daring daylight raid against the bastion of Neolympian power was the kind of thing super-villains dreamed about. If the attackers had deployed even a small number of parahumans alongside their swarm of drones and missiles, they could have inflicted far more damage. That they hadn't implied this was a primarily – maybe even solely – human affair.

Anti-Neolympian hate groups were as old as Neolympian themselves. Almost eighty years ago, Aldous Huxley had written a brilliant and vitriolic novel about a dystopian future where humans were the slaves and pets of a superhuman aristocracy. The future described in *Prospero's Playthings* had not happened, but the fear it had engendered was all too real. A number of organizations had become obsessed with combating Neolympians. Even the Ku Klux Klan, after being targeted by Janus during the civil rights struggles of the 1960s, had switched its focus from minorities to parahumans. The US government itself was notoriously schizophrenic about its 'heroes,' doing its best to recruit Neos into military and federal agencies while demanding registration and monitoring powers over the rest, not to mention quietly researching ways to destroy them should they become impossible to control.

And now someone with enormous resources had engineered an attack in which a human crew willing to sacrifice their lives had inflicted severe damage on the most powerful parahuman organization on Earth. Was this a harbinger of something worse?

Confronting a threat to all Neolympians took precedence over her personal problems. It was also easier to deal with emotionally. Larry and his guilt would have to wait.

Olivia shifted in her seat, turning away from her husband, and got back to work.

Hunters and Hunted

New York City, New York, March 14, 2013

One by one, all possible tomorrows winked out of existence until only one remained. A dead world, no longer blue, spun quietly around an uncaring sun.

Most choices led down to that final fate. Cassandra would not give in to despair, however. She fought on, seeking an alternative.

Among the myriad powers bestowed over the blessed – and cursed – few, precognition was one of the least common. Not many were given the ability to peer into the unformed chaos of what yet was not and come back with coherent visions. Of those few, fewer still managed to retain their grasp on reality when confronted with near infinite possibilities. The temptation to stay and watch all the things that might be often proved overwhelming. Most precognitive talents fell into comas and never returned to the here and now. Cassandra had barely escaped that fate herself, and only by deliberately limiting her visions.

She had often tried to explain to Marco how she chose what to see. "It's like fishing," she had told him. "I cast my lure into a vast ocean, and try to reel in one vision at a time. Sometimes it's a big fish, and we can stop great disasters from happening. Other times it's a small fish, and we save a handful of lives, or even a single one."

It had been a weak explanation, but it had served for the time being. In other conversations, she had explained how the mere act of observing the future could alter it, and how she often had to look again and again, hunting for unintended consequences before she could recommend a course of action. And why at some point she had to stop looking, lest she become lost In the vastness of all possible futures.

This time, she had caught a very big fish. Her biggest catch would also be her last.

The long struggle finally paid off. There were tiny temporal streams that led to alternate outcomes, rivulets set against the torrent aimed towards an inevitable doom. Cassandra ignored the pain growing out of the base of her skull and forced herself to look further and delve into those hopeful futures. After some time, she saw, and understood. She had felt from the beginning that some ultimate price would be required on her part, but she had hoped there might be an alternative if she looked hard enough. Those hopes had been slim even before she sent Marco away; her last vision dashed them altogether.

She didn't want to die, but every future where she ran away and lived through this day led to that dead, lifeless world. She might as well make the most out of her inevitable demise.

Cassandra sighed as she waited for her executioners. After a few seconds, she picked up her old Stradivarius and started playing. She began with a few desultory arpeggios before settling on Chausson's *Poème*. It had taken her a long time to master the E flat minor scale on that piece, and she was justifiably proud of the result. The melancholy notes fit her mood and would provide a fitting accompaniment to what was to come. The music helped ease her mind and accept her chosen fate.

She would miss the boy most of all. Marco had been a friend and ally for only a few years, but he had been a source of great comfort to her. As her partner, he had been able to do a great deal of good, averting many a vision of tragedy and death. Cassandra liked to think she had helped channel the boy's bloodthirsty rage towards largely positive ends. How would he fare without her?

The answer to that question remained elusive. Marco's fate was now intertwined with that of the girl from another world. Cassandra's gift could only catch scattered glimpses of Christine's future. The ultimate fate of the world depended on the decisions she would make in the next few days. If those decisions were wrong, the lifeless future would come to pass. Marco would be a great help to Christine, but his most likely reward would be pain or even death. Cassandra had hoped the boy would earn some measure of happiness for all the good he had done, but she knew better than to expect justice or fairness in this world.

Justice and fairness exist only to the extent we create them, she told herself, and sent forth her mind to create a psychic lure even as she played on. She would lead the hunters to her. She would fight them.

And she would lose.

C.J. Carella

The Freedom Legion

Chicago, Illinois, March 14, 2013

"It is an honor, Mr. Clarke," Doctor Cohen said, shaking John's hand. The therapist was a tall, slender man, nearly matching John's six foot three. A fringed beard and short black hair surrounded a narrow face dominated by large, kind eyes that regarded his new patient with friendly interest. Beneath his calm demeanor, however, John could sense nervousness. His enhanced hearing could pick up the doctor's quickening pulse. While that reaction could be simple jitters from dealing with a prominent figure, John felt a twinge of suspicion.

"Please have a seat," Doctor Cohen continued after the usual pleasantries had been exchanged, indicating a comfortable sofa; there was no traditional reclining couch in his office. John did so, casually looking around. In addition to the usual diplomas and credentials that sprouted like mushrooms in all physicians' offices, there was a rather unusual collection of African and Asian artifacts, all of them seemingly genuine, along with several old black and white pictures showing the doctor in assorted exotic locales.

"Mementos of my misspent youth." Cohen said. "I went on safari quite regularly back in the Thirties. I used to have several trophies on the walls, but they disturbed some of my patients and I had them removed."

John also noticed some portraits of Cohen wearing a US Army uniform. The good doctor had done more than go on safari; during the 1940s, his traveling had been arranged by Uncle Sam and his adventures had been provided by the Wehrmacht. Knowing that his therapist had seen the elephant comforted John somewhat.

Doctor Cohen noticed John looking at his service pictures. "Yes, I was with the 29th Infantry at Omaha beach," he said. "A bad day. It would have been much worse if you hadn't been there, of course."

John nodded –

He was a near-indestructible object, moving faster than a bullet. Smashing through a concrete bunker barely slowed him down. Human beings were killed by the mere wind of his passage, their limbs torn off, their lungs shredded, their very skin ripped off along with their clothes. When they were directly in his path, they splashed away like bags of red liquid hit by a cannonball. He veered up for a few seconds and looked down at the carnage he'd inflicted on the fortifications overlooking the beaches. Tracer fire and artillery shells reached for him, the impacts from direct hits as bothersome as mosquito bites. He swooped down again and reaped another hundred men in a handful of seconds. It was so easy...

- and realized he'd gone into a daydream again.

"You just underwent one of your fugue states," Doctor Cohen said. "This one lasted twenty seconds or so."

"They are getting worse," John replied. Being out of control terrified him. He knew how much damage he could inflict in twenty seconds. Combined with his increasingly shorter temper, the fugues made him a walking time bomb. He had come much too close to killing that idiotic blogger over a stupid question. To make matters worse, the blogger had been murdered by pro-Neo fanatics upon his return to the US; John had learned the news just before leaving for Chicago. The backlash from that death was yet to be felt, but it made regaining control of himself even more important.

"Tell me everything you can about the blackouts and the other symptoms you've been experiencing."

John looked into the man's eyes for some moments. He still felt some distrust for the therapist, kind eyes or not. He had no choice, however. He began talking.

C.J. Carella

Hunters and Hunted

New York City, New York, March 14, 2013

Archangel looked around the decaying neighborhood with slight twinge of nostalgia. Oh, this was not quite like the slums where he had grown up in the *Rodina*. For one, things were in less disrepair than in the world of his youth, the post-war Russia that had been abandoned by her erstwhile allies and left to wither and die. Still, the atmosphere of neglect and despair was similar enough to bring back memories. Here dwelt many with nothing to lose, and those with nothing to lose enjoyed a form of freedom that he could appreciate even if he no longer shared it. He had much to lose now, and even more to take.

"This is the place," Lady Shi said confidently, pointing at the derelict building that squatted forlornly on a seemingly uninhabited city block. "This is as close to a home as the Faceless Vigilante has ever had. I can feel it calling to me."

"Is he here?" Archangel asked.

Lady Shi shrugged. "Perhaps. There are psychic defenses in the building. I can sense he has come and gone in there many times, and fairly recently. The rest is hidden from me." She clearly did not like being thwarted even in this minor way, and her smile had a definite edge now. Archangel filed the information for future reference. He seldom let anything make him angry. Anger gave others power over you. He might need to make Lady Shi angry one day.

They had arrived in three cars, luxury versions of the Jeep Seven that the American military loved so much. The vehicles very obviously did not belong in this neighborhood, but the locals knew that it didn't pay to be too curious about the affairs of others. The three Neolympians and a dozen henchmen got out; four of the men were armed with the new special weapons that were supposed to neutralize Neolympian powers. Archangel gestured at the group and they took positions surrounding the building.

"Shall we?" he asked his fellow demigods. Lady Shi nodded. Medved only grunted. Archangel strolled towards the building's entrance and his new colleagues followed. Even as he crossed the sidewalk he felt a distasteful psychic ambiance around the building, a subtle working that made people want to stay away without knowing why. While most of his talents were physical, Archangel had studied under the most accomplished mentalists in the Dominion and he had learned to recognize and deflect many forms of psychic attack. He was also wearing a special amulet meant to ward him against such things. He did not waver at all. Neither did his companions.

The front door was open, and through it he heard music, a violin, playing a sad and beautiful melody. He smiled – someone was home, which made for a good start – and walked inside, ready for action. Nothing. No gunshots or bursts of energy welcomed him, just darkness and the sad music.

The interior of the building looked as dilapidated as it had outside. Either the faceless man preferred an ascetic existence or this was merely part of the façade behind which the real lair hid. He started up the stairs.

The front door shut behind him, a slam nearly as loud as a gunshot. The violin playing ceased at the very same instant, letting the echoes of the slamming door fill the ensuing quietness. Medved whirled around, his clawed hands at the ready, but there was nobody there. Archangel chuckled. A horror movie cliché used against three real-life monsters? How amusing. Medved was not amused. He lifted one leg and kicked the door open, snapping off its hinges and sending it flying into the street. Archangel smiled indulgently and started back up the stairs.

On the third step, the stairs changed. He changed. His perspective twisted, grew smaller. Day became dusk, and he was now on the third floor of the *kommunalka* where he had lived when he was a child. Where he lived now, for he was a child once again, a malnourished, ill-favored boy eking out a miserable existence in the slums of Leningrad. He was no longer walking up the stairs of an abandoned building in New York, he was running up the wider stairs of the ill-maintained apartment building in Leningrad that he called his home, and others were running after him. It was May 16, 1958, and he was eleven years old. Archangel was gone. He was little Feodor Igorovich. Feodor the runt, a weakling in a world where the weak were prey.

No.

The denial was weak and useless. The fear that drove him was much more immediate, the more so because he knew what was going to happen. There was an older boy waiting for him on the fourth floor, and even as he ran up he saw him. Sergei, the leader of the gang of semi-feral children who had decided to teach the defiant thieving runt a lesson once and for all.

"Where are you going, *hooyesos*?" Sergei asked him, and Feodor froze at the top of the stairs for a second before trying to push his way through. Even then he had thought things through clinically. Better to try to evade Sergei alone than to face the half-dozen boys below. Sergei was briefly surprised, but not for long enough. He grabbed Feodor before he could rush past him and pushed the smaller boy up against a wall. Feodor's face slammed into the wall, and blood started running down his nose. The pain was familiar and paralyzing. "Not so fast, cocksucker," Sergei hissed behind Feodor's ear. His breath stank of cabbage and cheap cigarettes. "I got you now."

Feodor struggled. Archangel knew what would follow, the savage beating he had barely survived, the nightmarish trip to the hospital where uncaring doctors and nurses had nearly finished what Sergei had started. The limp that had not healed until his Neolympian powers had manifested themselves years later. The part of him that was still Archangel braced itself for the pain to come.

"What will I do with you, *hooyesos*, little cocksucker?" Sergei wondered. "Ah, yes."

The agony when the knife pierced Feodor's kidney was enormous, all the worse because it was unexpected.

"You think you can steal from me and live? Fuck your mother!" Sergei hissed as he stabbed Feodor again and again.

No, that did not happen, that's not how it...

The pain paid no attention to his denials. The onrushing darkness as his life ebbed out was too real, too absolute.

His vision narrowed into a vanishing point, and he was no more.

Light returned and he found himself running up the stairs again. Thrown against the wall, again. "What will I do with you, little cocksucker?" Sergei wondered. "Ah, yes."

The older boy grabbed Feodor and flung him over the railing of the stairs. Feodor screamed all the way down. Impact. Bones broke. Blood streamed out of his mouth, choking him. Darkness. Death.

Again.

This time he survived the fall, became a cripple. His powers never manifested themselves. He lived a life of ongoing misery until the day he purposely pushed his wheelchair onto the path of the Petrograd Metro. Darkness. Death.

Again.

Feodor looked at the blade flashing towards his eyes, the last thing he would ever see. Suffered a beating that ended when one of Sergei's boys stamped on his neck until it broke. Was carried sobbing to the top of the building and thrown off from it. Had his pants pulled down and saw Sergei slashing at his genitals.

Again and again. Darkness, death.

The past became eternity, an assault of might-have-beens that became hell.

* * *

The men outside waited for several minutes. They saw strange lights flashing from the building, and heard faded and oddly distorted voices, and possibly screams. The minutes stretched into nearly half an hour. Eight men went in after their boss. They did not come out. More muted screams came from inside the structure.

The remaining four looked at each other and waited some more. Archangel did not encourage initiative among his underlings. After another hour had passed, they drew straws and the loser reluctantly approached the doorway, gun drawn. He passed the threshold, and did not come out. The screams, if that's what they were, continued unabated. The remaining three henchmen decided to wait some more.

The afternoon turned to evening.

One of the three suggested they draw straws again. The response from the other two was a chorus of "*Yob tvoyu mat!*"

A consensus was reached and the men continued to wait, trying to ignore the sounds coming from the building.

Chapter Thirteen

Christine Dark

Chicago, Illinois, March 14, 2013

Christine had never been to Chicago. She didn't even know offhand what Chicago's skyline looked like. She was pretty sure, however, that the Chicago of her universe did not have a shiny red skyscraper shaped like a gigantic dildo right in the middle of it.

"Holy crap!" The monstrous erection – no other word could describe it – towered over all the other buildings of the city. It shone with an oily sheen, its monochrome awfulness an assault with a deadly weapon on the senses. She looked at Mark, who was also watching Big Red raptly.

"Welcome to Chicago, home of the Tower of Power," he said. "I've seen it on pictures and video, but they don't do it justice." He leaned towards his seat's window to get a better look. Christine wanted to look away, but couldn't turn away from it. It was just too awful. "When the sun hits it right, entire parts of Chicago turn completely red," he added.

"What the hell is it? And who allowed it to be built?"

The Condor Jet made a stealthy run over the city, well away from normal flying routes. Its course took them a few hundred feet past the Tower of Power. Christine could not see any windows, seams or openings of any kind, just shiny redness everywhere.

"Short story is, an insane Neo built it in a matter of hours,' Mark explained. "It sort of grew and literally *ate* the building it replaced. Luckily it did so slowly enough that everyone inside supposedly managed to escape, although there are rumors that a couple people never made it out and are missing to this day."

"And why did the guy built that thing?"

"Why do you assume it was a guy?" Mark asked; she could sense a smile in his voice.

"That thing isn't even a phallic symbol, it's a freaking mega-dick on a stick!" Christine replied. "That's the most guy thing I've ever seen."

"Okay, yeah, it was a guy. The Crimson Overlord was his name, and he thought he was doing Chicago a favor. The Tower of Power is a giant electrical generator. It actually provides enough energy for most of Illinois and Indiana. The Overlord figured he'd get the keys to the city for his creation. Instead he got lawsuits and arrest warrants. That's when he revealed the Tower of Power could also be used as a weapon. It took just about all the Neos in the Midwest to take him down. Big mess, large death toll."

"So why is the tower still standing?"

"Nobody has figured a safe way to knock it down. For one, the material it is made of is extremely tough and it self-repairs. Also, it does provide free clean energy; nobody knows how it does it, even the big brains like Daedalus Smith are baffled, but it does. So now the Chicago Sentinels, the local Neo team, make their headquarters there. And people started calling Chicago 'the Tower City;' from what I hear the locals don't like that name one bit. Even mentioning the Tower of Power will get you dirty looks or worse. They like to pretend it doesn't exist."

"Good luck with that. It's like not noticing a, well, you know, right in your face. So just one guy did all that damage?"

"Yes, it was another Neo crime again humanity," Mark said bitterly, his good humor vanishing. To her empathy-sense, it was like a candle being snuffed by a sudden wind. His mood change actually hurt her a little bit. "We are a dangerous bunch."

"You tell her, killer," Kestrel piped in, breaking what had been a very nice spell of silence.

"I'm not trying to put Neos down or anything," Christine said apologetically. "It's that I keep seeing things that… well, they scare the living pee out of me. In my world, a crazy guy with a gun can kill a dozen people. Here, a crazy Neo can kill a dozen *thousand* people!"

"Yes, it happens, although usually the nutters get stopped pretty quickly," Mark said. "On average, about ten, twelve thousand people a year get killed in Neo-related incidents in the US. But," he added quickly when Christine gasped at the figure. "But, car accidents kill about twenty thousand people a year in the US. Used to be more like forty thousand, until, get this, a Neo by the name Doc Slaughter designed a crash survival system that cut fatalities from car accidents by almost fifty percent. Yeah, we do a lot of damage, but we do a lot of good, too. Some of us have managed to do things like cure several forms of cancer, which saves hundreds of thousands of lives a year. We – speaking loosely, I haven't cured anything except a few terminal cases of being an asshole – do a lot of good."

"But when we go bad, we go *really* bad," Kestrel said. "Cure a disease one day, unleash a plague that turns people into pink goo the next. Keeps vanillas on their toes."

Christine didn't need to ask what 'vanilla' stood for.

"Cut it out, Kestrel," Mark said before turning back to Christine. "I don't want to lay this on too thick. Sorry. "

"It's okay," Christine said. "I didn't mean to upset you."

Mark looked at Kestrel to curtail any more smartass commentary, but she had sullenly turned her back on them and was pointedly ignoring their conversation. He leaned closer to Christine and spoke in a soft voice. "Truth is, you didn't say anything that hasn't crossed my mind already. I don't want to sugarcoat things, okay? We're a mess, us Neos. We are smarter than humans – our average IQ is in the 140 range – but we also have a lot of mental issues. Something like mild autism is relatively common. OCD and the entire spectrum of personality disorders, ditto. We are all adrenaline junkies. Want to hear a great Neo factoid? There are about five thousand Neos around, but the total number should be closer to ten thousand; that's how many have been recorded over the last century or so. The others all got killed one way or another, typically while chasing their next thrill ride. We are our own primary cause of death, by the way. Neos killing Neos."

"Okay. Scaring me again."

"I'm sorry. I'm just trying to keep the bullshit to a minimum, and it's hard because I don't know if I'm bullshitting myself, or being too gloomy." He managed to sigh despite having no mouth. "I'm definitely the wrong guy to be a Neo cheerleader. I can see both sides of the argument, and which side I'm on depends on my mood that morning. I don't like being hated, but it's easy to understand why we are. Not that I want people to love me, just to leave me the fuck alone. But it's not a simple situation."

"I can see that. That's why I like math. It's all pretty black and white, or zero and one if you want to get binary about it. Except for a few annoying things like irrational numbers, but I mostly just round them up and ignore them. When it comes to people, well, they are all irrational numbers."

"After you work on the streets for a while, it's easy to start thinking of most people as either assholes or morons. You start expecting the worst from everyone." He shrugged. "If you do you're rarely disappointed, but it sort of sours you on everything."

"I tend to be a proponent of the 'People Suck' theory myself, but then you start finding exceptions to the rule," Christine said. Just like Mark, she wasn't really equipped to defend people in general. Even her fellow geeks were not exactly plaster saints: half of them had zero social skills, half of them were eternally horny in the grossest and most inappropriate ways, and half of them had annoying habits not even their mothers could love, and yes, she knew that was too many halves. "People can be a pain, okay." She paused, at a loss for words for a change.

"I'm assuming there is a 'but' after that," Mark said after a bit.

"Yeah, I'm working on it." Thank God she'd never volunteered at a suicide hotline, or she'd have garnered quite the body count. "But, really, when you get down to it, most people aren't evil. They just want to do their thing and be left alone. Even in high school, the a-holes were a minority. They are just noticeable because, well, they are a-holes."

"Yeah, I keep telling myself something like that," Mark agreed. "Thanks to Cassandra and Father Alex, I believe it most days."

"If you don't, it's going to be too easy to become an a-hole yourself," Christine said, and he nodded.

"We'll be landing shortly, kiddies," Condor said from the cockpit. "No need to fasten your seat belts."

Christine looked out a window. The Condor Jet was hovering over what looked like a warehouse section of Chicago near Lake Michigan, having left downtown and the giant red dildo behind.

"So, this friend of Condor's, he's on the up and up?" Christine asked, trying to change the subject, which was getting way too emo for comfort.

"Yeah, Lester Harris has worked with the Lurker all his life," Mark replied, also glad to talk about something else. "It's a family thing; his great-grandfather was with the Lurker back in the 1930s. The Lurker's had a lot of human helpers over the years. A lot of the old-time mystery men did – they were Type Ones, and they didn't know they weren't normal humans at first. Eventually the vanilla sidekicks kept getting killed so often that most Neos stopped using them. The Lurker still has a network of informants and investigators, though."

"I see. That reminds me of, surprise squared, another question: do you have a lot of normal humans putting on costumes and trying to be superheroes?"

"Used to happen a lot at first, but not that much anymore. The lucky ones get a close call or two and realize that if you can't heal from injuries like a Neo, you aren't going to last very long in this game. The others... I'm sure you can figure it out."

Christine nodded. In the real world, a normal person would catch a bullet sooner or later, or end up totally messed up from assorted injuries or even repetitive stress syndrome from all the ass-kicking. And if the wannabe hero ran into someone who could melt someone's face off with a glance or whatever – yeah, that would suck.

"The Lurker's people mostly stay out of harm's way. Lester helped Condor and the Lurker coordinate their hunt for a Neo serial killer. He did a lot of the legwork but didn't join in the action. Condor and the Lurker inflicted all the violence. Much safer that way."

While they talked, the Condor Jet, still invisible, descended until it was facing a large warehouse and hovering – and vibrating again, much to Christine's discomfort – a few feet off the parking lot. A wide rolling door in front of the warehouse rolled up. The entrance didn't look quite big enough for the Condor Jet, but Condor expertly guided the aircraft through it and set the ship down as the door slowly rolled shut behind them.

"All right, we are here. Thank you for flying Condor Airlines. Now get the hell out," Condor announced.

As they exited the aircraft, Christine could see the ship's insides and the ramp leading out. The rest of the aircraft remained invisible except for a very vague shimmer around the edges, better than the camouflage screen in *Predator*. *How does he do it?* Christine wondered, and as the exit hatch closed and the aircraft became completely invisible again, she decided to use her Christine senses on it. She still hadn't quite figured out exactly how to trigger her super-vision thingy, but after she squinted long enough it kind of just happened.

She got an eyeful. The Condor Jet looked very visible to her Christine-vision. Another bundle of swirling lights was overlaid over the frame of the aircraft, and it was somehow connected to Condor, as if it was an extension of him. She was beginning to get a feel for how super-gizmos worked; the creator somehow used his own aura or Chi or whatever to empower the devices. Pretty cool.

Condor and Kestrel were carrying luggage, so they probably had brought along some civilian clothes, but they currently were wearing their skin-tight outfits. Good thing they were indoors; the locals would have probably noticed two people in costumes appearing out of an invisible plane. Mark was in civvies, so he looked fine except for the faceless bit. Christine had politely declined to wear her Condor groupie costume in favor of her regular second-hand clothes, which unfortunately were all she had. She'd been in New York all day yesterday and she hadn't done any shopping. That was just wrong. Maybe after they had set up an appointment with the Lurker she might get to buy something else to wear.

The warehouse looked like it hadn't been used for anything for some time. There was a large Humvee-like vehicle next to the roll-down door. Christine wondered if there was enough clearance for the car to drive out now that the Condor Jet was filling up most of the warehouse space. An older guy — forty-something at least — in a business suit was standing next to the car. Said older guy shook hands with Condor. They made their introductions while they loaded their luggage into the car.

"Good to see you again, Lester," Condor said after they were loaded up. Lester did not look particularly happy to see Condor, or happy about much of anything for that matter.

"Wish I could say the same," Lester said. "I almost called you to tell you not to show up, but then I figured the boss could use some backup."

"What are you talking about?"

"I just found out this morning. Somebody's looking for him. Somebody who's not afraid to leave bodies behind if they don't get what they want. And they want the Lurker."

Condor glanced at Mark. "What do you think, Face?"

"I think I don't believe in coincidences. We are looking for the Lurker and now it turns out someone else is? What are the odds the two things are unrelated?" Mark turned to Lester. "Why don't you start at the beginning?"

"Okay," Lester said, looking nervouser and nervouser. "When you called last night, I left word with the boss that you were coming to town. We don't exactly socialize, you know. We mostly communicate via dead drops and coded messages. There is something else we use for emergencies, but he hasn't gotten back to me. I'm getting worried."

"Yeah, I know how he operates," Condor agreed. "What happened this morning?"

'I got a call from one of my people. Said he'd heard about some tough guys asking about the Lurker and spreading cash around for information. Also, a local police informant was found late last night. Dead. Someone had used a blowtorch on him. It wasn't pretty. The dead guy's worked with my people before; going after him would be a good place to start for someone who's trying to find the boss. I think you can do the math."

"Yeah, and it's not adding up to anything good," Condor said. "Any ideas on who might be looking for the Lurker?"

"I'm not sure. My guy thinks it might be the Russian mob, but that makes no sense."

Christine picked up an emotion spike from both Condor and Mike when they heard the word 'Russian.' Kestrel didn't seem to give a crap either way, although she'd been the one who had told them the Russian mob was looking for Christine in New York.

"What made him think it's the Russians?" Condor asked.

"The blowtorch stuff. It's sort of a signature move of the local Russian outfit. They weren't very subtle about it."

"Oh, this is no fucking good at all," Mark commented, seconds before one of the warehouse walls exploded.

Things got really not effing good after that.

C.J. Carella

Hunters and Hunted

Chicago, Illinois, March 14, 2013

Vladimir Vladimirovich kept his cool, much as he wanted to start blabbering like his men were. "Shut the fuck up," he growled, and his men did. People usually did what Vladimir told them to if they knew what was good for them.

"That's the Condor," Grisha, his second in command, whispered, pointing at the screen showing the interior of the warehouse. "He's got his invisible plane in there. I read an article on *People Magazine* about it."

"You're reading *People* now, Grisha?" one of the men in the back seat said.

"Fuck you, it was my wife's and I was bored."

"If you fucked your wife more often, you wouldn't be so bored."

"I said shut the fuck up," Vladimir said, but without much heat. He was too busy trying to think of a plan of action.

Vladimir Vladimirovich wasn't a tall man, but he made up for it with his personality. He was over sixty years old, but thanks to his Neo abilities he looked about half that age, and thanks to those selfsame abilities he could take a grown man and break him in half with his bare hands. His position as a major player in the Russian Outfit in the United States was due to his skills more than to his Ne-olympian powers, however. He had been in one of the last graduating classes of the KGB, which even during the final days of the Soviet Union had remained a highly effective intelligence agency. He had risen high in the Russian underworld afterward, although he obscurely felt he had been denied a greater destiny in the process. Serving the Ukrainian motherfuckers who kept the Motherland weak and in disarray had always stuck in his craw, but a man did what he could and not a bit more. It couldn't be helped.

His Neo talents weren't many. Stronger than most men, but not very strong by Neo standards, he had a gift for languages that could be natural, and was a superb marksman with any ranged weapon, from bows to RPG-16s. Most of his achievements had been a result of his human ability to asses a situation and devise ways of dealing with it, regardless of who got hurt in the process.

He considered the situation at hand. The plan had been to follow that Harris cocksucker to see if he made contact with their target, the Lurker. Harris was meeting with other superheroes instead. Condor and three others. The woman in the whore's outfit and the man with no face he knew. Kestrel and Face-Off, both crime fighters like Condor and the Lurker. The young girl was not familiar to him, but he would assume she was one of them as well. The most likely explanation was that the newcomers had shown up to help the Lurker. They might know where he was, or at worst they might provide useful hostages. Either way, that made them valuable targets. But could he take them? Besides him, he had his fellow Neo Boris in one of the other cars, plus fourteen men and the special weapons they had been given for the mission. Would that be enough?

Vladimir tried to contact his handler. Archangel did not respond. He left him a brief voice mail, hung up and went over the objective conditions he was dealing with. Should he continue to follow Harris and the new arrivals? If he did, nobody would blame him; those had been his instructions. Following a human lackey was one thing, however. Condor's name was a legend with the underworld. What if the Neo discovered the robot device he was using to track Harris? It would be best to grab them now, before they were on the move. He made his decision.

"We take them. Alive, you hear me?"

"I hear you," Grisha replied. "Now we find out if those fucking toys we got from the Ukraine are any good."

"They are good."

"And if they are not?" Grisha asked.

"Then we're fucked, every last one of us," Vladimir responded, and all the men in the car laughed. Good. Keep their morale up, and maybe most of them would live. "So stop blabbing and get ready. Grisha, get the others."

Grisha nodded and stepped out of the car to gather the rest of the team. They were parked in a shut-down auto shop half a block from the warehouse where Harris had been waiting for his friends. Vladimir had been observing the inside of the warehouse through the electronic eyes of a little mechanical flying bug that sent audio and video right into Vladimir's wrist-comm, one of the many toys they had been given for their mission. The little device had followed Harris to the warehouse and filmed the arrival of Condor and his friends.

Vladimir had everyone out of their cars for a quick group conference. "Grisha and me, and you three," he said, pointing at his best marksmen. "We use the special weapons. The rest of you, you have the Ukrainian blasters; those things are better than rocket launchers. Go in and keep the cocksuckers busy. Boris will lead the way." Boris, the other Neo in the team, was a strongman who loved to use a huge mace-and-chain on his enemies. "Shoot at them, but remember, we want them alive." Neos took a lot of killing, so he was willing to let his men shoot them up a bit if necessary. "Once they are down, don't finish them off. Understand?" As long as one or two of them survived, he would be happy.

His men nodded. He looked them over. They were all tough and experienced, either ex-military or career criminals who had spilled blood long before their balls dropped, men who had grown up in the tough streets of Moscow and Saint Petersburg. None of them looked very eager to get into a firefight with several Neos, which proved they weren't complete idiots, but they weren't pissing their pants about it, either. That was good enough. They could handle this.

"Let's go."

C.J. Carella

Face-Off

Chicago, Illinois, March 14, 2013

When things go wrong, they go wrong fast.

A whole section of wall exploded, close enough to shower us with flying, burning debris. A hot piece of brick bounced off my head. I ignored the impact and the pain, moving to interpose myself between Christine and whatever would be coming through the hole in the wall. Condor and Kestrel were on the move too. "Stay down!" I shouted at Christine. She wasn't ready to get into a real fight. If her concentration lapsed during a crucial second, she could get killed. She did the sensible thing and dropped to the ground next to Lester, who was lying down already.

Men burst in through the shattered wall, shooting from the hip. They weren't using regular guns. Their muzzles emitted blinking lights like camera flashes, and whatever they aimed at exploded. Ukrainian A-75s, copies of the ray guns that had wrecked the Wehrmacht and the Red Army. Serious artillery, and rare as hell. I might survive one direct hit from them, but probably not two.

One of the men didn't have a gun. He was wielding a morning star, a spiked metal ball at the end of a long chain. He was whirling that thing so fast it was a blur. A Neo, all right.

I had to duck and roll, narrowly escaping several blasts that carved deep trenches on the concrete floor of the warehouse. The Neo with the whirling ball and chain moved closer and the shooters spread out and kept a steady barrage of energy fire on us.

They'd come in ready to dance, and we were happy to oblige them. Condor reached into his utility belt while dodging around, and his hands came out full of stylized throwing knives – his claws, he liked to call them. He flung them all in one volley. Ball-and-chain used his spinning weapon as a shield, deflecting a few of the claws, but two of the attackers went down, twitching uncontrollably. The claws had built-in capacitors that released enough electricity to knock down a charging horse. Condor was feeling downright charitable if he was using his Taser claws on the fuckers. The electrical shock was unlikely to be fatal unless the target happened to have a pacemaker or a bad heart.

I wasn't feeling charitable at all. I shot two of them while ducking their blaster fire. Nothing fancy, two in the chest for each of them. Then ball-and-chain tried to whack me with his toy. I sidestepped the spiked mace and managed to snag the chain before he could pull it away. Tug of war time, asshole. The idiot was a big guy, a good six seven, six eight, and probably weighted three hundred pounds' worth of muscle and high-density bones. All of which meant diddly-squat when I pulled on his chain and yanked him clear off his feet and right towards me, where he masked his buddies fire for a couple seconds. I welcomed him with a head-butt and an elbow to his face and he went down like a ton of bricks, dead or unconscious. Big and ugly was a lightweight, a mid-level Type One was my guess. I would have made sure he stayed down by snapping his spine with a kick or shooting him in the face, but when he fell his pals started blasting me again. I rolled away, moving too fast and erratically for them to get a hit.

In the meanwhile, Condor got one more and Kestrel, her trademark whip slashing out at supersonic speeds, beheaded three of the assholes. She wasn't taking prisoners, either. Condor was probably going to be upset with her.

Another group had entered the warehouse while we slaughtered the first bunch. They had some sort of long, bulbous weapons attached to backpacks. I'd never seen anything like them before. Whatever those things were, I figured they had to be something worse than the Ukrainian ray guns. Even as Condor and Kestrel finished off the last two survivors of the first wave, I managed to shoot one of the newcomers. Four men with the backpack contraptions lived long enough to shoot back. That was enough.

Most energy weapons don't create a visible beam. These things did. Twisting, almost tentacle-like streams of purplish-dark energy erupted from the weapons' barrels and reached towards us. I rolled away, and saw one of the streams twist in the air and follow me. It struck.

I've been hurt before. Quite a few times, actually, but nothing like this. What I felt when the twisting energy hit me was like a full-body terminal toothache, only worse. And that was only a side effect. All of my voluntary muscles stopped working and I collapsed in an ungraceful heap on the ground. I couldn't even scream.

What with all the agony and suffering, it took me several seconds to realize my face was back. My real face was back and my powers were gone. Everything went dark and quiet after that.

Chapter Fourteen

Christine Dark

Chicago, Illinois, March 14, 2013

She was scared to look, but even more scared not to look, so she watched the carnage from the floor. Not too far away, Lester Harris had done the same and seemed to be trying to make himself as small a target as possible.

Condor, Kestrel and Face-Off charged the men coming into the warehouse. Condor was flinging some sort of throwing knives, Face-Off was firing a gun and Kestrel, unsurprisingly, was swinging a whip-like weapon. The bad guys were not using regular guns, but some sort of boxy short-barreled weapons that made things burn and blow up a lot better than guns. Phased plasma rifles in the 40-watt range or something like that, was her guess.

Funny, if someone had asked her how she would deal with a firefight taking place a few feet from her face, Christine would have guessed she'd be curled up in a fetal position, losing bodily fluids from every available orifice. Instead, scared as she was, Christine was watching the action with the same rapt attention a football fan would during the Super Bowl.

The good guys and gal were fast and graceful, like ballerinas in a speeded-up video. They went through the bad guys like chainsaws on a bunch of papier-mâché mannequins, despite the fact they were dodging energy blasts and a guy swinging a spiked wrecking ball along the way. Except those weren't mannequins, those were people, people who bled and screamed and died. It happened too fast for the horrible sights to really sink in. It didn't seem real.

A new bunch of bad guys armed with something that looked for all the world like those things in the *Ghostbuster* movies came in, and started shooting some weird energy streams. She saw Condor and Face-Off get hit, and they went down like a ton of bricks. Next thing Christine knew, one of them started shooting at her!

As the energy stream reached for her, Christine raised her force shield. The result was nothing like stopping the fast-balls during her tests the night before. The strange swirling energy reached for the shield and started... *eating* it. She felt the shield being drained of power. Never mind the shield – she was being drained of power, heat, life itself. It felt like someone was sucking her blood through every pore. She had to –

Get

OUT!

She felt a painful impact around her head and shoulders, and the world grew dim for a few seconds. The next thing she knew, she was being buffeted by freezing winds, and she was surrounded by... fog?

No. Not fog. Clouds.

Holy mother of crap, I'm somewhere up in the air!

Like way up in the air. Like, so high up all she could see were clouds and darkened skies.

For a second or so, she seemed to hang up in the air. Then, in the best Looney Toons tradition, gravity took over and she started to fall. She hated flying, but she suddenly realized she hated falling even more.

"Ooooohh sheee-it!!!" Christine screamed as she plummeted back to earth.

C.J. Carella

Hunters and Hunted

Chicago, Illinois, March 14, 2013

Vladimir Vladimirovich roared laughter as the vaunted Neo bastards fell under the power of his gang's special weapons. The fucking things worked! Then his delight turned into anger when one of the Neos, the girl he had not been able to identify, flew up, smashed through the roof of the warehouse, and disappeared from sight. Not good.

The other Neos were down, but they had dropped almost every one of his men. His good humor vanished, and he cursed loudly while he, Grisha and Josef – the only ones still on their feet – checked on his people. Four men were unconscious but alive. Boris was getting to his feet, his face a mask of blood. With a grunt, the big man reached for his dislocated jaw and snapped it back into place so it could heal properly. Everyone else was dead. Without the special weapons, the entire team would have been wiped out.

"Grisha!" Vladimir's shout stopped his second in command, who was about to plunge a knife into Condor's face. "I said to take them alive!" Grisha stepped away from the Neo and shrugged. "Go help the men! Boris, stop fucking around. You and Josef, bring the cars here. We need to go before that flying bitch comes back with reinforcements!"

The survivors were shaken up by the deaths of their comrades, but they did as were told. Soon everyone, including the unresisting Lester Harris, were inside their vehicles. Before leaving, Vladimir marked the position of the still invisible

Condor Jet. The fucking thing had taken a few blaster shots but it was still in working order. He would have to come back for it later, after he got Condor to tell him how to work it.

Vladimir flipped open his wrist-comm and called his contact to report as his team sped off. Once again, Archangel did not answer. He tried one of Archangel's henchmen, and was curtly told the boss wasn't available. What the fuck was going on? The man in white was a fellow Russian, a strange bastard who dressed like a faggot to be sure, but a powerful Neo who knew how to get things done. Vladimir had a few ideas on how to proceed, but he was hoping for some guidance from his higher-ups. You didn't want to stick out your neck too much in this business. If you didn't cover your ass and something went wrong, you would be the one getting the chop. Vladimir was fond of an American expression: shit rolls downhill. It was all too true. He tried Archangel's number again. Once again, it went to voice mail.

He was about to hang up when the comm screen went dark. Vladimir frowned at the damn thing; was it dying on him? That'd be all he needed. The screen flickered back to life after a few seconds, revealing a slender man with graying black hair and dark glasses. Vladimir's eyes widened in shock. He knew the man. Mr. Night, Archangel's liaison with their American partners. He had met the man with the dark glasses twice, and each time Vladimir had gone away feeling angry, frustrated and, though he would never admit it to anybody, scared. The strange little man always seemed to know too much, and the way he moved and talked always seemed wrong somehow. It made Vladimir think of an actor who didn't quite have the talent to stay in character. It was as if Mr. Night couldn't pretend to be human very well.

"I believe you have something to report, Vladimir Vladimirovich," Mr. Night said in flawless Russian. "It seems that Archangel is currently occupied, so I took the liberty to contact you and hear any news you might have."

There was nothing left to do but to comply and report. "We got Harris," Vladimir said. "He was in the company of four Neos. We captured three of them."

"You were supposed to follow Harris, not capture him," Mr. Night said. The image on the screen dissolved in a burst of static for a second, and Vladimir felt certain it was the man's doing. "My dear, dear Vladimir. Why would you disobey your instructions? We wanted to locate the Lurker and strike him in a manner and time of our choosing. Now he will come to you, looking for his friend. You're quite unlikely to have a pleasant time when making his acquaintance."

"We have the special weapons. If he comes to us, we'll take him down," Vladimir replied confidently. "We'll be ready for him."

"We will see. Or rather, you will," the man said. His smile was a hideous lopsided thing that did not express humor or any other human emotion. "The other Neolympians. Please describe them, if you don't mind."

Vladimir did so. There was another burst of static. When Mr. Night's visage came back, the smile hadn't changed, but something about the man had. "The girl. Did you capture the girl?" There was a sense of urgency in his voice that Vladimir had never heard before. It worried him.

"She's the one who got away," Vladimir admitted, suddenly getting the creeping feeling that he had fucked up.

Another burst of static, and when the image came back the little man looked – distorted. As if the image had been stretched, except the backdrop didn't change, just his face. "The girl must be found."

"She flew away. How are we to do this?"

"Never mind. I'll deal with this myself," the man said, and Vladimir felt shameful relief coursing through him. The little man had to be a Neo of some sort, and one of the strangest ones he had met. Getting on his bad side could not be good for one's health. Mr. Night switched back to English; he appeared to be talking to himself at first. "Oh, dear. Things are getting complicated. Our cherubim seems to be indisposed, and now the girl is in Chicago. But never mind that, Vladimir. Carry on with your plans. Expect the Lurker to try something soon. I strongly doubt you will enjoy the experience." The screen went blank.

Vladimir shut off the wrist-comm. Nobody had said anything about a girl. How the fuck was he supposed to know she was important? Unfortunately, if you got blamed for something in this business, it didn't matter if you were guilty or innocent. You'd get fucked no matter what. Shit always rolled downhill.

He'd better take down the Lurker, or things would not go well for him.

Christine Dark

Chicago, Illinois, March 14, 2013

Her hair kept getting into her eyes, and she was spinning and tumbling in the air, falling and flailing her arms and legs. And screaming. Screaming more loudly than she ever had.

For once, her brain did something useful. *You got yourself up here, Dumbo. You can fly. I believe I can fly!*

R. Kelly lyrics? Thanks a lot, brain!

But her brain was right. She had catapulted herself God only knew how many thousands of feet in the air. And if she didn't do something she would hit the ground a lot sooner than she would like. She'd studied aerodynamics in school, lift and thrust and drag and all that jazz. She needed to provide some thrust to stop the good old thirty-two and a bit feet per second squared stuff from doing its thing on her. She didn't know if she could survive a fall from this altitude and she really, really didn't want to find out the answer the hard way. Since Neos were denser than humans, they had a higher terminal velocity, too, so the fall would hurt pretty badly. She could figure out how badly by doing some off-the cuff calculations – figure out her drag coefficient, plug it into the terminal velocity equations, run the numbers and she'd have the answer before she hit the ground, she was sure. Or she could spend her time learning how to fly. *Yeah, let's try that instead.*

Her power allowed her to accelerate objects, and clearly she could accelerate herself, so all she had to do was concentrate...

Hmm, still falling.

Concentrate a bit harder. Fear is the mind frakker. Push, pull, whatever.

It kind of worked. She stopped falling and instead moved suddenly at an angle, up and to one side, very fast. The sudden reversal in direction gave her a severe case of whiplash, the kind of thing that would have put her in a neck brace if she wasn't all super and stuff. It still hurt like heck. Unfortunately, the sudden burst of speed ended after just a moment or two, and she started falling again.

Epic failing so badly.

Okay, I can provide thrust, just need to figure out how to make it constant and steady. No problemo.

It took several tries, darting up and down, side by side, and pretty much in every possible angle and direction. She bounced back and forth like she was a tennis ball at a Venus versus Serena match. Her body felt like she'd been used as a punching bag after some quality time at a torture rack. By the time she figured out how to push herself just enough to sort of float without moving, she'd lost enough altitude to see Chicago once again, including the rather noticeable Tower of Power. She was somewhere off to – check the sun – the east of the city proper. There was water directly below her, which should be Lake Michigan. And she'd been jumping all over the sky, thankfully not in the path of any passing airliners, and now she had no effing clue where her friends were. And they probably weren't there anymore. The bad guys had been winning when she ran away like a scared little b-word.

They could be dead.

Grip, acquire. She couldn't afford to think like that. First things first. She needed to get down to earth, quite literally. After that little achievement was unlocked, she'd figure something out.

Christine felt and heard a major disturbance in the air above her. She looked up and saw a jumbo jet not two hundred feet over her, soaring by. Yeah, definitely get down to the ground. Well, she'd figured out how to stand still. Now how about a little push?

The words 'little push' weren't in her vocabulary, apparently. The weakest one moved her a few hundred feet in an indecently short span of time, and the direction always seemed to be somewhere random. She really could use some flying lessons. Of course, neither Condor nor Mark had even mentioned the possibility that she could fly. In retrospect, that little oversight was peeving her off pretty badly.

She looked longingly at Chicago. Getting there wasn't going to be fun.

C.J. Carella

The Invincible Man

Chicago, Illinois, March 14, 2013

"Whatever does not kill you, makes you stronger," Doctor Cohen quoted. "I'm sure you have heard that cliché many times."

John nodded. Confession had turned out to be good for the soul, something his Lutheran upbringing had not taught him. Unburdening himself to Cohen left him feeling more relaxed than he had been in a long time. He knew this was probably only a momentary relief, but he welcomed it. At least all the cards were on the table. No more denials or attempts to avoid his problems. He had always preferred to face his enemies head on. Telling the therapist everything he could remember about the fugues and his other problems had taken a good while, but it had been worth it.

"It's largely bullshit, I'm afraid," Doctor Cohen continued, drawing a startled laugh from John. "Whatever does not kill you mostly just leaves you fucked up beyond all recognition."

"Unless you are parahuman," John replied.

"Not even then, unfortunately. We can recover from almost any form of damage physically, but trauma still leaves some marks in our minds. Even when we are physically unscathed, how can we witness the things we have and pretend we are unaffected?"

No kidding, John thought but did not say out loud. Yes, he had seen more death and desolation than any hundred normal humans. Eighty years, five major wars and a few dozen minor ones, not to mention thousands of crime scenes: those experiences were going to make an impression on anybody who wasn't a complete sociopath. But he needed to know why it was affecting him so much, and at this particular time.

Some of his feelings must have shown on his face, or Doctor Cohen was empathic enough to sense them. The therapist chuckled ruefully. "Sorry. That sounds like an empty platitude, doesn't it? And in fact the Neolympian psyche is remarkably resilient. Our experiences affect us, but not as badly as they would a normal human, which is fortunate or our subspecies' mental health issues would be even worse than they already are. We recover from mental trauma very rapidly, not least because of the way our memory works. We forget pain more quickly than normal humans, you see."

"Do we?"

"You know the old joke, mothers don't really remember the pain of childbirth, otherwise the human race would have died out a long time ago? Well, Neolympians generally distance themselves from traumatic memories faster than most humans. We suffer and grieve, and we remember the experiences that caused that sort of mental trauma, but the impact of such trauma lessens rapidly, often in a mere matter of weeks or months, or in some cases days."

"Except that is not happening to me," John replied. *Not happening to me* now, he realized. Before, he had recovered from even Linda's death, although not as quickly as Doctor Cohen had suggested. He had grieved, and he had never felt truly happy since her passing, but he had learned to live with the loss. It was easy when most of your life was spent going from one crisis to another, of course, and

John had never believed that wallowing in your misery did anything useful for you. Of late he was wallowing whether he wanted to or not, however.

"That is correct," Doctor Cohen agreed. "Something is making your mind relive painful and traumatic memories, and doing so vividly enough to cause a disconnection from reality. I have a couple of ideas as to what is causing this."

Finally. John forced himself to stay quiet and not play Socratic Dialogue second fiddle with the doctor.

"One possibility is that this is a factor of old age. Memory problems are common in humans as they senesce. Perhaps Neolympians are not immune to this. However," he continued quickly as John's eyes widened in alarm. "I don't think it's likely in your case. Alzheimer's disease and other forms of dementia have a physiological component, and Parahumans are able to repair any damage, including brain damage, rather thoroughly. My suspicion is that the flashback episodes are being deliberately induced."

John felt his entire body tense with anger. Knowing someone was responsible for his state of mind had him on the verge of screaming with rage. It took all of his self-control to remain sitting down. His emotions were getting frayed beyond what he could control.

"The induced memories are the most likely cause of all the other symptoms," Doctor Cohen went on. "You are being forced to relive moments of pain and anger, and that is keeping your emotions in turmoil. Unless we find a way to stop this, you will become a danger to everyone around you."

The blunt assessment was sobering. "How is it even possible? Mind control..."

"...is nearly impossible even with normal humans, let alone Neolympians, especially against someone as highly resistant to psychic attacks as yourself, yes," the doctor jumped in. "But 'nearly impossible' is a slippery term when dealing with our kind, wouldn't you agree?"

"So how can we deal with this?" John said. What he wanted was to find the culprit and deal with him, and once again he was surprised by the depth of his anger. He'd been less worked up about people trying to kill his loved ones.

"I would like to try some relaxation techniques on you. I've been able to get some surface empathic readings off you during our conversation, and I might be able to monitor your fugues if we can induce one of them right here and now."

That was more than John had bargained for. But if he could finally come to grips with this… condition? Madness? Yes, this madness that was plaguing him. It was worth the risk, he decided. Hell, he'd already gone into a fugue state during this session. What harm would there be in going through another one? He looked intently at Doctor Cohen. That hint of nervousness was back, barely perceptible to his enhanced senses, but still there. It could be perfectly innocent, of course. If John lost control during this experiment, the results could be deadly, and that would make anybody nervous. John had to trust someone. Reluctantly, he nodded.

"Let's do this."

Chapter Fifteen

Christine Dark

Chicago, Illinois, March 14, 2013

"Okey-dokey," Christine muttered to herself (not that she could hear herself flying through the air) as she planned her final descent – not too final, she hoped – onto the unsuspecting city below. Her flying skills hadn't improved one bit above 'erratic;' it was like her very first driving lesson, when she had driven her mother crazy by having one foot on the gas pedal and another on the brake and stomping on both nearly at random. But she was more or less going where she wanted to go, and that was pretty good, considering she'd had zero preparation. Stupid Condor. She was going to lodge a formal complaint when she saw him again.

The question was not 'to be or not to be,' but where the frak to land? If Christine went downtown, she was going to end up on YouTube by the time she hit the ground, and if those Russians were looking for her that would be un-good. Staying up in the air would also get her noticed sooner or later, though; she needed to land, hopefully somewhere not too public. She angled for somewhere a bit off the beaten path. Smaller buildings, less traffic. She went sideways and up and down as often as she flew forward, but she more or less zigzagged her way there.

Christine ended up somewhere off to the south of the city. A few people lounging outside some not-so-nice looking buildings looked at her as she descended. Well, tried to descend and ended up shooting upwards for a hundred feet, over-corrected and darted down much faster than she'd intended to. She clipped a street light and tumbled into an alley behind a bodega. Or, to be more accurate, she tumbled right into the dumpsters in said alley. Luckily, the dumpsters were locked shut – apparently people would steal your garbage around those parts – so when she hit one of them she made a Christine-shaped dent on it but did not end up swimming in garbage. Neat. Not.

Christine bounced off the dumpster and ended up on the ground. If she had to pick a superhero name, she might try and see if Captain Banana Heels was taken. Amazingly, neither her close encounter with the street light nor her crash into the dumpster had hurt much. No damage, even to her clothes, as long as she didn't count her dignity. Her defensive shield and energy field or whatever were keeping her safe. Maybe she would have been able to survive hitting the earth at terminal velocity. She still didn't want to try it unless she had to. Oh, well, at least she was back on the ground.

An angry Asian guy came out of the back door of the bodega wielding a baseball bat and screeched something at her in his native tongue, whatever it might be. He seemed to have a vested interest in the well-being of the dumpster, so he was probably the owner of the bodega, which probably wasn't called a bodega but the Unidentified Asian Language equivalent.

"I'm sorry," she said as she got to her feet – no more flying until she got the hang of it, she decided. She was lucky she hadn't flown into a building and killed a roomful of kitties and puppies.

"You get out now!" The Asian bodega owner replied, making poking motions with the baseball bat. Christine backed away, more scared of accidentally hurting him than anything else. She was clearly in a bad part of town and the locals had little tolerance for tomfoolery or hijinks. The poor man must not have seen her fly in, or he wouldn't be so confrontational. If she were a mean person, she'd take to the air for a few seconds just to show him who he was messing with, but she wasn't a mean person, and she'd decided there'd be no more flying for now.

"Okay, I'm going. Peace!"

The angry store owner half-chased her down the alley and onto the street, but after she had left his home ground he contented himself with shaking a fist at her and unleashing another torrent of Unidentified Asian Language at her. Christine made it to the sidewalk in one piece.

Um. Bad part of town. You could tell from the potholes and the boarded up buildings and the graffiti and the littering. On one corner a group of clearly disaffected minority youths were playing loud music on a boom box and loitering. The music wasn't hip hop, but some weird form of… jazz? Kind of like if you took jazz and mixed in angry vocals in between the instrumental bits. Whatever that music was, she was sure plenty of middle-class parents around the country were bitching about their kids listening to it.

She would have liked to listen to it for a while, or to any music in general; one of her most missed possessions was her I-Phone with all her playlists. *Oh, Florence and the Machine, I miss you so.* No Tegan, no Sara. The butterflies had gotten them all. Christine hadn't really had time to do a thorough Hyperpedia search on the state of music in this brave new world, but the little she had done had made it clear the musical divergence was pretty steep. The Beatles were still touring (her mom would have loved to hear that), and so was Elvis Presley, but that was all Grandpa music; actually Grandpa was more of a Bruce Springsteen kind of guy, so more like great-grandpa stuff. She'd gone through Condor's playlist, and most of his jams were some folk-country-rock mix that reminded her of Mumford and Sons. None of the bands of the last decade existed here, or at least the bunch she'd Googled didn't, except for, of all things, The Dropkick Murphy. Bizarro Sunnydale was Bizarro.

Christine's attempt to appreciate the local street music didn't last. For one, the disaffected youths were staring at her, and not in a friendly hugs and kisses way, unless the hugs and kisses were on the nonconsensual side. This group hadn't seen her fly down, since she had come from the other side of the block, so as far as they were concerned she was a normal girl in the wrong part of town. She looked around. Not a cop to be seen, and the only other people she could see were an older couple looking out a window and showing no interest in coming out and a couple of skinny teenage girls in skimpy clothes standing by another corner under the careful watch of a guy in a fur coat sitting in a car. Christine didn't think they were selling Girl Scout cookies. She hadn't felt this out of place since Sophie had accidentally driven them to a bad area of Detroit during freshman year.

Not as big of a biggie, sure, since worst case she could fly away, not to mention she had enough kewl powerz to take out the entire cast of a Quentin Tarentino movie. But she still felt very uncomfortable. The skinny girls were ignoring her and concentrating on the occasional slow-driving car. The disaffected youths were looking at her and making jokes she couldn't make out over the music. Their laughter was loud enough to hear, though, and it didn't sound very nice.

Okay, walking away now. Moving away from the corner with the youths and their intriguing music. She went past the bodega and caught the owner giving her the evil eye. *Okay, not waving goodbye to him.* Christine walked down the street and tried to look like she knew where she was going. That would take some acting skill, since she had no clue where she was, where to go or what to do. Mark and Condor had been nice as hell, but they kind of had forgotten to give her some, you know, money or a wrist-phone thingy. And even if she got someone to lend her a phone she didn't know who the eff to call! The big dumb macho guys hadn't even considered the possibility they might get separated. She was going to have some pointed words about that with them. If she saw them again. If they were all right. *Please be all right, big dumb macho men. And Kestrel, too, I guess.*

She turned a corner and ran into two heavily tattooed white men wearing red leather jackets and wraparound mirror shades, also red, with their heads shaved except for three stripes running front to back, dyed red as well. Bikers? Earth Alpha's version of skinheads? She didn't get to find out. One of them grabbed her by the waist and pressed her against his body. He was either packing a gun or was glad to see her. "Where you goin', mama?" The urban slang sounded different, but the misogynistic elements seemed to be pretty much the same.

Non-consensual hugging, check. For a second, she froze in terror. The man spun her so her back was against a wall. Assault, check. "You lost, mama? Need some guidance? You lookin' for the Tower of Power?" Huggie's pal laughed at that.

"Please let me go," Christine said in a firm tone. The fear was still there, but there was something else welling up behind it, and it wasn't fear at all.

The man grinned down at her, displaying a mouthful of gold teeth with dollar signs carved on them. "Oh, mama, we's gonna have fun."

Christine put a hand on the man's chest and pushed him off her. The look on his face when he went sailing all the way onto the street was hilarious. "I said please," she told the crumpled form on the pavement. He seemed to be mostly okay besides some bumps and scrapes. Hopefully that would be the end of it.

The fear was gone, and she felt *great*. Nobody puts Baby in a corner, or Baby's gonna get medieval on your ass!

"Fuckin' cunt!" Huggie-man's friend yelled. He was reaching for something in his back pocket, and she didn't think he was going to pull out anything nice and/or cuddly. And he'd used the c-word, which she hated with a passion. She stepped towards him just as he pulled out a gun – Holy Crap – and delivered a high round-house kick to his face that sent him spinning off in a spray of blood and teeth, gold and regular. The man landed limply on the sidewalk. She had no idea how she'd managed that kick. Maybe all Neolympians knew Kung Fu instinctively, kinda like Vampire Slayers.

The guy she'd kicked was twitching feebly but otherwise wasn't moving much. "OMG!" She hadn't meant to hit him so hard. Christine knelt by the man and rolled him over. His jaw clearly was off its proper place, and his eyes were rolling in his head, but he was breathing. Holy crap, she had really hurt him. She felt terrible – but she also felt like laughing and clapping her hands. Guilt and joy made for a crazy weird mix. "Sorry for pwning you," she heard herself say.

A loud metallic bang made her jump. She turned and saw Huggie pointing a gun at her. He shot at her again – and missed her again.

"What are you, a Storm Trooper?" she taunted him. Huggie screamed and emptied the gun in a blaze of semiautomatic fire. Her shield flared when two of the dozen or so bullets he fired came close enough to hurt her, and she felt the bits of lead bounce off it. Huggie screamed again, this time in terror, flung the empty gun at her – it missed her by several feet; dude seriously needed some Lasik or at least prescription glasses – and took off running.

"Oh no you didn't!" she yelled at him. She reached out with one hand and felt energy gathering around it. One little blast and…

And you'll put a hole the size of a basketball hoop all the way through him!

Oh, God, no. Christine checked herself before she wrecked herself – and more importantly, before she wrecked the crap out of Huggie. She let him go.

That was the first time she had raised her hand in anger, or even annoyance. Huggie's friend was going to need an ambulance and thousands of dollars' worth of dental care. Even worse, people were staring at her. Some of them had those goggle-cams. YouTube, here we go. *Way to draw aggro, Christine.* She'd better get out of there before she made the news.

She started running.

Thaddeus Twist

Washington, DC, March 14, 2013

The man who would save the world closed his eyes and thought about Faustian bargains and the cost of doing business.

The conference room was rather Spartan as such places went, especially given the rank of the men and women who would be joining him momentarily. The chairs were comfortable but unremarkable, the mahogany table with its inlaid computer screens stoically functional, the paneled walls plain and unadorned. One of his staffers had put a framed copy of his *Time* magazine's Man of the Year cover on a wall but Thaddeus had it taken down. Such displays were silly and unproductive, and did not help cultivate the image he wanted to project among his associates, that of being first among equals, not their absolute leader. The best way to lead people who were used to holding the reins of power was to make them think they were partners instead of followers. Lies and illusions were the strings to use with this particular assortment of puppets.

Of course, at this level nobody knew who the puppet was and who pulled the strings, not until the end of the performance. Perhaps not even then.

Thaddeus Twist knew that at least two of the men about to sit at this table thought they were the puppet masters. They were certainly deluded in that respect, and they didn't worry him at all. The one person who worried him would not be attending the meeting. If his putative peers even suspected that Thaddeus had made a deal with his secret partner, they would tear him apart with their bare hands. This was, after all, a meeting of the secret leaders of the Humanity Foundation. Its goal was to cleanse the Earth of the Neolympian plague.

Thaddeus's silent partner was Daedalus Smith, one of the world's best known Neolympians. Smith doubtlessly believed that Thaddeus was his dupe, a tool to be used to further his goals. Thaddeus believed the exact same thing in reverse. Only time would tell who was right.

News reports about the Freedom Legion attack droned on from one of the computer screens on the table. The new Global News Network anchorman's voice annoyed Thaddeus. It was too bad he no longer involved himself on the day to day operations of the network, or he would have quietly had the man replaced. To add to Thaddeus's dislike of the anchorman, the news he was delivering did little to cheer him up. The damage to the Legion had been substantial, but far less than what he had hoped for. Billions of dollars, irreplaceable assets and several dedicated men and women had been lost, and they had done their enemy a small injury at best. None of the major players had been destroyed; the icons of the Legion still lived. Ideally the carrier vessel would have reached the island itself before detonating its built-in nuclear device, but the initial attack to disable the local defenses had elicited a faster reaction than expected. The plan allowed for this, of course, but he had wanted to do more, to show the world that human ingenuity and courage could match the monstrous powers of the false gods seeking to rule humanity.

Thaddeus had reached his epiphany in 1964, a few months after his father's death in a hunting accident had left him in charge of the family's small network of southern radio stations. Thaddeus had been twenty-two, forced to drop out of Harvard during his senior year to take over the family business. Young Thaddeus was a staunch – some might say fanatical – supporter of J.F. Kennedy. The man was the embodiment of the hopes of a new generation: a human war hero, a champion of the new ideals desperately needed by a world still recovering from global war and destruction. The hopes for a new Camelot had been dashed that year, however. Tainted by a sex scandal and painted as an idealistic incompetent, JFK had been cast down by one of the very New Olympians whose influence he had tried to curb. As he heard Kennedy's concession speech on one of his own radio stations, Thaddeus had realized humans no longer ruled the planet. They had become playthings, flies for wanton boys to kill for their sport.

Kennedy had left the White House a broken, bitter man. The dream had been crushed. The ex-President had written books few read and retreated into seclusion, plagued by ill-health and regrets until his premature death. His son had barely won the 2012 Democratic primaries, only to suffer an ignominious loss in the general election to yet another Neolympian. The destruction of the Kennedy dream had spurred Thaddeus to craft a new vision for the future.

If something was not done, a miniscule aristocracy of *ubermenschen* would take over. The process was less than a century old, and already close to a fifth of the world's heads of state were Neolympians, including the current US President. Neos dominated the world's militaries, media and technology. This very conference room, its plain exterior concealing the most advanced security systems money could buy, was a product of Neolympian minds. Thaddeus had turned his family's small network of radio stations into an international media conglomerate and become one of the world's richest men, and yet his power and influence paled in comparison to freaks of nature who had gained their exalted status through a mere accident of birth. That could not be allowed to stand.

The others started coming in, individually or in small groups. The need for this meeting's secrecy could not be overstated. Many of the people sitting down around the table would lose their positions, their freedom or even their lives if their involvement in the Humanity Foundation became known. It had taken exquisite care to 'coincidentally' schedule conferences on half a dozen different matters that would explain his partners' presence here. Fortunately Washington DC was a natural focal point for the wealthy and powerful. Gathering them all in one place and time had been a logistical nightmare, but for this business long-distance communications would not do. The risks of interception might have been small, but at this stage even small chances were too risky.

After a few minutes, nine men and three women sat around the table, with Thaddeus at its head. No assistants were allowed, and their absence was a clear source of discomfort to most of the gathered VIPs. Too bad, Thaddeus reflected. They would have to take their own mental notes, and make decisions without some flunky whispering in their ears. If they weren't prepared to participate in this meeting on their own, they had no business being there.

Thaddeus waited for a couple of minutes while his guests exchanged pleasantries or, in one or two cases, angry glares. He loudly cleared his throat and all conversation ceased. "The operation has begun successfully," he said to open the meeting.

"Somewhat so," Mitsuo Fuchida said. He was the oldest man at the meeting, and at one hundred and ten years old, one of the oldest humans on the planet. Fuchida claimed his longevity was due to God's grace; others suspected Neolympian intervention, but nobody could deny the man's dedication to the cause. Thaddeus thought Fuchida was something of a Jesus freak but he was one of the most influential people of the impoverished and bitter Empire of Japan, and a true believer in the war against Neo-humanity. Fuchida's epiphany had taken place on a lifeboat from the doomed aircraft carrier *Akagi*, sunk along with most of its crew by the Neolympian Janus. "The attack failed to do more than thirty percent of the anticipated damage, did it not? Only a handful Legionnaires perished, and none of the greater ones."

"The damage is beside the point," Boris Chernenko answered before Thaddeus could do so. Chernenko was the son of the last General Secretary of the Soviet Union, and he had managed to parlay his family's fading influence into control of Russia's burgeoning oil and gas industries as the Russian Soviet Republic became the plain Russian Republic. His wealth and influence existed only on the sufferance of the Dominion of the Ukraine, however, since the Iron Tsar's empire controlled the pipelines that transported said oil and gas to Russia's European customers. Chernenko has seen his country and his own interests suffer at the hands of Neolympians. He had been instrumental in providing the Humanity Foundation with technology and intelligence. He also had a Russian's love for chess and the mindset the game developed. "This was an opening gambit, and its success was never contingent on the damage it inflicted."

"Just so," Thaddeus agreed. "The connection between the attack and the Chinese Empire will be made very quickly or has been made already. The stage has been set for the coming conflict." He turned to Fuchida. "I'm sure you have the next steps well in hand."

Fuchida nodded. "My men are ready. They will not fail in their duty to humanity and God Almighty."

Thad had never quite understood how a Christian fanatic could command so much power in largely Shinto Japan, but there was no doubt that Fuchida always delivered. "Things are well in hand here in the US," Thad continued.

"Everything is going well," Art Blood confirmed. The former Senator from Georgia was best known for his best-selling anti-Neo book, *Mortals in Olympus*, which in turn had led to the highest-grossing movie documentary in history. His political career had not been quite as successful, with no less than four unsuccessful runs at the Democratic nomination to the presidency, the last one ending with his accepting the role of JFK Jr.'s VP for what turned out to be the fiasco of 2012, where the Democrats had barely gotten 30% percent of the popular vote (that they edged out the GOP by over ten points had been cold comfort).

While Blood had been a dud politically, his influence over public opinion was undeniable. His efforts had been instrumental in pointing out the clouds inside any silver lining related to Neolympians. One in every three Americans was convinced Neos were a clear and present danger to the country, in no small part thanks to Blood's determination, aided by Thaddeus' careful use of his media empire to drive home the message. Thaddeus wished the anti-Neo poll numbers were better, but it was hard to compete against the glamour of the costumed freaks and the rival media empires that worshiped and celebrated them.

"We have enough votes in the House to approve additional troop deployments to the ROC," Blood went on. "If we can get the Majority Leader to do his damn job, we'll have the Senate too. The calls and letters are pouring in. That last movie about POW torture victims during the First Asian War has really gotten people stirred up." Blood made an appreciative gesture towards Thaddeus.

Thaddeus nodded modestly. He'd helped produce that little screen gem, and he thought Richard Gere's portrayal of a heroic American's torment at the hand of sadistic super-powered Chimps had been inspired. It was a pity that the starring role of the movie had been a fictionalized version of Daedalus Smith – he allowed himself to savor the irony for a moment – but that was all right. As long as the movie generated anti-Neo feelings, even if it only was towards other countries' Neos, it still helped the cause.

"You may stink at the news game, mate, but you can make a good movie," Matt Braddock admitted ruefully. Braddock's international news empire had been at war with Thaddeus' for decades, but the two men agreed unconditionally on finding a solution to the parahuman problem. "I did my part, too. Public sentiment in Europe is with us. Same in the Pacific Rim." The media magnate frowned. "But you knew all this, Twist. So for fuck's sake, why did you call this meeting? Unless you're planning to kill us so we don't blab about our little projects," he added with a chuckle.

Thaddeus laughed politely at the joke. That was the kind of thing Neo supervillains did for any reason or none, and one of the few things that had kept them from amassing more power than they already had. Humans were more rational. "I have learned some new information that I knew I had to share with all of you in person. Something that will make the Third Asian War into little more than a sideshow when the history books are written."

Everyone at the table leaned forward intently. Thaddeus, ever the showman, let the silence hang for a couple of seconds before continuing.

"I have discovered the source of Neolympian powers. And I have a plan to destroy it."

C.J. Carella

Face-Off

Chicago, Illinois, March 14, 2013

I woke up to pain.

I was lying on damp concrete. My hands and feet were shackled and tingling painfully. Class III restraints fired electrical impulses to disrupt motor control and make concentration all but impossible. The electrical pulses felt like the proverbial pins and needles you get when your arm falls asleep, except the pins and needles were industrial size. They were expensive as hell and illegal as shit. And they would keep almost any Neo from moving their limbs at all or gather their minds enough to activate non-physical powers. These guys weren't fucking around.

Condor and Kestrel were lying next to me, also chained up, still unconscious. Lester Harris was bound with cheap and mundane duct tape. He was awake.

"Face-Off! Are you all right?" he whispered.

"I'm just dandy," I growled, and tried to sit up. It wasn't easy, with my arms dead from the shoulders down, and legs likewise from the knees down, but I managed by crawling up to a wall and leaning on it. "Thanks for the set-up, by the way."

"I didn't know they were following me!" Harris pleaded. "I followed all the counter-surveillance procedures I knew."

I sighed. "These guys clearly have the best toys. You probably were being tracked six different ways. Not your fault. Sorry." No sense making Harris feel bad, considering he wasn't going to live to see the next sunrise. None of us were.

"I'm sorry too. I didn't think they were going to do something this blatant."

"Did they get Christine?" I asked Harris. The thought of her enduring the tender ministrations of the Russian mob made me sick with fury.

"No. She managed to get away. She flew right through the warehouse roof."

Christine could fly? She really was full of surprises. And she had gotten away, that was the important thing. Except she would be alone and without any resources in a strange city in an alien world. Still, maybe she would make it. Her chances were better than ours.

We were fucked.

Kestrel was stirring. She looked at me, then at Condor. "Condor! Kyle!" she called to him. They had taken their helmets off, so I could see her face clearly. I'd never seen that expression on her before. She was afraid and concerned. She usually acted as if she didn't give a shit for anybody but herself and her little pleasures, and it mostly wasn't an act.

"He should be all right," I told her. "Whatever they zapped us with doesn't seem to last very long." My featureless head was back to normal, for one, which made me feel a little better despite the situation. I had felt naked and defenseless without it.

"He'd better be." She turned to me. Her eyes filled with rage, a more familiar sight; she glared at me. "This is all your fault, dragging us into this mess."

"Nobody held a gun to your heads, baby. You should be thanking me; you're in for a full night of all the bondage and sadomasochism you can take, and more."

"I'm not into snuff," she replied. "At least not with me on the receiving end."

Yeah, Condor was a lucky guy. "We're not dead yet," I said.

"No thanks to you."

"Has anybody told you you're beautiful when you get bitchy? Because if they did they were lying their ass off."

"Can you two shut up and let me suffer in peace?" Condor said.

"Kyle!" Kestrel dragged herself over to her boyfriend and cuddled next to him as best she could. I guess she'd found her mate, and harpies mated for life.

"Hey, Mel," Condor said, looking around. "Guess this time the bear ate us."

"So much negative thinking," I said, despite the fact I felt the same way. I'd rather fake some optimism than admit defeat, just to be contrary. "We just got hit with a new hyper-gadget. We'll figure something out. What would your buddy Ultimate do?"

"He's not my buddy, and he'd have wiped out those mooks in three seconds or so. Captured them alive to boot."

"I'm not so sure. Those backpack blasters disrupted our powers somehow. They might have done a number even on a Type Three."

"There's that. I hadn't even heard that was possible. Did they actually disrupt our powers, though? I know they knocked me out, but plenty of things can do that."

"Trust me," I told Condor. "For a few seconds before I went down, I got my old face back. That's never happened before."

"Shit."

"The question is, where the fuck did the Russian mob get a Neo power disruptor?"

"Where else? They get all their high-tech toys from the Doms," Condor replied, using the slang word for agents of the Dominion of the Ukraine.

Shit. Well, at least we had a clue who was behind the manhunt for the Lurker – and the hunt for Christine, for that matter. With the Russian and Ukrainian mobs, you never know if they are just trying to make money like any other criminal or if they are running a caper for the Dominion. But if they had that kind of firepower that meant their metal-headed overlord or one of his lieutenants was involved. In other words, it was safe to say that we were well and truly fucked. You can try to make a deal with criminals, but you need more cards than we had to make a deal with the Doms.

The only feature in the concrete box we were in was a reinforced steel door. It opened noisily and a man entered, not tall but athletic, with blonde hair and a mean-looking Slavic face. He was followed by a big bull-necked badass type, his head shaved, prison tattoos sneaking out from under his black turtleneck's collar and sleeves. He'd been the Neo swinging that ball and chain at us during the attack at the warehouse, and he looked like he'd bounced back from the beating I gave him. Behind him two other thugs stood at the ready, one with an A-75 blaster, the other with one of the backpack guns that had ruined our day.

The thug-in-chief moved warily through the room. We might be chained up and helpless, but people have learned to worry about being in an enclosed space with hostile Neos even when we're supposed to be under control. We're like tigers that way. He quickly placed himself so his henchmen had a clear field of fire from the doorway, and then knelt in front of me, staying at a safe distance in case I tried to go for a head-butt. In the mood I was I in, I might just have tried it.

Blondie went right to the point. "Where is the Lurker?"

Ask a stupid question... "Have you checked with your mother? Last I heard he was giving it to her pretty good."

Blondie stepped away and Prison Tattoos kicked me in the face hard enough to send me spinning away. I felt my face bone crack under the impact. Blondie grabbed me by the scruff of the neck and dragged me back against the wall with one hand, demonstrating he also was Neo strong. A couple of Type Ones with delusions of grandeur, I figured, not that they weren't plenty dangerous when dealing with three shackled Type Twos. The Russian gestured towards the door. His flunkies briefly moved aside and another guy came in with an acetylene torch. Just the thing to mutilate Neos past the limits of their regeneration abilities.

When you make it your business to hunt down murderous sociopaths, there's a damn good chance you'll meet a gruesome end sooner or later. One of the worst things that can happen to you is to get tortured for information you actually don't have, because there is nothing you can say that will stop the pain. All you can do is wait for a chance that will likely never come while praying the interrogators fuck up and manage to kill you sooner rather than later.

I tried to change my face to mirror Blondie's. Some guys get creeped out when torturing someone who looks exactly like them. I wasn't expecting that would stop him, but maybe it'd give him nightmares afterward. It's the little things that mean so much. I couldn't quite make it, thanks to the shackles. My face rippled and Blondie's face emerged for a second or two before my concentration broke and I went back to being me.

Blondie smiled and punched me a couple of times to make me mind my manners. "I will ask you again. Where is Lurker?" His Russian accent got thicker, either because he was getting pissed off or excited by what was going to happen. Probably the latter. You don't have to be a sadist to work with the *Mafiya,* but it sure helps. He smiled at me and waited for an answer.

"He's touring Vegas with Don Rickles. And your mother." I know, not the best crack. I needed better writers.

The grin on Blondie's face got bigger. He gestured to Prison Tattoos, who leaned over and grabbed Kestrel.

"You touch her and you're a dead man," Condor said in his most threatening growl. Prison Tattoos ignored him and forced Kestrel face down on the floor. She didn't struggle or say anything. I caught her eyes; they had gone flat and distant. Blondie walked over, produced a switchblade and used it to saw through the back of Kestrel's costume. It took some effort – the flexible material was both bullet- and knife- resistant – but he managed to cut through it and the skin beneath it as well. The shallow slashes on her back bled for a few seconds after he was done, then closed up and disappeared, leaving nothing but bloody smears behind. Her regen was better than Condor's or mine, which under the circumstances was a mixed blessing at best. Kestrel's breathing accelerated minutely while she was getting cut up, but other than that she elicited no reaction. Boris grabbed the blowtorch and started fiddling with it.

She was tough, she got off on pain, and she was brave. But when the metal-melting jet of flame started doing its thing, she would break eventually. We all would.

"Stop," I said.

Blondie turned to me.

"You got me. I don't know where the Lurker is right now, but I know where he will be later tonight. We were supposed to meet with him." All pure BS, of course, but when in doubt, lie your ass off. Buy some time, hope the camel learns how to sing. "I'll tell you where and when if you leave her alone."

"Shut up, Face!" That was Condor, backing my play. "They'll kill us when you tell him."

"*Da*," Blondie said. "You are all dead. You should be smart enough to know death is the thing you should be hoping for." He nodded to the guy with the torch. "Mind the spine, Boris. We want to keep her alive."

Prison Tattoos – Boris – nodded. He was the happiest guy I'd seen in a while, except for Blondie, who also looked like a kid at a birthday party. Boris leaned over Kestrel with his torch, and there was a clearly visible bulge in his pants. "I'll be careful, Vladimir. All meat, no bone. Yes."

"Wait! I said I'd talk, motherfucker!"

"*Da*. You will. This is just a demonstration."

Skin and flesh sizzled, a sickening sound. It lasted for fifteen seconds before the screaming began.

Chapter Sixteen

The Invincible Man

Somewhere Not Quite Real

"If you had been serious about keeping your identity a secret, you would have worn a mask," Linda Lamar said as she lit a cigarette. She considerately blew the smoke away from his face. "Take the Lurker and his gas mask. Nobody has any idea who the man really is. Or the Dreamer and his Greek Theater face mask, ditto. If you don't want your name to be in the papers, you need to cover up your mug. Dummy." Her smile took the sting out of the words.

"I didn't think – " John Clarke began to say.

"That's right, you didn't. Did you really believe that silly fake mustache and changing the way you part your hair were going to fool me for a second after I got a good look at you? Darling, you had your picture on the front page of the *Post* wearing that ridiculous circus acrobat costume with the cape and the boots. Half the bullpen knew you were Ultimate the second they saw that picture, and they told the other half lickety-split."

"So that's why everyone has been staring at me all week. I kept wondering about that."

"Yes, everyone knows your big secret. It wasn't because I told them," Linda said. "I've known for over a month but I sat on the story, and it wasn't easy, let me tell you. The story of the year, it would have been."

"I think the European war is going to be the story of the year," John said sadly. "The identity of yet another mystery man isn't such big news anymore, is it?" John glanced around the eatery, wondering if their conversation had attracted eavesdroppers. People at Gino's Diner were good at minding their own business, which was why a lot of the reporters from the *World Journal* used the place to conduct discreet interviews. At the moment no other reporters were in sight, but John was beginning to think having his first date with Linda there had not been the best idea.

"Damn the war, and damn Hitler, too," Linda replied hotly. "That overstuffed chimpanzee and his Aryan Supersoldiers! Did you hear about those poor Polish lancers and the Teutonic Knight?"

John nodded. They both read the same wire reports, after all. The Knight, a hulking brute going by the name Panzerfaust, had faced an entire regiment of Polish cavalry and destroyed it single-handedly, killing the helpless soldiers almost to the last man while laughing at rifle and machine-gun fire, as well as a heroic but futile mounted lance charge. Panzerfaust had been such a hit with the Nazis that a couple years later they would name their version of bazookas after him. A part of him wanted nothing more than to wipe the arrogant smile off that Hun's face.

And he had done just that a bit over four years from now. An image of Panzerfaust collapsing lifelessly at his feet somewhere in France flashed through his mind.

He shook his head. *France? Why would I be fighting Nazis in France? And a bazooka is a musical instrument, not any kind of weapon. Bob Burns plays it.*

"Are you all right, darling?" Linda asked.

"Just a stray thought," John said, dismissing the weird images from his mind. Here he was, with the girl of his dreams, the girl who not only had agreed to go on this date but who had protected his secret identity even though her life's work was to reveal such secrets. He should be lost in blissful happiness. Instead he was experiencing false memories from the future. What was the matter with him?

"Thinking about how to reveal Ultimate's identity to the world?" Linda continued. "I think I should get the byline for that one."

"I think you should too," he said, and watched her face light up like a Christmas tree. "I couldn't think of anybody better suited to write that story, sweetheart."

"It may not be the story of the year, but it will be on the front page, unless the Nazis pick that day to do something especially heinous." Linda gave him a mischievous look. "I'll have to try and get a quote from Edgar J. Hoover, now that he's finally stopped telling everybody that Neolympians are nothing more than tall tales and Nazi and Communist propaganda. And as soon as it's official, you can hit those clowns at Buck Comics with a lawsuit for back royalties."

John smiled. Buck Comics had been 'chronicling' his exploits – making up most of those exploits and grossly distorting the rest – for over a year. "I'm not in it for the money, my dear. I might ask them to give some of it to charity, though."

"How about when Hollywood comes knocking? I've heard rumors Universal might be interested in doing a feature about you."

"Maybe I can get them to have Cary Grant play my part."

"No dice, darling. Cary Grant is with Paramount."

"Too bad. Hepburn could have played you."

Linda snorted. "That'd be a hoot. Or maybe Rosalind Russell, except she's already played a brassy reporter."

"I still think they based *His Girl Friday* on you," John teased. "Maybe you should sue *those* clowns."

"I didn't marry the editor of my paper," she said. "Can you picture me saying my I-dos to Mr. Wilkins?"

John had to laugh at that. Mr. Wilkins – he could not imagine using his Christian name even at this remove – was a heavyset, profane and bulldog-faced Great War veteran with as much charm as the set of brass knuckles he kept on his desk as a paperweight. If Cary Grant's role in *His Girl Friday* had been based on Mr. Wilkins, the writers had taken poetic license to dramatic extremes. He said as much to Linda and got a good laugh in return.

"Well, if I do end up in a serial or, God forbid, a serious movie, I'll try to see if they can set a little something aside for charity, too."

"So you won't take a dime for risking your life to save people?" Linda asked, somewhat incredulously.

"For one, I'm not risking as much as all that," he said, faintly embarrassed. The first time he had been shot, he had flinched, expecting the worst, and been as shocked as the shooter – a bank robber with a Chicago typewriter and an itchy trigger finger – when they both realized the bullets had bounced clean off his skin. One of the .45 rounds had ricocheted right into the shooter's shoulder, too, which took care of him until the cops showed up. Since then people had used knives, billy clubs, speeding cars and every type of gun on him, to no visible effect. He wasn't risking his life, not really.

During the war, the Nazis had tried everything from 88s on to an assortment of super-weapons. He'd been hurt a few times, but not very often.

He shook his head again. What Nazis? He hadn't fought any Nazis. The European war was none of his business, or America's either. More phantom memories of things that hadn't happened. Or things that hadn't happened yet? Was he catching glimpses from the future, like that Gypsy fortune teller he'd once met? That was worrisome.

"And for another?" Linda said after several seconds of silence.

"Uh, yes. For another, I wouldn't feel right taking money for that kind of thing. I try to help people. That's all."

"You're a swell fella, John Clarke," Linda said drily. "A little too swell, if you ask me. You don't see Doc Slaughter stinting on himself. He owns an entire building right downtown!"

"Only the eighty-fifth floor," John corrected. "Okay, and the eighty-third and eighty-fourth, too. But he's earned his money honestly. The man has patents on half the gizmos of the last decade. The Garand-Slaughter automatic rifle the Army is looking into buying, just to name one."

"Yeah, a neat invention, except how's Roosevelt going to pay for all the ammo those guns burn through? Twenty-round magazines – it's like giving a Thompson to every grunt. Uncle Willis was livid at the very idea, let me tell you." Linda's uncle was a retired Marine general, a man not disinclined to voicing his opinions on a plethora of subjects. "Not that the jarheads ever get the latest toys, but for him it's the principle of the thing. But you digress, mister," she told John accusingly. "I didn't think you were in it for the money, either, or the glory. Although you could have fooled me when you started busting heads wearing that circus outfit. Whatever possessed you to do that?"

"I hate to say it, but it first occurred to me watching the Olympics: Hitler's Knights in their gaudy costumes. They became an inspiration to Nazis everywhere. I thought maybe I should try to create our own symbols. And that's also why I didn't wear a mask. I didn't want to look like I had something to hide."

"So you ended up wearing a mask – a fake mustache, anyhow – when you were playing at being an average Joe. I don't know if that's funny or sad or just a bit bonkers."

"Well, that's all over. John Clarke, reporter, is going to be dead and gone as soon as the story goes public."

"John Clarke, a.k.a. Ultimate the Invincible Man will still be here. Who stuck you with that moniker, by the way? Ultimate? Sounds like a new car model, a Ford Ultimate, or something like that."

"That was one of the Buck Comics kids, Joe or Jerry, I forget which one. They had a couple of other ideas but they sounded too much like the *ubermensch* stuff Hitler loves."

Linda said something in return, but her words were drowned out by strange music blaring throughout the restaurant. John's enhanced hearing would normally have pinpointed the source instantly, but the sound seemed to be coming from everywhere at once. It lasted for several seconds before stopping, replaced by the ordinary sounds of the diner. For some reason, the music made John think of a telephone, even though it sounded nothing like a telephone's normal ringing.

" – at least have them spring for a fancier costume," Linda finished.

"Did you hear that?"

"Hear what?"

"That music..." John began to say, but realized from Linda's expression that she hadn't heard a thing. He was hearing stuff that wasn't there, having visions of things that hadn't happened. His mind – or something else – was playing tricks on him.

A man's voice echoed through the diner, once again drowning out all other sounds. "Yes." A pause. "It is working. He's wholly unaware." Another pause. "Yes, I could do it if necessary." The voice was familiar somehow, but John couldn't place it.

"John, you look like you've seen a ghost," Linda said, a concerned look in her face. "What is wrong?"

"This is wrong," John heard himself say. "All wrong."

The overwhelming voice came back. "She's here? And I should take care of this? How? Oh, you mean use him. Yes, I can keep control for at least several hours. There are risks, however."

This was all wrong. This wasn't real.

The omnipresent voice returned. "Go back to sleep, you stupid oaf."

The world shifted. John's doubts dissolved away.

Linda touched his hand. He looked at her, and saw her smiling at him, radiant in her wedding dress.

"You may kiss the bride," the priest said, beaming from ear to ear.

"Not if the bride kisses him first," Linda said, and did. John found himself standing up in a tuxedo by the altar in St. Patrick's Cathedral, being kissed by the woman of his dreams. Hadn't he just been in a diner on his first date with her? Memory could play funny tricks when you were fighting wedding jitters, he told himself, forgetting the weird feelings and giving in to happiness.

Christine Dark

Chicago, Illinois, March 14, 2013

Christine stopped running after she had put a handful of blocks between her and that little scene from *Sons of Anarchy*. She'd heard a police siren out in the distance but she couldn't tell if it was headed towards her. She hadn't run so far so fast in her life, and she wasn't even winded. After a quick look around, she felt confident nobody had followed her. People around here minded their own business, apparently.

And the madness continued, Day Two, or was it Three? One really loses track when living in a roller coaster ride. Funny, she'd been in two firefights in the last hour or so, and she was mostly worried about finding her friends, which would probably lead to Firefight *Numero Tres*. She'd never even seen or heard a real gun being fired before today, let alone had one shot at her. Stupid guns. They were so frakking loud.

The neighborhood still looked pretty bad. Maybe she should try and get on the El and head uptown, or downtown, or the Loop or whatever, except she didn't have a dime to her name. Maybe she should have gone through the pockets of the guy she'd punched out, what's a little mugging after assault and battery? What kind of gamer was she? Always loot the bodies after you take them down! She'd probably missed out on some phat loot.

Brain...

Her train of thought slowed down a bit and she kept walking. It was beginning to get dark. Hopefully she'd be out of the worst part of the neighborhood before night time, when she guessed things got even livelier. They had to have shopping malls in this universe, right? She would find a mall, sit at the food court after ordering some free water, and think things through. There, a sensible plan.

"Excuse me, ma'am!"

The voice was loud, male, very serious and authoritarian, and coming from somewhere up and to her right. Christine looked up and saw a costumed superhero standing on a hovering metal disk and looking down at her.

Oh, no.

People on the street were clearing out in a hurry like this was High Noon in your typical good old Western. Somebody must have snitched on her. Whatever happened to the code of silence? Christine had never been busted for anything before. This was bad, so very bad.

The guy on the flying metal Frisbee was wearing a scarlet and gold costume, complete with a half-mask that covered the upper part of his face, thigh high boots (*not butch at all, dude*), sculpted abs that she couldn't tell whether they were real or built into the costume, and a freaking golden bow and quiver of arrows on his back. He wasn't very tall but had freakily huge biceps.

"Ma'am, please come with me. I am placing you under arrest for assault and unlawful use of parahuman abilities."

And where were you when those creeps tried to assault me with their human abilities? "Umm, ah, I didn't do anything?"

"I have video footage of the assault," Frisbee Man said. "Please come with me peacefully."

Crappity crap. Face-Off had said they couldn't go to the authorities or bad things would happen. On the other hand, where else could she go? Maybe this guy could help. Christine shrugged. "Okay, I give up, you son of a Katniss."

"Son of a what?"

"Sorry, nothing." *This is not a good idea,* her brain whispered, and she agreed, but what else could she do? "Listen, some of my friends are in big trouble, and maybe you can help. I didn't mean to hurt anybody, those guys back there started it, and I'm really worried about my friends." Maybe Frisbee Robin Hood would help, even if he looked like the king of a Gaudy Pride Parade.

"I'm sure we can help, ma'am. We can sort things out when you are in custody," Gaudy Man said, sounding very sure and confident. Face-Off hadn't sounded like that but she trusted him a lot more than this officious guy. *Mark, are you okay?*

"Thank you, and you look fabulous, by the way, er, what's your name?"

Frisbee guy looked a bit put out by the question. Christine guessed people who dressed like that wanted to be recognized, promptly and without room for doubt, and she had lost points for not being in shock and awe of him and his Lady Gaga-esque outfit, even if she had complimented him for it. "I'm the Crimson Fletcher, of course."

"Of course." All the good names must have been taken, what with superheroes running around for seventy-odd years. She was amazed someone could run around in scarlet thigh-high boots and call himself the Crimson Fletcher with a perfectly straight face, but that wasn't important now.

"Here," the Crimson Fletcher said as he tossed something to Christine. She caught it by reflex – by brand-new reflex, since before her rise to superhumandom the only things she caught were colds and pop culture references.

She'd caught a shiny pair of ultra-tech handcuffs with electronic circuitry etched on their surface.

"If you can kindly put them on, hands behind your back, we'll be on our way," the Fletch said pleasantly.

Not a good idea at all. "Uh, thanks, but I've already been tied up once this week, and that's like my limit."

"Please do as instructed, ma'am."

Getting peeved now. Nobody had called her 'ma'am' so many times in a row. She dropped the handcuffs; they clattered on the pavement. "Sorry, but no."

Frisbee guy didn't like that. He drew and shot faster than the eye could follow. Well, faster than the normal human eye could follow. Christine followed the move just fine, and she got a shield up in plenty of time to catch the arrow. An arrow with what looked like a trank dart on its tip.

"CF here. Need back-up, pronto," the Fletch said, clearly not speaking to her. "I gave you a chance to surrender peacefully," he continued, this time definitely talking to her. He had another arrow on his bow's string, ready to go.

"So many *Hunger Games* references, so little time," Christine muttered to herself. Once again, instead of feeling like was about to pee herself she now felt a thrill of excitement. She decided to give peace one more chance. "Hey, I said I'd come along peacefully, just not in handcuffs, okay?" Especially not handcuffs that looked like they did something to cancel out people's powers.

Frisbee Fletch didn't bother replying with words. Instead he shot her again, with an arrowhead that exploded into a dozen metal bands clearly intended to wrap her up from shoulder to ankles. This guy really wanted to tie her up. Maybe she should introduce him to Kestrel. She expanded her shield and the metal bands recoiled away in a shower of sparks. Electrical metal bands? They probably would have hurt a lot if they'd wrapped around her. Gaudy Pride Fletch was turning out to be quite a prick, and didn't she just sound like Face-Off in her head when she thought that? She was beginning to understand why Mark didn't like costumed heroes.

"Quit shooting arrows at me!"

"Quit resisting arrest," El Fletcho replied even as he shot yet another arrow at her, this time something that burst onto her shield in a cloud of thick smoke. Or gas; she probably shouldn't inhale that stuff. She felt her shield *thickening* somehow, and the gas could not get through. Air-tight shield. Cool. She held her breath anyway and scampered away from the gas cloud.

It kept raining arrows. The Scarlet Prick fired a spread of five blunt arrows that hit way harder than the bullets her shield had deflected earlier that afternoon. He must be using a gazillion-pound draw. "Dammit, Legolas! Stop being such a d-bag!"

From the way Fletch-boy's lips tightened, he knew who Legolas was, had been called Legolas before, and didn't like it one bit. He shot her again.

This arrow exploded.

Christine got picked up and smashed into a wall by the shockwave. She felt bricks crumbling under her shield and she found herself lying in the ruins of a building lobby, right next to a row of mailboxes.

"Dude! This is someone's *home* you just blew up!"

Frisbee Prick had to come closer to the ground to see her through the hole he'd blasted into the building. Christine didn't give him a chance to shoot again.

In the marathon practice session at Condor's lair, she'd practiced shooting different kinds of energy blasts. A narrow one would probably blow a hole right through El Pricko, so she smacked him with a wide beam instead, more like a slap instead of an icepick stab. It still knocked him clear off his Frisbee and sent him flying in an arc that ended right on top of a parked car. The car crumpled pretty badly under the impact. He wasn't too badly hurt, though. In fact, he sat up and started reaching for another arrow. Christine visualized a giant fist above his head, and drove it down, smashing Gaudy Prick right through the roof of the car so only his legs were showing. They were twitching a little bit, so she guessed he'd be all right after a while.

Christine started running again. Maybe she should fly away, but she had to really concentrate to fly, and she didn't know if she'd be able to defend herself. What she needed was a fast-flying gryphon, and nobody was handing those out in this universe. Crap. She stayed on the ground, running away from Hunger Fletch at full speed.

Running at full speed right into a living metal guy.

This guy was shiny and looked like a statue, if you put a statue in a metal crusher and pressed it down until it looked like a fireplug on short legs, about five foot two or so and almost as wide as it was tall, and removed any hint of charm and good looks. Oh, and painted it Day-Glo orange. Metal dude's face was almost as featureless as Mark's, with only a hint of nose and mouth, and eyes that glowed like molten iron.

C-Fletch's back-up had arrived.

A metallic fist the size of a Thanksgiving turkey flashed towards her face. She tried to dodge but didn't make it in time, and the lights went out for a second. She came to leaning next to the stump of a streetlight pole, about a hundred feet from where she'd been just a second ago. Holy violence against women! Her shield had absorbed most of the impact, but she still felt like someone had punched her in the face. Nobody had ever done that to her, not since she was a child, and she found she didn't like it any more than she had then.

Day-Glo Man was charging her, bounding thirty or forty feet with each stride.

"You a-Hole!" Even as peeved off – no, pissed off – as she was, she still tried to think things through. Day-Glo Dick's last jump placed him right over her head: he was clearly planning to stomp her like a *cucaracha*. Christine let him have a giant-fist style blast straight up. She put more power into it, too.

There was a very loud – as in thunderous, car windows exploding all around kind of loud – clang, and Day-Glo Man went off in a very high ballistic arc that, if Christine's calculations were correct, would put him somewhere in Lake Michigan. Or maybe Canada; her calculations were pretty tentative. At least he wouldn't be plowing through any buildings and obliterating innocent housewives and/or toddlers.

OMG, how many people get killed in these fights?

She didn't have time to consider things. Lightning struck her from behind, and she found out what sticking your finger in a light socket felt like. Her shields did their stuff, but she still found herself on her hands and knees, twitching like she had the Tourette's. The shock went away quickly, thank God, and she jumped to her feet and looked for the source of the lightning bolt.

Christine's new tormentor was a flying woman in a golden string bikini, thigh high boots almost identical to the Crimson Fucktard's, and electrical arcs crackling all around her. Christine mentally dubbed her Lightning Stripper.

"Surrender or we'll be forced to use lethal force," Lightning Stripper shouted. Even her voice sounded electrically-charged.

Lethal force? So when the Hulk's ugly brother punched me he wasn't playing for keepsies?

"This is your last chance," Hoobaskank said, sounding very serious and authoritative, which was weird coming from a woman in a thong so skimpy the whole world would know if she'd missed her Brazilian wax.

"Sorry. Fletchgolas already gave me a last chance, and I blew it," Christine replied – and by the time she was halfway through saying 'Fletchgolas' she blasted Lightning Lassie straight up, hopefully into Low Earth Orbit. She would have said something about the outrageous outfit, but that'd be adding slut-shaming to injury.

Three days before, she would have cowered in her bus seat if some stranger looked at her funny, and now here she was, trading quips with superheroes and blasting them into next week. Having super powers was doing wonders for her self-esteem.

Christine turned around just in time to catch another exploding arrow with her teeth.

Okay, not quite her teeth, but she felt the impact all over her face even through the shield. She hit a storefront, went through the metal bars on the window display, and smashed into a drinks cooler, destroying a few hundred bucks worth of beer in tall cans. Thanks to her shields, she didn't even get wet, but she was feeling a bit battered, ill-used and very upset. Freaking Crimson Legolas had bounced back a lot faster than she'd expected.

This was insane. They were going to wreck half the city. She probably should have let Le Fletchier handcuff her and be done with it.

Christine came charging out of the store, shields at one hundred percent, but they were waiting for her. Fletch, Mini-Metal and Lightning Slut were all back in action, and they had been joined by something that looked like a cross between several breeds of dinosaur and Billy Bob Thornton and a woman in a blue jumpsuit surrounded in a nimbus of pale light that looked a lot like Christine's own force field. She barely had time to register their presence when they came down on her like a waterfall of anvils.

Lightning bolts and smoke arrows distracted her until she got clobbered by Day-Glo Boy and Billy Bob Dino, who smacked her back and forth like she was a Ping Pong ball. One smack, two smacks, three. They hurt. She smacked back. She pictured two giant fists closing down on Day-Glo from opposite directions. There was another deafening clang and Day-Glo tottered and went down. Christine blocked Dino-Bill's next claw attack and gave him a blast in the face that sent him reeling. Her shields shimmered and crackled under more electrical attacks from Storm Skank, which made her miss the fact that Blue Jumpsuit was coming up from behind her with a giant mallet of made out of blue energy in her hands. Christine turned around just in time to see the mallet coming down on her –

Ouch.

– head.

Christine found herself lying in a small crater. Water from a busted water main was splashing down on her, and her shields were weak enough that the water was getting through to her. The Power Strangers were coming after her, and everything hurt. Something felt broken on the right side of her chest, and every breath she took hurt like someone was poking her with a knife. Lethal force was on the menu all right. She was about to get zerged into oblivion.

A silver and red blur flashed overhead. Bam. Day-Glo was lying next to her now, and he wasn't even twitching. Bam, bam, and Mallet Bitch and Fletchorino were gone from view. Lightning Beotch started flying up, and the blur caught up with her. Bam, and she was down too. Dino Bob managed to land a punch on the blur. It didn't seem to do anything. Bam. Dino went down.

The blur became a tall man in a bright costume, a tall man who could have posed for a Greek sculptor. He loomed over Christine, looking at her with a maniacal grin on his face. She recognized him from Hyperpedia, except in the pictures she had seen of the man, his expression hadn't looked as crazy as it did now. He was looking at her in a way that made her want to blow a rape whistle.

Bam.

Armageddon Girl

C.J. Carella

Face-Off

Chicago, Illinois, March 14, 2013

The lights went out.

The only illumination left in the room was the blowtorch flickering over Kestrel's twisting body. The stench of charred flesh was overwhelming. Boris stood up, the torch in his hand still flaring but no longer burning Kestrel. Her screams died out, replaced by harsh, panting breaths. You could kill her but you couldn't make her cry.

Cold, unearthly laughter echoed outside.

The radio show producers hadn't done justice to that laughter. Maybe they hadn't done it justice on purpose. That sound was not something you wanted in your living room at any time of the day or night, even if you knew it was a silly make-believe radio program.

Nothing sane could laugh like that. Nothing human, either.

"The Lurker's here!" Blondie shouted before giving out a stream of barked orders in Russian. Boris turned off the torch and everyone trooped out and shut the door behind them, leaving us lying in the dark.

"Mel! Melanie!" Condor said. I had never heard so much anguish in his voice. He flopped towards Kestrel – Melanie Bauer; I'd never called her Mel, and she'd have punched me in the throat if I'd tried. Kestrel grunted, took a deep breath, exhaled. "Let me suffer in peace for a sec, lover," she said finally, and if her voice wasn't as steady as it normally was, I couldn't blame her. She took another breath. "I couldn't stay in subspace, dammit. Sorry for the screaming."

"Sorry for..." Condor's voice broke in a harsh laugh, with more than a bit of a sob mixed in it.

Outside the door, gunfire and the sharper sound of energy weapons started out, single shots at first, followed by long fusillades. Interspaced amidst the gunshots, the laughter continued.

"Those sorry bastards are so screwed now," Lester Harris said.

"Couldn't happen to a nicer bunch," I commented. Someone started screaming in terror and agony, more loudly than anything they had gotten out of Kestrel. The scream died with a gurgling sound that sent a chill down my back.

The buzzing sound that the backpack disruptors made joined the symphony of destruction playing outside. Shit. If they took the Lurker down, we were done. "We have to do something." I turned to Lester. "We'll get you loose first."

"How?"

"You are tied up with duct tape. Condor should be able to chew through it. I'd do it, but I can't make a face right now."

Lester crawled towards Condor, who gnawed through the duct tape binding Lester, and after a few seconds the Lurker's sidekick was free and rubbing his wrists. "I'd love to return the favor," Lester said. "But how? Those shackles are solid steel."

"The Russkies didn't think things through," I said. "They left their toy behind."

Kestrel managed to laugh at that.

It took some blind groping for Lester to find the acetylene torch in the dark, and some fumbling to get it working. He'd never used a blowtorch before but

Condor had, and he talked Lester through it. Lester didn't even have to cut all the way through the cuffs, just burn through them enough to destroy the circuitry zapping our nervous systems. He did my cuffs first, and he burned me pretty good while doing it, but after what Kestrel had gone through I didn't make a peep. As soon as feeling returned to my hands, I tore the shackles off me and freed everybody else.

Under the blowtorch's flickering light, we examined Kestrel. The burns were horrible, and her spine had been damaged; her legs wouldn't work even after she was free. I had no idea how long it would take for Kestrel's regenerative abilities to repair the damage. She certainly was out of this fight.

"Stop crowding me," Kestrel said after a few seconds. "I'll heal sooner or later. Now do me a favor, get out there and kill them all."

"Can do," I replied. Condor squeezed Kestrel's hand one more time and whispered something into her ear. That let me deal with the metal door on my own, which was good, because I had a lot of energy to burn. One kick and the door buckled enough I could get a good grip on it. I grabbed one of the door's bent corners, braced myself against the wall, and ripped it clear off its hinges. We walked out.

Condor and I found ourselves in a utility tunnel, pipes and cables running all along the walls and ceiling. Emergency lights had come on, illuminating everything in a dull red hue. Above us we could hear the muted sounds of loud Euro-Tech music. We must be underneath some *Mafiya*-owned nightclub.

"I'll go left," I said. Condor nodded and went right.

The tunnel made a turn some fifty feet out. As I rounded the corner, I found Boris' body. He'd traded the blowtorch for a large machete. It hadn't done him much good. The blade and the tattooed arm and hand that had been holding it lay six feet away from the rest of him; other pieces were scattered around the tunnel. Much as I'd wanted to kill the sick fuck, I didn't enjoy the sight. There were other bodies strewn around. They were all very messily dead, as if someone had run them through various industrial devices, the kind that crushed, shredded and chipped whatever was thrown into them.

More gunfire rattled further on. I ran towards it.

I turned another corner and saw two Russians advancing slowly and trying to look in every direction at once. One had an assault rifle, the other an A-75. They started to turn the guns towards me.

They never had a chance.

I closed the distance before they fully realized what was going on, grabbed them by their faces and smashed their skulls together. The guy with the A-75 managed to squeeze the trigger before he died, and I got a nasty flash burn on the side of my head. The blast also set the corpses' clothes on fire. My own clothes, even though they look normal, are highly resistant to fire, so I was only singed a little. The energy rifles really weren't meant to be used in an enclosed space. I stomped on the smoldering corpses until the flames went out, just to be a good citizen.

Another corner, and lots more bodies. At the other end of the tunnel, I saw a Russian fly towards a wall and bounce off it before landing limply face down. A second later, Condor came into view. We had cleared the tunnel, except for the one corridor between us. Sporadic gunfire was still coming from there.

I backpedaled and picked up the A-75. Its finish was a bit crispy from the back blast, but it was still in working order. They made them tough in the Ukraine.

Condor saw me pick up a gun, nodded and grabbed a submachine gun off another corpse. We approached the central corridor from opposite sides, and I took a quick peek around the corner.

It was a very quick peek, since somebody started shooting the second they saw me. I ducked back as gun and blaster fire tore through the corridor, punching holes and blasting chunks of concrete into the wall. I managed to get a good look before ducking, though.

The corridor led to a large storage area. Blondie and half a dozen thugs had made a rough barricade with boxes and crates and were forted up there. I crouched low to the ground holding the A-75 by its pistol grip, and fired a couple of blasts in their direction. The return fire was pretty heavy, but someone started screaming in pain. Even a near miss from a blaster would do serious damage. On the other side, Condor fired a couple of bursts at them, letting them know I wasn't alone.

This could take a while. The Russkies had too much firepower for us to charge in. And one of their disruptors was still in play. I could see the twisting energy coiling against the wall – and reaching towards me. Luckily there was a limit to how far the energy stream could bend, but I really didn't like how it seemed to be alive. Just for shits and giggles, I shot the stream with my blaster. The back blast would have singed my eyebrows off if I'd had any, but did not seem to have any effect on the disruptive stream. Oh, well.

A couple of seconds later, the energy stream ceased abruptly. Someone kept shooting short bursts with a regular gun, but they were not being aimed in our direction.

The laughter was back.

I risked another peek just in time to see Blondie shoot at a cloaked figure as it closed in on him. Nobody else was standing. There was a pulse of darkness that swallowed the emergency lights for a second. When the lights came back on, the cloaked figure stepped back and what was left of Blondie dropped to the floor. From the sternum down, Blondie's body looked like it had been run through a meat grinder. No Type One Neo could survive that. His face was grey and had been twisted into something that you knew could not be alive even without any evidence of injury.

The Lurker laughed again and turned to face us.

His cloak was long and had a hood that shrouded his head. There was something wrong with the cloak's edges: they seemed to get longer or shorter between eye blinks, and they fluttered as if caught by a breeze that wasn't there. The Lurker's trademark Great War-issue gas mask protruded under his hood like some monstrous snout. Unlike the one I'd seen on dozens of magazine covers and trading cards, this mask was covered with glowing geometric patterns that made me queasy if I looked at them for more than a few seconds. The glowing symbols were new, that was sure.

"Lurker. It's good to see you," Condor said, sounding a lot less certain than he usually did.

"Condor," Lurker said, giving him a brief nod. His voice had the same creepy, whispering and echoing undertones as his laughter, like it was being distorted by distance – or as if it was traveling through a medium other than air.

Having performed as many pleasantries as he was going to, the Lurker turned to one of the backpack disruptors the late Russians had been packing. He started disassembling it – and the pieces remained floating in the air as he took the device apart, linked by thin lines of dark light that seemed to create a blueprint around the pieces.

"No, no, this is all wrong. All wrong," the Lurker hissed. "He's tapping into the Outside, the fool." More disturbing laughter. "What's his plan? His plan. My plan. He knows too much. Have to fix that."

Oh, boy. I glanced at Condor, and he looked as disturbed as I felt. The Lurker was not playing with a full deck, which thrilled me to no fucking end.

The mystery man finished dismantling the back-pack component of the disruptor. A ball of swirling dark energy emerged from it, the same twisting sinuous stuff that had taken us down at the warehouse. The Lurker saw it, clapped his hands in delight and did a little hop. "Pretty." He sounded like a child – a child who'd shambled back from the dark lake where he had drowned to share something cold and terrible with his dearly beloved.

I don't creep out easily, but this was doing the job just fine.

"Go get Lester and Kestrel," I told Condor. "We need to get out of here." Sooner or later more Russians were going to show up, and if they had more of those disruptors the Lurker was so enthralled with, they might bag us again, him included. Condor nodded and left.

"Ah, Lurker," I said, and he turned towards me. The blob of swirling lights vanished the second his attention was diverted, along with a buzzing sound I hadn't quite noticed. The disruptor's pieces clattered loudly on the ground.

"Thanks for the help," I continued. He said nothing, just looked at me through his disturbing gas mask, his head slightly cocked to one side. "These assholes were after you, and there's probably more where they came from. We need to get out of here."

The Lurker cocked his head the other way. An eye blink later, he was right in front of me. I was positive I didn't see him cross the intervening distance. "You were with her," he said. "Where is she? Is she here? She's not here. Not here but near. Where?"

I wanted to step away from the whacko in the gas mask – hell, I wanted to run away – but held my ground. Turning one's back on the insane rarely turns out well.

"Christine?" I said. "You know Christine." I didn't like where this was going.

"Christine," the Lurker repeated. "Where is she? Where is my daughter?"

Chapter Seventeen

Christine Dark

Somewhere over the Eastern Seaboard, March 14, 2013

So cold. Everything hurts. She didn't want to wake up. Something bad was on the other side of her closed eyelids, and she wasn't looking forward to knowing what it was.

The universe doesn't give a rat's ass about what you want, her brain helpfully whispered. *Do, or do not, and all that crap.*

Christine opened her eyes and regretted it immediately. She was moving through thin clouds that rushed by at ludicrous speeds. Down below she saw glimpses of the earth below, at about the cruising altitude of a jetliner. Wicked high, to be technical about it. She felt cold, but nothing like she should be feeling that high up. She also was being held at the waist by a very well-muscled arm and hanging face down. They were moving fast, so fast she could see the ground moving below her, moving faster than she'd ever seen from an airliner. Strangely enough, her hair wasn't even fluttering – and at those speeds her hair should be not just fluttering, but being ripped clean off along with her face.

"Don't try to move, little girl, or I'll break both your arms," Ultimate the Invincible Man snarled at her. Conversation shouldn't be possible when moving through the air at those speeds, either, but she could hear his voice perfectly clearly.

Force field around both of us? She wondered. Next time she tried flying by herself she'd try that trick. Of course, first she had to deal with her current predicament or there wouldn't be any next times or first times for anything.

"Good girl," Ultimate said when she stopped squirming. Her current position wasn't very comfortable, but having her arms broken would be worse. She'd seen him wipe the floor with the super-gang that had wiped the floor with her, which in superhero math meant she was in deep doo doo. "This will be over soon," he continued.

"Where are you taking me?" That was such a damsel in distress phrase she wanted to puke, but bad guys were supposed to like to talk. Maybe she would learn something useful.

"You'll find out soon enough, little girl." Crap. Creepy.

Christine had watched some Ultimate video clips on the computer during her Hyperpedia-gasmic experience the previous night. He sounded nothing like this creep carrying her off to wherever. Something wasn't right. Mind control, alien puppet masters or a cloning experiment gone horribly wrong might be involved. Trying not to squirm too much, Christine twisted her head until she could see Ultimate and turned on her super-duper senses. As usual, she got more than she bargained for.

Ultimate was sheer power made solid, glowing like a halogen lamp on steroids, shiniest of all shinies. His aura was blindingly bright for the most part, but there were dark spots embedded in it like malignant tumors. The sickening purple-black spots reminded her of the weird energy beams that had taken her friends down during the warehouse firefight. Bad as that was, there was more.

Somebody was riding Ultimate like the proverbial back monkey.

Her Christine-sight revealed a psychic image of the body snatcher: a man in an old style suit and hat, with a laughing ceramic mask covering his face. Tendrils of slimy-looking green energy emanating from the masked man surrounded Ultimate's body and head and sank into the dark spots in his aura. Christine could sense Ultimate's mind somewhere under all the tendrils. Ultimate was blissfully unaware anything was wrong; he was happy, as a matter of fact. Happy as a clam, maybe happier than he'd ever been, because Christine sensed that Ultimate and happiness were at best passing acquaintances. The big guy had no idea that someone else was on the driver's seat.

The masked man somehow realized she could see him. Maybe he had his own version of Christine's senses. "I think this warrants one broken arm," he said in the same tone he'd been using through Ultimate's mouth.

Something went *ding* inside Christine's head. She understood what Laughing Mask was doing. The green tendrils worked like her own empathy. They created a connection between him and his target, except where Christine sensed a target's emotional state through that connection, Laughing Man could actually go in and manipulate stuff inside his victims, stuff like thoughts, emotions and memories. The dark spots in Ultimate's aura had created openings that allowed the masked man to enter his mind and take over.

Her captor reached for her with his free arm. Christine pushed with her mind, using her special sight as a guide. Maybe she could break the connection. Maybe —

She wasn't being carried through the air by a psycho controlling Ultimate anymore. She was standing in a large office space, filled with desks cluttered with piles of paper and ancient typewriters and telephones. There were newspaper clippings affixed to just about every wall. The biggest headline she could see read 'Hitler Invades Poland.' Second place went to another headline: 'Ultimate's Identity Revealed.' The newspaper's name was *The World's Journal*, which she'd never heard of before.

That was all pretty weird. But not as weird as the fact that she was dressed like her favorite gaming character, an Elven rogue named Snipe, all decked out in her Tier Ten leather armor, with twin epic daggers glowing right through the scabbards belted around her waist. The armor looked great, but it was riding up in places where it really shouldn't. She touched her ears. They were long and pointy and elf-y, or was that supposed to be elfin? WTF?

I didn't break the connection, she realized. *But I think I hitched a ride inside Ultimate's brain.* She was in Dreamland, and in Dreamland she was Snipe. It made sense if you were a little bit crazy to begin with.

Christine didn't get much of a chance to appreciate her situation. One of the walls of the newspaper bullpen started bulging inward like a plastic membrane being pushed from the other side. The man in the laughing mask burst through it. Laughing mask or not, he was pissed. She was picking up his emotional state in here just like she did in the real world.

"You insufferable bitch!" he screamed. "You are going to pay for this. I'm not allowed to kill you, but here I can hurt you as much as I want."

Her daggers were in her hands now, and she felt an irresistible urge to let fly with sinister strikes and all her other rogue tricks. "I'm going to gank you like a n00b," she hissed, and she sounded just the way she imagined Snipe would.

The man pounced like a cat, long claws at the end of his fingers reaching towards her. Christine's daggers flashed in a blur of light, and she severed both of his hands off at the wrist. From out of nowhere, 'Kiss with a Fist' started playing, one of the songs she liked to listen to while gaming. In the land of the Mind Trip you got your own soundtrack, apparently. It would have been more awesome if she wasn't so pissed off.

The masked man roared in pain and recoiled, stumps spurting dark blood. Christine followed him, daggers whirling. She stabbed him in the chest just as new hands grew out of his stumps. The wounds didn't seem to make much of an impression. She had to duck under a haymaker that felt like it would have taken her head off if it had landed. Christine hacked and slashed, and Laughing Mask shouted in rage, but he didn't go down. Dreamland unfortunately did not provide a hit point counter over his head, so she couldn't tell how much she was really hurting him. She was sure she was hurting him, though. Every time she landed a hit, she felt a flare of pain and fear from the a-hole.

When she didn't duck fast enough, he landed a punch and she discovered that he definitely could hurt her back. She went flying across the bullpen, hit a wall and bounced off it. No force field protected her. Christine ended up on her hands and knees, coughing up blood.

Urk! Healz, please!

The pain disappeared. She looked around to see if she'd conjured a healer out of thin air. She hadn't, but she had managed to heal all the damage she had taken anyway. Awesome.

The masked man had been about to gloat when he saw Christine get up. His shock when he saw her recovery felt like a bucket of cold water to her empathy senses. *Surprise, d-bag.* Surprised or not, he was ready to keep playing. He went after her, his hands turning into clawed limbs once again. This could go on all day. Which was just what Laughing Boy wanted, Christine realized with a sick feeling. In the real world, Ultimate might be still flying her to wherever the bad guy wanted to take her, and she didn't think she'd like it there. Time to get the eff out, find the big guy and wake him up. This bullpen must be from Ultimate's past. They were dancing around Ultimate's memories: he had to be somewhere in there.

"Peace out, bitches!" Christine yelled and tried to go into her rogue's stealth mode. She disappeared in a puff of smoke and rolled away from Masked Man, who looked confused and started turning around, vainly looking for her. Ha! Okay, where to go? A door stood out in the office. It didn't match the other doors, and it was glowing faintly. Christine reached it and started opening it. An angry shout from behind her made her look back. Laughing Mask had managed to spot her. Crap. She ran out the door.

She ran out the door right into a scene from *Saving Private Ryan*. The door was gone and she was wading on shallow water on a sandy beach littered with broken equipment – and dead people. Unlike the bullpen, there was a full cast of characters, props and FX there, mostly screaming American GI's, explosions, dead bodies and pieces of dead bodies on the blood-drenched beach, and Nazis raining death from the high ground overlooking them. Not good. She ducked into a shell hole as bullets flew all around her. Christine had never been a big fan of war movies, and she quickly found out that being inside one sucked a lot worse than watching one.

"Catch."

She looked up and saw the masked man dropping a grenade-on-a-stick right into her shell hole. She jumped out as with the full grace and speed of her rogue reflexes, but the blast got her before she was clear. She was knocked sideways and felt shrapnel ripping into her. It hurt a hell of a lot.

Healz...

It worked again, thank God, but she had to keep moving – dodge and weave around soldiers and barbed wire and bursts of automatic fire, and it wasn't half as much fun as it sounded, especially with a masked maniac chasing her. She put him down for a few seconds when she grabbed a big rifle-like thingy she thought was called a BAR and shot him up pretty good, but he didn't stay down for long. She went into stealth mode again and managed to leave him behind for a bit while he tried to find her again.

Wasting time here. Have to find Ultimate.

She tried to use her Christine senses. It didn't work the same way as it did outside Dreamland. The scene didn't change very much, but she saw a golden light shaped like a six-foot tall oval, hovering a few inches off the ground near the remains of a landing craft. It felt like the door she had used to get out of the newspaper offices. Hopefully this one would get her to Ultimate. She ran through it.

The beach battle bingo went away. Christine came to a stop in a bedroom, watching a man and a woman screwing like bunnies.

Armageddon Girl

Very embarrassing.

C.J. Carella

Face-Off

Chicago, Illinois, March 14, 2013

"Lurker, we've got to get out of here," Condor said, interrupting our little chat before I did something I would almost certainly regret. He had Kestrel in his arms. Lester Harris was behind him.

"Condor! You'll tell me where Christine is."

"Yes. Sure. But we need to go back to my ship first. Kestrel needs medical attention."

"Oh, that." The Lurker walked over to Condor and examined Kestrel for a second. Before anybody else could react, he took Kestrel's head in his hands. The air around the Lurker *shuddered*. It was like a mirage, or heat daze, but I didn't just see it, I felt it in my bones. Kestrel's body convulsed as if she was being electrocuted.

"What..?" Condor started to say, too surprised to react.

"She's fine now," the Lurker said, stepping away from them.

"He's right, Kyle," Kestrel confirmed. She stood up, stretching her arms and shoulders.

"My daughter," the Lurker repeated.

"I put a tracer on her," Condor said. "If we can get to my ship, I can find her."

"Where?" Lester Harris gave him the address to the warehouse.

The Lurker spun around. His cloak spun, grew larger, and became a sheet of solid darkness. It swallowed us. I felt surrounded by something like a very thick fog, almost liquid in consistency, and cold. I couldn't see or hear anything. For all I knew I could be the only living thing in the dark. For a couple of seconds, I stood in the cold blackness, wondering what the fuck was happening. Luckily, the darkness dissipated, and I saw we were back at the warehouse where we'd been ambushed. I was impressed. Teleports were fairly rare. Instant or near-instant teleports were incredibly rare; it usually takes a while for teleports to visualize their destination and move themselves there safely. The only quick jumpers I could think of offhand were Janus, who was among the top ten most powerful Neos in the world, and the Scourge, the Holocaust survivor who had gone on to help found Israel.

The Lurker had been hiding quite a few things, or had learned some new tricks recently. He'd certainly grown more eccentric, or, more accurately, batshit crazy.

There was no time to deal with that now, though. We had to find Christine and arrange a little family reunion. That was probably going to end in tears, but it had to be done. Cassandra, as usual, had been right. I'd have to remember to grovel a little next time I saw her.

Condor rushed into his ship, the Lurker right behind him. Kestrel, Lester and I followed a bit more slowly.

"How are you doing?" I asked Kestrel. She might be a pain slut – her own and everybody else's – but nobody enjoys having their flesh seared off with a blowtorch.

"I'll live. All I need is a bit of killing to work off some stress. You guys had all the fun back there."

She sounded like she was back to normal, at least. "I'm sure we'll find all the action you'll ever want before this is over," I said.

"I always want more," she replied. "It's the only thing that keeps me going." Yep, back to normal, all right. She gestured towards the ship. "The Lurker is something else, isn't he?" She didn't sound like she was interested in learning more about his powers. "I love crazy weirdos. They have the most interesting hang-ups."

"You really don't want to go there," I growled at her. "Jesus H. Christ, that's the last thing we need."

"I wasn't really serious," she said, grinning. "That would be biting more than even I can chew. Besides, it would hurt Kyle."

I looked at her. "You really do give a shit about him, don't you?"

Her smile had an edge now. "More than I ever did for you, killer."

I nodded. "Fair enough." What else could I say? I wished them the best.

Condor was at a communications console, a dozen screens lit in front of him, the Lurker looming behind him, his cloak taking more room inside the Condor Jet than it should. Weird shadows formed around him and gave the ship a gloomy, Gothic feel. The screens I could see were all tuned to news channels. There were Breaking News signs on every one. A video feed showed a street that had clearly been the site of a Neo brawl. Burning cars, shattered concrete, broken water mains, sparkling electrical arcs from downed power lines. Your basic shit storm, in other words. Another screen showed shaky video from someone's cheap Goggle-cam. In it, Christine was kicking a gang banger in the face. I gave her a mental thumbs up and fervently hoped I'd get to see her again.

"She's on the move," Condor reported. "Moving fast, Mach Four and still accelerating." He pounded a fist against the console, denting the metal alloy. "We'll never catch up."

"I will," the Lurker said.

"... reports that Ultimate himself joined the fray remain inconclusive, but somebody disabled the entire roster of the Chicago Sentinels and made off with the young woman who had been fighting the heroes," a TV reporter said on one of the screens.

Ultimate? Fuck.

Even if Condor let loose with every gadget in his arsenal, trying to fight Ultimate would be like spitting into a hurricane. I looked at the Lurker. Maybe the old mystery man had more tricks up his sleeve than he'd shown so far, and what he had shown was impressive enough. Even so, if Ultimate was involved in this, we were in for the fight of our lives. And very possibly our deaths.

Dying didn't bother me all that much. I'd been living on borrowed time since that night on a kitchen floor where I'd been choking on my own blood and teeth fragments while my stepfather pounded my face into hamburger. Dying a failure, that bothered the shit out of me. I'd found Christine. She was my responsibility. If that meant I had to figure out a way to take down the Invincible Man, I'd have to think of something.

"I'm going to go get my daughter," the Lurker announced, and did his spin the cloak trick. Just like that, poof, he was gone.

He didn't bother taking us along.

Fucking hell.

C.J. Carella

The Invincible Man

Dreamland/Somewhere Over the Eastern Seaboard, March 14, 2013

John looked at Linda and smiled.

"Again? You're insatiable, you know," Linda said, but her grin matched his. Two years of marriage later, and it still felt like they were on their honeymoon, whenever they could find the time to be together. They were both incredibly busy, but they always made the most of the time they spent with each other.

"Try and break me, big boy," she said playfully, an old joke that still made him chuckle as he took her in his arms. Their first night, she had wondered out loud whether she would survive the experience. Discovering John's ability to turn off his inhuman strength at will had come as a relief to her. "I was worried this was going to turn into a tragedy – Titanium Man versus Paper Woman," she'd said, painting an image that had made him shudder at the time.

As always, he was exquisitely aware of everything about her, from the warm flush on her face and neck as he entered her to the rhythm of her breathing, the racing heartbeat that his thrusting motion matched, the crescendo their bodies built together. Her first orgasm was a brief eruption; he changed his rhythm to match her body's reaction. Her delighted moans were music to his ears. He was home. Peace and joy enveloped him.

"Holy mother of crap!"

John rolled off the bed and landed in a fighting crouch. A young woman dressed in an outlandish leather costume was standing in their bedroom, gaping at... well, at him. "Oh, my," she said, her eyes wide.

"What the hell?" he yelled, his erection pointing at her like a gun.

"Should I shoot her, darling?" Linda said steadily, pointing an actual gun at the intruder. She'd reached into the nightstand and grabbed her .15 auto pistol, a Doc Slaughter design that fired several types of ammunition. Linda looked mad enough to spit, and John was pretty sure she wasn't planning to use the non-lethal rounds in the gun. John's first impulse was to attack, but the intruder was not making any aggressive moves, so he held off for now. He shook his head at Linda, who held her fire for the time being.

"What are you doing here?" John said. He belatedly covered himself with a pillow.

"Oh, God. I'm so sorry, but I've got some really bad news, and now I know why you were so happy, but... But, it's not real. None of this is real!"

"What is she talking about?" Linda said.

"Damfino. What do you mean, not real?" Even as he asked the question, John felt a sinking sensation deep in his gut. Wrenching horror gripped him; it felt as if a man expecting to celebrate his wedding had stumbled into a wake for his dead fiancé.

"He's mind-controlling you, Laughing Mask Man is; he's a, uh, a puppet master, a mind frakker. And he's right behind me, so you've got to snap out of it. Sorry. I know this was the worst possible moment, and I'm sorry, but I had to find you and tell you, because right now you're kidnapping me, my real body, your real body is kidnapping my real body, and if you don't wake up we're all in deep crap."

"You're out of your ever-loving mind, whoever you are!" Linda snapped. She looked like Linda, sounded just like Linda, but... John blinked. Suddenly he could see right through his wife as she became ghost-like and translucent. Shock washed over him. He blinked again and the woman on the bed was a skeletal scarecrow with a bare hint of the features of the woman he loved, dying alone and afraid. He remembered, and felt his heart break all over again.

"No."

"You little bitch!" said a man in a theater mask and clothes that had gone out of fashion when John first arrived to New York City. John hadn't seen him enter the room, but there he was. He slapped the woman in leather and sent her flying through a wall.

John recognized him immediately. They'd only worked together a handful of times. The masked man had been one of the early mystery men. He'd been featured in the pulps and had a short-lived comic book. John had never liked or trusted him much, not least because he was a master of illusion and misdirection, abilities that always struck John as dishonorable, no matter to what ends they were used.

The Dreamer.

"Back to sleep, you imbecile," the Dreamer commanded. John started to move –

John was back in bed with Linda. "Again? You are insatiable, you know." Linda smiled and kissed him deeply and passionately as he held her in his arms. He was home. He was happy. She gasped as he entered her...

"OMG, do guys ever stop thinking with their dicks? Wake up!" the girl's voice cut through his happy daze like an icy knife.

Linda was gone. Linda was dead, long dead. He felt his heart break all over again.

Linda vanished, leaving only the girl and the Dreamer. The Dreamer had overpowered the girl and was trying to strangle her.

"Healz, please…" she choked out.

"Shut up! Shut up! Shut the hell up!" the Dreamer shouted, smashing her head against the floor over and over. He seemed to have forgotten about John.

The punch should have been immediately fatal. John did not restrain himself. He gathered all the fury and sorrow that were flooding back into his soul and released it into one blow. The Dreamer's head snapped back and he was knocked off the girl. That was all.

No, not all. The blow had knocked away his mask. The Dreamer's identity had remained a secret throughout the decades. He had disappeared in the Seventies, dead or retired, nobody knew. Until now.

"Doctor Cohen," John snarled.

"The name's Muller. Dietrich Muller," the Dreamer spat back. "The *Juden* doctor was just another mask. The real Cohen has been dead for a while. Pity, isn't it?"

"I am going to kill you now," John said in strangely calm voice.

"I don't think you can," the girl said, getting up. Her wounds were gone, and she looked grimly determined. "We're in Dreamland and nothing lasts very long in here, even death."

"I'm putting you back to sleep, boy," the Dreamer said, a savage grin in his face. "And then that little bitch and I are going to spend some quality time together. There is some incipient trauma in her mind that is going to be a pleasure to explore."

"We can't kill him," the girl said. "But if we beat the crap out of him enough, we'll kick him out of your head."

The Dreamer's grin wavered. He looked at John and concentrated, but nothing happened. "*Was ist das?*"

"That's me, stopping your mind-frakking crap," the girl replied. "Time for some tank and spank." She charged the Dreamer.

John reached him first. Being able to hammer someone with all his strength filled John with savage elation. For a while he was able to wash away his grief in blood.

The Dreamer tried to fight back, but it wasn't much of a fight. The girl kept stabbing him in the back, and if he tried to turn towards her John smashed him down. It wasn't much of a fight, and it didn't last long. The Dreamer seemed to deflate and he faded away.

"Pwned you! Can't wait to do it for real next time," the girl said.

"Ditto," John agreed. "We were never properly introduced, by the way. I'm John." He offered her his hand. Now that he had time to actually look at her, he realized her eyes and hair color were almost identical to Linda's. The realization brought another pang of sorrow, but it was somewhat muted now.

The girl shook John's hand tentatively. "Christine. Nice to meet you."

"Nice to meet you, Christine. Ah, do you know how we get out of here?"

She furrowed her brow in concentration for a few seconds. "I think... Like this." She snapped her fingers.

John found himself floating in mid-air, holding Christine with one arm. She was dressed in regular clothes, looking much the worse for wear. He shifted his grip on her so they were facing each other. Their eyes met.

"Hi," he said.

"Hi," she replied, smiling at him; she was flushing. John smiled back. She was beautiful.

"Let her go," someone said in an inhuman voice that echoed with strange whispers.

John turned towards the sound. The Lurker stood in the air facing him, floating and surrounded by an aura of dark energy.

"Another creepy guy in a mask?" Christine said. "How many of them are there?"

"Wait. I know him," John said, but even as he tried to reassure her, he wondered. He'd known the Dreamer, too. And who had sent John right into the Dreamer's trap? Kenneth Slaughter. His best friend. He couldn't trust anybody.

"Let her go, Invincible Man, or I will show you things," the Lurker said, and tittered. "Things you won't like."

"What do you want with me?" Christine shouted at the Lurker.

In lieu of an answer, the mystery man removed his gas mask.

Christine's face froze.

"Dad?"

Chapter Eighteen

Hunters and Hunted

New York City, New York, March 14, 2013

Cassandra was dying.

For decades, paranoids everywhere had feared the day when Neolympians with the power to control and manipulate the minds of others would take over the world. Some of them claimed that day had already happened, and people did not realize it. The truth was that mind to mind communication of any kind was a two-way street. To control or even affect another mind, you had to become intimately linked to it. The targets' memories and emotions touched the controller. Their pain became the controller's pain. Telepathy begat empathy. The effect was magnified by the number of minds affected. The psychic trauma caused by trying to affect too many people was prohibitive. No Neolympian could control more than a few minds at once, and even that would bear a terrible price.

Below Cassandra, eleven men and one woman died time after time, as she forced their neural pathways to experience alternate realities. She experienced each death in turn. Thought was becoming reality, and she was bleeding from multiple spontaneous wounds, far beyond what her limited healing abilities could handle. Soon they would overwhelm her and she would fall.

It was worth it. She had held the hunters at bay for crucial hours, time for Marco and his friends to do what was necessary.

* * *

Archangel crawled up the stairs. They kept disappearing, replaced with scenes from his past. He knew they were there, however, and he forced his body to move even as he died yet again.

The amulet he wore under his neck had finally started working, muting the effect of the visions. Each new death felt less real than the last. Horror had been supplanted with rage. Only one thing mattered: to find his tormentor and destroy her. Archangel had sensed her presence through the kaleidoscope of death. A woman, a little Gypsy witch, was responsible for this. He would make her pay. He would make her scream.

Another step. Another death, this one wholly impersonal: a young woman with hard eyes and a bruised face going to a doctor to take care of her little problem. It took him a while before recognizing the young woman as his mother. Archangel spat blood and ignored the psychic feedback tearing his body apart. He would heal or he would die, but he would keep climbing for as long as he lived. He grinned, revealing red-stained teeth.

Almost there.

* * *

The dance of possibilities was coming to an end. Two alternatives remained. The man called Archangel would reach her and kill her, or she would die of her wounds before he did.

It had been a good life, a worthy life. She had enjoyed some of it immensely, and left the world a better place than she had found. What more could be asked of anybody?

There was one last thing she wanted to do. She gathered her nearly depleted reserves even as the Russian staggered towards her, and sent forth the last of her will and power. A last message for Marco.

Cassandra said her goodbyes, and let go.

* * *

"No!"

The roar of denial was useless, futile. He had been mere steps from her, savoring what he would do to her. He could almost taste it. The torn burning flesh, the screaming and pleas for mercy. They all begged in the end, if they had enough breath left. He had begged and pleaded a hundred times during his climb up the stairs, and now it was her turn. He wanted, no, he *needed* to hear her scream.

He held the slight, lifeless body in an almost tender grasp. The Gypsy bitch had sighed and died seconds before he reached her. She had died peacefully like an old *babushka* at the end of a long life. She was covered in wounds, should have perished in agony, but her face told a different tale. She had been smiling at the end. Had felt no pain at all. Had not revealed any information. Had *fucked* with him like no one ever had.

He tore apart her corpse with his bare hands, not even bothering to call forth his divine fire. Useless. The bleeding carcass could not feel anything. He could never make her pay.

"Did you love anyone, bitch?" he whispered to the severed head in his hands. "The faceless man, did you care for him? He will pay for what you did, him and everyone you ever loved. You owe me a thousand deaths. I will collect every single one."

Useless. She could not hear him. He carelessly tossed the head aside and went back downstairs. He would do all the things he had promised her corpse, for he was a man of his word, but they would provide him little satisfaction.

Nichevo.

He found Medved kneeling over Lady Shi. The Bear's breath came out in shuddering spasms. Tears were still running down his face. Lady Shi was lying so perfectly still that Archangel thought she was dead, but just as he reached the landing, she opened her eyes.

Lady Shi giggled like a schoolgirl. Giggled and did not stop. The giggles became savage laughter, not sane in any respect. Medved held her tightly and continued to sob while she laughed.

They would recover, or not; at the moment, he could care less. Archangel walked past them and gave them their privacy. He checked the time. They had been trapped with the witch for hours. Where were his men? Where were those useless pieces of shit?

Nine of them were scattered around the building's lobby. Eight of them were dead. Six of those bore a myriad phantom wounds. The other two had killed themselves, one by the simple expedient of bashing his head against the wall until his skull had cracked open, the other by disemboweling himself with his bare hands, something Archangel had not thought was humanly possible. The ninth one was kneeling down, breathing shallowly, his eyes glazed over. Useless. Archangel casually broke his neck and put him out of his misery.

He found the last three survivors standing by the cars outside with their thumbs almost literally up their asses. It was only by the Devil's luck that the police had not shown up to find out why exactly three expensive cars were parked outside an abandoned building in this neighborhood. His first impulse was to take out some of his frustration on the cowardly assholes who had decided to wait and see, but their losses had been heavy enough as it was. Anger was counterproductive. He had already lost his temper over the Gypsy bitch, and that had been one time too many. Instead of going into a murderous rage he walked up to them as if nothing had happened.

Nothing, after all, had happened. He'd seen phantoms that had never been, and endured some psychic feedback. He'd lived through worse. He'd inflicted worse. If he told himself those words enough times, one day he might come to believe them.

"Report," he said curtly.

"Nobody left the building until you did," replied one of them, trying desperately to be helpful. He failed miserably, of course, but he did not know his life had already been spared. Let him keep trying.

"Anything else?"

"Nothing here. Vladimir in Chicago wanted to speak with you. I said you weren't available."

Archangel shrugged. That had been true enough. He checked his wrist-comm – his very secure, signal-encrypted wrist-comm – and saw he had two voice mails from the ex-KGB man, his point man in the operation to capture or kill the Lurker.

They were juggling too many balls at once. The operation in New York to recover the lost subject, and the Chicago mission; those were the two he was overseeing directly. He knew of at least two more operations in different parts of the world, and suspected of at least one or two more. Not all of them had to succeed for the Project to come to fruition, but there were still too many things left to chance. The technical expression was multiple failure points. Not all of the operations were essential, but some were, and if any one of those failed, the whole Project would collapse.

Nichevo. Great rewards required great risks.

Grisha, Vladimir's second in command, answered the call. He had news. All of it was bad.

While the Gypsy witch kept Archangel and his team busy, Vladimir's main team had found Face-Off and the bloody girl! They had stumbled upon them purely by accident, while following one of the Lurker's henchmen. The idiots hadn't even known about the girl, and in any case she had managed to escape. Vladimir's team had captured Face-Off, but even that small triumph had turned into shit very quickly, however.

Archangel controlled his breathing while Grisha listed all the ways things had gone to hell. Vladimir and everybody on his team except Grisha – he had been lucky enough to be running errands when the Lurker struck – dead. The girl, apparently captured by Ultimate – how the fuck had that happened? – and whisked off somewhere unknown. The Lurker, Face-Off and two other Neos gone, also to parts unknown. Archangel's search efforts in New York had been rendered moot, unless their quarry decided to return to the city, which wasn't bloody likely. Grisha was nearly hysterical: Archangel had to calm him down, something he was not used to doing, and something he did not do well. It took some doing, but he managed to steady Grisha enough to start acting professionally, at least.

In his business, failure often meant death. Both missions had failed rather spectacularly. Archangel considered his options. He could run. He could contact his handler and offer another possible course of action. Or he could try to take down his bosses before they put him down. None of his choices were optimal, and none offered a great chance of success. It was a challenging situation.

Medved and Lady Shi emerged from the building. They looked calm and composed, almost back to the way they had been before facing the witch. There were subtle differences, however. There was more distance between them than before. Archangel wondered if some of their visions involved one of them meeting a bad end at the hands of the other. That wouldn't surprise him one bit.

"What now?" asked the Bear.

"We leave here. I will contact our superiors and ask for new instructions," Archangel replied as a decision crystallized in his mind. Running would be futile. So would be trying to strike back. Much as the idea bothered him, he would place himself at the mercy of his superiors. He was a valuable asset. They would seek to use him.

He had made a promise to the dead witch, and he intended to keep it.

Armageddon Girl

Face-Off

Chicago, Illinois, March 14, 2013

"She's stopped somewhere over New York State," Condor reported. "Damn me, but Ultimate is *fast*." He sounded envious.

"Fast isn't always good," Kestrel purred.

"The Lurker must have caught up with them," I said before the happy couple could trade more pleasantries. "I wonder how that's going." I found it hard to believe that even the creepy, seemingly supernatural Lurker could take out the man J.R. Oppenheimer had dubbed 'Shiva Incarnate, Destroyer of Worlds.' "Can we go after them?"

"Even if I go on afterburner the whole way, which I don't have the fuel to do, it wouldn't matter," Condor said. "We wouldn't get there in less than forty-five minutes."

"Shit."

"Look, the Lurker may not be able to take down Ultimate," Condor said, then visibly reconsidered. "That is, I don't think he can. But he's tricky. He could easily grab Christine and disappear. Ultimate is a tough guy and no dummy, but he's no Doc Slaughter. The Lurker can fool him."

"Maybe. Did you get a good look at Mister Creepy? Did he look like the sneaky, tricky guy you used to know?"

Condor didn't say anything. We all turned towards Lester Harris, who had been sitting quietly, enjoying some local sedatives courtesy of the Condor Jet's sick bay. Unlike us, the cuts and bruises he had sustained during his capture had not gone away. Sucks to be human.

"Okay, yes, he's changed," Lester said defensively. He paused, clearly debating how much to tell us. "I don't know exactly what's happening to him, but for the last few years he's been doing… I don't know what to call it, exactly. Magic, maybe."

Magic? I almost snorted at the word. Sure, there were a bunch of Neos who called themselves sorcerers and magicians and masters of mysticism or what not, but all their 'magic' was nothing more than Neo powers with fancy names. Most of them were just trying to be more impressive and scary than they really were. A few really believed they were real witches and warlocks, and sometimes became so deluded their powers would only work through some magical doodad or another. Some couldn't perform unless they chanted spells in Latin or Esperanto or some other weird language. Crazy Neo shit, in other words.

"I know how it sounds but I don't know what else to call it," Lester continued. "He draws these symbols, like the ones he started carving on his mask last year, and they make things happen."

"Some sort of Artifact," Condor said reasonably. "He must have developed the ability to make Artifacts at some point. That's nothing new. It's the same way the Iron Tsar makes a lot of his super weapons."

"The symbols work even if a human draws them," Lester said.

"What?"

"Do you know any magic tricks?" Kestrel said, switching from playful kitten to ice queen instantly. "Were you holding out on us, Lester?"

"I only know one," Lester admitted. "The Lurker showed me how to do it. It's not easy, when you are drawing the symbols you start to see things, hallucinations or something – at least I hope they are hallucinations. The mark I know lets me send mental messages to the Lurker. That's how I let him know you were on your way here. I could use it now but he's probably busy right now."

That was new. There were rumors the Dragon Emperor empowered normal humans and turned them into Celestial Warriors, but most people dismissed those stories and asserted that the Emperor simply had found a way to identify latent Neos and trigger their abilities. Who knew? Maybe the Lurker did. There was definitely something strange about the guy. The weird symbols etched on his gas mask had felt supernatural enough.

"Look, I wish I could help out more, but this is all way out of my league," Lester said. "I think I'll be going now."

I nodded. I felt bad for the guy. He had gotten mixed up in Neo affairs and could have easily gotten killed a dozen different times in the last few hours. We said our goodbyes and he drove off in the slightly dinged car he'd brought to the warehouse for our ill-fated meeting. I wished him well. With most of the Russian mob in Chicago dead, he would probably be all right. I figured he'd have the sense to lay low for a while until things settled down.

Meanwhile, we had plenty of problems of our own. Christine's father was a possibly insane Neo sorcerer. I hoped she'd be able to handle it. I hoped she would be in a position to have to handle it.

I started to say something to Condor – and felt my mind being yanked right out of my body.

* * *

Cassandra smiled at me from her stuffed chair. She looked like shit. She looked like she was dying.

I was back at her building. People were screaming downstairs. I saw a pale man in a white outfit crawling up the stairs, bloody and battered and with a murderous look on his pasty face.

"What the fuck's going on?" I blurted out. Cassandra had been shot, slashed, struck with a dozen nasty wounds. A long cut ran down the side of her face, and blood was running down from it, staining her silk shirt. I saw a large red pool spreading out from under the chair. I rushed towards her. "What happened? Who did this to you?" *I'll kill them.*

"I did," Cassandra replied. "Marco, we don't have much time. I called you to say goodbye."

I wanted to do something to help, but I wasn't really there. The scene had that fuzzy around the edges feel you got from a psychic contact. "Fuck that. The Lurker can teleport now, when he gets back I'll bring him here and he'll heal you. All you have to do is hang on for a little while. We'll take care of you," I said in a pleading tone. "You have to hang on."

Cassandra shook her head. "All this has already happened. It's a little time trick; I borrowed some time to reach you, but my tab is about to come due. I am gone, Marco. I'm sorry I couldn't tell you what was going to happen, but if you had stayed here all would have been lost. And it was worth it. Christine and the Lurker have met. The world has a chance."

"You lied to me. You knew this was going to happen and you sent me off to find the Lurker." I felt numb. I was talking to a dead woman. I glanced at the man in white. He had reached the room, and when he reached Cassandra he would kill her.

"The poor man was rather disappointed, I'm afraid," Cassandra said. "I took my leave before he reached me. No doubt he desecrated my body, but I was done with it."

"Are you a ghost?"

"This is a bit of me I sent out as I died. Come closer." I did, and she took my hand. "Don't be mad at me, Marco."

"I am. That was a fucked up thing you did. Christine would have been fine with Condor and Kestrel. I could have helped you."

"You would have died with me and achieved nothing. Christine needs you, Marco. She is going to need you very badly. Your presence may make all the difference in the world. Listen to me closely. Something is going to happen that may turn the entire planet into a lifeless wasteland. Billions of lives snuffed like candles struck by a tornado. I kept seeing that future. If you and Christine make the right choices, there is a chance we can avert it."

"Great. You sent me off to be with Armageddon Girl and never bothered to tell me. I get to be Sam Gamgee to her sexy version of Frodo, is that it? Do I even get a kiss out of it?" I tried to keep things light and ignore the fact this was going to be last conversation I was going to have with Cassandra. I had to set it aside and not think about it.

She looked at me. "I don't know. Maybe. I know you are developing feelings for her, but that doesn't mean anything. The white knight doesn't get the girl all the time, or even most of the time."

"That's good, because I'm no white knight. I kick white knights in the balls and stomp them when they're down."

"Good. But try to be her knight anyway, white or otherwise."

"I will."

"I always loved you like a son, Marco."

"I know." I was going to say more, but she was gone. I never got a chance to say goodbye to her.

* * *

"You all right, Face? You looked like you went away for a second or two."

A little time trick. "Yeah, I did."

Unless I make a face people can't tell how I'm feeling. That suited me fine right now.

Christine Dark

Various Times and Locations/Chicago, Illinois, March 14, 2013

A Brief History of Christine and Her Dad:

Age eight. Christine put down the copy of *Harry Potter and the Chamber of Secrets* she'd been reading in bed when she heard her mother's angry voice coming from downstairs. She slipped quietly out of bed, stepped into her Marvin the Martian slippers and tippy-toed her way towards the bedroom door to listen to what was going on.

"... she's sleeping anyway," her mother was saying. Christine had never heard her sound so angry, not even when Ellen Weathersby had given Christine a black eye and Mom had been ready to go to Ellen's house and, in her words 'Kick that fat b... bad girl's as... butt!'

It sounded like someone's ass-butt was about to be kicked.

Christine heard a man talking, but he was mumbling in a low voice she couldn't quite make out. "Who the fuck cares what you want? Do you think the monthly checks give you the right to see her?" Mom replied. She wasn't screaming, but her furious whispering voice carried very well. Christine gasped; she'd never heard Mom say the F-word before. "You can't see her now anyway; she's sleeping, and it's a school night." Another mumbled response. "We'll see. You can't abandon us and come back years later like nothing happened. I got your damn number; maybe I'll call you. Maybe. And if I don't call you, take it as my final answer and fuck off!"

The front door slammed shut.

Christine made it to the stairs and saw her mother leaning against the front door, breathing heavily. She looked very, very mad.

"Mommy?"

Mom looked up, and Christine saw tears running down her face. That scared her more than the cursing. Her mom only cried when something really bad happened, like when their cat Princess Fuzzybuttons had gotten hit by a car and gone to Kitty Heaven.

"Oh, Chrissy, I'm so sorry." Mom came up the stairs and hugged her. "It's okay, honey. It's okay."

Christine wanted to believe her, but she remembered the words Mom had said, and something clicked in her head. Who had abandoned them years ago?

"The man..."

"Don't worry about the man, honey. He's gone now."

"That was Daddy, wasn't he?"

At first, Mom didn't say anything. Christine could feel her mother getting all stiff in her arms. Was she getting mad again? Mom let go of her and crouched down so she could look Christine right in the eye.

'Yes, Chrissy. That man was your biological father. He wanted to see you."

"He did? Can I see him?" Christine said and then wished she could take it back. Her mother almost never talked about Daddy, and when she did she almost got at least a little mad.

She didn't get mad this time, but she looked like she wanted to cry again, and Christine leaned forward and hugged her. "It's okay, Mommy. If it makes you sad I don't have to see him."

"Oh, Chrissy," Mom said again. They held each other quietly for a bit. Mom stood up, wiping her eyes. "It's okay, Chrissy-bear. If you want to see him, it's okay. We'll set it up. Maybe tomorrow after school we can all go for ice cream. Would you like that?"

Ice cream and Daddy? Christine nodded enthusiastically.

The next day went by in a blur. Christine always did well in school but that day she didn't pay attention to anything. Even when Ellen Weathersby called her names Christine barely heard her. Nothing really registered until Mom picked her up and took her to the Dairy Queen. Her father was already there, sitting by one of the outdoor tables, sipping on a milkshake. He saw them and stood up.

"Is that him?" Christine said.

Her mother's hand tightened on hers. "Yes. His name is Damon, Damon Trent. That's your father, Christine."

He was short and skinny. He was barely taller than Mom, and Mom was shorter than most adults. And he was old. Not old like Grandpa, who had no hair on his head and a beard that was gray and white, but pretty old. Dad's hair was red just like hers; it was cut short but kind of messy, and there was no gray there and no wrinkles on his face, but that was Christine's impression anyway. Old. Old and sad, with a snub nose a bit like hers and a few freckles on his cheeks. Christine got freckles when she got too much sun, too. He was wearing a suit that didn't fit him very well.

Mom let go of her hand and Christine took some tentative steps towards the old, sad man who was her father. He came down on one knee and reached out with his hand, offering to shake it.

She did. "Pleased to meet you," she said politely.

"Hi, Christine." His voice was hoarse, as if he had a sore throat. "I'm glad to see you."

"Why did you abandon us?" Christine asked. She hadn't known she was going to say that until the words were out of her mouth.

Her father's face looked as if he had bitten on a lemon. "I had to do important things, in places far away," he said. "I wish I hadn't, but sometimes we have to do things we don't want to do." He didn't sound sad, just very serious.

"That's okay, then," Christine said, but she was kind of lying. It wasn't okay. Still, this was her Dad. She hugged him. He hadn't been hugged much, she guessed, because he didn't hug her back very well at first, but he did after a bit and it felt like being hugged by her Dad, the way it should, and she felt happy.

They had ice cream — her favorite flavor, mint chocolate chip — and he asked her about school and what classes she liked, and she told him about Harry Potter and how she'd gotten an A in her last test. Mom didn't say much, but she didn't look as mad as before. Dad told her stories of far-off places and lands, of climbing mountains in the Himalayas and traveling through the jungles of Borneo. Mom invited Dad over for dinner and he said yes, and dinner was also very nice.

"You're a very special girl, Christine," Dad said when they were saying their goodbyes after dinner. He didn't call her Christie or Chrissy, but Christine, the way she liked it, although she would never tell her Mom about that because she knew it would hurt her feelings. "You don't know how special." He hugged her and left.

Age sixteen. High school, braces, acne and enough petty evil to drive a saint insane. Dad had been back a few times — two Thanksgivings, one Christmas, and one birthday. He would call ahead, and her mother would agree to his visit; he would show up and they would have dinner and chat for a bit and he would give them presents or money and after that he would go away for nine months or twelve or twenty-four. He'd always been civil to Mom's boyfriends, polite to Mom, and nice to Christine in a distant, cool way. He never spent more than a day with them, and he was gone without a trace afterward. It was weird. She'd Googled his name a bunch of times and found a few Damon Trents, but none of them had been her father. Sometime she wondered if that was his real name or whether he was a spy or drug lord or something.

That day, Christine had been having a quiet cry in the empty classroom where the Chess Club usually met. Nobody was around, and that was just fine. She didn't want to see anybody. She just wanted to curl up and die.

The Halloween Dance was scheduled for the next day. Halloween was one of Christine's favorite holidays, a chance to let her freak flag fly in relative safety. The dance party had been the community's way of rounding up as many teenagers as possible and putting them in a relatively controlled environment so they didn't go forth and enact their own version of Devil's Night, but Christine didn't care. It would be a good night to dress up (she had spent days working on her costume: Princess Giselle from *Enchanted,* with the critter from *Alien* bursting from her midsection), sip non-alcoholic punch and hang with her homies from the D&D, Math and Chess clubs. Geeks of the world, unite. Yay. She knew Harry Yang was going to ask her to be his date to the dance, and she was going to say yes, even though poor Harry was now and forever stuck in the Friends Zone. Things were looking up, but as they so often did, they turned to crap at the worst possible moment.

Christine had been in the bathroom when the cheerleader death squad came after her.

"Look who it is," Ellen Weathersby said. Over the years, Ellen had lost the baby fat but kept the bad attitude. She'd made the cheerleading team last year. "Pissy Chrissy Dorko." Her three friends laughed nastily. An eleventh grader who'd also been in the bathroom made a hurried exit; she knew things were going to get ugly in there.

Sinking feeling in the pit of her stomach. These were the times that tried women's souls. These were the times when she hated her last name. Dark was a perfectly nice Anglo-Saxon name. A derivation of the 7th Century Old English word *deorc*. But in 21st Century America, Dark was a weird name, and weird was punishable by mocking and abuse.

Christine tried to leave the bathroom. One of the cheerleaders blocked her way, and when she tried to go around her, another one body-checked her and sent her staggering back. "Did anybody say you could leave, bitch?" the cheerleader snarled.

Christine didn't say anything. Nothing she said would do any good, and most likely would only make things worse. Plus Christine could be a chatterbox normally, but in this kind of situation her words went away, not that she could produce enough breath to speak even if they hadn't.

Ellen Weathersby got right in her face. "This is how it is, Dorka. You are cordially disinvited to the Halloween Dance. We're going dork free this year. You feel me?"

Why? Christine thought but didn't ask out loud. What had she done to get Ellen on her case? She'd even tried tutoring her when the cheerleader was failing math. Okay, Ellen had failed anyway, but some people just refused to think, and Ellen's face could be on the national flag of the People's Republic of Non-Thinkers.

Maybe Ellen blamed Christine for failing. As the Laws of Thermodynamics say, you can't win, you can't break even, and you can't get out of the game.

Christine's silence wasn't good enough for Ellen. She leaned close enough to Christine's face for her to smell a nauseating combination of bubble-gum and tobacco wafting from behind the cheerleader's Invisalign clear braces. "This is where you say 'Yes, Ellen. Thank you, Ellen.' Or things get really bad."

"Yes, Ellen. Thank you, Ellen," Christine said dully, tears of humiliation burning in her eyes.

Ellen patted Christine's head like she would a dog's. "Good Chrissy, good girl. So we won't be seeing you tomorrow night, right?"

Christine nodded, looking down. Submission display mode, all in the hope the alpha bitches would be satisfied and saunter away. And saunter away they did, laughing and giggling amongst themselves. They'd shown Pissy Chrissy Dorko what was what, and all was well in their world.

All of which led to her quiet cry in the Chess Club meeting room. She had a free period, which she normally spent in the library, but today's plan was to turn on the waterworks for a while.

"Christine?"

The gravelly voice made her jump like a goosed cat. Her father was leaning against a wall, dressed in the same ratty suit he always wore. He looked the same as the last time – or for that matter, the first one: old, sad and tired. And short: Christine was five three but if she was wearing heels she'd be able to see the top of his head.

"Dad? How the frell did you get here?" He wasn't wearing a visitor's badge, and George Washington Carver High School frowned (as in call the cops frowned) on unsupervised visitors roaming around its hallowed halls of learning.

"I have my ways," he said by way of explanation, which wasn't much, but typical of dear old Daddy. "You're crying."

"Nothing gets by you, Dad. Sorry, that was rude. I'm not having a good day, today. Or a good week, not really. Definitely a sucky month, since it's almost over. Next month will probably suck, too. Speaking of next month, are you going to come over for Thanksgiving?" she asked, hoping to change the subject.

"No." That was also pure Dad, Christine had discovered in the dozen or so hours she had spent with him over the years. He said what he meant, meant what he said, and if you didn't like it you could go pound sand. He also didn't let other people change the subject, although he himself did it all the time. "Why do you let those girls bother you? They are nothing. Tramps."

"How did you know about the cheerleaders?" Christine said. Had he been spying on her? In the bathroom? Frelling creepy, Dad.

"I saw them leaving the bathroom, and I saw you leaving afterward. Nothing gets by me," he said, the closest thing to a joke he'd ever uttered, and she thought he was smiling. It was hard to tell; Dad seemed to have only two expressions and both of them would make a Marine drill sergeant look like Mary Sunshine.

How come I didn't see you in the hallway? Christine thought. Granted, she was upset and mostly looking at the floor, but it was strange she hadn't noticed him.

"You shouldn't let them scare you," he went on.

"I know: fear leads to anger, anger leads to hate, hate leads to suffering, yadda Yoda."

"That's one of the stupidest things I've ever heard," Dad said, starling her into a burst of laughter.

"You know what? You're right." She gave him a weak smile. "See? All better now. Thank you, Dad."

"I wish I had been around more. I would have taught you how to fight," he said.

"That would have been cool. Like that line from *The Stand*: 'Give me kung-fu in the face of my enemies.' I could use some kung-fu lessons."

"Oriental fighting styles are fine, but you don't need them," Dad said, and went on before Christine could mention that 'Asian' was the preferred term this century. "Attitude is essential. And ruthlessness. You need to be willing to do whatever it takes to win, and show it."

"And if the other girl or guy has attitude and ruthlessness, and is bigger and stronger?"

"Then you will lose, of course. But at least they'll know they were in a fight."

Christine snorted. "Dad, you don't just not sugarcoat things, you don't even Splenda-coat things. And why did you sneak into my school? You know Mom doesn't like surprise visits, or unsupervised visits." Even now that she was a couple years away from voting or serving in the military, Christine's mother didn't want her to be alone with Dad.

"I wanted to show you this." 'This' was a cube he held out in his hand. It was made of some sort of brightly polished red stone, and was covered in little carvings, weird symbols she'd never seen before. "Here." He handed it to her.

It felt heavy, like lead or gold, and it was warm. Her fingers tingled where they touched the stone. The symbols were pretty interesting. They were important, she was certain of that, although she had no idea why. She thought she could figure them out if she just looked at them long enough...

Dad took the cube away, and Christine felt like she'd just woken up from a nap. "What was that?"

"Something I made. I wanted to see what impression it made on you."

"Well, it kind of hypnotized me, I think. It..." Something had happened between the moment she'd started looking at the symbols and when Dad had removed the cube from her hand, but she couldn't remember it, just the way sometimes she would wake up knowing she'd had an intense dream but was unable to remember it. "You made a cube that plays Jedi mind tricks?" *Or you made a cube and coated it with some really good drugs?* Christine wanted to trust Dad – yes, he never was around but he'd sent money to her mother every month, and he seemed to give a crap about her in his own curt non-people person way – but let's face it, she didn't *know* Dad.

"Something like that." He seemed disappointed in her somehow. "It was nothing. Forget about it."

And she did. The memory would only come back five years later, floating forty thousand feet above the Earth while held in the arms of the Invincible Man.

"So no Thanksgiving," Christine said. "Maybe next year?"

"I won't be here next year," he said.

Christine did not ask about the year after that. She had the feeling she wouldn't like that answer, either.

The school bell rang. Her free period was over. Weird. Even counting her little encounter with the Cheerleader Death Squad and her chat with dad, it had only been like ten or fifteen minutes, hadn't it? She looked at the time on her cell phone. Nope, an hour had come and gone. Time flies when you're spending quality time with Dad.

"I have to go," she said. "Or I could commit some truancy and we could go out for ice cream." She'd never been absent without leave, but there's a first time for everything.

Dad shook his head. "I have to go as well." He did something very unlike him next: he hugged her tightly. "You will be all right now," he said cryptically. "Take care, Christine."

"You too, Dad." This didn't sound good. It sounded like goodbye. She felt tears gathering behind her eyes. She'd thought she'd cried herself out, but here was Dad sounding like he wasn't coming back. Like ever.

He stepped away, and his eyes looked a little moist, too. Without another word, he left.

She didn't go to the Halloween Dance, much to Harry Yang's disappointment. The Princess Giselle Has an Alien Baby costume never got worn. Just as well, because the dance turned into a real-life horror story. Ellen, the rest of the Cheerleader Death Squad and their boyfriends had all gotten killed in a freak car accident on their way to the dance. The deaths were blamed on drugs, and the rest of the school year was a mess, between grief counselors and D.A.R.E. speakers and all that happy crappy. Christine felt sad and guilty for months. She'd often fantasized about Ellen meeting an untimely end, and that was a fantasy she now wished she'd never had. She never connected the deaths with her father, not until years later at forty-thousand feet yadda yadda.

Christine didn't see her father again. Not on that world, at least.

* * *

"Dad?"

Maybe Porta Potty Man wouldn't have been so bad.

The emotional Space Mountain ride was really getting to her. She'd been dealing with Ultimate's feelings in the dream world, massive grief followed by massive anger; thank God he'd calmed down a little after beating the living crap out of the Dreamer. Then she'd had this little moment with him when they'd woken up, and her heart was still doing a little hippity hoppity thing. She didn't go for jocks at all, but Holy Crap! Something about him just made her blush like a schoolgirl. And now, this:

"Last chance, Ultimate, or whoever is controlling him," Dad said. His voice sounded kind of like she remembered, if you hired a sound FX team that loved to use reverb and had read the complete works of H.P. Lovecraft and put it to work jazzing it up. It was the scariest voice she'd ever heard. It made Darth Vader sound like Jessica Rabbit. Then Dad laughed, and *that* was the scariest laugh she'd ever heard. She didn't want to even imagine what his yodeling would sound like.

"Dad!" she called to him, and he stopped laughing, for which she felt immensely grateful. "It's okay. He was being controlled, but I helped him break free. He's fine now."

"She's telling you the truth, Lurker," Ultimate – John, that's his name, use it – said. He didn't sound overly impressed by the Lurker's – by Dad's, that's his name, use it – scary special effects.

Dad considered this for a few seconds. When he spoke next, his voice sounded a bit less scary, almost the way he sounded during his visits back on Planet Normalcy, a long time ago in a galaxy far away. Christine desperately wished she was back there.

"Very well," he said. "She must come with me."

"Fine," John said. "But I'll be coming along."

"Wait!" Christine said, intruding into the superhero equivalent of dogs sniffing each other's butts. "My friends. Face-Off and Condor." And Kestrel, she guessed. "They got captured by the bad guys. Russians with weird ray guns. We have to find them!"

"Already taken care of," Dad said. "I'll take you to them."

He floated closer, and she felt John tensing up, but he let Dad get to within arm's reach. Lurker-Dad did some weird trick with his cloak, and things went dark and cold for a very disturbing second or two. Christine most definitely did not try to use her super-senses inside that darkness, and even without them she got the feeling there were things there, things she most definitely did not want to see. The darkness thankfully went away quickly and Christine, still in John's arms, found herself in the now fairly crowded passenger compartment of the Condor Jet. Condor was leaning over Mark, who was slumped on a chair. Kestrel was looking away. Nobody looked happy.

Mark… Christine broke free from John and rushed to him. Mark's pain was as bad as what John had experienced in Dreamland, and it hit Christine even harder. When he saw her, he hugged her convulsively, like a drowning man reaching for life preserver. "What happened?" she whispered as he squeezed her hard.

"Cassandra's dead," he said. The tone was flat. He was trying to bury the grief away. Christine let him do it for now. He wanted to be cool in front of everybody, and she could understand that. "I'm glad to see you in one piece," he added.

"I'm so sorry," she said. Cassandra had been so nice. Christine wanted to cry but this wasn't the right place or time. "And I'm glad to see you in one piece too. I feel like crap for running away. That was not heroic at all."

"No, that was the smart thing to do. Those assholes want you for some reason. You never give assholes what they want."

"Too many words to put on a t-shirt, but I approve of the sentiment," she said, and felt him smile a little. But then he saw John and the invisible smile disappeared.

Crap. She'd forgotten that Mark was an unlicensed vigilante. If John decided to arrest him, things might get messy.

"John, this is Face-Off. He saved my life. Face, this is John. He was being mind-controlled, but he's all better now." She disentangled herself from Face-Off, who went over to John and shook his hand. Condor and Kestrel also exchanged greetings. Condor and John had already met, of course, although the vibes she got off them weren't all warm and fuzzy. Kestrel was looking at John like a cat looking at a Red Lobster special. Was there anybody on Earth Kestrel didn't want to screw? She was like a man with a vaj.

After greeting time was over, there was an awkward silence. Dad had put his gas mask back on, the one covered in symbols that hurt her head if she glanced at them for a few seconds – and which looked much like the ones in that cube he had shown her the last time she'd seen him. She was picking no vibes off him. Either he didn't have any emotions or he knew how to block her senses. Probably just as well. She was pretty sure she didn't want to know what was going on inside Dad's head. She still needed to know what was going on, however.

"So, Dad," she said casually. "What's new?"

Chapter Nineteen

Hunters and Hunted

New York City, New York, March 14, 2013/Kiev, Dominion of the Ukraine, February 28, 2013

"... and we returned to the safe house to await instructions," Archangel said. On the phone's view screen, Mr. Night's expression did not change, his asymmetrical smirk seemingly frozen in place. "I have Medved and Lady Shi standing by, and the remnants of my team. Should we proceed to Chicago?"

"Things are moving fast, my dear cherubim." Archangel's jaw clenched at the mocking tone but he remained silent. "I'll be there shortly." The connection went dead.

Archangel started at the desk phone's blank screen for several moments. Mr. Night was the middleman for his superior's American partner, and in overall charge of the operation. Even on short acquaintance, he had come to intensely despise the old man with the uneven features and grating voice. To have to answer to him was nearly unbearable, and yet...

"And yet one does what one must," Mr. Night completed Archangel's unspoken thoughts. Archangel whirled on his chair and saw the man who had been in Chicago moments ago standing behind him.

"I decided it would be best for me to fetch you," Mr. Night explained. "Things are not going well, dear boy, not well at all. We lost the girl, we lost Ultimate, who could have made such a great puppet, and I must presume that the Lurker and the girl have been reunited by now."

"Is all lost, then?" Archangel asked cautiously. He would have to strike swiftly and with all his strength if he had any hopes of overcoming Mr. Night. If failure was total, there was no point in waiting for the inevitable punitive measures that would follow. He'd tried to intimidate Mr. Night once before, and that had ended up badly. This time he would not be posturing but fighting for his life, however. It was probably futile; the man in the black suit could read his thoughts and would be ready for his attack, but it was better to go down fighting than to meekly await his fate.

"Lost? Not at all, my murderous cherubim," Mr. Night replied before Archangel could act. The words stilled any thought of action, for the time being, at least. "My adversary is sure to try to induct his precious little girl into the mysteries of the Source," the strange man in black continued. "He will take her somewhere he deems safe, of course, but the process will create a very powerful energy signature. I will be able to locate it and take us to them. Then you will have your chance to redeem yourself, dear boy. You may even have a go at the faceless freak you want to slaughter so badly."

Archangel had learned that his deepest thoughts and emotions were like an open book to Mr. Night, for all of his training in countering such forms of mental intrusion. This time he didn't care. The chance to fulfill his promise to the dead witch made him surprisingly eager to do Mr. Night's bidding. "What do I need to do?"

"The very words I wanted to hear. Splendid! Let me go gather our lovelorn couple: the Bear and the deadly lady have just completed renewing their carnal acquaintance and are cleaning up. Their experience at the hands of Cassandra was a bit harrowing for them, the poor things." Mr. Night's smile didn't change, but something seemed to shift behind his sunglasses. "Ah, Cassandra. If I only I'd dealt with you when we first met." Mr. Night left the room, leaving Archangel alone with his thoughts.

Two weeks ago he had been in the court of the Iron Tsar, as content as one can be in a den of snakes where courtiers and favorites jockeyed for position and despised him for being a Russian parvenu. He had made his place there by strength and cunning, and he had no further ambitions beyond enjoying himself as much as he could while safeguarding his position. This assignment had changed everything.

* * *

Archangel answered the summons and arrived promptly to the Golden Spire, the 850-meter tall structure that dominated Kiev's skyline and served as the Tsar's home. On the lengthy lift ride up, flanked by two motionless Automaton guards, he forced himself not to think about what awaited him above. The Tsar rarely gave personal audiences. Most of his interactions with the Dominion's monarch had been ceremonial: state dinners, parades, and special celebrations. Archangel was not a member of the court's inner circle, and he never expected that to change. An ethnic Russian – or a German, Pole, Rumanian or Jew for that matter, for all that they made up a large proportion of the Dominion's population – could only advance so far at court, with very few exceptions. This meeting was an unusual event.

Archangel retained his impassive demeanor and spent some time looking at himself in the gold-framed mirror on one of the lift's walls. Not a hair out of place, his ghostly-pale persona intact. Good. Style was substance in the world of living legends and demigods. Whether this unusual meeting presented a danger or an opportunity, he would face it looking his best.

The lift's doors opened, revealing the Wall of Enemies, a honeycomb of glass-covered cases containing thirteen severed heads in a pyramidal arrangement. Pride of place was given to two heads: Nikita Khrushchev's and Stepan Bandera's. Khrushchev, the Ukrainian Communist Party leader, had been killed by the Iron Tsar's own hand in 1940, an act of open defiance to Stalin and part of the campaign to avenge Russian crimes against the Ukrainian people, a campaign that continued to this day. Stepan Bandera, the former leader of the largest Ukrainian nationalist group on the eve of the Great Patriotic War, had died for the crime of being in the way of the Iron Tsar's ambitions.

The other eleven heads changed from one year to the next, as new enemies were executed and put on display. The replaced trophies were in a museum-like room a lower level; the last time Archangel had bothered to check the Gallery of Enemies had contained ninety-seven heads. He noticed a couple of new faces at the bottom of the triangle: a Russian general caught plotting against the Dominion and a young woman, the former leader of a pro-democracy movement. She was fairly attractive. It was a pity she had chosen to become an enemy of the Throne.

Other, less gruesome trophies lined the walls of the crimson-carpeted corridors leading to the audience chamber. He walked past several historical art pieces, including portraits and busts of Vladimir the Great, Saint Olga, Yaroslav the Wise and many other rulers and heroes of Ukraine's past. A modern painting depicted the Iron Tsar accepting the surrender of Soviet general Zhukov in 1944. The look on Zhukov's face was that of a man trying to wake up from a terrible nightmare. Archangel could sympathize. The world had been living in a terrible nightmare since the New Olympians had become the masters of the planet. In such a state of affairs, of course, it paid to be one of the nightmarish beings rather than their victims.

A sliding steel door at the end of the corridor opened, revealing the audience hall. Blue-and-yellow flags unfurled on every wall in between windows that looked down on the city and the Dnieper River. The floor was gold-rimmed marble, with purple-and-gold carpets stretching towards the gilded throne. The ruler of Ukraine sat casually on the golden throne, his consort sitting on his lap.

The Iron Tsar was a tall man wearing a dress military uniform with the tabs and insignia of High Marshall. His face and head were covered by an iron and bronze great helm, a medieval design that completely covered its wearer's face except for a thin eye slit. The stories and rumors about the helmet were legion. He had never been seen without it. Some claimed the helmet was permanently affixed to his head, and to remove it would mean his death. Others thought it concealed some horrible deformity or injury and that is was vanity that kept his features forever hidden behind the metal mask. Or maybe the helmet helped contain his godlike power, acting as a safety valve to keep the Tsar from obliterating his surroundings with his mere presence.

Archangel did not know whether any of the rumors were true, or care overmuch. All he knew was that the few times he'd been close enough to look into the Tsar's eye slit, a red glowing light had been shining within. Whatever lay behind the metal mask was no longer human, he was sure of it. That would have bothered Archangel if it were not for the fact he was no longer human as well.

Archangel was one of the most powerful beings on the planet, a 3.1 in the PAS system, but the Tsar's mere presence humbled him. There was an unmistakable aura of power and confidence around the man. After meeting the ruler of the Dominion in person, nobody had to wonder why entire Soviet Army Groups had surrendered and switched their allegiance to him.

In addition to the platoon of Automatons standing guard along the walls, there were two other people in the audience room. Baba Yaga was embracing the Tsar and smiling languidly. The Witch of the Pripet Marshes was in her more pleasant guise: she appeared to be a beautiful young woman with long black hair and flashing blue eyes, wearing a diaphanous purple gown. Archangel knew her other two shapes were far less lovely; she could look like a hideous crone when she so wished, and in combat she became something utterly monstrous, a misshapen chimera of animal and human body parts. Only a madman or a god would consider taking such a being to his bed. She was the Tsar's consort and chief adviser, and men would suffer and die by her whim, with no regard to their station and rank.

A short distance from the throne stood a fat man with an oversized head and squinting mismatched eyes, one far bigger than the other, clad in the green tunic of the Ukrainian Science Corps. Archangel barely avoided an angry sneer at the sight. The Mind was a German, one of only two foreigners in the Tsar's inner circle. The obese Neolympian had defected to the Ukraine shortly after murdering Hitler, knowing his life was forfeit if the Allies captured him. It was a pity he was so useful and that he had managed to ingratiate himself into the Tsar's confidence over the decades. His presence at the meeting was not reassuring; the Mind's schemes and devices were always brilliant and they almost always worked flawlessly, but when they went wrong they did so spectacularly.

One of the Automatons announced Archangel as he walked in, stopped at the requisite fifteen steps from the throne and went down on one knee, bowing deeply as protocol demanded.

"No need for formality, Feodor Igorovich," the Iron Tsar said. His voice sounded perfectly normal, even pleasant, nothing like the reverberating metallic tone he used when trying to intimidate others. "There's important work to be done, and you're just the man for the job."

"You do me honor, my lord," Archangel replied, using the informal form of address as ordered.

"I have forged an alliance of convenience with an American, an artificer of some skill," the Tsar explained. "You will bring some special equipment to him – to his underlings, rather – and will assist him in any way he requires. You will also supervise the shipment of some new devices to our people in America."

"As you command, my lord."

"The Mind will provide you with the details," the Tsar added, gesturing towards the German.

"If I may, my lord?" the Mind said in badly accented Ukrainian. At the Tsar's nod, he went on. "The equipment will be loaded in two containers. One is to be delivered to the American's agents in New York. The other is to be distributed among our men in New York and Chicago. Everything must go according to plan. We are on the verge of a momentous event. Soon we will have access to the Source!"

"No need to bore Archangel with the details," the Tsar said mildly, and the Mind shut his mouth, looking guilty. Archangel wondered what the Source was, but realized the German had already said more than the Tsar wanted him to hear. Something important, obviously.

Baba Yaga rose to her feet and walked sinuously towards him. Archangel watched her coldly as she approached. Her beauty did not affect him much; it would not have even if he didn't know what lay beneath it. He preferred his women to be properly subservient, and her wanton expression and smug smile only made him want to beat her until they were gone from her face. That was not an option here, of course, even if they were not at court. Baba Yaga's power level was unknown, but she had always bested him every time they had sparred. She was a trickster and deceiver, an expert at finding one's weak spots and striking at them.

Baba Yaga embraced him and pressed a cold cheek against his. "I made you a little gift, Archangel," she whispered in his ear. As she disentangled herself from him, she placed something heavy and metallic on his hand. It was a metal bracelet. "An amulet of sorts," she explained. "Keep it close, and it will serve you well."

"Thank you, my lady," he said politely.

"Consider her gift as a reminder of the importance of this mission," the Tsar said as Baba Yaga returned to his side. "Failure cannot be countenanced. Do you understand, Archangel?"

"I do." But he hadn't, not until much later.

* * *

Archangel looked up and saw Mr. Night walking back into the office, Medved and Lady Shi behind him. The killers were fully attired for battle. The Bear had replaced his street clothes with a black jumpsuit, metal gauntlets that left his clawed fingers uncovered, and heavy metal-banded boots. Lady Shi was wearing a one piece black bodysuit that left her arms and legs bare, accentuated by a golden belt, vambraces and boots. Her hair was gathered in a tight topknot. Archangel smiled. If this was to be their final battle, at least they would enter it in the full panoply and pageantry expected of the gods of the twenty-first century.

"Now we wait," Mr. Night said. "The Lurker and his daughter will be reunited soon, if they haven't already. He will try to initiate her into the mysteries of the Source."

His twisted smile grew wider. "And that's when we will strike."

C.J. Carella

The Freedom Legion

Hong Kong, Republic of China, March 15, 2013

Chastity Baal smiled pleasantly at her quarry.

"You have exquisite taste," she said in Cantonese before taking a sip of the rather nice vintage her host had poured for them before taking their conversation to a more intimate venue.

Kuo Wei-Fang smiled back. "I merely appreciate beauty in all its forms," he replied. "That is why I could not refuse you an audience."

Kuo was officially a prominent and quite legitimate financier and industrialist whose contacts with the Republic of China had helped usher a new age of prosperity for Hong Kong after the British handover in 1997. Unofficially, he also ran a large smuggling network between the Dragon Empire and the rest of the world, bringing proscribed items into the Empire in exchange for assorted illegal goods produced there. The smuggling network generated enormous revenues which were in turn skillfully laundered through his legitimate business operations.

Chastity had met Kuo in his sanctum sanctorum, a three-level penthouse on an eighty-story skyscraper that provided a god's eye view of the burgeoning city below. The ten floors below the penthouse were occupied by offices where a small army of managers worked on the many enterprises that made up the overt face of the Kuo commercial empire. Kuo himself had two sprawling mansions in the city, but he spent most of his days here, overseeing his business concerns and receiving worthy visitors, like a well-known international adventurer who had contacted him with an intriguing business offer.

The penthouse was as opulent as one would expect, combining modern conveniences with ornaments that would have befitted a mandarin or emperor. Artifacts from various dynasties – including a pair of imposing terracotta soldiers placed on each side of the entryway to the formal dining room – shared space with the latest creations of the best designers and artists from Shanghai and Beijing. Chastity noted that everything in the palatial penthouse seemed to come from China, from Kuo's perfectly tailored suit down to the smallest fixtures. "Thank you once again for your hospitality," she told her host.

"It is the least I could do," Kuo said as they strolled through the penthouse. He was a tall and handsome man in his mid-fifties, brimming with charisma and arrogance. "When I heard the notorious Chastity Baal was acting as a go-between for an international cartel wishing to conduct some discreet business with the Empire, I could not resist. Even if we cannot do business, perhaps we can still have an enjoyable evening."

Chastity's smile widened, suggesting the financier's hopes were not unfounded. "That would be most entertaining, I'm sure. But business first, yes?"

"As you wish," Kuo said. "What is it your partners have in mind?"

Chastity started her spiel, a purely contrived scheme to provide technical services to the Empire in return for trading concessions, some of them of dubious legality. Even as she spoke, the highly sophisticated sensors built into her contact lenses conducted a thorough scan of Kuo's home. The penthouse was protected from outside intrusions by a very sophisticated security system. Once inside, however, Chastity was quickly able to detect several hidden compartments built into the penthouse. One of them had a computer that had no physical or wireless links to any networks. That would be the device Kuo used to record his illicit dealings, and that's where the information she needed would be stored.

Kuo asked her several shrewd questions. Chastity answered them without missing a beat even as she mentally commanded her wrist-comp to initiate a covert invasion of Kuo's system. It was difficult to carry out a conversation while at the same time directing a computer raid through a neural interface, but Chastity was well-versed in multi-tasking. Kuo, determined to charm and impress her into his bed, was blissfully unaware that she was peeling away layers of electronic security and learning his darkest secrets while she flirted with him.

"Your offer is highly tempting, especially if I've guessed correctly as to the identities of your silent partners," Kuo finally said. "I will consider it carefully. I hope we now can turn towards more pleasing matters."

"I regret to inform you that will not be the case," Chastity said. The last of Kuo's private files had been downloaded into her wrist-comp. She mentally sent a signal to the awaiting Chinese Secret Police and her fellow Legionnaires. "Acting on information provided by an Imperial defector, the Chinese authorities have issued an order for your arrest. I suggest you come along peacefully."

"You have made a grave mistake," Kuo said, his friendly expression vanishing. "You and the foreign devils that have divided and enslaved the Middle Kingdom for far too long." His eyes started to glow, and Chastity's widened in surprise. Kuo was a normal human; his dossier had included detailed medical records.

He was certainly not a normal human anymore. He moved with unnatural speed, and Chastity barely ducked under a high kick that drove his foot through one of the bedroom walls. She rolled away and hoped her backup would arrive in time. They had expected Kuo might try to escape and possibly summon armed bodyguards. Nobody had expected this.

Gunfire and the sharper report of energy discharges erupted outside the apartment. Her backup had run into Kuo's guards. She rolled away from a stamping kick that smashed a hole through the penthouse's floor. Kuo came relentlessly after her. His files mentioned he was a martial arts aficionado, but he clearly was not used to his newfound strength and speed. His attacks were slightly off-balance. Chastity dodged another kick and landed a punch before the magnate could retreat. Kuo flew off his feet under the impact and crashed into a wall hard enough to embed himself into it. Daedalus' words came back to her: the dagger had indeed transferred some of the dead Celestial's power to her.

Kuo forced his way through the wall's wreckage. He casually ripped off the expensive suit jacket and silk shirt off his chest, revealing an Imperial Sigil. The mark on Chastity's hand tingled as if in recognition. She blocked a kick and used her grip on Kuo's leg to flip him face-first onto the floor. She stamped on his unprotected neck as he struggled in her grip, but the lethal attack did no apparent damage. Kuo twisted around and kicked at her, knocking her away. The blow should have killed her instantly. As it was, it left her bruised and winded. The two combatants leaped back to their feet.

Reluctantly, she considered reaching for the dagger in the hidden sheath strapped to her upper thigh. The mark on her hand started tingling as soon as the thought crossed her mind, and she felt something akin to lust surging through her. A part of her wanted to wield the dagger, to feel it cut into Kuo's flesh and drink his life and power. Her hand started moving towards the weapon.

The penthouse's front door exploded inwards and Swift and Chasca rushed into the bedroom. Swift smashed into Kuo like a humanoid missile; the two crashed through a wall. Chastity stopped reaching towards the dagger with a feeling of relief.

"Are you all right?" asked Chasca.

Chastity nodded. "I'm fine. Go help Swift, he might need…"

Swift's unconscious body shot through the walls of the penthouse, disappearing into the night. A second later, Kuo soared past them and flew away from the skyscraper.

"On it," Chasca called and darted after Kuo.

Chastity could not follow – or could she? What other powers had she stolen from the Celestial? She would have to find out sometime soon. For now, however, she would leave the chase to the other Legionnaires.

She did not trust her new powers. She did not trust herself.

* * *

Olivia O'Brien saw Larry's limp body falling off the skyscraper, but resisted the urge to go and help him. Other Legionnaires would rescue him. Olivia needed to deal with the developing situation, not worry about her husband. Once again, the Legion had been caught flat-footed, and she was getting sick and tired of it.

Things rarely went according to plan: the opposition always had its own plan, after all. Still, the Legion rarely got blindsided so badly. After being briefed on the situation, she had organized a team to back up Chastity Baal as she tried to extract information from Kuo Wei-Fang. They had expected the possibility Kuo would call out armed guards and possibly Neo mercenaries. The smuggler's display of superhuman abilities had been wholly unexpected.

Olivia wasn't one hundred percent sure the defector's allegations were true – Chastity Baal's misgivings had been persuasive, despite the antipathy Olivia felt towards the spy – but there was enough damning proof to get the Republic of China to issue arrest warrants for one of its most prominent citizens. The Legion had hoped Chastity would persuade Kuo to give up and cooperate, but now they would have to arrest the man and try to scare him into giving up more information.

Olivia altered her flight path to join in the aerial chase over Hong Kong. Kuo was flying at high speed, with Chasca not far behind. As she caught up to them, Olivia saw Chasca fire several powerful light blasts at their quarry. He dodged some of them, but was hit twice. Both times, the light bolts dissipated in a coruscating energy release, leaving the man apparently unharmed, although his flight trajectory wavered a little under the attacks. The financier and smuggler was not just a Neolympian but a very powerful one. Few beings could survive Chasca's energy attacks.

She closed into range and hurled a flame spear towards him. The financier had been too distracted with Chasca's attacks to notice Olivia's approach. The spear struck Kuo squarely in the back but the fiery impact did not seem to damage him any more than Chasca's sun rays. The smuggler's naked torso gleamed with sinuous glowing symbols shining brightly in the evening's growing darkness. Olivia recognized them at once: they were Imperial Sigils, the marks of a Celestial Warrior.

The Emperor had long claimed to have the power to create Neolympians. The spectacle of a middle-age businessman flying through the air and shrugging off attacks that would have obliterated a tank confirmed those claims. The implications of finding a Celestial involved in supplying the attack on the Legion were terrifying. The war the Legion's Council had been blithely discussing mere hours before had just become nearly inevitable.

"To all units: converge on my position," Chasca called through her communication implants as she kept up a barrage of energy discharges. Olivia did so as well, striking the fleeing smuggler again and again. The impacts were beginning to tell; Kuo's flying became erratic and wavering. The chase had led them away from the city and over the surrounding sea, which thankfully would reduce the chances of collateral damage. She was thankful for that; subduing someone with Kuo's powers would take a great deal of force, and she didn't want innocent civilians anywhere near the upcoming fight.

Twinkling points of light over the horizon grew closer and resolved into man-sized figures flying straight at Kuo and his pursuers.

The enemy had plans of his own.

* * *

Isabel Quispe, code name Chasca, was angry.

Anger was a natural emotion for a woman of color in Peru, where the social divide between whites and the *cholos* – the Quechua Indians that made up much of the country's lower classes – ran deep. Things had changed a great deal over her lifetime, but she still seethed when remembering the genial contempt she had endured as a *cholita*, a little Indian girl good for nothing more than cleaning the houses of her betters, and that under supervision, because everyone knew that *cholos* would steal anything not nailed down if they were not watched closely.

She would have ended her days as just another anonymous brown face if not for the random chance that turned her into a demigod. The more superstitious among her people believed she truly was the reincarnation of the goddess Chasca, Lady of Dawn and Twilight, protector of virgin girls. In reality, her code name was a bitter joke. Her own virginity had been gone before her Neo powers manifested themselves, taken by a family friend who had caught her alone one day. She had never told anybody about the rape, nursing her rage and hatred in private. Even the possibility of vengeance had been taken from her: the family friend had died in a drunken car crash months before her ascension. Those *cholos*, you can't trust them with liquor, either.

Anger had driven her even as she became the darling of the press, the heroine who had winkled out gangs of bandits in the Andes, death cults in the Amazon, and helped defeat international criminal Hiram Hades, although it had been the *yanqui* demigod Ultimate who had finished off the villain. Ultimate had sponsored her entry into the Legion, but whatever gratitude she had felt had been tainted with frustration and rage. Look at the nice *cholita*. Let's make her an honorary member of the Legion of White Aristocrats. She had used her position to fight for the rights of the poor and oppressed, and to stamp out the racist and paternalistic tendencies within the Legion itself, but she had never been satisfied, never felt content or happy. Despite all her achievements, Isabel often wondered if her rise to the ranks of the Legion Council had been another pat on the head rather than a reward she truly deserved. Those doubts only made her angrier.

The pursuit of the rich Chinaman was stoking her anger in a way the attack on the Legion had not. The Legion *should* inspire hatred: privileged genetic aristocrats looking down their noses at the rest of humanity deserved whatever they got. The fact that she was one of them did not affect her judgment. But to find out the attack had been engineered by yet another elite – a billionaire who had never done a day's honest work in his life and had enriched himself by exploiting millions of oppressed workers – was infuriating. The attack had not been a blow for freedom, just part of a power struggle between two oligarchies. She would make that filthy capitalist pay for his crimes and for confirming her worst suspicions about the state of the world.

Chasca pushed her powers and unleashed a much stronger blast of concentrated photons. Kuo thought he could take it; let's see how the *puerco* liked this! She struck dead on, and Kuo's defenses nearly broke under the onslaught. Soon he would fall.

She was too intent on finishing off the capitalist to notice new enemies had arrived.

The newcomers were wearing some sort of powered armor with rocket packs for propulsion. They opened fire on her just as Artemis shouted a warning through their communication system. Belatedly, Chasca went into evasive maneuvers. The attackers were using Imperial fire lances, artifacts that lobbed balls of plasma at bullet speeds. She dodged all but one of them; the single hit did not pierce her protective aura. Those attacks had been a decoy, however. A twisting stream of purple-hued energy reached out to her, changing its trajectory when she tried to evade it and reaching for her like a living thing. The energy tendril broke through her defenses as if they didn't exist. Excruciating agony paralyzed her. No longer held aloft by her will, her powers stripped away, she began to fall.

Isabel Quispe was no coward. She glared hatred at the armored figures as they leveled their weapons at her.

Chasca died snarling her defiance.

* * *

This was shaping up to be a really bad day.

The awkward silence on the flight to Hong Kong seemed to confirm Larry Graham's worst fears. Olivia knew. He'd been too much of a pansy to try to talk to her about it, however. As it turned out he would rather not know for sure: doubt was better than certainty when certainty meant the love of your life thought – no, *knew* – that you were a cheating, lying son of a bitch.

To make things worse, Chastity Baal was the Legion's point woman in the operation to discover how somebody had managed to smuggle out a flying carrier from the planet's most notorious rogue nation. Did Olivia know about his fling with Chastity? Larry couldn't tell: his wife had been downright grim the entire night, which could mean nothing or everything.

The operation to get information from Kuo Wei-Fang had turned into a fiasco. Larry had tried to subdue the financier and had gotten knocked into next week for his troubles. Luckily a telekinetic operative of the Chinese Secret Service had caught him before he could land on someone or something important. By the time he had woken up, the fight with Kuo had gone aerial. Larry had hurried up to join the fray.

Running on air was a pain. His ability to go out of phase had to be fine-tuned to let him grip air molecules and use them as a surface to run on. He had no idea how he did it, and neither did anyone else, although there plenty of theories that made for entertaining bull sessions. When he ran while intangible on the ground, he only needed to hold on to solid molecules on the ground or other solid surfaces. It took a great deal more concentration to do so in the air, and the effort translated into overall lower speeds and bursts of agony when the occasional errant nitrogen or oxygen molecule passed through his semi-tangible body, inflicting painful albeit short-lived injuries. He'd learned to grin and bear it, but it was no fun.

He had the feeling that no fun was just what the foreseeable future had in store for him.

Larry caught up with the action somewhere over Deep Water Bay. He arrived just in time to see Chasca torn apart by plasma fire from the armored fliers that had joined the fight. Olivia exploded one of the fliers with a fire spear just before being hit by a strange energy attack, a fluid, tentacle-like stream of purple-black light that he'd never seen before. Olivia's flame aura disappeared and she fell limply through the air. She would end up like Chasca if he didn't move quickly.

Only two of the armored attackers wielded the unusual energy weapons; he went after them first. Larry accelerated towards the closest one, ignoring the pain, and became solid long enough to ram into him at supersonic speeds. Larry felt the impact distantly; he knew he'd shattered the suit of armor and the human being inside, but all he cared about was going back out of phase to correct his course and hit the next target.

If the power armor pilots had been Neos, they would have had the reflexes to track and hit him before he could turn back towards them. They weren't and they could not react in time to deal with him, although the bastard with the strange beam weapon came close. The energy stream twisted around as if it was alive and almost hit him. *Close but no cigar. Better luck next time, buddy*, Larry thought coldly before he smashed into the shooter and turned him into a mix of metal confetti and meat puree.

The surviving three fliers engaged him with their fire lances. A direct hit burned him painfully – his intangible state did not protect him against some forms of energy attack – but inflicted no permanent damage. He wiped them out in a few seconds. It turned out to be a few seconds too long: by the time he was done, Kuo was nowhere to be found. The son of a bitch had gotten away. The other Legionnaires just arriving to the area would have to look for him; Larry needed to look after his wife.

Olivia's emergency beacon still worked. He found her bobbing unconscious in the water. Alive. He could breathe again. The thought of losing her was more than he could bear.

Why are you driving her away, then? He had no answers.

C.J. Carella

The Invincible Man

Chicago, Illinois, March 14, 2013

John Clarke wanted to sit down, cradle his head in his hands, and close his eyes for a few moments.

He couldn't do that, of course. Not in front of others, especially not in front of other Neolympians. The Invincible Man couldn't show weakness. He stood up straight, towering over most of the gathering, and watched the Lurker and his daughter's rather awkward reunion while trying to make sense of it all.

The encounter with the Lurker had been a shock. John had not seen the vigilante in decades; the two of them had run in very different circles after the war. The man in the gas mask had never been a pleasant fellow on his best day, and he clearly had not improved with age. After his own brush with madness, John found the obvious instability of the Lurker profoundly disturbing, especially when combined with the powers the mystery man had demonstrated. He was certainly not the kind of ally John would have chosen.

He considered the other members of the gathering. Condor was a talented crime fighter and he'd worked with the Legion on several occasions, even though he was technically an 'illegal.' Face-Off and Kestrel had been linked to a number of murders and disappearances around New York City, although not enough evidence to press charges had ever been found. The alleged victims had all been hardened criminals, and the authorities hadn't pursued those cases very vigorously. Neos who wantonly murdered innocents were a priority for law-enforcement; relatively discreet vigilantes like those three were relatively safe from prosecution.

From Face-Off's body language, he'd expected John to start reading him his rights. Or perhaps he was still bothered by the sight of Christine in John's arms. The crime fighter might not have a face, but his body language clearly showed he felt protective – and possessive – towards the girl.

The girl... She'd made quite an impression on John. But there was no time for that at the moment.

The Lurker hadn't said anything after Christine's initial greeting. He seemed to be deep in thought. Christine turned to Face-Off. "Okay, can *you* tell me what happened? Dad's gone to his happy place, apparently."

"We got grabbed by the Russkies. The Lurker showed up and rescued us."

"I guess we're doing the Cliff Notes version," Christine grumbled. "Me, I learned how to fly, despite not having been given any flying lessons, thank you so very much for that, got lost in Chicago, got mugged, sort of, and then the local superheroes tried to arrest me."

"Yeah, I saw you on the news. You were kicking ass and taking names," Face-Off said and Christine smiled. "You too," he added, nodding towards John.

"Oh, yeah," Christine said, looking uncomfortable. "When that masked guy..."

"The Dreamer," John said.

"The Dreaming Dude, when he took over your mind, he used you to smack down the other guys."

Condor pushed a button and a replay from an earlier news report came on one of the screens. "We can now confirm that Ultimate the Invincible Man has attacked the Chicago Sentinels. This is exclusive footage from an eyewitness' Goggle-Cam." The viewpoint switched to a wavering view of a street. A silver and red streak moved past. It was replayed in slow motion: John had never seen that manic leer disfiguring his face before, but the face itself was perfectly familiar and recognizable.

Whoever was behind this had played his cards all too well. John was already under suspicion after his erratic behavior in the past several months. Now he had publicly attacked a renowned hero group. He could go back to Legion HQ and try to explain himself, but who could he trust? None of this could have happened without the connivance of someone inside the Legion. Kenneth Slaughter had recommended Doctor Cohen. Had he been duped? Could he be under a similar form of mind control? Or was he a conspirator? Going to the Legion was too much of a risk.

John had felt alone before, but he belatedly realized how petulant and childish he had been. This was what being alone was like. Before this madness had begun he had been one of the leaders of an international organization, a man with dozens of friends and hundreds of associates, all of whom would risk their lives for him, as he would for them. And he'd dared to feel alone? Alone was not daring to contact any of his friends out of fear they would be targeted by the traitors in the Legion – or that they would be traitors themselves. He could trust no one.

John couldn't even trust himself. He forced himself to speak. "I think I've been under some form of mental attack for some time now," he told the gathering of vigilantes. "Christine helped me break free, but I don't know if that's a permanent situation."

"You're still a puppet, man of metal," the Lurker said, and chuckled. "They sank their hooks into you, sank them deep."

"Dad!" Christine said. "Could you cut down on the creepy and be a little more helpful? Please?"

The mystery man stood silent for a moment before speaking again. "It's hard holding on to things. You start slipping away, and then all you can do is laugh."

"I said *helpful*, Dad."

"Help. Yes, help's on the way." The Lurker walked towards John. "I can help. Who sees the darkness in all men's souls?"

"The Lurker does!" Kestrel shouted. Condor covered her mouth with both hands, but the Lurker did not seem to hear. All his attention was on John.

"One does not bring down a god in a day," the cloaked man muttered. "Baby steps, little traps, little tricks. Little hooks for a big fish." He reached up towards John's face. John let him. The Lurker's gloved fingers touched the sides of his head.

There was a brief flash of pain. John blinked. The Lurker was holding John's cochlear implants, the communicators everyone in the Legion was issued. The old vigilante had ripped out his implants, somehow bypassing John's near-impregnable protective field without any apparent effort. The implications were disturbing.

"Do you see?" The Lurker turned to Christine and was showed her the bloodied implants.

She squinted for a second. "Yeah, I can see some swirling energy thingy around them. It's like those energy streams the Russians used on us."

"Yes!" The Lurker's tone was triumphant. "You can see the truth. That's why they want you. That's why you're here." He turned back towards John. "You are not free and clear, Invincible Man, but this will help. These are the hooks they put into you. They could whisper things into your ear. Make you remember things. Make you relive them. Make you dream. Listen to you." The Lurker made a fist and crushed the transmitters. "They can find you through them. They know where we are."

"We'd better get the hell out of here, then," Condor said.

"Yes," the Lurker agreed. He concentrated, and his cloak stretched and flowed out, enveloping them in darkness yet again. When they emerged from it, they were still in the Condor Jet, but the aircraft was listing slightly to the left. The ship was no longer in a warehouse in Chicago. "This is my island," the Lurker said. "Come on in, the water's fine. We can talk and plot."

Talk and plot indeed. John followed his newfound allies out of the craft.

Chapter Twenty

The Freedom Legion

Atlantic Headquarters, March 14, 2013

Kenneth Slaughter walked into the Legion's main communication room, where Daedalus Smith, Hyperia and Meteor were already gathered. Meteor had flown to the Atlantic Headquarters to serve as a replacement for Swift and Artemis. If someone tried to attack Freedom Island again, they might need his help. Under the current circumstances, they might need more help than was available.

A dozen communication technicians sat behind large screens covering one third of the oval room. Kenneth nodded to one of them, and the comm call Kenneth had received minutes ago was transferred to the largest central screen, revealing the battered face of Doctor Cohen.

"You're on, Doctor," Kenneth said. "Please repeat what you just told me."

"It's Ultimate," Cohen said anxiously. "I'm afraid he has suffered a psychotic break of some sort. He didn't exactly attack me – I wouldn't be alive otherwise – but he rushed past me as if he didn't see me, and I was slammed me into a wall and knocked unconscious for some time. He was talking about a plot against him from within the Legion's ranks. He specifically blamed you, Doctor Slaughter, but he appeared to blame most of the Legion as well."

"To that we can add the reports that Ultimate attacked the Chicago Sentinels for unknown reasons," Hyperia said, her dark blue eyes bright with concern. She absently played with her jet black hair as she continued her report. "They were subduing a rogue Neolympian when he struck them down and carried her away, also for unknown reasons. The Sentinels suffered minor injuries, except for Devolution Man, who had to be hospitalized."

"I am extremely worried," Doctor Cohen continued. "If he has been consumed by paranoid delusions, it may be nearly impossible to reason with him."

"Thank you for your help, Doctor Cohen," Kenneth said. "We will be in touch." The therapist's face was replaced on the screen by a replay of Ultimate's attack on the Sentinels. Ultimate's expression in the news footage was wholly alien to the man Kenneth knew. That raised his suspicions. Could John change so much, so quickly? Or was there another factor in play?

"I'm going to go out on a limb and say this isn't good at all," Daedalus said with his usual flippancy. Kenneth knew that his counterpart used humor as a tension reliever, but it still never failed to irritate him.

"Ultimate's gone bloody barking mad," Meteor said, with more than a hint of schadenfreude in his tone. "And you don't look very much surprised, Doc," he added, glaring accusingly at Kenneth.

Feeling like he was betraying John's confidence, Kenneth spoke. "Some of us have noticed that John seemed to be suffering from some emotional problems. Nobody had any inkling things were so bad, let alone that he could become a danger to others. I still find it hard to believe."

"He seems to be dangerous enough. He stomped on the Chicago Sentinels pretty good," Daedalus said. "Of course, none of them is rated higher than 2.8. They never had a chance against him."

"Do *we* have a chance of stopping him, if it comes to that?" Hyperia asked. In many ways she was Ultimate's female counterpart, immensely strong and nearly impervious to injury. However, she had always come a distant second to John in terms of raw power. Kenneth found the PAS system deeply flawed, a facile and largely inaccurate attempt to quantify parahuman powers, but the numbers provided an easy point of reference. Ultimate's number was 3.6. Hyperia was a 3.2. Four 'points' did not seem like a lot until one understood that each point represented a large increase in power. John was three times more powerful than Hyperia by most measures. "Can we take down Ultimate?"

"That's the sixty-four thousand quid question, isn't it?" Meteor said sourly. His one fight with Ultimate had not gone well. "We could bury him in bodies, if it comes to that, but we'll lose more people than we did on yesterday's attacks. Many more."

"I've been making some tweaks to my Myrmidon Armor," Daedalus said. "I think I might surprise dear old Johnny if he's really flipped out. And we can reactivate Janus and get him here PDQ; he can probably take down Ultimate all by his lonesome. Even then, it's not going to be a walk in the park."

"We'll have to find Ultimate first," Kenneth said. "His communication implant went dead a few minutes ago, somewhere in the Chicago metro area. He had flown all the way to the Pennsylvania-New York border before reappearing in Chicago an instant later."

"I didn't know Ultimate could teleport," Daedalus commented. He was listening to something via his comm implant even as he spoke.

"As far as I know, he cannot. We do not have enough information. In any case, if we must confront him, we need to do it as far from populated areas as possible, or we risk a humanitarian crisis of unprecedented proportions."

"Speaking of humanitarian crisis," Daedalus broke in. "I just got news from the Pacific branch. Plenty of news and it's all bad."

Kenneth's expression remained impassive, belying the turmoil within. Too many things were going wrong at the same time. Suspiciously so. He listened to the initial reports coming from Hong Kong. Chasca, a Councilor and one of the most respected leaders of the Legion, was dead, killed by weapon that could apparently neutralize parahuman powers. Artemis had been severely injured as well. The investigation had revealed more evidence that the Dragon Empire had been responsible or at least complicit in the attack on the Legion. War with the Empire was becoming more likely by the moment.

"We need to prepare for the worst," Kenneth said. He was the current team leader, a rotating position that would have gone to Ultimate the following month, ironically enough. "Daedalus, please take Hyperia and Meteor and any other active members you need and prepare a plan to subdue Ultimate should it become necessary. I want to emphasize we must attempt to communicate with Ultimate before taking any hostile actions. This could still be a misunderstanding or some form of deception."

"Sure thing, Fearless Leader," Daedalus replied. "Trust me, the last thing I want to do is to go *mano a mano* with ol' Shiva Incarnate. By the way, when are you going to call the President? I hope he didn't have any plans for the weekend, 'cause he's gonna be busy."

"Why should we contact the US President directly? We're not a US appendage, much as the newspapers like to pretend we are," Meteor broke in.

"Sure, matey," Daedalus said mockingly. "But who else are we going to call? The UN doesn't exactly have a hot line. Someone's got to call an emergency meeting of the Security Council. It's probably a good idea if it's not the Legion doing it. Do you want the media accusing us of instigating the Third Asian War? And our most famous Legionnaire just wiped the floor with a licensed super-team on American soil. We have to get in touch with the White House, pronto."

"Daedalus is right," Kenneth said, forestalling Meteor's angry response. "I will contact the White House and offer to brief the President or anybody he chooses to speak to me."

"Better you than me, Doc." Daedalus said; he and US President Colletta did not get along. Daedalus' unwavering support of the Republican Party and his efforts to strangle the Reform Party in its cradle had a lot to do with their mutual dislike. Unlike his fellow inventor, Kenneth had made a point of remaining thoroughly apolitical throughout his career, which was very helpful whenever he had to deal with the US government. The choice of messenger would not make these particular news any more palatable, of course.

Everybody went off to play their roles. Kenneth could not help feeling those roles had been scripted in advance by someone else, and that whoever was doing so was no friend of the Legion, or the world.

Hunters and Hunted

New York City, New York, March 14, 2013

The fateful moment was near.

Mr. Night could sense something momentous was nearly at hand, an event so powerful it was creating echoes through the fabric of time itself. His ability to peer into the future was limited at the best of times, but he could feel the appointed time's presence like a sudden variation of pressure announcing the imminent arrival of a powerful storm. Every precognitive Neolympian in the planet must be convulsing and foaming at the mouth, overcome by visions forecasting the end of everything they held dear.

That normally pleasant image did little to amuse Mr. Night. The girl was too close to becoming the ruination of all his plans. Her capture would make the foreordained end of humanity a certainty. Her death would make for an acceptable alternative outcome, delaying the inevitable but only for a relatively short time. But if she escaped, if she was allowed to roam free and learn, everything he had worked for could be ruined.

Mr. Night looked at his henchmen with a critical eye. Medved was sitting on a couch that visibly sagged under his weight, with the Lady Shi curled in his arms like a kitten and whispering sweet nothings into his ear. Archangel was behind his desk, lost in thought. They were ready for action, relaxing as experienced warriors do, turning their minds away from the possibility of death and getting what rest they could. They were a formidable trio, but Mr. Night was not sure they were up to the task.

The girl had somehow gathered several champions along the way, including Ultimate himself. The murderous misfits at Mr. Night's disposal were powerful and capable, but he didn't think they were up to the task. Mr. Night expected to have his own hands full with his old friend Damon Trent, better known as the Lurker; Damon, the treacherous meat bag who had learned of Mr. Night's grandiose vision and devised his own scheme to thwart it. He needed his three little puppets to take care of everyone else and capture or kill the girl.

He needed to stack the deck a little, even if it meant making a few changes here and there.

Archangel was the most powerful of the lot, but he was also the most unreliable, a man dedicated only to his own survival at the expense of all else. Trying to improve him was likely to be counterproductive, not to mention difficult: the Russian's mind and will were well protected by an artifact of some sort. Mr. Night was surprised that little Cassandra had managed to snare Archangel, even at the cost of her own life. The woman had shown unsuspected depths. He really should have killed her when their paths crossed all those many years ago. In any case, it would be left to leave the cherubim the way he was. He would do well enough on his own.

Mr. Night considered Lady Shi. He could see the brutalized little girl she once had been quite clearly, and the years of trauma that had broken her mind over and over. What had emerged from that cauldron of degradation and torment was a beautiful killing machine, but there were a few too many twists and turns inside that pretty little head. You couldn't tell which of her mental building blocks could be altered safely. He decided to spare her as well.

Medved, on the other hand, was a simple man. He was happy when things went his way, and angry when they didn't. He cared nothing for most people, but when he made a friend or a lover he was fanatically loyal. He wasn't an imbecile – few Neolympians were – but he was not a man given to thought or introspection. That made him an ideal subject for Mr. Night's purposes.

"Mister Bear," Mr. Night said. "Front and center, if you please."

Medved rose ponderously from the couch. "What do you want, little man?" he growled.

"In a very short while, we are going to face Ultimate the Invincible Man. How would you like to be known as the man who killed him?"

The massive Slav considered this. His frown became a smile. "That would be good. Everybody loves him, the pretty man in his fancy costume. I would enjoy tearing him to shreds."

"What are you going to do to Medved?" Lady Shi asked. She wasn't smiling. The Japanese killer knew enough about Mr. Night not to trust him when he came bearing gifts. Smart girl.

"Nothing he won't like," Mr. Night said in what he considered to be a reassuring tone. Nobody seemed reassured. Well, he *was* lying, so he couldn't blame them for not believing him. "I'm going to give him power, woman. Far more power than he's ever known. And you are going to follow orders like a good schoolgirl and not interfere, *wakarimasuka*?"

Lady Shi tensed. One never knew when the pretty woman with the sharp smile was going to lose control and start severing limbs with the fiery throwing stars she conjured with her mind. Mr. Night had been on the receiving end of one such tantrum some years ago, and it had been a stressful experience for all concerned. Lady Shi remembered how things had turned out then; she had not enjoyed the results. She stayed her hand and silently acquiesced to Mr. Night's little experiment.

Mr. Night considered the problem. Power given was power lost, so he was forced to be parsimonious. He examined Medved's massive hands and especially his fingers, the blunt digits that could produce two-inch long black talons capable of shredding steel. Against Ultimate, they might draw a little blood, inflict some shallow scratches, and no more. Medved's strength was but a fraction of the Invincible Man's. And yet, with a little infusion of the darkness inside Mr. Night's soul, things would be different.

He held the brute's hands with his own. Medved grunted as coldness rushed up from his hands and arms into his body. The darkness found the man's inner rage and intermingled with it. Mr. Night nodded in satisfaction. The Outside had found an agreeable place to nest and grow.

Medved took a step back and pulled his hands away, but it was too late. If he survived the night, the giant's body and soul would undergo a number of changes. He was strong, and he might even live through the process for longer than a fortnight, but he was unlikely to last much longer than that. The Source and the Outside were opposing forces, and their interactions could best be described as corrosive. Only Damon Trent had managed to survive for long under those conditions. It was a pity such a historical figure had to be sacrificed, but needs must when Mr. Night drives.

The time to act was getting close.

Face-Off

Somewhere in Lake Michigan, March 14, 2013

The island was a wind-swept rocky wasteland, consisting of two hill surrounded by a beach barely large enough to fit the Condor Jet. A handful of scrawny trees on the hills were the only sign of life; other than that the island was a misshapen mound of dirt protruding from the lake like an infected pimple. It fit my mood perfectly.

The Lurker led the way. He took us down a natural path between the hills into a cave that did not look natural at all. It was a round tunnel carved into the rock, with walls so smooth they reflected the moonlight at the entrance almost as well as mirrored glass. As we went underground, the Lurker's mask started glowing with a bluish light that provided enough illumination for us to find our way. We went down the spiraling tunnel for quite a ways, certainly well below the lake's surface. Nobody spoke as we walked down. I guessed everyone had stuff to think about.

I didn't want to do any thinking. If I let myself think, I would have to face the fact that Cassandra was gone. She would never again let me know when I screwed up, or laugh at my jokes. I'd been halfway through reading *The Wide Sargasso Sea* to her. She didn't need me to read for her, but she liked hearing me do it. Now I would have to finish the book by myself. Alone. I tried to spend the walk down checking the tunnel walls, admiring how smooth they were, wondering if the Lurker had built it or had found it the way it was.

We arrived to a large chamber below the earth. The ceiling was fairly high, about twenty feet, but the place still felt claustrophobic to me. Maybe it felt that way because almost every square inch of the walls and ceiling were covered with glowing signs that waxed and waned in a steady pattern. The signs were larger versions of the ones on the Lurker's mask. I couldn't look at them for very long before my head started to hurt. I ended up keeping my gaze mostly on the nice, ordinary dirt floor. No wonder the Lurker had gone batshit crazy. If I had to look at that kind of wallpaper for very long, I'd be bashing my brains out against a rock faster than you could say Charlotte Perkins Gilman.

The walls were making an impression on everyone else, too. Kestrel was staring at them while swaying her head back and forth, looking hypnotized. Condor was pointedly looking at her rather than the walls. Ultimate was trying hard to look unimpressed. A little too hard, I thought, but I wasn't feeling particularly charitable towards the All-American Hero.

Christine was shaking.

I rushed towards her as soon as I noticed her reaction. I had to get past Ultimate, and I shouldered him out of the way – he might be a thousand times stronger than me and a good five inches taller, but unless he willed himself not to be moved, I could move him. He didn't react, not that I was paying attention to him. I tentatively put an arm around Christine. She did not seem to notice. Her attention was fixed on those symbols.

"It helps if you don't look at them for very long," I said.

"They are words," she whispered. I wasn't sure if she knew she had spoken out loud. "And the words can change reality. I can almost read them." The shaking grew stronger, as if she was having an epileptic attack.

I turned to the Lurker, who was just standing there, looking at us as if we were so many lab rats. "Hey!" I said in a tone that usually preceded violence and bloodshed. He did not seem to hear me. "Hey, asshole!" That got his attention. "Turn those fucking things off or take us somewhere we don't have to look at them. Or I'm leaving and taking her with me." If he tried stopping me, we were going to find out exactly how much of a badass he really was.

The Lurker shrugged. A second later, a sheet of darkness spread through the walls and ceiling, obscuring the constellation of mind-fuck doodles from sight. The illumination level did not change somehow. 'Somehow' is a very useful word when dealing with Neo powers. Christine staggered a little when the signs were hidden away. I held on to her until she felt steady on her feet. "That was the weirdest thing I've seen," she said. "And after the last couple of days, that's saying a frak of a lot." She smiled at me. "Thank you."

"It's just a bunch of shiny chicken scratches," Kestrel said. "Just some sort of hoodoo your daddy's conjured up, that's all. He sees the darkness in all men's souls." She laughed. The laughter sounded less amused than hysterical, spoiling the attempt at nonchalance.

"What are those things?" Christine asked her father.

The Lurker had taken his mask off. Without it, he looked like a skinny man with a mop of reddish hair and incongruous freckles on a face lined with either years or a stressful life. The family resemblance to Christine was there, if you took away the wrinkles and insanity. "I do not truly know," he said, sounding a little more normal than usual. "I suspect many things. They make up a language, but much more than that. I suspect they may be access codes to reality itself."

Whatever the hell that meant. It sounded impressive enough, though.

"I also believe they come from the same source as our powers."

"Aliens! I knew it!" Condor said triumphantly. That was one of those perennial arguments people with time to kill loved to get into. Where did Neo powers come from? Schools of thought included Aliens Did It (we had so far met no aliens who could deny or confirm it; no aliens at all for that matter), Divine (or Infernal) Origins, Natural Evolution (highly discredited since the Human Genome project came to fruition and found no Neo Gene), Cosmic Rays, They Were Always Here But Hid Themselves, and Someone Put Some Weird Shit in the Water. I usually argued in favor of Nobody Knows and I Don't Give a Fuck; Let's Order some Pizza. Condor was an Aliens Did It man.

"I have a question," Ultimate said. "How did you come to gain this knowledge? I know people who have been studying Neolympian powers for nearly a century. Nobody I know of has made any meaningful discoveries."

"I was shown," the Lurker replied; he was reverting back to the muttering, batshit crazy guy we all knew and hated. "I had eyes, but did not see. I could only understand the simplest words. I needed fresh eyes." He was looking at Christine when he said that. "That's why I made you what you are, to see and to help me understand. You will be my eyes, Christine."

"Oh, God," she said. "Is that all I am, Dad? Your interpreter? Living prescription glasses so you could read the writing on the wall?"

"I had to see," he said as if that explained everything. I guess if you were batshit crazy, it did.

"So now what, Dad?" Christine almost shouted. I'd never seen her so angry before. "You want me to read the words out loud while you take notes? And when

I'm done you can send me home and forget about me? Mom was right about you. You're an asshole."

If her words hurt the Lurker at all, he showed very few signs of it. His eyes narrowed a little, and his grim expression got a tiny bit grimmer. "There had to be the right elements in one person," he explained. "It had to be someone hidden somewhere the others could not find. It had to be you."

"Well, find someone else, Dad. Screw you, and screw this." Christine started walking back up the tunnel.

I started to go after her. So did Ultimate. I tried to push him aside, but this time he had braced himself and I bounced off him. "Get out of my way," I told him.

"She and I have fought together," Ultimate said. "I owe her. I'll go talk to her."

He and Christine had fought the Dreamer together. She and I had chatted for a bit. Maybe he was the guy who should go see if she was okay. Hell, Ultimate was the guy to call if you needed help. I was the guy to call if you needed to murder some asshole. He was the right man for the job. I didn't give a shit. "Get out of my way," I repeated.

Ultimate gave me a pitying, understanding look that made me want to punch him in the face. Only the certainty I'd just break my hand without messing a hair on his head stopped me. He stepped aside. "Give it your best shot," he said. He was so sympathetic, so contemptuous, I wanted to vomit all over his silver costume. But I went. He let me go after her and I went.

C.J. Carella

Christine Dark

Lake Michigan, Illinois, March 14, 2013

She didn't know where she was going. Anywhere but the Island of Doctor Moron, she supposed. She would get to the surface and fly away. She'd almost made it to the mouth of the tunnel when he called out to her.

"Christine."

She turned around. Mark had caught up with her. He was worried.

"Hey."

"Hey. Just wanted to see if you were okay."

"I haven't been okay since I went to that stupid frat party I can't even remember how many days ago." *I'm never going to be okay.* "So what's up? Did they send you to talk some sense into me?"

Mark shrugged. "Nobody sent me anywhere. And I don't know if anything makes any sense." He paused for a second or two. "I'm sorry your father's crazier than a shithouse rat," he finally said.

Christine actually laughed at that. "Yeah, Dad turned out to be a dud, didn't he?"

"Dud you just make a pun?"

She started to laugh again, then sat down on the tunnel floor as the laughter turned into sobbing. He sat down by her side and she hugged him. He let her cry quietly on his shoulder. She could feel him crying too, just on the inside. Christine might have found her father was a whacko who had bred her to be his Seeing Eye

Bitch, but Mark had lost the closest thing he'd had to a mother. So they just sat on the cavern floor for some time, two hurting people grieving together. Having someone to grieve with helped a little bit.

"Thank you," she said after a while.

"Thank you," he replied. She guessed it had been good for him, too. "Wish I was better at the pep talk shit. Ultimate wanted to come talk to you. He's probably great at talking people off ledges and consoling the bereaved."

"Heh." John probably would have had a great spiel or three. She started to grin at the thought but suppressed it quickly when she caught a spike a pain from Mark. Oh, God. Things were getting complicated. Just the kind of thing she liked to read about sometimes, but which was no fun at all when it happened to you in the real world, or even in this effed up version of the real world.

They got to their feet. Christine looked at the exit. It was so tempting, to just take off and see how far she could fly. Timbuktu was probably nice this time of year. "Got any ideas, Mark? I'd love to go home. Maybe we can hunt down Porta Potty Man and see if he can get me there. Do you want to come along?" Christine tried to imagine introducing Mark to her friends and relatives. That would be a trip.

"I'll back you up whatever you decide," he said. "But people are still looking for you. People with enough muscle to use Ultimate the Invincible Man as a meat puppet, not to mention drag you from your home universe. The Lurker is nuts, and a dick, but he might be able to help us. Maybe all he wants to do is to use you. But we can use him, too."

"I really don't want to have anything to do with him," Christine said, knowing even as she spoke that she was going back down the effing tunnel. "He is crazier than you know. Looking back, I think he murdered half the cheerleader squad in my school because they were mean to me. Thanks to him, I'm a complete mess and I'm probably going to die in some horrible, stomach-turning way."

"Sure. But thanks to him, you are."

"Am what?"

"Here. Existing and shit."

"The saving grace of every father, eh? I fertilized some eggs with my man-juice, so you'll have to forgive me for being an absentee insane murdering freak from another universe. Worst daddy issues ever."

"My father got killed when I was seven," Mark said, shocking her into silence. "He was a nice guy, from what I remember. Had a temper, but never raised a hand to me or my mother. His temper got him in a bar fight, though. Somebody punched him in the chest and he just keeled over. Dead before he hit the ground. Turned out he had a bad ticker and the punch hit him in just the right spot to stop it."

"Oh, God, Mark. I'm so sorry."

He shrugged. "I don't know why I just told you that. Trading daddy stories, I guess. Or maybe I'm trying to say your father ain't perfect, but he's still alive, so there's still a chance you two can work shit out. And maybe he's not just using you. People aren't that simple; they almost always have more than one reason for whatever the hell they do. So yeah, he was building himself a translator, but on the other hand he wouldn't have killed those cheerleaders if he didn't give a shit, right?"

"That's just horrible."

Mark shrugged. "Well, yeah, I didn't say he wasn't batshit crazy and probably should be institutionalized or even put down, just that he cared about you in his own batshit crazy way. Oh, Cassandra also said if we don't make the right choices, the world is going to end. Does that count as a pep talk?"

Christine patted him on the shoulder. "It was good enough. Let's go back down to the Lurker's Lair and see what Dad Vader has in mind."

Nothing good came to mind all too readily.

Chapter Twenty-One

The Invincible Man

Lake Michigan, Illinois, March 14, 2013

Condor filled John in on the story behind Christine's appearance and the events that had led them here. The fact that she came from another world, one where Neolympians did not exist, was fascinating. If given the chance, he wanted to hear more about this alternate Earth. Had the absence of Neos been a blessing or a curse? Many people believed only Neo intervention had prevented the triumph of Nazism and Communism: Christine could help confirm or deny those theories. Unfortunately, Condor hadn't had much time to learn about her world. The girl had been hunted from the start. The main culprit appeared to be the Dominion of the Ukraine, a troublesome bit of news.

John had learned to distrust coincidences. Christine's arrival, the attack on the Legion, the Dreamer's attempted takeover of John's mind, the hunt for the Lurker – all those things had happened within a few days of each other. If all or even some of those events were parts of the same puzzle…

"… and that's when the Lurker came back with you and Christine in tow. We'd just heard from Face that the Russians killed Cassandra." Condor shook his head sadly as he finished his story. "I'm going to miss her, even if we never spent all that much time together. She always knew what she was talking about, and she was convinced Christine was important. She was also certain contacting the Legion would lead to disaster."

"She was right. The Legion has been infiltrated," John reluctantly agreed. The psychic had to be the same Cassandra John had met decades ago. Their encounter had been brief but memorable. She would be missed.

"When Cassandra told us to go look for the Lurker, it never occurred to me he could be Christine's *pater familias,* although Christine actually thought about it. No offense, Lurker, but you never struck me as a family man."

The Lurker did not respond. He had remained silent throughout, staring at the tunnel like a puppy waiting for his master to return. John could hear Christine and Face-Off talking near the tunnel's entrance, but he had resisted the temptation to eavesdrop. The girl just needed to blow off some steam, that was all.

Sure enough, they came back after a while. Christine looked grim but determined. "Well, here I am," she said. "What's the plan, Dad?"

Instead of responding, the Lurker removed something from his pocket: a small cube made of some red material, covered with symbols similar to the ones decorating – or, more accurately, infesting – the chamber's walls. "The last time I showed this to you, it didn't work. I thought I had failed. I thought you'd live a normal life and never know about any of this. I tried to do things myself, and that didn't work. But now you are here. Maybe I tried to show it to you before you were ready."

"What is it?"

"A key and a test. I made it for you."

"Never a straight answer," Christine complained. "Would it kill you to just say what it is, maybe toss in a nice PowerPoint presentation? Fine, let's see it." She took the cube and looked it over. "So what happens next? Do I go invisible and start saying 'Gollum, Goll...'" She trailed off. Her gaze was fixed on the cube.

John heard the faint thrumming emanating from the cube first, but it quickly grew in intensity until the very air seemed to vibrate along with it.

'You okay?" Face-Off asked Christine. She didn't answer. He turned to the Lurker. "Is she going to be okay?" The Lurker paid no attention to him, either.

The sound was getting louder, and it was changing in a way that suggested speech; it was as if a string instrument was trying to speak. Christine started to glow with a reddish light. Everybody but Christine and her father looked at each other. Nobody seemed to think the sound and light portended anything good, but nobody came forth with any ideas of what to do about it. John kept a close eye on Face-Off, just in case he tried to take the cube away from her. The vigilante seemed to accept this was what Christine was there to do, even though he didn't look at all happy about it.

The thrumming and the light reached a crescendo and leveled off for several minutes. Christine didn't move at all. The Lurker was swaying slightly back and forth, but otherwise remained as intent on Christine as she was on the cube.

To make things worse, the glowing symbols on the walls and ceilings came back into view. Either the Lurker had forgotten to keep hiding them, or the process affecting Christine had brought them back into sight. John concentrated on Christine and tried not to think about them. The girl's expression never changed. She was in a trance.

John lost track of time. Eerie as the scene was, after a while it started to become tedious. John found himself wishing for something, anything to happen.

He should have known better.

Armageddon Girl

A blast of cyan energy struck him from behind and flung him into the nearest wall. John felt a nasty burn on his back where he had been struck. As he turned to face his attackers, several glowing starry shapes spun towards him and hit his face and eyes. Those impacts hurt but did not pierce his defenses the way the first one had but dazzled and blinded him. A large figure smashed into John before he could recover. Clawed hands struck his chest and abdomen, ripping through his defenses as if they weren't there, tearing into flesh and bone, overwhelming him. Pain like nothing he had ever endured paralyzed him.

Agony became darkness, became oblivion.

Christine Dark

Lake Michigan, Illinois, March 14, 2013

In the beginning, there could be only one. One thing that held everything. A Monoblock, which come to think of it would be a cool name for a band. Monoblock. It was the whole universe, every bit of space-time compressed into a single point so small and so dense the most massive black hole was like a butterfly fart by comparison, except things like small and dense meant nothing, because things like spatial dimensions did not apply to the Monoblock. It was all very Zen and Zany. She skipped over most of that part of the history lesson because, well, it looked like it might be kinda boring and, if she thought too hard about it her brain started skipping a beat or three.

Then came a big 'Poof!' moment, your basic Big Bang and rapid expansion thingy, cosmologists had gotten that right, but missed the part that in the beginning there had also been a Mono-Mind inside the Monoblock and it too had gone bang and fragmented. The other thing they had missed was that when the universe expanded, it stepped on some toes along the way. The universe expanded into something else, something completely different from anything within it, utterly alien.

That alien something – those alien some-things, actually, because they had identities – got smacked by the universe's bubble as it expanded faster than the speed of light, and they didn't like it one bit. A few got crushed, turned into cosmic road kill by the expanding universal bubble. Others packed up and headed off somewhere else, angrily shaking their figurative fists and vowing to come back. And still others got swept up by the new universe and hid in the more-or-less empty spaces between matter and energy, plotting their revenge.

She didn't look very closely at those things, those Outsiders. Even thinking about them for too long hurt her mind and something else that she thought was her soul. A couple of sidelong glances at the Outsiders had shown her things that made Great Cthulhu look as threatening as a Hello Kitty doll. Just knowing they existed was bad enough: there was something Outside, something beyond the stuff of the universe.

Things settled down in the Cosmic Bubble. Stars were born, the hot gaseous ones, not the paparazzi magnet ones. Planets and other celestial bodies followed, you might as well cue in the *Big Bang Theory* theme song. Life was all over the place, if by all over you counted the tiny lumpy bits in the bubble that held most of the non-dark matter and energy. And each piece of life, from the smallest virus to the biggest space whale – okay, she didn't see any space whales during her Cosmic PowerPoint Presentation, but there were some pretty big things floating around gas giants that she dubbed space whales, thanks for all the fish and all that – all life had a connection to the Mono-Mind.

Fast forward to the time when some of the living critters became self-aware and started learning the rules of the game, fun stuff like the Laws of Thermodynamics, algebra and the joys of cooking. Some eventually figured out even neater tricks like splitting the atom for fun and profit or how to milk anti-matter and bottle it for easy access. The smartest ones, the ones who didn't blow themselves up or kill their biospheres or run out of gas before learning how to do without gas, they packed up, left their birth planets and headed for the center of their respective galaxies. That's where the action was, where matter and energy and fun things like black holes and supernovas were concentrated and within easy reach.

And there's the answer to Dr. Fermi's question: all the smart aliens leave the dirtball planets and most of the galaxy to the rubes who are still figuring out that putting sharp pieces of flint at the end of a stick made it easier to kill buffalo, or that *e* was equal to *m* times *c* squared, you know, basic stuff like that. They go forth and join the big treehouse at the center of the galaxies.

The smart guys in said treehouses figured out how to read reality's programming language and made their own cool apps; they folded space and tap-danced with time, and knew things that Christine couldn't even name, let alone understand, much like a caveman or a cheerleader couldn't understand how a computer worked, or even what a computer was.

Knowledge that Stephen Hawking would have killed for flooded into her mind. Her brain, annoying nerdy thingy that it was, had not evolved enough for most of it, but as long as she was touching the cube, her ability to comprehend things had grown exponentially. She knew that the carvings on the cave and on the cube were symbols and referents in one: the words could create the things the words described. Say 'Let there be light' in that language and light there would be. Learning the words would take a long while and many sessions with the cube, but even the little bit she'd picked up in this lesson was enough to scare the bejesus out of her.

The worst part was, all that was just the tip of the iceberg.

The universe was at war.

Armageddon Girl

The smart kids – let's call them the Cosmic Nerds, Bill Gatii and Mark Zuckerbergers of the Universe – at the center of all galaxies were fighting the Outsiders that were trying to pop the Cosmic Bubble by expanding it until it grew too thin to hold reality down. And that war was the reason us puny Earthlings had been handed super powers and the magic writing of the gods. The Cosmic Nerds needed all the help they could get. They had started sending little starter kits out to the Lesser Races to give them a little push in the right direction. Unfortunately the Outsiders had caught on and were trying to sabotage the project. Which led to…

Lesson interruptus! Christine felt her brain being compressed down to its regular human size: the sudden loss of hyper-cognition was painful and humiliating and incredibly sad, a *Flowers For Algernon* moment that brought tears to her eyes as she desperately tried to retain ideas and concepts that slipped like oil from her mind and left her with pathetic generalities. Coming back to reality was like being made to sit back at the little kids table at Thanksgiving, times a million.

To make things worse, reality just happened to be sucking big time at the moment.

Somebody had knocked her to the ground pretty effing hard. Christine saw the cube she had been holding clattering away on the ground. Mark was lying next to her. "Look out!" he wheezed, as if he couldn't gather enough breath to shout.

Christine looked up and saw a pale guy in white about to slice into her with what looked like a freaking light saber.

"Frak me."

C.J. Carella

Face-Off

Lake Michigan, Illinois, March 14, 2013

The freaky sounds and lights had been nearly hypnotic. No wonder some assholes sneaked up on us without being noticed. I got my first clue that something was wrong when Ultimate was mowed down by a barrage of energy attacks and pounced on by a seven-foot plus bearded man-mountain that tore into him like a rabid organic chainsaw. Ultimate went down, guts and pieces of flesh and bone flying everywhere, and stopped moving. It really sucks when the toughest guy in your gang gets taken out right off the bat.

Big Ugly went after Condor next, and an Asian chick somersaulted into the chamber and launched a barrage of glowing spinning stars at Kestrel. I couldn't pay a lot of attention to either fight because Asshole Number Three was making a beeline towards me. A short man, white from head to toe, an energy sword in his hand. I recognized him right away: he was the motherfucker I'd seen in Cassandra's last vision.

He's mine. I'd never wanted to kill someone so much.

From the look in his eyes as he rushed toward me, the feeling was mutual.

I sidestepped his flashing blade, which went on to carve a molten furrow on the cave floor, and tried to drive my fist right through his face; I was aiming for a point about six inches on the other side of his head. Instead, my knuckles hit a heavy-duty protective field, the kind that absorbs and dissipates energy. In other words, the punch didn't hurt him very much at all. I rocked him back a step, and I broke his nose. That was it. Fucking force fields.

His energy sword would hurt me plenty if it hit me. Even the first near miss gave me a mild case of sunburn. I did a little dance around a flurry of furious slashes, trying to avoid getting skewered and deep fried while I looked for an opening.

If Pasty-Face hadn't been so eager to carve me a new asshole, it would have been a short fight. He was pissed off and trying too hard. A particularly wild swing left him wide open and I got him with a spinning kick right on the throat. I put everything I had on the kick. He got rocked back and was stunned for a second or two, long enough for me to land the best punches on my repertoire on all the vital points I could reach.

I hurt him, but nowhere near enough. I managed to kick him in the balls, which got me a few more seconds to try to kill him, but he bounced back much faster than he should have and kept me at bay with his fucking sword.

To make things worse, after he recovered he stopped fighting stupid. The frenzied cuts stopped, and he started coming after me like a professional, cool and collected, using the greater reach of the sword to make me keep my distance. And the fucker healed all the damage I'd inflicted. The blood on his nose and lips disappeared, and he looked like the picture of health just again. I was fighting someone who could take my best punch without going down and could heal at least as quickly as Kestrel.

This is how most Neos buy the farm. Sooner or later you run into someone several points higher in the pecking order, someone you can't beat, and that's all she wrote. I knew this was it, and so did he. As long as he didn't completely fuck up, I wasn't going to last very long.

Not that I was going to roll over and die for him. The asshole was going to have to work for It, and I was going to do my best to take him with me.

I ducked under a horizontal slash that would have cut me in half and tried to sweep his legs off under him. He jumped up, avoiding the sweep – fucker was fast – and tried to pin me to the ground with a downward stab. I rolled away from that, but not quite fast enough; the energy sword touched me on the upper arm, burning and slicing through my armored jacket and the flesh beneath.

I rolled until I was far away enough to leap to my feet. He came after me, swinging his sword in a figure eight pattern, leaving behind bright after-images like a sparkler from Hell. I had to backpedal away from him. A quick glance to the side told me things weren't going great for the rest of the crew. Condor and Kestrel were also on the run from their respective dance partners. The Lurker was engaged in some sort of staring contest with a creepy little guy in a black suit. Dueling creeps. Not my kind of spectator sport but I'd rather be watching it than running for my life from a guy who powdered his face like a fucking mime. I needed to come up with something.

Sometimes a good idea can be used more than once. I cartwheeled backwards to get some space and pulled out my gun. I didn't even bother shooting Pasty-Face with it; I flung it right at his head. He took a moment to slash the gun out of the air, and I used that moment to close in on him. We grappled, and I got the first bit of good news of the night: I was stronger than him. I grabbed his sword hand and pushed it away while I gripped him by the throat with my other hand and head-butted him a few times. The blows didn't do much, but at least I had the initiative. Maybe I could rip his arms off, snap his neck, something.

The energy sword in his hand disappeared. I had just enough time to realize that couldn't be a good thing.

The dazzling blade reappeared in Pasty-Face's other hand, the one that I didn't have a grip on.

He ran me through.

I felt the burn all the way through my lower torso; things burst and popped inside of me and I smelled my flesh being roasted. Pasty-Face kicked me away and had the sword reappear in his right hand. I landed in a heap with a wide round hole burned clear through me, front and back. I could have put a whole hand in it. I could feel air blowing through my insides. I tried to move, but nothing seemed to be working at the moment. It hurt to breathe. It hurt to exist. The world was beginning to get dark around the edges, and a part of me wanted to close my notional eyes and go to sleep. I told that part of me to fuck off.

Pasty-Face looked down on me. "I could have killed you just now," he said. He had a nice stage-actor voice, for a murderous pissant asshole in white-face. "My name's Archangel. I owe your Gypsy bitch a debt I intend to repay. Before I kill you, I will show you something interesting." He gestured towards Christine, who was still standing in a trance, looking at her father's freak show cube. "I have to capture her alive, but she doesn't need to have arms or legs when I take her in. Watch this." He turned his back on me and strode towards Christine, sword at the ready.

Nobody else was in any position to do anything. I saw Condor leap over the giant and kick him in the head, which didn't even muss the fucker's hair. I couldn't see Kestrel anywhere and the Lurker was still busy. The last thing I was going to see before I died was Pasty-Face mutilating Christine.

Fuck that.

I sat up, ignoring how bits and pieces of me were moving around the hole in my midsection; some were falling right out. I kept moving. No guts, no glory, and I don't need guts to live, Condor told me so. I gathered my legs – my leg; the left one wasn't working for shit – under me, and jumped. It was the most painful leap I'd ever made; I felt stuff tear up inside and I was positive a good percentage of my body didn't make the jump with me. It a crappy leap, but I slammed into Christine and knocked her down before the killer mime landed a cut that would have taken off both of her hands at the wrists. As we rolled on the ground I felt the last bits of energy and blood leaving my body. I felt cold and thirsty and very sleepy.

Christine was awake. My peripheral vision caught a glimpse of Pasty-Face walking up to us, sword in hand. "Look out!" I yelled. Tried to yell. It came out pretty garbled. Next I tried to scream. It sounded pretty bad.

Neos in pain can make the most curious noises.

Chapter Twenty-Two

Christine Dark

Lake Michigan, Illinois, March 14, 2013

Shields up, Giordi!

The freaking light thingy – Lucasfilms should sue the guy – slammed into her shield in a pyrotechnic display that would have looked much prettier if it didn't mean someone was trying to chop her up like a carrot.

Whiteout Man tried a couple more slashes; she felt her shield weaken, and when her shields went down she was going to get effed up for real, yo. She blasted the guy, and he was knocked back a couple of steps, which put a stop to the hacking and slashing for a couple seconds, but he didn't go down. "Not bad," he said. "I think I'll have to put your eyes out as well." He gestured with the sword at Mark; he was lying face down and he wasn't moving; smoke was coming out of a huge hole in his back and he was making a horrible howling noise that terrified her and broke her heart at the same time. "He might even live long enough to watch," the killer mime commented. Mark fell silent a second later. "Or maybe not. Pity."

"Fuck you very much," Christine hissed and let him have it. Her anger and terror at seeing Mark down – *not dead, he can't be dead* – all exploded out in the strongest blast she'd ever fired off. She visualized a mental spear – a gigantic, mammoth-size spear, the kind of harpoon you'd use on killer whales or dinosaurs – and threw it at him with all her inner strength, propelled by a glare of pure hatred, moving fast enough to generate a supersonic crack as it struck. It went right though the man in white in an explosion of blood that should have sickened her but instead filled her with savage satisfaction. The man clutched at the huge hole in his chest with an incredulous look and fell flat on his back. His feet kicked a couple of times and he was still.

"Mark!" There was fighting all around her – Christine saw Kestrel wrap her whip around some Asian woman's throat and send her spinning off in a move that should have broken her neck but somehow didn't – but she needed to help Mark first. There was a huge smoking burn that went all the way through him, worse than the one she'd blown through the white dude. She could see *inside* of Mark and it was gross and horrible and who could survive that? *Neolympians, that's who*, her brain said. Neos didn't need to eat or breathe. They didn't need their organs, not really, not in theory at least.

She knelt by his side and gently turned his head so he was facing her. Mark had a face on. It looked very young. Light brown hair, narrow nose, softer features than she'd have expected. His eyes were closed. He wasn't in pain anymore, that's why he'd stopped howling. She picked that up with her Christine-sense. He was also getting sleepy and about to let go.

"Mark! Wake up!"

His eyes opened. They were green. He saw her and he smiled with his lips and his mind.

"You got the fucker?" His voice sounded like he had a really bad case of asthma. She nodded. "Fuck, my face's back, that's twice today." He tried to take a breath, and she heard air escaping through the hole in his torso. "This can't be good," he wheezed. He closed his eyes.

She felt him start to slip away. "No way. Mark, do you hear me? No fucking way!" Christine turned her special sight on and saw the bundle of colors that was Mark Martinez. The colors were draining away, replaced by a dull gray the same shade as the inert ground under him. It was a terrible thing to see, the end of life, but she forced herself to look, to figure out a way to stop it. The more she looked, the more she understood what the colors meant. One set of colors – a bluish-green hue – embodied all the healing power all Neos had to some degree or another; the green light was tapping energy from somewhere in a desperate attempt to undo the damage before his body stopped working altogether, but it wasn't enough, and the green light was fading and turning gray as well.

Christine looked at her hand with her sight and looked through the colors within herself. She found the one that matched the healing force and tried to send it to Mark. Nothing happened. Most of Mark was gray now, except around his upper chest and his head.

Come on, think! She touched his face, saw her colors flowing near his, not touching, not mixing up. They were separated by something, some sort of membrane around her soul, or aura, or whatever. *Okay, then. Break it.*

She did, and it hurt like nothing ever had. She involuntarily pulled her hand away. *This is so not a good idea*, her brain warned her rather pointedly. She ignored it and did it again. This time she breathed through the pain like she was doing Lamaze exercises and dealt with it, worked through the agony wracking her, and now her colors were mixing with his colors and that hurt even worse.

She recoiled again and was almost overwhelmingly tempted to just give up. She'd done as much as she could. *Just let him go.* The pain had been bad, but the realization he might take her with him when he died was worse. She was terrified of the pain, of dying. *Just let him go.* Mark's colors had made a brief comeback, but they were fading away again. His eyes reopened; she'd be the last thing he saw. He was cool with that.

She wasn't.

Christine screamed as she let their auras flow together once again. Now they were both dying. She pushed back against the empty oblivion she saw ahead of them. In her mind, she pictured herself dragging his limp body out of a twisting dark tunnel. He was so heavy, and it would have been so easy to just drop him and walk out by herself. She didn't.

When it ended, it was convulsive, explosive, a shuddering cold quasi-orgasm that made her body and mind spasm. The pain vanished. The walls around her soul snapped back into place and she was once again alone, no longer connected to him. She felt drained and weak.

Christine opened her eyes. Mark's no-face was back, and he was breathing normally. "What the fuck just happened?" he muttered. He turned around and sat up. His clothes where still torn up and bloodied, but the wound was gone. "Holy shit."

"Was it good for you?" Christine said, trying to sound like Kestrel and failing miserably.

"How... Look out!"

She turned and saw Pale Face. He was back on his feet and his wounds and the blood around them were gone. She barely got her shields up before he blasted her with an energy beam that looked like a ranged version of his light blade thingy. The blast hit her shield hard, knocking her on her back. Ranged and melee, that was so unfair.

The white bastard charged her, blasting her with one hand, sword held high on the other. She had to concentrate on her shield and couldn't hit back, and she was still weak from whatever she had done to Mark. Her shield was collapsing.

"Fuck this," Mark said. He moved just as the energy blade came down on her. He grabbed Pale Face's hand, stopping the strike – and then pushed the hand back. The energy sword cut into the man's neck, but he managed to stop the motion before the energy blade went too deep. Mark was still too weak to force the man's hand beyond that point. Christine was almost out of juice too, but she sent forth one more push, adding her strength to Mark's. The sudden push drove the sword all the way through the man's neck.

Christine felt Pale Face's mind/soul/whatever go poof as his head rolled off his shoulders and landed between her and Mark. He was dead, for real this time. The energy blade disappeared and the headless body collapsed.

"Burn in hell, motherfucker," Mark said, always ready with a *bon mot* or two. He struggled to his feet and looked around. "Shit, we have to help the others!"

He was right. Kestrel and Anime Amy were in full catfight mode, but Anime Amy had shredded Kestrel's whip with her energy thingies and seemed to have gained the upper hand. Condor was in even worse shape; she looked his way just in time to see him tase a guy who made Rubeus Hagrid look like Tyrion Lannister. Condor's Taser was industrial strength: sparks and arcs of lightning flared everywhere and giant dude staggered back a step, but only a step, and he bitch-slapped Condor and sent him tumbling away.

Christine gathered all the power she could muster and blasted the hairy giant in the back, knocking him down, and caught Anime Amy with another blast just as she was trying to deliver a flying jump kick. Ninja Chick rammed a wall face first and stopped moving. The two attacks just about did her in, though. She needed some time to recover.

Mark jumped the bearded giant and started pummeling him, but the big guy came to his feet, knocked Mark away and jumped after Anime Gal, who was lying down semi-conscious while Kestrel kicked her. While Christine desperately tried to gather enough power for another blast, the big guy forced Kestrel back with a few wild slashes with his clawed hands. He used the breathing room to grab his friend and start fleeing towards the cave's exit. Christine was about to blast him again when she noticed John's body lying on the floor. There was blood and worse stuff everywhere. She rushed to him. Was she going to have to do the healing thing she'd done with Mark? She didn't know if she had it in her to do it again – okay, she was positive she didn't have it in her – but she turned on her Christine-vision anyway.

John was alive, and still shining like a multimillion watt bulb. She could see his healing energies swirling all around him, fixing him up, washing away the last traces of the evil dark energy that had poisoned him and temporarily neutralized his invulnerability. It was going to take a while – someone had really pwned him – but he would recover. Relieved, Christine looked up.

And saw her father and an even creepier guy facing each other. That would have been bad enough, but her special senses were still up. She saw what the two men really were, what they had become. The one time she'd used her Christine-vision near her Dad, she'd gotten nothing; he must have some sort of ability that blocked her power. This time, however, nothing blocked her sight, and she saw the thing that wore the face of her father.

Next thing she knew, she was on her hands and knees, throwing up and wishing she was blind.

Face-Off

Lake Michigan, Illinois, March 14, 2013

I got up. Man Mountain hadn't hit me with his claws or my guts would have ended up all over the cave for the second time that evening, but his punch had broken several ribs and given me a mild concussion. Compared to the radical laser surgery I'd just survived, it wasn't much, but it had left me a bit wobbly. The giant retreated up the tunnel, his little friend slung over his shoulder. I don't believe in letting people who try to kill me or mine get away to try again another day, but I wasn't eager to mix it up with the guy who had gutted Ultimate like a fish. I'd probably regret it later, but I let him go.

Kestrel was checking on Condor. "He's going to be all right," she said.

That left the Lurker and the guy in the black suit. I turned towards them just in time to see Christine collapse and start to sob and vomit at the same time. I ran to her.

She was dry-heaving now. "Oh, God," she said over and over. Her eyes were tightly closed and tears ran down her face. "Oh, God, Dad."

I didn't know what to do. I held her and she shook in my arms and sobbed hysterically. Condor and Kestrel were back on their feet; they warily approached the Lurker and his psychic sparring partner. "Don't get too close," I warned them. I wasn't sure why, but I didn't think touching either of them was a good idea. There was a faint dark purplish glow around them, and the last time I'd seen that glow was when the Russians' disruptors had fucked us up all to hell. "But do me a favor and kill that asshole at range, would you?"

"Roger that," Condor said, producing a couple of his claws. His throws were fast and precise, aimed at Black Suit's throat. The claws spun forth at speeds only a Neo's enhanced reaction time could follow – and disintegrated three feet away from the target. "Shit. Guess you were right about not getting close."

"We have those energy rifles we took from the Russians," Kestrel suggested. "I can get them from the Condor Jet."

"Good idea," Condor said. She nodded and rushed off.

I turned my attention back on Christine. "Hey," I said softly. "Christine. Come on." Yeah, I was being fucking useful all right. I'd be trying prayer next to see how that worked out.

"Oh, God," she said again, but she'd stopped crying, and that was something. "Okay. Okay, I will not go crazy. I will not blow my sanity rolls."

She was chattering again; that was a good sign.

"My father..." She shuddered. "Ugh, it's still bad, but the worst of it is fading away. I'm repressing it, I guess. I'm sure it'll come back to me in my sleep. Great. Not. Dad's been in touch with the Outsiders, uh, Big Bads from outside the universe. That's why he's batshit insane. He blew his sanity rolls – game term, sorry – and they got to him. And that other guy's worse. He gave himself to the Outsiders, body and soul. There's nothing left of him."

"Sounds like he needs killing," I said. "Can you blow his head off?"

"I don't know, but I really should try." She got to her feet.

"You have to get out," the Lurker said in his inhuman voice. Some of the disturbing symbols carved on his mask had started to melt off, along with the skin and flesh underneath. The mixed smells of burning flesh and rubber added a little extra something to the evening's festivities.

"Not without you," Christine said. "You need help, Dad. The Outsider stuff is killing you. Let's take out that a-hole and get out of here!" She started concentrating.

"Don't," her father said. One of the symbols on the mask exploded, burning a hole right through his forehead, but he didn't seem to feel it. "You're not ready to deal with him. I will deal with him, but you may not survive the energy release when I do it."

'May not survive' sounded pretty serious to me. As if to emphasize his words, the whole island shuddered. Earthquake or energy release? I knew which way to bet. "Let's get the hell out of here!" I shouted. "To the Condor Jet! Now!"

Condor took off running – he needed to get the aircraft up and running if we were going to get out of this fucking rock. Christine was still standing there. "Come on!" I yelled at her.

"John! He needs help," she replied, pointing at Ultimate. He was unconscious but alive, and his guts were mostly back where they belonged. All-American Heroes were built to last.

"I'll get him. Go!" I said, tossing the Not-So-Invincible Man over my shoulder and urging her on.

She looked at the Lurker, who was now levitating a few inches in the air, his arms outstretched, facing the soulless asshole. Dark energy was swirling around him, and his mask was a melting mess. I noticed that some of the symbols on the walls had also started to melt and explode. I wasn't sure what that meant, except that it was all bad. "Dad?" Christine said.

He turned towards her. One of his eyes was visible now, the mask having melted off half of his face. That eye was a solid pool of darkness. "Go," he said in his inhuman voice, and Christine went.

I was right on her heels, stopping only for a couple of seconds after she left to pick up a little keepsake. The tunnel shook as we ran. It was my first experience with an earthquake, and I didn't care for it. When we came out, the whole island was shaking hard enough to make it hard to stay on our feet, and the lake's waters were splashing all around it, making some impressive waves. The Condor Jet's engines were all fired up. Ultimate and I were the last ones in. I unceremoniously dumped him on the rear seats and went to sit down near a window as the Condor Jet started rising. The tunnel's mouth spewed fire mixed in with the swirling darkness that was becoming much too familiar for my taste. Christine was looking out as well; she was biting her lips hard enough to draw blood.

We managed to get far enough not to get obliterated when the island exploded like a soda bottle stuffed with cherry bombs. The shockwave nearly sent the craft spiraling towards the water, but Condor managed to keep us in the air. When things settled down enough for us to look out the windows again, we saw a mushroom-shaped pillar of fire and ash rising majestically over Lake Michigan. People in three states and Canada were getting a treat for the eyes.

The world was more fucked up than I had ever imagined, but at least we were alive.

"Any ideas where to go?" Condor asked from the cockpit. "No offense, but I'm not bringing this mess to New York if I can help it."

"How about somewhere off the beaten path?" I suggested. "You're the rich playboy, bud. Don't you have a shack or a cabin or a time-share somewhere in Upper Bumfuck or something?"

"Well, yeah. A few places. There's an old hunting lodge in Canada that's pretty remote."

"Sounds like a place to regroup," I said. Everyone agreed, except Christine, who seemed to be in shock, and Ultimate, who was still sleeping off his near-death experience, the wimp. I turned to Christine. She was pale as a ghost, and beginning to suffer from reaction aftereffects. So was I, for that matter. My hands were shaking a bit, but I ignored them. Comes with the territory. We overdose with adrenaline during a tough fight, and this one had been the toughest one yet.

"Hey," I said.

It took a while before her eyes would focus on me. I didn't rush her.

Christine Dark

Lake Michigan, Illinois, March 15, 2013

"Hey," Mark said, extending a hand towards her. Christine took it.

"Hey-hey," she replied. Images of dead worlds orbiting dying stars flashed inside her head. She forced them to go away. She'd deal with the visions and premonitions and the heebie-jeebies later. She glanced at one of the wall screens and noticed the time. "Hey, it's past midnight. The worst day of my life is finally over."

"Mine too," Mark replied. "I'm sorry about your father," he added.

"Me too," she said. Her eyes were dry this time. *I'm all cried out*, she guessed. "I wouldn't count him out, though. He could pull a Gandalf and show up in a few days. The White Lurker or something like that."

Mark chuckled. "Sure. Weirder shit has happened. Hell, weirder shit has happened in the last fifteen minutes."

"I didn't get to see the whole message Dad prepared for me," she added. "I dropped the cube when you tackled me. Not that I'm blaming you, since the Big Bad was about to slice and dice me at the time, but I still don't know what's going on."

"Got a riddle for ya," he said with one of those awesome internal grins only she could see. "What have I got in my pocket?"

"What..? You got the cube?" She could read his no-face like a book. "You got the cube!" Christine leaned over and hugged him. *He wants to kiss me*, she suddenly realized, but he didn't.

"I noticed it on our way out, when I was rescuing the All-American Hero," Mark said after a second of awkward silence. "Figured you might need it. It's the least I could do after you saved my ass in there. I didn't know you had healing powers too."

"I guess I'm a multi-class multi-talented freak of nature," Christine said, trying to sound more confident than she felt.

Mark produced the cube for a second, then stuck it back in his pocket. "You should probably hold off on using it until we are relatively sure it's not going to attract more gangs of homicidal maniacs."

Christine resisted a sudden urge to pretend to look angry and start demanding he give the cube to her, maybe throw in a couple 'my preciouss' for extra drama. It would have been funny, but too much bad crap had happened for her to feel right making a joke. "You're right," she said. "But at least we have it. That's something."

She thought again about the two sides of the war. Cosmic Nerds versus the Outsiders, with Earth a little colonial kerfuffle out in the boonies; there was bound to be lots of collateral damage. She turned to Mark. "So what do we do now?"

"We fly to Condor's hunting lodge and if the place has the fixings, I'll make us some pancakes. You like pancakes?" Christine nodded and he went on. "Pancakes, then we relax for a few hours. After that, we'll see."

"After that, we figure out how to save the world," Christine said with conviction. When in doubt, act like you know what the frak you are doing.

"Always wanted to do that," Mark replied.

They sat side by side, and after a bit she leaned her head against his shoulder and fell asleep.

Epilogue

Medved emerged from the waters of Lake Michigan and gently deposited his beloved on the beach's sandy soil. His lady had been badly hurt, but she would recover. Rage filled him, but confusion as well. He had wanted to tear the evil bitch that had hurt his lady, but instead he had run, fled like a coward. He had never run away like that. He did not understand why he had done so, and he hated things he did not understand.

He did not have time to ponder such things for long. A violent convulsion seized his body and he collapsed next to Lady Shi. The convulsions went on for a long while.

Some time later, Lady Shi came to and saw Medved's inert form lying on the ground. "Darling?" she asked tentatively.

Medved opened his eyes. A strange lopsided smile that did not fit his coarse features slowly formed on his face. "I'm afraid not, my dear," he said in a reedy, tremulous voice. "I'm sure you haven't forgotten me.

"I'm your good friend, Mr. Night."

THE END

TO BE CONTINUED IN *DOOMSDAY DUET*

C.J. Carella

Special Thanks

To all of you who helped launch the Kickstarter project that produced this novel. My deepest thanks to everyone!

Steven Andres, Kevin Aug, Benjamin Barton, Trentin C. Bergeron, Drew Bittner, Brian Bolinger, Alba Olivieri De Bortesi, Jason Bontrager, David Brown, Adam Canning, Robbie Corbett, Scott Coady, John Michael Davis, Kim Dong-Ryul, Damian Elder, Javier "Intkhiladi" Escajedo, Erik Fischer, Travis Foster, Patrick Fowler, Delia Gable, Scott Galliand, William Gunderson, John D Kennedy, John Lambert, Moe Lane, Jorel Levenson, Mike Lowrey, Michael Magliocca, Scott Maxwell, Noe Medina, Theodore Miller, Andy Munich, Duane Oldsen, Scott Palter, Paul R. Partridge, Michael Pierce, William Reich, Roxanne Richards, Joshua Richardson, Felix Shafir, Mendel Schmiedekamp, Paul Singleton, C. Ryan Smith, D.G. Snyder, C.J. Stott, Derek Swoyer, Richard Taylor, David Terhune, Nancy Thurston, James Van Horn, Morgan Weeks, Jennifer Whiteside, Charles Wilkins, and Micah Wolfe.

Coming In December 2013

New Olympus: The Armageddon Girl Companion features several short stories set in the world of Armageddon Girl, as well as the notes on the history, politics and society of the setting and guidelines to use it in roleplaying game campaigns. Available in print and Kindle Versions. See www.cjcarella.com for more information.

Made in the USA
Charleston, SC
09 December 2013